WHEN WISHES BLEED

CASEY L. BOND

ISBN: 9781698251479

Book Cover, Map and Interior Formatting designed by The Illustrated Author Design Services

Edited by The Girl with the Red Pen

Praise for When Wishes Bleed

"Spellbinding and bewitching, When Wishes Bleed is the perfect mix of magic, danger, death, and love."
- # 1 New York Times Bestselling Author Jennifer L. Armentrout

"The Selection meets The Hunger Games in this MUST read!"
– Tara Brown, International bestselling author

"Witchy, witty, and wildly addictive. Bond's twist on Fate is imaginative and fun. Cinderella meets the Hunger Games in this magical tale of family, tradition, and deception."
- Tish Thawer, best-selling author of The Witches of BlackBrook series

"Spell-binding and delicious, with magic that's absolutely magnetizing. An unforgettable story with breakneck pace, enchanting characters and a dynamic plot. A real page-turner!"
- Misty Provencher, author of the Cornerstone series

"Casey crafted an intricate magical tale into a masterpiece. Be ready to be enthralled."
– Mary Ting, International bestselling, award-winning author Mary Ting

"A magically phenomenal tale with a bewitching modern spin."
– Brittany Hively of Books Babble

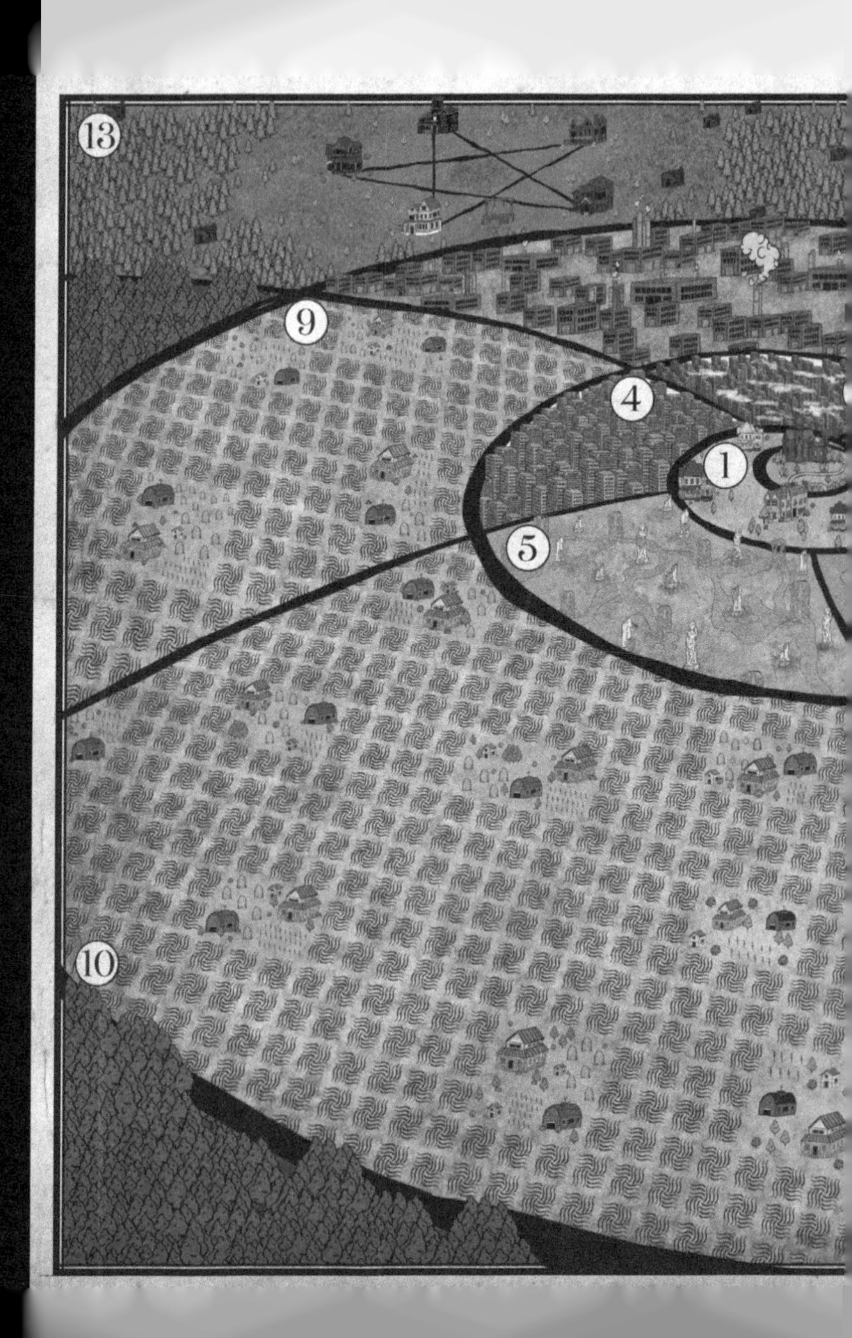
13
9
4
1
5
10

WHEN WISHES BLEED

CASEY L. BOND

The Sectors

1 through 4
The Core Sectors

5 and 6
The Arts

7 and 8
Industrial

9 through 11
Farmland

12
Timber

13
The Gallows

To Misty,
For showing me the magic in friendship.

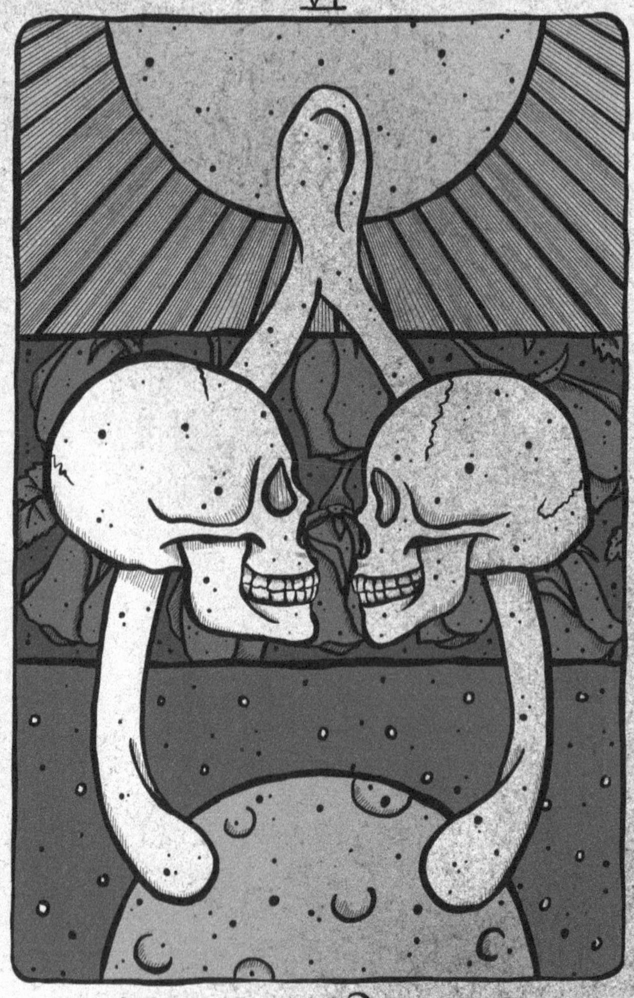

THE LOVERS

PART ONE

WHEN WISHES BLEED

one

The tips of my fingers, even my nails in their beds, were glacier blue despite the hot, dry autumn air. They ached and throbbed as I pumped water into a kettle and prickled as I carried it back inside and hung it over the fire. Nothing but death would bring them back to life at this point.

I wrapped my icy fingers around my middle and waited patiently for her to arrive. She was almost here, thankfully. I had important business to see to today, but the two readings Fate demanded would take precedence.

I took out the tea leaves and piled a heap on the counter, then sat three saucers behind them. To the witches I read for, they probably looked nearly identical, but each had its own markings and secrets only it could reveal.

Today was my birthday, and my power and I were now considered mature. Fate, I knew all too well, was real. He wasn't an obscure concept of destiny, or a dream of what the future might hold. And he certainly wasn't luck or a wishing well. He was sentient and very much alive. I was Fate's daughter, and he lived inside me.

As a child, he was gentle with his demands, but today there was no gentleness left in him. His easy whispers turned to shouts, and lately, his nudges of guidance had become harsh shoves.

Fate shoved me now, evidenced by my icy, dying fingers and the stiffness settling into my joints, but I had learned to push back. He almost always listened when I promised to do as he wanted in time, but today, he was impatient. He wanted a man to swing from the gallows, and for me to hang him there.

I wanted to hang him there, to be honest. I wanted the needle-sharp pain to go away, to be able to extend my bones, and for the feeling to fully return to the parts that felt numb. The only thing holding me back was the fact that no crime had been committed yet. I always checked first to be sure. Fate warned me that an offense *would* happen, and that if I waited, whatever occurred would upset every witch in The Gallows, but I refused to hang someone when there existed the tiniest chance the offender might choose a different path. And I was a firm believer that until a line was crossed, there was hope.

Fate… felt differently.

Today was not a day I could hang someone unless I wanted to be exiled. It was the Equinox. Marring such a reverent and sacred day, even for Fate, was unwise. He would have to forbear his anger for a short time, and I would have to learn to better tolerate pain.

I blew warm breath into the middles of my stiff fists.

The girl stepped onto the porch, the worn planks creaking under her weight. She pushed the door open, lingering just inside as she surveyed my small, cluttered cabin. From head to toe, she wore red. Her robes, cloak, and even shoes represented the fiery color of her House. On her arm was a small basket, where the scent of fresh garlic wafted toward me: her payment.

"Set the basket on the bench beside you."

She jumped and glanced at the basket as if she'd forgotten it hung from her arm. She gingerly sat it on the old wooden relic, careful that its unevenness didn't allow the bottom to turn and spill the fragrant bulbs. Then she stood up straight and smoothed her skirt anxiously. She fussed with her cloak until she was satisfied with its position, the sides thrown back over her shoulders.

"Tea, wax, or bones?" I asked, waiting for the answer I already knew she'd give.

The girl chewed on her bottom lip while considering the three options. The smattering of freckles across her nose and cheeks made her appear younger than she was, but her indecision was what truly showed her immaturity. Every witch in The Gallows knew what I preferred to read. The girl was no exception.

The auburn shade of her hair was the same hue of the heap of loose tea leaves lying on the counter. Across the room, the kettle leaked steam. Loose, languid tendrils curled and entwined with one another. I could get lost in their silken dance if I stared long enough, so I snapped my eyes back to her to refocus.

The water wasn't heating for her; it warmed for the boy in the woods. He stood behind my cabin, clinging to the rough bark of a tree, desperately trying to talk himself into knocking on my door and asking me to read his fate, and berating himself for considering leaving before gathering it.

Eventually, he would garner enough gumption to approach and ask me for the favor he coveted, but not before witnessing the girl's hasty exit. He would emerge from the woods as she left through the back door, probably to keep from sullying his reputation should anyone see him here. And he would choose a tea leaf reading because he feared the color of candle that might choose him, and that the bones might tell him something he wasn't prepared to hear; guide him where he was yet afraid to step.

He was a boy who wrestled with intense self-doubt. A boy who would rather cling to a tree than let go. I pushed him out of my mind and watched as the girl inched farther into the room as if she was easing into a lake of cold water. There wasn't much to see in the small, open space. A couch to her left, and a simple square table and chairs in the far corner. The kitchen lay to her right. Inside were only a few cabinets, and the stained, somewhat warped countertops were littered with precious stones and potted herbs. Her eyes caught on the hearth with its flickering fire, and the thicker slivers of steam pouring from the kettle.

She turned away from the hearth and the tea.

Her pale amber eyes caught on the casting cloth stretched over the table's top. She noticed the wishbones piled high in a silver bowl, desperately wishing she weren't so weak. I couldn't hear her words in my head, but followed the way her delicate features revealed a swell of emotions that built and crashed over her countenance.

"Fate doesn't favor the weak," I warned the girl as she shifted her weight back and forth, worrying her fingers. Her eyes met mine. In their depths swam both guilt and confusion. I elaborated for her. "You shouldn't fear the bones. They can reveal things the wax and tea leaves cannot."

She was a girl who wouldn't take advice even when it was in her best interest, a girl who gave fear dominion over her decisions. Her eyes flicked to a nearby shelf and the colorless candles it held. She refused to look away from the pale tapers, afraid the bones would call out to her again. They always did.

"I choose wax, please," she said, her voice quivering. The little mouse was terrified, not of the tea or wax, or even the bones… but of me.

I gave her a smile to put her at ease, all too aware that it might do the opposite, and moved to the shelf, gathering the mound of slender tapers and bringing them over to the table. "Would you care to remove the cloth?"

She hesitated, but gently pinched the corners of the dark silken square and pulled it from the wooden surface. I lay the tapers down, steadying them so none rolled off, then took the cloth from her. During the exchange, the tremble in her fingers rippled through the fabric into mine.

Her eyes flicked to the plate of wishbones again, then back to me. I wouldn't offer them to her again. She had made her choice, and my time was as valuable as my reading. I wouldn't waste it on indecision or fear.

I folded the dark casting cloth, tucked it into the wide pocket of my dress, and removed the bowl of bones from her sight. Tension oozed out of the girl's muscles as soon as they were gone. I scooped a basket of mismatched candleholders from the shelves, handing it to her. "Place a taper in each, and arrange them in a circle."

She shifted her weight from her left foot to her right, then back again. "Which one do I start with? They all look the same."

"You'll find they don't *feel* the same. Hold each one, and then place it where you feel it belongs. The pattern is yours to design."

Her lips pinched together.

"Think about a question to which you'd like to know the answer. Focus on it and the feel of the taper in your hand, then place it. If you allow it, the wax will show you the answer in the pattern you make. Let me know when you're satisfied with the circle. The colors will reveal themselves, and I will decipher them for you."

She swallowed thickly and then picked up a taper, closing her fist around it and shutting her eyes for a brief moment before popping them open. She placed the first taper in the candleholder located at the twelve o'clock position. Slowly, she formed a circle, guiding each taper around the circumference in varying positions until every holder was full. She couldn't see past the opaque wax to the color lying beneath, but I knew each one by heart. Her arrangement surprised me. It contained jarring combinations of yellow and black, violet and green, orange and white. When she'd completed the circle, she glanced up expectantly.

"You're satisfied?" I asked.

She looked over the circle she made and nodded. "This feels right."

"I didn't expect this from you," I revealed, waving my hands over the sacred circle. The tapers lifted from their holders and began to spin around in the air. Their true colors absorbed into the white wax from the tip of each taper to its base. I expected to read her pattern, but again, she surprised me. Or rather, her future did. One candle in particular chose her, which was a rare gift.

Her eyes struggled to keep up as the tapers slowed, and she watched warily as a single candle left its position in the wheel and drifted into the center. The wax was the color of eggplant, or a deep and long-lasting bruise – an unfortunate fortune for any witch to garner, but a wise witch would heed the warning and might be able to change her fate…

"What does it mean?"

"It's a warning."

She gulped.

"Foresight is a gift of Fate. If you heed his warning, you can make choices to avoid a catastrophe."

Her lips barely moved, but I saw them form a soundless 'catastrophe'.

"What will happen to me?" she asked.

I whispered an incantation. Flame seared its wick, growing tall and flickering. Dark smoke drifted toward the ceiling. She watched the flame, the element and source of her power. The reflection of fire shone in her eyes. "Extinguish it," I said softly.

She closed her eyes and the flame died instantly.

"Stay away from the border."

"For how long?" she was quick to ask. Too quick.

I quirked a brow. She shouldn't be going there unaccompanied, anyway. "Why are you leaving without permission?"

The girl swallowed.

Gripping the taper, I read the lingering breath she'd blown onto the wick. "A boy in Twelve? You've been sneaking across for months."

Her eyes widened. "Please don't tell the Priestess. I'll be banished from the House."

"The young man's heart is as black as his words are sweet. He's luring you into a web of lies. You should never see him again."

Her lip began to quiver.

Oh, no. I could already feel the punch of emotions roiling through her. There was nothing I could do to stop a feeling as strong as love, but if I could get through to her, make her see that it was a love that had never been reciprocated... "Do you love him?"

"Yes," she croaked.

"He does not love you." A fat tear fell onto her cheek. She looked down at her shoes. Ashamed. "Deep down, you already know this."

A second tear fell from her eye. This one splashed onto the tip of her leather boot.

"The occasional tryst might be overlooked, but you know that to be with anyone outside The Gallows means you can never return. Without your House, your power would dwindle. Do you wish to lose your flame?"

She shook her head. She had to know that whatever fling she'd been having with the boy couldn't last, but forbidden fruit was a temptation some couldn't force themselves to turn away from.

I softened my voice, hoping she could see reason. "What about your life? Do you wish to have it snuffed out?"

The girl began to cry in earnest. She knew I couldn't and wouldn't lie to her, but the feelings she harbored for the malicious young man were as strong as his will to break her.

"I can see his will," I revealed, "and its only purpose is to hurt you." The truth often stung.

Her eyes snapped to mine. "He wouldn't do that."

"He will kill you. If you see him again, you will die by his hand."

She shook her head defiantly and wiped her nose. "He would never hurt me."

"It's the truth. Now, you must make an important choice. The most urgent of your life. Will you heed my warning, or accept your fate?"

She pushed by me and flung open the back door. A loud slam rattled the walls. I almost chastised her for rudeness, but in her defense, her reading was rather shocking. Most of the time, I held a sliver of hope that the person I read for might change their fate, but I didn't think that would hold true in her case.

If she went to him tonight as planned, this moment – and I – would be one of the last things she recalled before death claimed her.

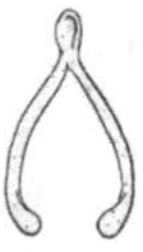

I hadn't finished clearing the tapers away before the boy from outside entered the cabin. His cloak and robe reflected the blistering color of the House of Fire, but the clothes weren't his. He had no flame. *How strange...* I'd never seen him before, and I thought I'd seen all the witches at one point or another. Still, there was something familiar about him, although I couldn't put my finger on it. His eyes were downcast as they searched my cabin.

"Would you like something sharp to dig the bark out from beneath your fingernails?" I asked, returning the wax and basket of holders to their rightful place.

He bristled. "I want you to read my fate."

"What payment do you offer?"

He fished into the left pocket of his cloak and withdrew a crystal. "Amethyst."

I plucked the pale purple stone from his hand. It was as big as my palm. I would never decline such a beautiful crystal. "Tea, wax, or bones?"

"Tea," he answered quickly. "Can you hurry? I need to get back soon."

"Before someone discovers you've come to me?"

"Exactly." His eyes darted from item to item in my sparse kitchen as I moved through the space.

I gestured toward the countertop. "Choose a cup and saucer, then place three spoons-full of tea leaves into the cup. I'll pour the water."

He moved to the counter and quickly scooped three lumps of leaves into a cup. His eyes flicked to me. The pupils were strange. Not round, but slitted... like a snake's.

I crossed my arms and leaned my hip on the counter. "Why did you come here?"

"I'm sorry," he asked, his brows furrowed.

"You clearly don't want to be here."

"I need my fate. Fast. Nothing more. And I don't owe you an explanation beyond that, Daughter of Fate."

Kettle in hand, I paused over his cup. "You would be wise to be more respectful."

He inclined his head and muttered an apology. "It's just that I've been plagued of late. Strange dreams. Voices…"

I let the water flow into the plain white tea cup he'd chosen. All my teacups were white to the common eye, much like the tapers. But each had a distinct handle, and each chose the recipient of the fortune in a like way, as well. This cup reflected change. His life was about to be dramatically altered.

He watched the surface as the leaves swirled, sank, and rose. His eyes flicked to me, but quickly darted away. "What now?"

"Think about the question you need answers to as you blow the steam away."

"All of it?" he asked.

"All of it."

"I've been called a windbag, but even *I* couldn't blow all the steam away. It's piping hot."

I leveled him with a glare until he gripped the counter's edge, puckered his lips, and blew. The steam disappeared, and with it, so did the water. The pattern of leaves left along the bottom and sides began to morph into shapes.

"How…?" he asked.

"Watch. Don't turn away."

He followed my instruction, watching until the leaves settled. They formed a straight line that ran east to west, from him to me.

"How do I know you?" I asked.

He opened his mouth. "I shouldn't have come."

"What are you hiding? I know the robes you wear are stolen. I can't sense an affinity, yet I feel something powerful inside you. Something dark." *Something that could be beautiful or deadly*, I didn't tell him.

"What do you see in the leaves?" he demanded firmly.

"Your entire world is about to be upended, and somehow, it has to do with me. You will need me for something. And this is not just *your* fate. Something... dire will occur."

He muttered something unintelligible.

"What was that?" I asked, quirking a brow.

"Just... never mind."

This was getting tedious. "The choices you are about to make are the most important of your life. Choose well."

The boy stormed out through the back door just as the girl had, the stolen red cape swirling behind him.

two

Prickles of pain flitted through every muscle as I climbed the three hundred-year-old, stone steps of the House of Earth. At the landing, I steeled my rib cage and stared at the door. My frigid blue fingertips lifted the iron knocker and struck the plate. Once. Twice. Three times.

I turned around as I waited for an answer, hiding my hands in the pockets of my skirt, but there was no way to conceal the matching hue of my lips. It felt like there was a noose cinched around my middle, tugging me toward the House of Fate just across the Center's cropped lawn. I didn't have long to study the structure, because squeals came from inside the freshly-painted moss-green house, heralding the answer to my summons.

Twin girls with fawn-brown hair wrenched the door open, although their giggles and smiles faded when they saw me. Beyond them, bundles of drying herbs hung from wooden frames suspended from the ceiling. The walls beyond were as green as their robes.

Their eyes raked over my clothing, so different from theirs. Despite its age, my dress was black as tar, and a pinch too tight now. Awkwardness oozed between us and it became apparent that neither of the young witches was going to greet me.

I took a step forward and lifted my chin. "I would like a word with your Priestess, please."

I wasn't invited in and the door slammed closed, stopping an inch from my face. I took a step back and waited patiently for it to open again, turning to look out over the heart of The Gallows.

The hearty hue of summer leached from the grass of the Center more and more each day. It crunched under the feet of the witches walking across it. To the south were the gallows. A graying noose swayed in the wind as if it were dancing, as if hopeful that it would soon be useful again.

It wouldn't. I preferred my own rope. The graying one was my mother's. It was the one with which she'd been hanged.

I refused to touch it.

The door opened behind me and the High Priestess of the House of Earth stood across the threshold. Ela was older than the house itself, old enough to have seen three of them erected and demolished.

She was my maternal grandmother, though she disowned my mother before I was born and by extension, had disowned me before I drew my first breath.

"*Daughter* of Fate," she woodenly greeted, bowing shallowly at the waist. Her sage green robes were gathered at her ample waist by a simple belt threaded with clay beads, each inscribed with a different protective rune. The ivy pattern in the fabric of her robes writhed, stretched, and receded, settling down again as she spoke.

I returned her bow. "Priestess, Fate requires a quorum. And while we're gathered, I have a personal matter to discuss with the Circle."

Her wizened brow furrowed and her eyes sharpened. "Surely both matters can wait until the Equinox has passed."

I flexed my fingers in my pocket. It would've been less painful if someone had stuck a thousand pins into them. "I'm afraid they can't." The words were more choked than I expected them to be, full of the pain lancing through me, coupled with the feeling of defeat. I couldn't hold Fate off any longer.

She straightened her hunched back as much as she could, her vertebrae popping in succession. Her bony toes curled against the lacquered wooden floor slats. "Very well. I'll call the Circle together."

"I'll await you in the Center."

As she pressed the door closed, less rudely than the girls of her House had, the fragrant smell of herbs and soil was carried away by the crisp, warm breeze. I turned on my heel, feeling eyes on me. When I glanced over my shoulder, the curtain in the front window swayed.

The Center of The Gallows was criss-crossed by well-worn, converging pathways that formed the shape of a pentagram. Situated at the tip of each point in the star sat one of the Houses. Earth and Air to the left, and

Fire and Water to the right. The pointed tips of my worn leather boots pointed toward what I wanted most, as if they were a compass pointing northward.

At the star's tip, the House of Fate sat empty and dilapidated. It withered away every day it went unoccupied and unwanted. The past seventeen years hadn't been kind to it. Chunks of scalloped shingles were missing. The siding had faded from black to ghostly-white, occasionally interrupted by splotches of bright green algae. Every salvageable plank needed to be scraped and repainted. And that was just the outside.

I stepped into the grassy Center and turned my face toward the warm sun. Its rays seeped into my skin. I was doing what he asked, but Fate wasn't eager to release me from the ever-present reminders of his power… including the fact that he always got what he wanted, one way or another. The bones of my fingers felt like they might snap at any moment. They felt brittle, as weathered as the decrepit House of Fate.

The sound of crunching grass came from the four directions behind me as the Circle members drew near. I turned in a circle and greeted each of them with a slight bow.

"You called for a quorum?" said Wayra, High Priestess of the House of Wind, the youngest of the four Circle members. She was never one to beat around the bush. The breeze that accompanied her everywhere stirred her blue robes and long, white hair. Flanking her were my grandmother Ela and Ethne, High Priestess of the House of Fire. Her robes were made from a living flame. Blue at the bottom and deep orange at her middle, licking yellow at her neckline. Popping and sizzling sounds accompanied her wherever she stepped.

The only High Priest stared at me from a respectable distance, a few feet behind his female counterparts to honor them. Bay was Priest of the House of Water, and his eyes and robes were the deep blue color of the ocean where it fell off the sandbar and stretched deep into the earth. The fabric of his robe ebbed and flowed around his feet, pulling and pushing the blades of dried grass. His wavy gray hair was tucked behind his ears, and his arms were folded across his chest.

The Circle never hid their disdain of my presence, but were too afraid of upsetting Fate to deny me, or him, when I requested a quorum. I abided by their rule of law, and so far, Fate had allowed me to live within their constraints. It was a precarious balance of power, the scales of which were always teetering back and forth ever so slightly.

Today they would tip violently, and I didn't know if the scales would right themselves.

"Fate has called for the life of someone who will cross the border today."

Most of the witches believed Fate was Death and that I was his hands, but Fate was exactly what his name implied. Sometimes he demanded that a person forfeit their life. Sometimes he urged a person onto a better or more prosperous path. I often wondered why he chose the people he favored, but rarely questioned him about the lives he called me to take or felt guilty for being his hands. Perhaps he was merciful enough to take that feeling away. Or maybe their actions warranted the swift hand of justice.

Bay's lips pursed. "Will Fate allow you to stay the execution until tomorrow? Today is a sacred day. Within hours, the Center will be filled with people from every sector."

"He will not be kept waiting." Truthfully, I was no longer strong enough to hold Fate's wishes at bay. And apparently, he wanted the crowd to witness the person's death. Bay's eyes fell on my blue lips, then my icy hands. He gave me a knowing look and inclined his head ever so slightly.

He was the only one of the four who seemed to at least attempt to understand my position and duties. The others couldn't care less what it meant to be the 'daughter' of Fate, let alone to hold him inside.

Ela, my grandmother, spoke next. "There will be many who cross the border today. Perhaps you won't find the person you seek." She hoped I wouldn't find my mark, but I would. Fate would not budge on this execution.

"Fate will reveal his mark to me," I told them, my fingers curling in. He always led me to the ones he craved. In my mind, a vibrant orange sky sliced through the densest part of the forest near the border separating Sector Thirteen from Twelve... "I must carry out his sentence at sunset."

Wayra gasped and a gust of wind blew through the center. Pale ribbons of her hair thrashed back and forth, flapping wildly. Her robes faded from sky blue to cloud white in an instant. I flashed a warning glare at her, and she schooled herself quickly. I wasn't afraid of any of them, despite the clout and powers they held, because ultimately, Fate was more powerful than all of them combined, and he'd made me his equal.

"Can't it wait until after midnight?" Ethne blazed, her skin becoming ruddy to match the flaming hues of her hair.

"It cannot," I bit back at her. *Do they think I enjoy this?*

I didn't ask for this curse; I had no choice but to fulfill his will. Even when it conflicted with theirs, even when it conflicted with mine. "The citizens of the lower sectors know what happens in The Gallows. That's why the King sends their criminals through Thirteen into the banished lands." He hoped we would deal with them before they made it to any semblance of freedom they might carve out for themselves.

"That arcane practice will end soon enough," Ela promised sharply, taking a threatening step toward me.

Bay held his hand out as if to block her from reaching me, and with a warm, cautious expression, offered me a gentler reply. "Knowing a thing is different from witnessing it. The citizens in the Lower Sectors have never *seen* anyone hanged."

Grandmother Ela pushed Bay's hand away and bared her teeth. "Do as you must, Daughter of Fate. You clearly aren't seeking our permission to carry out your task."

Ethne and Wayra nodded their assent, each staring at me with equal parts fear and anger. Bay remained neutral, as always. They turned to leave, each facing their respective Houses. I stopped them before they fled. "There is another matter I wish to discuss."

The heads of the Houses stopped and turned to face me once again.

"Today is my seventeenth birthday."

Ela's jaw ticked. Grandmother knew what I wanted, and she didn't want me to have it.

I clenched the muscles around my stomach and ribs. "I claim the House of Fate."

Ethne started toward me, stopped only by Bay's outstretched hand – again. "The House of Fate has not been occupied since your mother's death. It's practically uninhabitable," she growled. Her flaming robe licked at Bay's hand, but never burned him.

"I am of age to claim it," I asserted, "and as Fate's chosen, now that I am of age, it is my right to do so."

Wayra cleared her throat, pushing her colorless hair behind her ears. "Claiming your inheritance will not entitle you to a seat in the Circle."

Yet, I wanted to add.

I glared at her until the silent wind surrounding her roared. Even so, I refused to back down. She turned to her peers. "We can forbid it," she suggested. "We can demolish the House."

Bay stepped forward, his dark robes thrashing in Wayra's blustery fury. "Demolishing the House would weaken the Circle. We draw some power from the residue of spells worked inside its walls. For that reason, we cannot demolish it. And, as Sable is the rightful heir, she is within her rights to claim the House as her own." Ethne boiled and opened her mouth to spew her hatred as a caldera did lava. Bay put a hand up to stop her and continued, "But, we do not have to recognize it as anything more than a structure, and continue to reap the benefits of having the House remain intact. The House of Fate was stripped when Cyril died, as was the House's Circle seat. It is a building constructed of wood and stone, nothing more."

I expected Ela to continue the fight, but was surprised when she said, "Let her claim it, then. And let it be known that the *accursed* will no longer be welcome in any of our Houses."

I stifled a smile. I had never been welcomed inside them and wasn't welcome now, so literally nothing would change.

Grandmother felt that it would have been better if I'd never been born. I'd always seen the truth of it in her eyes. She was waiting to witness the day Fate turned on me and called for my life instead of asking me to take or change someone else's. After all, she'd told the story a hundred times with me in earshot, of the day Cyril crossed Fate and how he rose against her. The way she swung from a rope she'd somehow secured and hoisted herself.

My grandmother's hazel eyes, for all the warm tones they contained, were cool as she dismissed me, glancing among her peers for their opinions on the matter.

In the end, the Circle decreed the House mine. I could repair it as needed, decorate it as I liked, and would reside in it – alone. And it would only ever serve as a residence. Never again would the House of Fate be represented in The Gallows' Circle.

Not that it made sense. What could my mother have done to anger Fate so much that he would kill her? And what did she do to the Circle, to her own mother, to make them so angry with her?

Bay called my name as I turned to leave them in the Center. "See that you carry Fate's plan out swiftly on this night. We should not mar the Equinox longer than necessary."

I'd never drawn out a hanging, and I wouldn't do so tonight. I wanted it over as much as everyone else. Well, everyone except the one who would hang.

Instead of telling him that, I inclined my head. Perhaps I could sweet-talk Fate into allowing me to hang the young man in the wood, away from the eyes of our visitors. Surely, he could make that concession.

A young girl from the House of Earth emerged from the woods, robes hiked around her calves, her steps fueled by fear. My stomach sank. "Priestess Ela!" she shrieked, her voice jolting with her steps. "Priestess!"

My grandmother turned to receive her with open arms, gifting the young witch with kindness she'd never bestowed upon me. She nearly knocked Ela down, but threw quivering arms around my grandmother, panting against her as tears streamed down her cheeks. "Priestess, a witch is dead. On the border," she stuttered. "It's Harmony, from the House of Fire."

Ethne gasped, racing just above the earth toward our border with Twelve.

Nausea coiled in my stomach as Fate confirmed that the girl who'd visited me earlier had indeed ignored his warning and made the wrong choice. My marrow ached for her. I closed my eyes and whispered a wish for her soul to separate and move on to the Goddess.

I turned my attention to the one I knew was responsible for her death. His hair was the color of wet sand, and he had twin dimples the murdered girl wanted nothing more than to see aimed at her.

On this eve, the witches will be avenged, Fate whispered.

Suddenly, the anxiousness I'd felt since he told me I would have to execute someone on this day faded away into a glorious, satisfying burn that I knew would soon be quenched. Justice would be meted out tonight. And not only would I make him pay, I'd send a strong message to anyone else in the sectors who even for a second considered harming one of our own.

three

Every House was somber as preparations began for the Equinox celebration. The Affinity Battle that was supposed to be resurrected today for the festivities was cancelled.

The young witch's body had been prepared by her House. As she was from the House of Fire, she would be laid on the altar of flame, and fire would guard her until Ethne instructed it otherwise. The witches of The Gallows would mourn her throughout the day, and then flames would consume her body at daybreak.

I attempted to pay my respects to her, but Ethne, true to her word, referred to me as the accursed and refused to accept me into her House. So, I watched from the steps of the House of Fate as witches from House after House lined up and filed into Ethne's home to honor their fallen sister.

When the last witch had exited and the front door creaked closed, I made my way to the cabin that had been my home for as long as I could remember and began to pack my things. I only needed to bring my essentials and supplies. The House still contained all of my mother's belongings.

The cabin sat alone in the woods far behind my mother's House – *my House*, I tried to correct in my mind. The only sounds along the trodden path came from the scampering squirrels, singing cicadas, and pairs of birds foraging for worms in the rich, dark earth. They flittered about as I began to pack.

I filled my cauldrons with my tapers and their holders, along with small burlap bags of tea leaves, tight bundles of white sage, and my collection of crystals. I'd smudge the House before I took my belongings inside. There was enough negative energy surrounding the House to smother a witch if she wasn't careful. And who knew what had been trapped inside?

Wrapping my wishbones in the casting cloth, I laid them on top of the pile and grabbed my broom. Once I'd gathered everything I wished to take, I closed my eyes and spirited myself to the warped back porch of the House of Fate. Taking a deep breath, I reminded myself again, *This is* my *House now.*

"Hey," a deep voice called out from behind me.

I jumped and whirled around, clutching my chest and dropping the substantial cauldron precariously close to my toes. "You scared me."

Brecan chuckled, striding toward me in his easy gait. He took up the heavy cauldron and pulled the weathered, squealing back door open for me. "After you. This is *your* House, after all."

I couldn't help but smile.

"And anyway, I hardly snuck up on you." His lavender eyes twinkled with mischief. "You should pay better attention to your surroundings."

He pushed his sky blue cape back as he stepped into the house, instantly at ease. "What else do you need from the cabin?" he called over his shoulder as he spun in a circle.

"Not too much. What do you think of it?" I asked.

"Needs to be dusted," he answered dryly, dragging his finger over the nearest table's surface. "But it looks like it always has, I suppose." It was a rite of passage to peek in the windows of the former House of Fate for little witchlings – though none would dare linger long. It was said that a curse might pass to them if they absorbed too much of the dark energy it possessed.

In reality, the House felt empty to me. Bay suggested that a residual magic abided here, but I couldn't sense it. The House was bones. A cage of ribs. And the heart it once held had long since decayed.

"Anyway," Brecan said, clapping his hands, "I'm at your disposal. Do with me what you will." There was more than the offer of help in his tone.

I decided not to answer. Instead, I turned my attention to my cauldron. I'd planned on smudging the House before I brought my belongings inside, but that was when I thought negativity dwelled in every corner. Now that I was inside, the House felt like a void. I wasn't sure it was necessary to smudge the rooms, but tradition called for it. It would be unlucky to start a life in a House that hadn't been purged, just in case.

"Tell you what, I'll be right back," Brecan finally said, marching out the back door.

The only other things I needed were my clothes, sheets and blankets, and pots and pans. I would have to harvest from my garden at the cabin until winter, and plant a new one here in the backyard next spring. I pinched my bottom lip, looking out over the overgrown lawn. Somewhere beneath the tall grass, in the rich earth, were the weedy roots of my mother's plantings. I leaned my broom into the kitchen's bare corner and sighed. There was much work to be done.

Brecan reappeared, tossing his long, icy blond hair over his shoulders. His locks were arrow straight and shone like silk. Tonight, all the girls who ventured into Thirteen from the lower sectors would cast lingering, longing glances in his direction. To them, Brecan was exotic; a feast for the eyes, in the middle of what must be a great famine.

"How did you know I would be here?" I asked.

He grinned, grabbing the top of the door frame and leaning toward me. "Word travels fast."

"Did Wayra send you to try to convince me to defy Fate?"

He shook his head. "I haven't even seen her today. Besides, I'm not worried about what she thinks; I'm worried about you."

I glanced at him in my periphery. "She would exile you for saying that."

He crossed the room in two long strides. "Only if she heard me," he leaned in to whisper in my ear, toying with a strand of my hair.

"Tonight, I'll hang the one who took the Fire witch's life."

Brecan's eyes sharpened. "Good. Not only will it exact justice for our fallen sister, it'll ease some of the tension building among the Houses."

The mounting tension... Perhaps I could help ease it, but would anything ever alter the other witches' perception of me?

Brecan placed a comforting hand on my shoulder. "Take time to get settled. I'll be back with the rest of your things, starting with your clothes."

With his touch, my heart skipped the slightest beat. Brecan and I had a strange relationship, one that was slightly more than friendship, but a lot less than love. It was one that every witch in The Gallows neither understood, nor approved of. My face didn't heat at the thought of him seeing my undergarments, but I knew him well enough to know there would be a spark in his eyes when he returned with them in hand.

He waltzed out the door with a smirk on his lips.

I lit the sage and its earthy aroma filled the room, rich and cleansing. I led the smoke, letting it waft into every corner of every room, on all five floors. Once I finished, I could finally breathe easier. Not because the sage expelled any danger, but because one task of the many I'd mentally listed was finished and I could begin another.

I made my way back downstairs, raising every window pane that wasn't stuck to the sill, and pushed all the dingy curtains back. A thick layer of dust hid the intricacies of every solid surface. Gusts from outside didn't dislodge a single particle as far as I could tell, but the musty smell that had settled into the walls began to drift away by the cleansing wind.

In the parlor, I lifted the sheets from the furniture, piling them in the room's corner. A deep purple couch with plush pillows propped against the backrest was flanked by twin mahogany chairs that hadn't been occupied since before I was born, but looked brand-new. Everything did. It was as if Mother had whispered a spell to preserve it all just as it was. Maybe she did. Or maybe Fate had taken care of my inheritance until I could claim it.

Maybe this was his gift to me. He warned me away from peeking in the windows like the other witches over the years, but today, he wanted me to have this. He wanted this House and everything in it to be mine.

This is your past and future, I told myself.

Brecan returned with my clothes, including boots and piles of gloves, with the wicked gleam I expected still twinkling in his eyes. "Which bedroom is yours?"

"I'm not sure yet. Just set everything in there on the bed," I suggested, gesturing to the nearest bedroom, located down the hall past the living room.

He complied and strode back outside. "I'll be back with more," he promised over his shoulder. If Brecan was anything, he was honest. By mid-afternoon, the cabin was empty, save for the bare furniture I no longer needed.

My only friend thought that quite enough work had been done for one day. Or maybe he was trying to lift my mood, considering the dark promise of the evening's events. "Come outside with me," he pleaded.

"If we go into the Center, everyone will stare at you."

He gave an ornery smile. "I'm okay with that."

"Wayra won't be."

He blew out a breath. "With all that has happened, perhaps it's not the time to push," he conceded. "Find me after?" *After you find and hang the young man Fate wants*, he meant. His eyebrows rose expectantly as he waited for my reply.

I swallowed. "Afterwards, I'll come back here. I need to perform a few readings."

Brecan hid his wince. He and I both knew that the likelihood of a single soul seeking me out after I hung a lower sector male would be absolutely nil, but Brecan was too polite to voice it. In any event, I had to try. This was one of the few times a year people from the other twelve sectors, which we called the Lowers, were allowed into The Gallows, and I needed any and all payments I could garner.

I looked around the House and blew out a breath. This place would take a fortune and another three hundred years to restore.

He nodded. "I'll find you after things wind down, then."

When he kissed my cheek, his lips lingered a beat too long. I pressed my eyes closed and wondered what it would feel like to really love him. To feel fire within my bones whenever he was near. There were spells for that.

I watched him quickly walk away from my House toward his own, where the House of Wind was being decorated with swaths of iridescent blue fabric, as delicate and sheer as the air itself. The female witches wore their best gowns and capes to match, held together at the neck by sculpted silver fasteners meant to mimic the swirling motion of the breeze.

From the window, I watched as my grandmother Ela oversaw the decorations for the House of Earth. The young witches called forth vines of ivy, guiding them as the new growth spiraled around the columns and railings. Great vines of cascading flowers bowed overhead, slowly showering petals that would never run out.

Ethne led the witches at the House of Fire as they formed pits that would later burn with colorful flames in every hue of the rainbow. At dark, they would light the entire Center with strategically positioned bonfires stacked vertically, so tall they'd overshadow the tallest of the forest trees.

Witches from the House of Water manipulated the fountains in front of their home. From the depths of their pools roared horses pulling chariots with angry, determined riders behind them. Bay greeted the first of the visitors from the lower sectors who gathered to watch a watery battle unfold. Their oohs and aahs echoed through The Gallows.

More people emerged from the wood and entered the Center.

I quickly dressed in my finest gown, a soft black velvet devoid of frills. Smoothing my hair, I hurried to gather my supplies.

I carried a small table outside and set it up in front of my House, covering it with a swath of black fabric. I arranged my casting cloth on top, placing a heavy crystal on each corner to hold it in place against the Wind witches' gusts. Citrine. Amethyst. Obsidian. Tourmaline.

The amethyst crystal that held down the far-right corner was from the tree-clinging boy. His strange familiarity pricked at me again, but I still couldn't place him. I stubbornly shoved thoughts of him away.

From my House, I brought out a deck of fortune cards, a crystal ball, and my silver bowl of wishbones. The cards and crystal were what citizens from the lower sectors expected, but the wishbones might call to someone.

I plucked a pair of chairs from the kitchen, situating them across the table from each other. I had no watery show, no petal-showering flora, no extraordinary twister or column of flame. Just the promise of a simple reading of fortune and a hope that someone – anyone – would want what I offered. And that the person would come to me soon.

Perhaps I could squeeze a few readings in before the condemned crossed into The Gallows.

Over the years, witches had paid me for readings in the form of scraps. Plants, when they had too many to fit in their perfectly measured garden rows. A ream of fabric when the dye clung too heavily to appropriately represent their Houses. Measures of rope they no longer needed.

Now that I lived in the House, I wondered if anyone would risk stepping foot inside, or even on the lawn in front of it, and defying their Priestesses or Priest. The cabin was located a discrete distance from the Houses, but here, I was among them, and privacy could not be ensured.

It doesn't matter, I told myself. *Fate will not let me starve. He will provide all I need.* My cabin's garden had flourished. I could make one flourish here, too.

Men, women, and children milled about the Center, racing from House to House and spectacle to spectacle. Soon, they would fill it until they spilt over its pointed edges.

On previous Equinoxes and Solstices when we welcomed any and all who wanted to join us in our Sector, I would make a mint. No one knew I was the "Daughter of Fate," or that I was different from every other witch in Thirteen. And if they did know the names by which the other witches called me, they assumed it was all for show. Merely another part of the thrilling, magical atmosphere we provided. It made them all the more willing to pay for a reading. They would smile at my crystal ball and sit down to hear what I might reveal, all the while wondering if it was real. In the end, they never truly cared. They just wanted to be enchanted for an evening.

Tonight, no smiles flashed in my direction. As the pit of my stomach began to roil and burn, I knew there would be no time. No readings beforehand.

It was time.

I stood from my table.

four

Fire writhed in my belly. The sun sank slowly to the west, inch by inch, until the hills swallowed it up.

He is here, Fate whispered. *Find him. End him. Make him pay.*

I held my stomach in a feeble attempt to extinguish Fate's fire. All I could taste was smoke. It burned my nostrils, charring the back of my throat. Even jumping into the fountains in front of the House of Water wouldn't quench Fate's flame. The only way to put it out was to find the boy.

The fiery sky blinded me for a moment. I turned in a circle, asking Fate to direct me.

The Center was full of people.

"Help me," I whispered.

Fate answered, *He is here*.

"Where?"

I searched every face for twin dimples, or for Fate's sigil. I would find it stamped onto the boy's forehead.

Musicians in the pentagram's Center struck up a jovial tune. Children squealed as they linked arms and skipped in circles through the grass. Witches from every House gathered in clusters, mingling together when so often they were kept separate. Their jewel-toned gowns and suits were the finest they had. I stood out among them like the sore thumb I was, dripping with a black velvet dress the same hue as my hair.

The Priestesses and Priest had been watching and waiting anxiously for me to emerge. When they saw me in the Center, they knew the time had come.

Grandmother Ela took control of the situation, commanding the crowd's attention. She explained that one of our own was found dead in the woods this morning, and that the culprit was among us and would be brought swiftly to justice. She warned them that this was no stunt, no skit. Those with children, she said, should take them behind the Houses so they would not witness the hanging that was about to occur.

Panicked murmurs bubbled through the crowd. Despite her warning, a few thought it was all part of the festivities, and waited with bated breath for something to occur. Others obeyed immediately. Mothers and fathers heeded her warning, guiding their children to the back porches of the Houses.

Slowly, the witches of every House began to chant, cleansing the atmosphere and casting a protective spell over the innocent.

They'd never assisted me in the least.

Although, to be fair, one of their own had never been so callously discarded.

My eyes found Brecan's. He gave a nod and I knew he'd told Ethne I was searching for the one who killed Harmony, the Fire witch. Brecan had always been a buffer between me and all the others, and I was thankful for his comforting presence.

A circle of young men from the lower sectors stood at the bottom of the Center. One threw his red head back laughing, clapping his two dark-haired companions on the back. Their two friends tipped back bottles, and I'd bet those drinks weren't their first, given their loose tongues and manners. "This is a joke, is all," one said. "A prank – and a good one, at that. *Beware... Hide your children's eyes...*" he joked, poking fun at Ela's legitimate warning.

I wondered how much fun he would be having if she removed his tongue, or even the ability to wag it for the evening.

They were the right age and build. Even though none had hair the color of wet sand, changing the color of one's hair was simple enough. I casually walked toward them just to be sure.

As I steadily approached, their laughter faded away.

The Lowers greeted one another, not by bows, but by shaking hands. I could learn much from a simple handshake. The only problem was that the residue of their touch would linger long past the initial contact...

The red-headed jokester saw me first and nudged one of the dark-haired boys, who turned to me with a roguish smile. His nose had been broken, but there were no divots in his cheeks. His hair was the same dark water hue of his friend. They were built the same. Gestured the same way. His eyes were the color of burnt toffee, a strange amber shade that was both warm and cool at the same time.

I realized the dark-haired men were brothers.

I turned to the other dark-haired brother, noticing his hair was a shade darker, a brown so deep it was nearly black. When he finally noticed me, I almost missed a step. His eyes were spun gold, the loveliest I'd ever seen. I told Fate right then and there that if it was him, I refused to do his bidding tonight.

Fate just chuckled in response.

"Good evening, Miss," the red-head greeted, extending his hand. "Thank you for allowing us to attend your celebration."

Flashing him a smile, I took his hand. "It is we who owe you thanks."

The flash of a shield entered my mind. He was a protector of sorts. Likely a soldier. And a good one, too, as the silver shield he projected bore scars, but none of them fatal.

The roguish brother opened his hand and grinned as I placed mine into it. "Pleasure to meet you," he said formally.

The golden-eyed brother watched silently as the others greeted me, but held his hand out. "Pleased to meet you," he rasped. When I took his hand, I couldn't suppress my gasp. In my mind, he kissed me. Feverishly. I wondered if he saw the same thing, because he pulled his hand away slowly, looking at me as if I'd hexed him.

I quickly schooled my expression, taking a deep, calming breath. *By the Goddess, what was that?*

"Excuse me," I told them, walking quickly toward the woods beyond them. I held my middle. My stomach was being singed. Fate had finally decided to show up and help me.

Fine timing that he granted me his favor only after *I made a fool out of myself in front of those young men.*

Not that I cared, I decided.

I was relieved his mark wasn't upon the golden-eyed boy. If he was the culprit, I might have been tempted to visit him in Twelve, just as the doomed young witch had sought out her lover. I picked up my skirts and jogged into the trees, letting the forest swallow me. Around my waist was a skinny length of solid black rope, stained with the last breaths of those Fate had damned and that I'd hung for him. I uncoiled it and quickly knotted the noose.

Fate whispered to me, *You have found him. Now, make him pay.*

Three young men huddled together, encircling a young witch from my grandmother's House. Her green gown and robes darkened in time with the sky overhead.

None of them realized I was behind them until I spoke. "Lovely evening," I remarked, staring up at the painted sky through the canopy. It was just as I had seen, just as Fate had designed.

"Uh, it sure is," one of them chuckled.

"Do you know these boys?" I asked the young Earth witch. *Madeline*, Fate told me. "Do you know them, Madeline?"

She shook her head rapidly, a tear falling from her eye.

"We know *her*," the dimpled boy fibbed. Fate's mark throbbed above his brow, the sigil pulsing with the need for me to conquer him.

I smiled. "You lie." I waved for the girl to come closer to me. "Madeline." She hesitated for a moment, her fear of me being overridden by her fear of the men, and strode toward me, tucking herself behind my back. "Go find Priestess Ela. Remain at her side. It's time." Her eyes widened as the meaning of my words sunk in. She glanced back at the dimpled boy who was no longer smiling.

"Time for what?" he braced.

"A witch was found dead just inside our border this morning. The one who killed her will hang in just a few moments."

The muscle in his cheek twitched.

Dimples was going to run. I could see him weighing his options, considering which direction to take

"What does that have to do with us?" his tall friend asked. He had no idea what his friend was capable of.

"Going forward, you should be more careful of the company you keep," I warned him.

Before my words had a chance to carry over the wind, Dimples took off at a sprint toward the border. I let him run, allowing his confidence and sweat to build and drip in rivulets down his face and back. I let him think he might actually get away as I kept a steady walking pace at his heels. Then I whispered a spell to strengthen his spine so it wouldn't snap prematurely, lassoed his head like he was a runaway steer, dug my heels into the ground, and gave the rope a strong yank.

Insects that had been singing to one another quieted as I reeled him in and began to drag him back toward the Center. His cowardly friends were nowhere to be found. They had long since scurried away, and were likely crossing the border back into Twelve at this very moment.

He gasped for air, clawing at his neck.

Fate wanted him dead. Every witch in Thirteen wanted the same. Myself included. How many more witches would have died at his deceitful hands? "I suppose it would be polite to tell you why you're about to die, but I think we both know the reason."

He tried to reply, but the noose had already crushed his larynx. *Oops.*

A normal Equinox celebration would be in full swing with tinkling bells, crashing cymbals, and witches dancing around fires they set and manipulated for the delight of the crowd, but this was no normal Equinox. Through the trees, I could see that the members of every House had formed a protective circle around the pentagram, encasing the citizens of the lower sectors and making a human barrier between them and the gallows where Dimples would hang.

The Lowers called Sector Thirteen 'The Gallows' for a reason, though few had ever witnessed a hanging here. We were the only sector who had them, and who punished those who committed crimes against us, with hanging. Citizens from the Lowers called us barbaric and inhumane for it, but Fate demanded it, and even if he didn't, the Priestesses and Priest would.

I knew the punishments were fair, but I wondered how effective the threat was when it was so far removed. No one from the Lowers normally witnessed someone being put to death, though the young man wriggling behind me obviously knew about our customs. Even though he knew more than most, not even the threat of hanging deterred the handsome, dimpled boy from asphyxiating the young Fire witch.

The boy was desperate for air, so I whispered a spell to loosen the noose just a smidge. He coughed and sputtered, sucking in deep, ragged breaths. I stopped and gave him a chance to catch his breath.

"Did you think we wouldn't find you?" I asked, curious to know the mind of the cruel boy.

His lips shook with rage. *If only he were stronger...* I saw the threat in his eyes.

The trees thinned and then came to an abrupt stop as we neared the gallows. The witches' chants were drowned out by the shocked gasps of those from the Lowers. When they saw what, or whom, I dragged behind me, the parents who hadn't heeded Ela's warning quickly covered their children's eyes, or scooped them up and carried them away toward the backs of the Houses to join those who had listened. The mouths of men and women, old and young, gaped as I dragged Dimples to the set of wooden gallows erected at the base of the pentagram.

Death was not welcome in the sacred circle.

Hovering over him, I waited for him to recover. "Stand up."

An inferno of hatred flared in his eyes. He tried to talk, but his crushed larynx only elicited flat shrieks from his mouth.

"Stand up, or I will drag you onto the platform."

He managed to get a knee up and pushed to his feet, sweat-soaked hair obscuring the upper half of his face. The coarse rope had cut into the tender skin of his throat. Rivulets of blood and sweat merged and sluiced down the skin of his chest, disappearing behind the buttoned fabric of his shirt. He panted, his lips puffing out with each breath.

"Now walk," I ordered, tugging on the rope as I ascended the stairs. At the bottom, he braced himself and resisted, refusing to budge. "I really thought we had an understanding. You were going to cooperate, and I was going to *consider* allowing your neck to snap when the floor falls out from under your feet... but now, you're irritating me."

His lips curled up into a cruel smile. "Witch," he mouthed, his throat squeaking like a rusted hinge.

It was my turn to grin. "Yes, I am. But do you want to know a secret? I am no mere witch. I am the Daughter of Fate. This evening, I am his hands, and his fingers want to crush the life out of you, the way you did our sister. Fate's hands never weaken, never falter, and they never fail."

I whispered a spell lifting the killer's feet off the ground. He sputtered as he floated, as I took control and made him hover up the steps while I walked alongside, as easily as one would guide a cooperative hound. Settling him beneath the top post, I ordered the spell to release him. He fell the few inches, nearly losing his balance. I righted him as Fate gave me his name.

Jenson. Jenson Renk.

Waving an arm through the air as one would clear a chalkboard, I whispered a spell to extricate Jenson's memory, projecting it to the crowd, where they saw what he'd done from his point of view. Saw his bony fingers wrap around her neck, watched him straddle her and crush her body beneath his. They witnessed her struggle against him. Her fear was so alive, I could almost taste it. Her desperation was palpable. The Lowers gasped as she floundered and then went still as the light and life faded from her beautiful amber eyes. Her fingers weakened and fell away from his punishing hands. Her head lolled to the side, but he held tight another moment to make sure she was dead.

"Jenson Renk, citizen of Sector Twelve," I announced, "you murdered Harmony, witch of the House of Fire, by means of asphyxiation. You are hereby sentenced to death by hanging. Fate has chosen to show you no mercy, because you showed none to our sister. As repayment for your crime, he demands your death."

I stared him down as I spelled the rope in my hands. The frayed end transformed into the head of a snake. It coiled around on itself, hissing at the guilty man before quickly slithering up the posts and across the beam. Usually, I would have made him stand on a stool and hefted his weight for him, but I wouldn't do anything to help a murderer of this caliber.

I didn't even bother with the doors that would break apart, giving way beneath him. No, there would be no mercy for him. I would not allow his neck to break. He would strangle slowly, the way he had strangled Harmony.

Bay stared at me from below with an unreadable expression. I likely hadn't made it quick enough for his liking, but I didn't care in that moment. Brecan stood at the fringe, his rigid posture a tell that he would gladly help if I needed it. It was a kind gesture, but I'd never required anyone's assistance for this. This... was what I was made for.

The snake coiled tighter and tighter over the beam until the condemned man's toes were lifted off the ground. He kicked, trying to find the planks beneath.

Jenson's face turned red and then purple as he scrambled to force his fingers between his skin and the serpent to ease the pressure. His heart beat faster, but the blood wasn't able to flow where he needed it most. His lips bulged.

He kicked out in a blind panic, sending his body swaying back and forth until his movements became uncoordinated. His grip floundered and his arms fell limply to his sides, twitching occasionally.

The thrashing and swinging slowed, and then Jenson stopped struggling.

The group of young men whose hands I'd shaken stood just within the collection of witches, lingering closest to the platform. With wide eyes and gaping mouths, their attention was fixed on Jenson Renk, staring like they could see his soul leave his body.

They couldn't, but I could.

A dark mist emerged from his flesh. It lingered as I whispered a spell transforming the snake back into a rope. His lingering last breath settled into the coarse fibers, darkening the length of cord, and then Fate's victim fell to the ground an empty heap, naught but flesh and bone.

There would be a fuss in the lower sectors tomorrow – tonight, if some chose to leave to spread the word about what they saw. Those who witnessed his hanging would never forget it, but Jenson Renk would be forgotten in time, and that was all that mattered.

Fate was pleased.

The fire in my belly was extinguished. My fingers and lips had thawed.

I descended the stairs and met a pair of golden eyes the moment my feet hit the ground. I looked away, unable to stomach the emotions blazing behind them, and made my way through the crowd that wasted no time parting for me.

five

From the steps of my House, I watched Ethne on the platform of the gallows where Renk's body lay prone on the weathered-gray planks. She waved her arms over the killer's corpse, causing a white-hot fire to consume it before the stench of him reached the crowd. She was a master of her craft, and could wield the flame so precisely that there wouldn't even be a char mark left on the planks. I could feel the heat of her anger wave across the grass.

Ela carefully climbed the steps to stand beside her. Her thick robes, now as dark green as the pines in the forest's middle, concealed her shrinking body. She'd shriveled just since this morning. Time had been kind to her for a very long time, but she had begun to pay the price for the unnatural extension of her youth. She looked positively brittle. Tonight's events had aged her significantly, though I wasn't sure why they'd taken such a toll.

Her hair faded more and more by the minute, leaching from newborn fawn to silvery white. The slight hunch in her upper back became a sharp mountain peak. Her skin wrinkled as she climbed, and her muscle withered away. By the time she reached the platform, she could barely fight the atrophy overwhelming her body to pull her weight up the stairs. She huffed and puffed, and I honestly thought she might fall over dead when she reached the top step.

It was immediately clear that despite the ravaging toll on her body, Grandmother's mind hadn't shriveled at all. Nor had her demeanor. But as she cleared her throat and her weak voice tried to calm the crowd, Fate gently whispered that her days were numbered.

As if she could read my mind, her hazel eyes snapped to mine.

A hush fell over the crowd. I wasn't sure if she'd spelled them, or if they genuinely wanted to hear what she had to say about what they witnessed.

The shaky words she spewed were spelled to calm and comfort those who heard them. She assured them that no witch would ever harm the innocent. The shoulders of the members of the crowd visibly relaxed, as did their breathing. The worry lines on their faces faded away. It was like they'd taken a collective breath and slowly expelled it.

I took a seat at my table once Bay helped Ela descend the platform's steps, and the musicians began strumming a soothing tune. The circle of witches that had surrounded the Center broke apart, freeing those within.

I searched for dark hair and golden eyes, but never found him.

Ethne lit the bonfires. A pair of witches juggled fire sticks, while another duo swung lit chains around in great arcs, slicing bright circles through the twilit sky. The scent of smoke filled the air as our guests finally began to form groups, talking and even laughing among themselves.

The witches of the House of Water called for miniature storm clouds to build. Lightning forked from them, creating small, intense bursts of light within the roiling thunderheads. The thunder they made complemented the musicians' drum beat.

Fragrant flowers in every color and shape emerged from the soil as the witches from the House of Earth were introduced. Topiaries of twisted vines formed next to a family of three, a father, mother, and daughter, perfectly mimicking their shapes down to the child's fine hair.

Those from the House of Wind sent a sweet, warm breeze to sweep across the space, plucking petals from stems and sending them whirling above the rooftops nearby, beyond the treetops and high into the sky, until they disappeared from sight. As they lowered their raised hands and snuffed out any trace of wind, soft petals rained from the heavens. Within minutes, the grass was carpeted in petals of every color of the rainbow. Children scooped up the delicate petals and flung them into the air, trying to imitate the Wind witches.

Tonight, here in this space, no one would scold them.

Tomorrow would be different. I'd heard that those who returned to Sector Twelve would advise their children not to speak about coming here, nor about the magic they witnessed. Where it was almost fashionable to attend years ago, cavorting with witches was becoming more taboo with each passing season. When I was a child, the woods overflowed with guests. Now, the Center was barely full.

Being a witch is nothing to be proud of, they would tell them. *Witches are dangerous creatures.*

They weren't wrong, but they also weren't right.

Children would ignore their own experiences and feelings if adults pressed them hard enough into the straight and narrow line. It was how prejudice and ignorance were perpetuated through the generations. But as long as it was only one night a year and they hid their purchased tinctures and herbs in their pockets, covering their heads and faces with the hoods of their cloaks as they crossed the borders and snuck back to their homes, there was no harm.

I whispered a spell, lighting the white candle on my table. I didn't have any of the elemental affinities, but I'd learned to conjure the elements to a small degree. I couldn't call down a tornado or flood a stream, but I could light wicks and fill my basins if the well dried. And, as long as I paid attention to my plants, they grew just fine.

For hours, I sat and watched. Anyone who ventured close to my table quickly found their way back into the anonymity of the crowd, placing as much distance between them and me as possible.

I sat quietly, alone, and watched the stars tilt around the blue-black sky. Blackberry wine was being passed around to anyone who wanted it, and the heavy atmosphere that I'd brought to the celebration of the Equinox was replaced by a more carefree one. The alcohol probably helped assuage the Lowers' feelings, and we were plying them with enough to drown an entire sector.

Someone wearing a heavy cloak finally staggered to my table, pulled out the chair opposite me, and flopped into it unceremoniously. The sweet smell of blackberries filled the air, along with something masculine and heady.

I rolled my eyes. "You're drunk. You should find whomever you came with and ask them to see you home."

Strong hands pushed back the hood, and with a start, I realized it was the handsome man from earlier. Looking into a pair of bloodshot, golden eyes that tried vainly to focus on mine, I noticed details I'd missed earlier. His dark brown hair was freshly cut; the hair at the nape of his neck hadn't even begun to grow back out. His shoulders were broad, and the cloak concealing them was made of thick, black material. In golden thread, a symbol was emblazoned over his heart, but it was wrinkled and I couldn't make it out.

"I'm not going nowhere," he slurred.

I crossed my arms and raised my brows. "You want a reading?"

"Reading? I don't see any books," he chuckled.

"I read fates."

"Futures?" He laughed and pointed a finger at me. "You're a witch."

"And you're obviously a genius." *A drunken genius, with pretty, molten eyes.*

"You're supposed to make love potions and hex dolls," he slurred. "Not hang people."

"Do you need a love potion? You're handsome enough to find someone on your own, I'd warrant," I said truthfully. He rewarded the compliment with a ridiculously wide smile that made my lips curl upward in response. "I didn't expect anyone to be brave enough to approach my table tonight," I told him. "And people rarely surprise me."

He grinned proudly and put his hand across his chest—the salute of the Kingdom's militia. He must be a soldier. "Glad to be of service, Madame. Perhaps I should offer *you* a reading, instead."

He was ridiculous and…sweet.

"Look, I can help you. Do you think you can climb steps? I have something that will help clear your mind, but you'll have to sit down for a few minutes after drinking it."

He scrutinized the stairs leading to my front door, and with a determined look, squared his shoulders and nodded his head. "Yeah. Yeah, I can do that."

Um, good. They're just steps.

I blew out my candle and gathered everything into my casting cloth, deciding I'd sort it all out later. It was clear that Fate had damaged any opportunity I might have had to make money tonight, not that I minded, in all honesty. Killing Jenson Renk was worth it. I wondered if it would feel the same in a month's time when I had no savings to provide what I couldn't, and the other Houses wouldn't.

Still, this young man obviously came from money. Perhaps he would feel grateful after the tincture I was about to prepare worked its magic.

I offered a hand in case he fell, but he made it up the staircase and stepped over the threshold and into my house. As far as I knew, he was the first outsider to ever step foot inside its walls.

I laid my things on a chair and pointed him in the direction of the couch while I went to rummage through the kitchen for the ingredients I needed. Brecan had left most of my herbs in a sack on the counter. Quickly plucking leaves from those I needed, I folded them neatly into a tea bag and grabbed a mug. I muttered a spell for it to fill with water, and for the water to heat but not boil. I was in a hurry. Something told me to help him and get him out of there as quickly as I could.

For this reason, I was thankful when the aromas of sage, rosemary, lavender, and mint filled the air.

As I walked toward the couch with the mug, the young man sat up clumsily, removing his feet from the oblong table in front of him, sheepishly apologizing and putting them back on the floor. He scrubbed a hand down his face as I handed him the mug.

"Drink. This should make you feel better."

He glanced from the steaming liquid to me and back. "How do I know it's safe?"

I smiled. "Why wouldn't it be?"

"You killed that young man tonight," he answered quietly.

My lungs expanded with a deep breath. Something about the way he said it made me wish I had somehow held Fate off until after the festivities, just so he wouldn't see the type of magic in which I was adept.

"That man was a murderer." Steam from the cup wafted into his face and I saw his eyes begin to clear.

Changing the subject, I asked, "You were with two others. Where are they?"

"We got separated. I don't know where they are."

"I have no intention of harming you," I told him honestly. "The tea will do nothing more than sober you up. Then you can go find your friends."

His fingers tightened on the mug's handle. "I hope I'm not making a mistake by trusting you." He brought the mug to his lips and took a tentative sip. His dark brows shot up. "This... this is delicious."

I tried to smile. "Glad you like it."

Within minutes the mug was empty, the spell had worked, and my guest was sober. He sat the mug on the coffee table and scrubbed a hand down his face, letting out a pent-up breath. "Thank you again. I hope I didn't do or say anything to offend you. I'm sorry to have intruded."

"You didn't intrude. I invited you in."

I had no idea why I did it, but I did. And now that he was here, I had the strangest sensation humming through me. My fingers tingled with the need to touch him.

He was quiet, his gaze focused but gentle. Then he surprised me by blurting, "I had no idea until tonight that beautiful women hanged fully-grown men."

I ticked my head back. "And who did you assume did it?"

He flashed a genuine smile. "I meant no offense. I just... my friends talked me into coming tonight to blow off some steam. My life is about to drastically change." He ran a flustered hand through his hair.

"How so?"

His knee bounced at the question. "I appreciate your hospitality, but I really should be going."

"Mom and Dad not know you snuck out?" I laughed as he stood.

"Something like that." His eyes caught on my silver bowl. A few wishbones that I hadn't carried outside remained on the bottom. "Why do you have those?"

"Wishbones are the best way for me to read someone."

"That's unusual. I expected cards or a crystal ball."

"I can use those, but don't prefer them." The bones called to me when I was just a girl. Wishbones, in particular, and I'd garnered all of them I could ever since.

"Is it difficult to read a person's fate?" He worried his hands.

"It depends on the person. Some fates are more complex than others."

He stared at the delicate bones, then turned his attention to me. "Would you read mine?"

"For a price."

"Name it, and it's yours," he promised.

I looked him over again, assessing his fine clothes and grooming. He had money.

"A bag of coin."

"Done," he chirped, rubbing his hands together.

That was easier than I expected. I thought he would haggle.

Where most people were easy for me to read, even from a distance, this young man was not. I couldn't pin down anything about him solidly, which shook me more than I would admit. "Sit at that table," I instructed, pointing at a small, square table in the corner of the room.

Perhaps it was me. Was I still rattled about the events of the evening?

He removed the sheet covering the chairs and table and sat in one, turning to watch as I gathered the iron bowl of wishbones. "Moving in?" he guessed.

"Just today, yes." Thank goodness I'd moved my clothes into a nearby bedroom. I didn't bother with the casting cloth. It wasn't necessary for a reading, it just added flair to the atmosphere; flair that most Lowers needed to make the reading feel more fun than true.

Sitting across from him, I placed the bowl between us. He studied the inscriptions engraved around the bowl's rim. "Choose a wishbone. Before you break it, wish for the knowledge of your future."

He plucked a bone from the bottom of the pile and closed his eyes. With a quick snap, the bone was broken in two, but something was terribly wrong.

I gasped at the sight of it.

His golden eyes snapped open.

My mouth gaped and I sucked in a shocked breath. Droplets of crimson blood dripped from the larger part of the bone, splattering onto the table. I felt a speck hit my cheek and wiped his blood away with my thumb. The smaller piece also bled, but to a lesser extent. I'd been reading fates for years, and had never seen a wishbone bleed. Three more large splatters fell before either of us spoke, and it was he who managed it.

"Why is it bleeding?" he asked, looking at me expectantly.

"Give me your hand." He dropped both pieces of bone and wiped his hands on his pant legs before proffering both. I placed my right palm against his and closed my eyes.

Scenes flashed through my mind. The first was a vision of him lying on his back, a foamy trail of blood bubbling from his mouth and his pupils dilated and still. Another scene swiftly appeared, of hands pushing him from a balcony or window… someplace high… and the sickening crunch that came when he hit the earth below. Another vision of him collapsing to the ground, a fountain of blood pouring over his lips and his skin pale as ice. That vision was erased by another, heralded by a wave of sharp pain as he looked down to find the tip of a blade protruding from his chest...

Every single fate pointed to one thing.

I called on Fate to confirm it and felt his warning warmth flow through my veins. The bone did not lie. There was no mistake. "Very soon, someone will try to kill you."

He gave a laugh of disbelief. "What? That can't be. You said yourself that some fates are more complex than others."

"You have no other fate than that."

I searched for any sign of hope and found none. His palm warmed mine, and through the connection, more scenes, each more disturbing and gruesome than the next, filled my mind. I couldn't see anything but his death as a product of murder. I grabbed his other hand and more scenes filled my mind, each more ghastly than the one before it. My lashes fluttered from the turmoil of seeing his body torn and empty.

He stared at our connected palms. "Could you be wrong?"

Our eyes met, and he knew the answer before I spoke. "No. I've never been wrong."

He was quiet for a long moment, clinging to my hands. When he cleared his throat, he croaked, "Does the blood mean they will succeed?"

I pursed my lips. The most difficult part of reading the fate of another was telling them they would die soon. "If you don't figure out who it is and stop them before they take action against you, then yes. I'm afraid they will succeed."

I pulled my hand away.

His mouth parted as he focused on the droplets of blood now speckling my table. "Can you tell me who it is?"

"No, I can't. I'm sorry."

"Okay, you said 'very soon'. How soon, exactly?"

I pulled the iron bowl toward me and ran my hands over the bones inside. "I wish I could tell you more, but I don't think it will be very long before they make an attempt. I take it no one has tried to kill you before?"

He glanced from my hands to my eyes. "No, they haven't."

"It's not pleasant." I knew that from experience; a rather unpleasant one I'd rather forget than have dredged up. Especially tonight, given the events of the evening.

"Given the bleeding bone, I'd say it won't be." He scrubbed his face again and let out a frustrated groan.

The young man was handsome. It was a pity he wouldn't live long, and even more of a shame he wasn't a witch. I'd never actually considered hand-fasting before, but if circumstances were different, he could make me reconsider.

He stood abruptly and extended his hand.

I looked at his palm. "Your fate won't change with another physical connection."

"No, I know. I was just going to shake your hand so I could thank you properly."

I quirked a brow. "You're thanking me, despite the news I've delivered?" My fingers itched to touch him one more time, knowing it may be the last time I would have the opportunity.

"I'm thanking you," he said, taking my hand in his. It had somehow floated up toward his without my knowing... "for your hospitality, for the information you provided, and I'd like to beg for your discretion."

"I don't know you, so I couldn't blab to anyone else."

He chuckled. "Right," he scoffed disbelievingly.

I pulled my hand away, stung. "I'm a witch, not a liar."

His smile fell away with his laughter. "You really don't know who I am?"

Crossing my arms over my chest, I scooted my chair away from him and farther into the corner. "Should I? Are you some sort of celebrity? Look around. You'll see no telecaster here."

"You must be the only person in Nautilus without one," he said beneath his breath.

"What was that?" I pretended not to have heard him. *He must be famous. With a face and build like that, the women in the Lower sectors would fawn over him. Any other witch would cast a love spell on him to make him hers for a time.*

Furtively, I looked at my herbal supply. I was tragically out of rosehips.

He hooked a thumb over his shoulder and shoved his hands into the pockets of his cloak. "I should go. I'm sure you're exhausted from the evening's events." His Adam's apple bobbed with his swallow.

"Do you need help finding your friends?"

He snorted. "Knowing them, they won't be leaving Thirteen until morning."

"I think you'll find that witches are nothing like the girls you've come to know in the lower sectors."

"How so?" he asked genuinely, his tongue wetting his full bottom lip.

"We're particular. And we *particularly* only pair with male witches – to whom we are hand-fasted."

"Hand-fasted?"

"It's what you would consider a marriage, except it only lasts for one year. Winter Solstice to Winter Solstice." There was no judgment in his eyes, just surprise. "You really didn't know that?"

"No, I really didn't. But... may I ask a question?"

"You just did," I replied sweetly.

He smiled. "What if you love the person to whom you're hand-fasted? What if a year isn't enough time to spend with them?"

I swallowed, trying to calm my thundering heart, and gave him the most honest answer I could, and the saddest. "I'm not sure witches are capable of loving someone for longer."

"Are you hand-fasted to someone? With someone?" he asked.

I shook my head. "No."

"Have you ever been?"

"No."

He quietly studied my face, his gaze locking onto mine. "Thank you again."

I gave him a small bow. He began walking backward, opened my door, and was gone.

six

"Wait!" I yelled. He paused on the step. "You promised payment."

"I'm afraid I'm out of money," he replied sheepishly. "But let me find my brother and our friend. They might have some."

I felt like throttling him. He was drunk when he stumbled to my table, but sober when he asked for the reading and promised payment. If our positions were reversed, would *he* happily work in exchange for nothing? Then again, he *was* about to die. I decided to take the high road—just this once.

"I will forgive your debt to me. You have more important things to worry about at this point."

"I'll repay you. I swear it."

Someone shouted, but I couldn't make out their drunken mumbling. His friends were in the Center, turning in circles and annoying all the witches trying to clean up.

"I'm here!" he yelled in response, throwing up his hand. "Thank you again," he said, locking eyes with me for a beat before jogging down the steps and crossing the yard to meet them.

He urged his friends toward the border. The three young men took to the woods, their dark cloaks flapping behind them.

All I could think was, *I hope he survives the night.*

As I pushed the door closed, a clock on one of the upper floors began to chime. I ignored the fact that it hadn't been wound in at least seventeen years and made my way into the house to wipe the blood from the table, and to cast that cursed bone out of my House.

I'd have to smudge again just to be able to sleep tonight… if it was possible to get the golden eyed boy out of my mind.

When I opened the back door and chucked the bone and shard out into the grass, I didn't even notice Brecan approaching. He ducked in time to avoid being hit. "Do I want to know?" he asked.

I opened my mouth, wondering if I should tell him about the reading and deciding against it. "Probably not."

"Wayra spoke to me," he casually mentioned as he stepped inside, his shoulder brushing mine.

"Do *I* want to know what about?"

"My future is finally looking a little brighter," he said, wagging his brows.

"Will you be hand-fasted?"

He pointed a finger at me. "You truly are a diviner of fate."

"And who is the lucky girl she's picked out for you?"

I followed him into the kitchen where he propped a hip against the counter. "You're unpacking this late?" he asked, looking at the bundles of herbs I'd used to make the sobering spell.

"I'm trying to. I can't focus."

He nodded, glancing from the herbs to me. "She said I could choose," he announced. "She said that as long as the young lady accepts, we will be fasted on the Winter Solstice."

"Who are you thinking of asking?"

Brecan gave me a smoldering look. *Oh, no. No, no, no.* "I was hoping you would be my first," he said boldly, crossing the room to stand in front of me.

"They would never approve," I told him. "I'm supposed to be isolated now that I've asked for my House back." *Not that I wasn't isolated before.*

"It's only for a year, Sable. It's not a lifelong commitment. By their own rules, they must approve if you accept."

"I think you'd find that a year is a long time to be sidled to the Daughter of Fate. Besides, if you fasted to me, no other witch would touch you after our year ended."

His eyes flicked to my lips. "Perhaps you're wrong, and our short-lived union would fuel their curiosity instead."

"You don't know what you're saying," I grumped, turning away from him and peering into the sitting room, at the spot on the purple couch where the golden-eyed boy had sat.

Brecan's hands found my waist. "I know you think I'm being ridiculous, but I'm not. And I know the consequences of my proposal as far as the Circle is concerned. You've always kept me at arm's length, but I think you'd find it much more pleasurable to keep me closer." He ran a hand down my upper arm. "Accept me, Sable."

I wished I felt something for him. Something like the tingle the mere sight of the boy with the bloody wish incited.

Brecan's hand fell away. "Would you even consider me?"

"It's not you, Brecan. It's…me," I answered lamely. "The witches hate me, and would hate you by extension if we were hand-fasted."

"They fear you. They don't *hate* you, Sable."

"It sure feels like hate to me."

When I didn't turn to face him, he stepped around to stand in front of me. "I'm too pretty to hate," he teased with a grin.

I couldn't help but smile. "You're not wrong."

"Do you feel anything for me at all? Even the slightest spark?"

A slight spark might be the best way to describe the way I felt. But a spark, however large, wasn't enough when I wanted an inferno. I wanted to want the man I hand-fasted to with every inch of myself. Every thought. Every breath. Every beat of my heart would be for him.

It was silly to think I'd ever have that, but I wouldn't settle for less.

I couldn't look Brecan in the eye.

"I see," he said quietly, tugging his cloak together. "I'll leave you alone, then."

"Brecan—"

"No, you've made yourself quite clear," he bit out before leaving the room, then my House, and then the yard.

He stomped to the House of Wind like a dark cloud. He didn't have to choose a witch from the same House and affinity, but it would make a smart first match, and there were plenty of talented, beautiful Wind witches for him to consider.

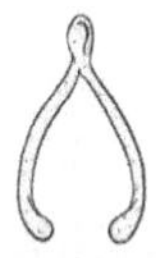

In the end, he would see reason, and would understand that he and I could never be. I just hoped I hadn't lost my only friend.

I paced the main floor, pausing at a portrait on the wall. My mother and I looked so much alike. I wasn't sure when the photograph was taken, but she must've been my age, or close to it. Her lips were shaped like mine, bowed at the top and full at the bottom. Her almond-shaped eyes were dark like mine. The portrait looked so real, almost like she could step out of the frame and join me.

I wished she could. It would be nice to talk to someone about Brecan and what had happened this evening between the two of us.

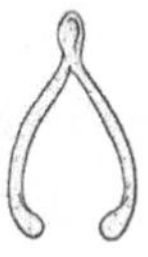

It took me hours to fall asleep after Brecan left. Hurting his feelings was never my intention, but I knew that lying to him would only cause more damage.

I stripped one of the beds in a room on the first floor and covered it with my sheets and blankets, but it still didn't feel right. The mattress was too plush. There wasn't a lump to be felt.

Tossing and turning for several hours, I finally fell asleep, just to have a strange dream wake me just before sunrise. Still, I couldn't bring myself to get out of bed and was hoping to fall asleep again, even though there was much to do. Stretching my arms and legs in the dappled sunlight that fell across my blankets made me feel warm where the dream left me cold.

It was of my mother. I didn't dream of her often, but when I did, it always unsettled me.

Closing my eyes, I slipped back to sleep, but didn't stay that way for long before a loud knock woke me. Sitting up with a grumble, I threw the blankets off and lumbered toward the door. Cracking it open and blinking against the bright morning light, I stared at the stranger standing on my steps.

"Daughter of Fate?" he asked. The man looked to be in his fifties, and his cropped, neat hair was equal parts gray and chocolate brown. I didn't know him, but I recognized the insignia smartly stitched into his dark cloak. The golden thread glimmered in the sunlight.

"I am she," I rasped, clearing my throat awkwardly. Straightening my spine, I waited for him to tell me what he wanted. I refused to invite him in.

"My name is Courier Edward Stewart. I have a delivery for you."

"A delivery from whom? I know no one in the lower sectors."

Courier Stewart didn't smile or show any emotion at all. His features were like iron as he held out his hands. In one was a small box, and in the other was a letter, sealed with golden wax. Pressed into the wax was the royal symbol, matching the one on his cloak – a spiraling nautilus shell. "The letter and parcel are from a member of the royal family," he replied formally.

The royal family? Why on earth would anyone in the royal family send me a package and a letter? Or anything at all, for that matter? Unless they heard about my role in last night's hanging...

I spied a cluster of Earth witches watching us from the Center, whispering to one another and giggling behind their hands. Brecan strode across the lawn to join them. His eyes met mine as I accepted the items.

"Is that all, Courier?" I asked, aware that the gaggle of witches watching the exchange had swiftly tripled in size.

"I will return before sunset to collect you. The letter will explain everything, but should you have any questions, I'll do my best to answer them then." He turned, jogged down my steps, and mounted a dappled mare I hadn't even noticed grazing in my front yard.

"What do you mean, *collect* me?" I asked.

He either didn't hear me, or purposely ignored my question, though I was fairly certain it was the latter. The nosey witch crowd giggled as I slammed the door closed.

Collect me? I don't think so.

I gave the palm-sized box a good shake as I walked further into the house. My fingers twitched to open it, wondering what I might find inside, but I broke the seal and unfolded the letter first. A separate, smaller rectangle of thick paper fell onto the table, but I ignored it.

Daughter of Fate,

I apologize for my lack of manners and decorum, and for not asking for your name last night so that I might properly address this letter. Or perhaps the greeting above is what you prefer. An intriguing title for an equally intriguing young woman.

In the box, you will find the payment I promised for your services. You read my future, saw my complicated fate, and didn't stretch my neck for not having the means to make a proper payment for services rendered. I trust that the contents of the parcel will cover any debt that I owe, in addition to an appropriate amount of interest for you having to wait to receive it.

As you have likely gleaned, I am a member of the royal family. My family and I would request your discretion regarding the revelations last evening, in the hopes that we can uncover and circumvent any attempt made upon my life.

During our brief time together, you made it clear that you neither have nor want a telecaster in your home, but you must have heard of our kingdom's traditions regarding royal matches. In case you aren't aware, the Prince of Nautilus must marry a woman from one of the Kingdom's sectors. As I am the eldest prince and of age to marry, I intend to do so very soon. Twelve young women have been chosen, one from each sector, and will arrive at the palace on this very evening. The women will reside with me and my family at the palace until I choose a wife from among the invitees.

Enclosed, you will find your invitation – the thirteenth.

My reasons for sending it are two-fold.

The first is more complicated than I care to put in writing. If you are curious at all, I would be more than happy to explain it in person.

The second is one you've probably intuited. I need the help that only someone with your particular skillset can provide.

I realize that a royal has never sent an invitation to a potential match in Sector Thirteen, and that even sending you this parcel and letter may cause you great trouble. If it is against your beliefs as a witch to marry an outsider, I will respect them, of course.

But I would be forever in your debt if you would come to the castle and remain close to me during your stay, as a means of possibly thwarting this threat and ferreting out those who seek to harm me.

Please help me, Daughter of Fate. Help me find the one who wishes me dead. Help me change fate's design.

Forever in your debt,
Prince Tauren Nautilus

What has he done?

My heart thundered as I bent and picked up the fallen paper from the floor and flipped it over. In swooping calligraphic letters, it read:

You are Cordially Invited to
Nautilus Palace.

Prince Tauren is to choose a bride. He has considered every eligible woman in the Kingdom and believes that you, above all the other women in Sector Thirteen, could become his wife and one day, reign at his side. One woman from every Sector has been invited to the palace so that he may spend time with each of you. It is an honor and privilege for you to represent your Sector as the Prince considers the best woman not only for his future,
but for the future of Nautilus.

Long may she prosper.

I let out a pent-up breath and flipped the card over. A small printed nautilus shell spiraled from the paper's center, spilling over the edges.

This had to be a joke. Did the royals truly think this was an honor? For a woman to be plucked from her home and life to parade around the palace competing for the Prince's attention?

Prince Tauren.

Why was the Prince of Nautilus in The Gallows? And how dare he order me to come to the palace? I didn't take orders from him. My orders came from Fate alone. I was sure *he* would have something to say on the matter. But when I whispered for him, he simply laughed, and immediately a sinking feeling filled my stomach.

Pinching my eyes shut, I knew in what direction he intended to push me before he began to shove.

This time, though, I dug my feet in.

"I am *not* going to the palace," I gritted as the taste of smoke filled my mouth. I would become a fire-breathing dragon before letting the Prince order me to stand at his side. And Fate could find a new Daughter if he cared so little about me that he'd subject me to something so abhorrent and chauvinistic.

The small, wrapped box began to rattle on the table. "Fine. I'll look!" I yelled at Fate.

I snatched it up, tore the dark string tied around it, and lifted the lid. Inside was a midnight blue sapphire the size of a robin's egg. The edges had been cut and every plane polished. The stone was so clear and perfect, every facet cast my reflection back to me.

Suddenly, my front door flew open. I quickly tucked the stone into my dress's pocket and went to greet my unexpected visitor.

Visitors, I corrected, as Wayra and Ela stood at the threshold.

"Why were you visited by the Courier of Nautilus, and what did he give you?" Ela demanded. My grandmother's now-rheumy eyes narrowed on mine. Her face withered more deeply as she scowled. She didn't spare a glance at the House her daughter had built and loved.

"I've been invited to reside at the palace for a time."

Wayra sucked in a breath. "Whatever for?"

"Your Houses have telecasters. Have you heard news that the Prince is looking for a wife?"

Ela scoffed. "Never has a royal sent an invitation to a witch."

"The tradition must have changed," I asserted, crossing my arms over my chest.

"Let me see it," she ordered.

I retrieved the invitation, but hid Prince Tauren's letter. It was my duty to keep his words private.

My grandmother tore the paper out of my hand, her eyes sliding back and forth across and down the invitation. "You will not accept," she finally declared, handing the paper to Wayra.

"You cannot marry," Wayra agreed, slicking her hands down the fabric of her sky-blue robes.

"Fate demands that I accept his invitation." Originally, I'd wanted to rebel against Prince Tauren's summons, but seeing how it ruffled the Priestesses' feathers made it tempting to go. I told Fate as much and sighed as the burn in my belly was quenched.

Ela's knobby finger pointed at my chest. "I forbid it."

Wayra straightened her back, looking from my grandmother to me. "It goes against our fundamental beliefs," she agreed. "Even Fate must understand that we cannot bend on this matter. If our foundation crumbles, what is to keep our Houses upright?"

"What if the Kingdom wants to unify the Sectors? Thirteen is treated as an outcast among them. The people in the lower sectors think we're evil and dangerous. What if I could show them that we are good? That we are vital to the Kingdom and its security? They don't have a clue what we do to protect them."

"It's better that they don't know," Ela argued. "Let them fear us. It does not matter what the Lowers think of us. We will not get involved in matters of state. We must remain sovereign."

"The Kingdom has changed, High Priestess. Perhaps it's time we change with it." I held my hand out and waited for Wayra to return the invitation. She placed the square of thickly embossed, white parchment in my palm.

Ela was not one to back down. "Change is dangerous. Change corrupts. Your participation in such a vile pageant will not help anyone in Thirteen. *You* are not representative of the Sector."

"The Prince believes otherwise," I replied stiffly, steeling my spine.

Wayra placed her hand on Ela's back. "I'll call forth the Circle."

Ela leveled me with a glare. "Know this. If the Circle decides that you're not to go and you defy our order, you will not be welcome back in The Gallows. And there is nothing the King, or even the might of Nautilus's military can do to persuade or force us to change our minds on the matter."

She looked around at the House of Fate, disgust curling her lips. I could almost see the moment she imagined it demolished. Wayra helped my grandmother down the steps as she wheezed and hobbled.

Her threat hung heavily in the air.

seven

The afternoon dragged on painfully slow, but I knew the moment the Circle's private meeting began in the forest. They cast spells to keep anyone from eavesdropping on the conversation. I knew this, because in the past, I'd tried.

It bothered me that they believed they had any power over my future.

I busied myself by dusting, which was a daunting task considering all the furniture, fixtures, delicate cobwebs, and stubborn dust.

My grandmother's ire fueled my aggravated cleaning. How dare she threaten to remove me from my House? How dare she threaten me at all? They'd said that my House would never again be represented in the Circle, but I begged to differ. I had just as much power as my mother. Maybe more.

I threw down the dusting cloth and moved on to a heavier chore. Angrily, I tore down more curtains and stripped all the beds, leaving the linens in balled-up piles lining the hallways until each were dotted with linens that desperately needed to be laundered.

Occasionally, the words of Prince Tauren's letter would resurface in my mind. I couldn't help but wonder what his first reason was… and when he might have the opportunity to reveal it to me. Or why it had to be explained face-to-face.

The fact that someone wanted him dead needled me. I wondered who could hate him so much that they'd risk their own lives to take his, and what he'd done to garner such hatred. Was it because of his title alone, or had he provoked someone?

Heavy was the head that wore the crown, though many coveted the weighty circlet.

Courier Stewart knocked on my door that afternoon, just as he'd vowed.

I'd packed gowns I thought might be remotely appropriate to wear at the palace, but still wasn't sure I should go. I approached the door to tell him so when Fate began to shove. By the time I reached the bottom floor, I was shaking violently. I had to twist the handle three times before I managed to grip it firmly enough to pull it open.

The courier wasn't alone. Beside him stood Brecan and a female witch from the House of Water. Her dark blue cloak complemented his sky blue robes. Was he here to introduce me to the girl he would hand-fast to?

I swayed on my feet.

"Whoa," Brecan said, rushing in to steady me. "Are you ill?"

"Fate wants me to go to the palace."

"That's why we're here," he said. "The Circle was split on their decision. Ela and Wayra were opposed to you going, Ethne and Bay were in favor. In the end, they agreed to compromise and allow you to choose your path. If you accept the invitation, Mira and I will serve as your escorts. The rules of invitation provide that two escorts can accompany each invitee."

"How do you know that?"

"The House of Water has a telecaster," Mira admitted. "We aren't allowed to watch it most of the time, but Bay does make exceptions. Most of the girls enjoy watching stories about the royals. We knew the invitations were about to be issued, but had no idea Thirteen would be included. It's the first time!"

Mira's blue-gray hair was braided, and she'd added a shell to the ends of each one. They clinked together when she spoke, making tinkling noises like a chime in the wind. Her ebony skin shone like silk and her clothing was structured, pressed to perfection. She was beautiful. Truthfully, she looked like she belonged in the palace. No wonder she'd been chosen to escort me.

"And I won't be exiled if I go?"

Brecan stiffened. "Ela pushed for it, but again, they were at an impasse. You will be welcomed back into Thirteen."

Welcomed was too kind a word. I would be let back in, but welcome? I would *never* be welcome here.

"What about my House?" I asked.

"It will remain yours and yours alone. The Circle will instruct all witches to keep away from it."

Fate squeezed. My ribs became so tight, I thought they might splinter.

I could do this. I could accept the invitation, go to the palace with Brecan and Mira, and try to figure out who was conspiring to kill Prince Tauren. Then I could come home. My House wouldn't be stripped from me. All would be well.

"There are two stipulations that all Circle members agreed to," Brecan said, straightening his back as he folded his hands behind him.

"What stipulations?"

"The first is that you will not marry or accept any proposals that Prince Tauren might offer."

That would be simple enough. Prince Tauren, as enchanted as he might be with my abilities, would never – *could* never – take a witch to be his wife.

"And the second?" I asked.

"You will hand-fast to a male witch promptly upon your return to Thirteen."

"Unless my stay extends beyond the Solstice, you mean." Which was exactly what I would attempt to ensure happened.

"No," he said. "The Circle has agreed to make an exception for you. You are to hand-fast upon your return to Thirteen, though you are free to approach whatever male you'd like for the honor of being your chosen mate for the duration of your time together. Your union would end at the subsequent Solstice, though."

I had enough to worry about with the Prince, the invitation, and my new House. Grandmother Ela knew this would make me dread returning here, and she was right. But I was seventeen. Perhaps this would not only be my first, but my *only* opportunity to hand-fast.

Courier Stewart shifted his weight on his feet as he pretended to watch the birds that plucked worms from the yard and flew to the tree limbs above to gobble them down.

"I accept the invitation," I said. The moment the words left my mouth, Fate released his grip on me and I took several restorative breaths.

Courier Stewart, who'd politely been pretending not to listen to our conversation, turned to me. "Have you gathered what you'd like to take with you, Miss Sable?"

Beyond the Courier, I saw two men hefting a large trunk onto the back of a carriage. Four more waited for them. They were discussing how to arrange them. "Whose trunks are those?"

Mira clapped her hands together, wringing them with a look of pent-up excitement on her lips. "Mine. I am to dress you."

"Dress me?"

"Oh, yes. Bay insists you represent us in style," she beamed.

Why would Bay care how I dressed?

Her eyes traveled from my head to my toes, causing her nose to wrinkle. "You aren't planning to wear *that*, are you?"

I looked down, smoothing my fingertips over the simple fabric of the best dress I owned.

She waved me off. "I have just the thing." Mira ran down the steps and threw open one of the trunks that hadn't been moved. She rifled around inside and pulled something out. Something poufy. Then she plucked out a pair of matching heels.

Royalty might require poufy, but, "I prefer my boots!" I yelled to her.

"Oh, no you don't," she replied breezily, jogging back up the steps. She shoved the pair of shiny heels into my hands. "Trust me."

Clutching the shoes against my chest with one hand, Mira used the other to pull me farther into the house, dragging me into the first bedroom we came to, and swiftly helped me change. The girl was a small tornado of energy.

I stood in front of the full-length mirror and sucked in a breath. "This is beautiful." I wore an impeccably tailored, black riding jacket that fell to my hips in the front, but cascaded to the backs of my thighs in the back. Underneath, layers of white ruffles spilled down in soft waves. Mira had added a pair of tight, black pants, and when I slid my feet into the perfectly fitted heels, she squealed and clapped her hands.

"You are so beautiful! You don't even need make-up, and your hair is like silk," she fawned, combing her fingers through the strands and placing them over my shoulders. "You look like you already belong at the palace."

I gave her a look of warning. I belonged in this House.

I wasn't going for some silly, romantic reason. I was going to help the Prince, to find out who wanted him dead and hopefully prevent their plan from coming to fruition. Nothing more. Didn't the Circle explain that to her?

Mira said she'd give me a minute to center myself and left the room. Why did Mira make such garments, and for whom? They fit me perfectly, as did the shoes. I wiggled my toes in the pointed tips and twisted my leg to see the back. Situated on the heel was a thin, silver dagger. Most would assume it was merely decorative, but it looked real. I slid the small blade from the sheath built into the heel, grateful that Mira had armed me.

Glancing at my discarded dress on the floor, I immediately felt better that she was coming along. She was far more adept with current fashions than I was. If she watched the royals on the telecaster, she'd know how I needed to look to fit in, and fitting in was the only way I would be able to remain at the palace long enough for Fate to reveal the would-be murderer.

The wishbone revealed that Tauren would die, but it didn't reveal exactly how. I couldn't sense the person behind the malice yet. And until I did, I would have to join the gaggle of moony-eyed girls vying for a scrap of the Prince's attention.

I smoothed a hand down my stomach, glancing at the mirror and admiring the way I looked in the coat and pondering whether it or the heels were my favorite.

What...? My breath caught. For a moment, I could've sworn my reflection shifted. I blinked, then waved my hand in front of my body and watched the mirrored me move the same way. Shaking off the strange sensation, I turned and headed toward the door to join the others.

In the living room, Brecan waited with his hands stuffed in the pockets of his cloak. He turned at the sound of my heels clicking on the wooden floor and his eyes widened. His mouth parted, and he sucked in a breath before quickly schooling his features. "Are you ready? Your trunk has been loaded. Though I'm not sure the horses will be able to pull us and all our luggage," he laughed.

"You don't have to escort me, Brecan. I know it's awkward."

He dropped his head. "It doesn't have to be. I volunteered to escort and protect you. Ela demanded a male witch go, to send a strong message that we stick with our own."

It would send no such message since I already accepted the Prince's invitation, but of course my grandmother had to push her will on me in some way. I just hoped Brecan understood that I still wouldn't choose him to be hand-fasted to when I returned.

"What if we aren't back by the Solstice? You want to hand-fast this year."

"It can wait. This is more important," he answered.

"How is Ela?" I dared ask.

"Quite frail, Sable. If you wish to see her..."

"It would only upset her. I just... I wonder why she's aging so quickly."

"I spoke with Wayra, and she explained it. You are of age, Sable, flesh of her flesh, blood of her blood, and the magic that has sustained her for so long has passed to you."

"Are you saying that she's dying because my power matured?" Brecan gave a gentle nod. That was exactly what he was saying. Though my grandmother and I shared no affinity, the harsh reality of magic was that it followed its own rules and demanded much from those to whom it was gifted.

I steeled my shoulders. There was nothing I could do to stop the course of nature now that the path had been established. Ela would have to endure her decline until death came for her, and I could not do a single thing about it – not even if I stayed in The Gallows. Not that Fate would allow it, at this point.

"Thank you for volunteering. I'm sure they would have had to order it of any other male."

He snorted. "On the contrary. I was the first to volunteer, but hardly the only one." He pointed outside where Courier Stewart waited patiently near the carriage. "They're ready if you are."

I grabbed the invitation and letter off a nearby table and tucked them into the pocket of my coat. Whispering a spell, I stepped onto the porch behind him and closed the door, sealing the House until I returned.

It wasn't until I started down the steps that I saw everyone. Every witch, male and female, from every House, stood in the Center, gawking at me. They watched as Brecan helped me into the carriage and climbed up after me, taking the seat beside Mira. She beamed to her sisters and brothers of the House of Water, waving to them as Courier Stewart climbed into the carriage and took the seat beside me. His men on horseback flanked us.

He gave the command to take us to the palace. As the carriage lurched forward, I saw something different in the eyes of my peers. Awe mixed with a touch of envy.

Ela and Wayra, Bay and Ethne stood in the middle of the crowd of witches, obvious alliances forged and lines drawn, with a different warning flashing in each of their eyes. Fate calmed my boiling blood, and the feeling that I was doing the right thing washed over me.

As the horses trotted, tugging us along the trail that led into the woods toward the border, the murmur of every witch in Thirteen melded together. The witches were excited to see one of their own leave for the palace – even if it was me. But I doubted the people of the lower sectors would be so quickly accepting of the Prince inviting a witch into the heart of their kingdom.

In the Kingdom of Nautilus, trade and travel among the lower twelve sectors was permitted. Citizens came and went as they pleased, as long as they checked in and out through the border walls. Thirteen was the exception to that rule.

Witches could pass to and from Thirteen with no issue, but no one from the Lowers was allowed into The Gallows unless it was one of our renowned celebration days. There were only two exceptions: the royal family, or former subjects exiled by the King, who were removed beyond Thirteen's borders into the wild lands.

Those two groups were periodically granted passage through Thirteen, with the caveat that anyone who entered Thirteen was subject to our laws and the penalties attached to them. Most of the exiles behaved, choosing a life in the wild lands over swinging from the gallows.

The border to each sector was walled, typically using natural materials mined from within its borders. Our border lay just on our sector's side of the Kingdom's official wall that separated Twelve from Thirteen.

Man-made walls weren't impenetrable and could be brought down, given enough force, whereas Thirteen's could not. Our wall wasn't comprised of stone and mortar, or crafted of thick pine from our forests. It was spelled by the Circle, shimmering with the magic collected within it. *To protect those within*, Grandmother would say.

When I needed anything from the lower sectors – and it was rare that I did – Brecan would retrieve what I needed. I had never set foot out of Sector Thirteen. As our carriage crossed the magical border, the spell sparked in the air, allowing us to pass freely, even as it made the hair on my arms stand up. I reveled in the intensity of it and couldn't help but scoot closer to the window to better see out.

When we reached the concrete wall belonging to Twelve, we paused until the gates rolled open. I wondered if the King's men felt the same spark I had, or if they felt it every time they passed into The Gallows. I wondered if it scared them.

Courier Stewart sat rigidly to my left. If he felt anything at all, he didn't comment about it. He kept his eyes trained forward, looking past Brecan and Mira. He hadn't moved an inch in miles, so when he spoke, it startled me. "The Kingdom of Nautilus is arranged like its namesake, a nautilus's shell. Do you know the creature?"

"I do." Every witch could appreciate the complexity and beauty of the nautilus, not to mention the fact it was a required ingredient to a few of the more intense spells I knew, and probably many others I didn't.

He gave an approving nod. "The palace is located at the center, and the sectors spiral out from it in ever-increasing waves. The first four are the smallest, but densest in population. As they are closest to the palace, they house the most affluent and influential persons in the Kingdom. A great deal of the Royal Guard is also stationed within the first four. The sectors begin to spread out from there, and each grows larger as the spiral expands to Sectors Five through Twelve. Twelve is best known for the timber industry. Nine, Ten, and Eleven for farming. They produce goods the Kingdom requires. Seven and Eight are filled with factories, and Five and Six are best known for their artwork. You'll find painters, writers, chefs, and sculptors there. Both Five and Six are very beautiful and worth visiting if you have the chance."

He watched me carefully in his periphery.

"Are Five and Six your favorites?" I intuited.

"They certainly are, Miss Sable. I'm fairly sure they're everyone's favorites."

"What are you permitted to tell me about the royal family?" I asked. I didn't know nearly enough. I hadn't even recognized Prince Tauren when he sat in my living room.

Brecan shifted in his seat. He and Mira watched for Courier Stewart's reply.

"They care very deeply about their kingdom, and have my utmost respect, Miss."

Stewart glared at Brecan until he finally looked away. *Did something transpire between the men before Brecan and Mira delivered the Circle's decision?*

His conversational skills depleted, Courier Stewart stopped talking after that. I watched as Sector Twelve, with its towering stacks of felled and stripped trees, along with mills and the smell of pine and sawdust faded away.

Eleven, Ten, and Nine were a patchwork quilt of fields, most of which had already been harvested; the similarity of vegetation made it difficult to tell the sectors apart. I was sure they grew different things, but the earth had been stripped and turned. The smells of fresh grass, manure, and rich soil pervaded the air.

Eight and Seven were filled with enormous metal buildings and concrete towers that shot into the sky. Some spouted clouds. Others breathed perpetual flame.

These sectors were loud with machinery churning violently and steadily. They were also the worst smelling, with sharp, indistinguishably unpleasant scents emanating from each factory. Some of the scents burnt my nose. I was glad when we neared the sector's wall.

Six... Six took my breath away. Even the wall encasing it had been painted in vibrant shades and scenes. Murals captured humanity and nature alike, including the most miniscule details. Other sections were abstract and strangely beautiful.

Five was more elegant and formal, showcasing a classic beauty. Its streets were lined with statue after statue; so lifelike, I thought they were watching us pass. The bridges were masterfully erected, bowing with elegant lines swooping over wide, shallow rivers and deeper, narrow canals. Flowers hung from every post, spilling lush petals onto the streets and sidewalks.

Before we left the sector, I got to see an artisan at work. His brow was sweaty and his muscles strained beneath his short-sleeved shirt as he chiseled away at a chunk of granite that stood three times taller than he did.

I didn't get to see nearly enough of Five or Six. I looked to Courier Stewart as we left the beauty behind us and were pulled into Four. "You were right."

He inclined his head and offered a small smile. "I'm glad you enjoyed passing through. You could spend a lifetime in each of those sectors and never tire of their beauty, nor see all the treasures hidden within. There is constantly something new being created."

"It's a wonder they're not the most densely populated."

"They're the most visited," he confirmed. At least that much was unsurprising.

Four passed much faster than the others had. There were buildings stacked next to buildings, rising high into the sky; rooftops were the only places large enough for gardens and small trees to grow. Three and Two were smaller still, with sleek, glassy buildings climbing even higher into the heavens. I could barely see the rooftops from the carriage window, but there was no green to be seen there. Only steel and metal and glass.

And One, I almost missed altogether. It was more a neighborhood than a sector, and the homes closest to the palace were enormous. Their yards were impeccably manicured, their gardens immaculate. They were what I envisioned a palace to look like. So, when Courier Stewart announced that we had arrived, Brecan, Mira, and I craned our necks to see where the royals lived, and where we would temporarily reside.

The palace was nothing short of breathtaking. The stone encasing it was a pale pink. The entire, magnificent structure glittered in the distance, set on a knoll and surrounded by the most luxuriant, green grass I'd ever seen. *The Earth witches would be in heaven here.*

And the witches of Air… the bright blue sky stretched on for miles. Brecan studied it, his eyes catching on every wispy cloud. There were no trees in the yards closest to the palace, but there was plenty of woodland. The palace was a city unto itself, a glittery star in a vast sky. Not even the homes and buildings in surrounding sectors could be seen in the distance.

"Wow," Mira breathed, scooting closer to the window.

Even Brecan was transfixed. The palace's scale could not be appreciated from so far away, but as the horses trotted nearer, it seemed to grow taller and expand. Rows of perfect steps swept up to a pair of grand, white doors, taller than ten men.

The driver yelled, "Whoa," and the horses slowed their pace, then stopped.

Two waiting guards opened the carriage door, and I accepted one of their hands as I climbed down.

Courier Stewart exited next and announced me. "Arriving is Miss Sable, from Sector Thirteen."

Brecan cleared his throat.

"And her companions," amended the courier.

Brecan and Mira exited the carriage.

"She travels light," one of the guards joked, glancing at the pile of trunks on the small platform behind the carriage itself.

I couldn't help but smile at him. He tugged at his collar and cleared his throat, looking away.

Courier Stewart gestured toward the immense palace door. "If you will allow me to see you inside, Miss Sable."

"Thank you."

Brecan and Mira fell in step behind us as we ascended the layers and layers of steps, climbing toward the first floor of the mountainous palace. For a second, I felt like a parcel being delivered. In a way, I was.

"It's so much bigger than it looks on the telecasts," Mira said in wonder.

Smartly dressed doormen pulled open the two doors a sliver, which was more than enough for us to comfortably enter. We crossed the threshold and stepped onto a stark white floor, whose mirror finish made me suddenly thankful for Mira and the magical clothes and shoes she'd loaned me. My simple dresses wouldn't have been enough for the floor, let alone the people contained inside these walls.

"Daughter of Fate," a familiar, deep voice called out. Goosebumps prickled on my skin as the smooth tone slid over me and my title echoed across the arched ceiling. Prince Tauren strode down the hall, stopping in front of me to offer his hand. I reluctantly shook it, but his grip seized my hand. He brought the back to his lips and pressed a gentle kiss onto my skin. As he did, his golden eyes glanced up to mine. "Thank you for accepting my invitation."

His eyes flicked meaningfully to the men at his side, one of whom was focusing a camera on the pair of us. *Uh… he said something. The invitation, right.*

"Thank you for extending it."

He looked me over and smiled. "I would have invited you sooner if I'd known you would arrive looking so beautiful."

There wasn't anything contrived about his tone. Though he wanted me to be aware of the camera, he didn't seem to be acting for it. "Thank you," I said, pulling my hand away.

"Prince Tauren!" a man called, rushing down the hallway. "Your father is waiting for you."

Tauren winked at me. "I'll stop by later, once you're settled." He finally noticed Mira and Brecan hovering behind me. His smile faltered just a little, but he quickly recovered. "I'm forgetting my manners. Welcome to the palace." He shook Brecan's, then Mira's hands and hurried after the man who'd come to retrieve him.

The fact that his suit was tailored perfectly for his body did not escape me.

The cameramen turned off their devices and scurried away somewhere.

"You can stop drooling now, Sable. The cameras are gone," Brecan said sarcastically.

Mira slowly shook her head. "I don't think we can."

I could almost hear Brecan's internal groan.

Our trunks were brought inside and loaded onto a large cart. Two men wheeled the cart past us while another gentleman in a stark white suit asked us to follow him upstairs, saying he would see us to our rooms. We climbed a wide staircase to the second floor, then the third where we were led down a long hallway lined with doors.

"This is the North Wing. Your rooms are situated at the end of the hall. Prince Tauren thought you might appreciate a measure of privacy. The Prince wasn't sure if you would be escorted, but we prepared rooms just in case."

"Thank you for your preparedness," I said to be polite.

He gave me a proud nod, then removed three keys from his pockets, unlocking Mira's door first and handing her the key to it. "Madam."

Her room was the color of buttercups. I didn't walk in, but knew she'd have ample space for all the trunks she brought along, and still have plenty more to move about the room. The bed wasn't visible from the door, but a plush, white couch with blue pillows was. Mira promised to come help me change soon.

"Why would I need to change?"

She rolled her eyes. "That's a traveling suit. You'll need to wear a gown this evening, and I have just the thing."

I bet she had shoes to match it. I hoped they concealed daggers in their heel, as well.

Our escort showed Brecan to his room and placed the key in his hand.

Brecan walked inside. "At least it's blue," he announced, walking farther into the room. "And huge... I have my own washroom." A few seconds passed before he added, "With running water."

At least Mira and Brecan were happy with their temporary quarters. The thought settled the nervousness simmering in my stomach.

The gentleman in white unlocked my room, which was situated directly across the hall from Brecan. He handed me the key and gently pushed the door open, holding the handle as I stepped inside. The faint smell of fresh paint filled the air. "Prince Tauren wanted you to feel at home," the gentleman explained. "He thought you might enjoy this décor in particular."

The walls were painted black, the trim stark white. A tall vase of red roses sat on a small table in the entryway, along with another wax-sealed letter. I grabbed it and held it to my stomach. The couch was black brocade, a plush red throw hanging over the back with matching pillows. The bed was covered in silky black fabric. Black. My favorite color.

The color I wanted the exterior and interior of my House to be repainted.

He noticed my House…

"He had this painted and decorated for me?" I asked.

The older man smiled. "You must be special to him, Miss Sable. He made no special alterations for any other invitee. In fact," he leaned in to whisper, "he hasn't greeted any of the other girls yet."

I was sure it was just a coincidence. I'd merely arrived at the precise moment he was passing by the door. Nothing more. Mira appeared at my side and nudged me, but I couldn't pay attention to her at the moment. I was trying and failing to quiet the moths flittering playfully in the pit of my stomach.

"I'll have your things brought in shortly," the man promised.

The man left me to stare at the room Tauren had designed for my comfort. Brecan stepped inside and stood behind me, every muscle tense. "It looks like you made quite an impression at the Equinox."

Mira made a noise and slipped away. I almost tried to grab her arm and force her to stay. Maybe Brecan would leave well enough alone if she were with us.

I pinched my lower lip, unsure of what to say.

"Is he why you won't hand-fast to me?" he asked bluntly.

I crossed my arms over my chest. "No. He's not."

Brecan made a noise to indicate he didn't believe me, then turned on his heel and left the room, letting the door snap closed behind him.

eight

The note was simple, written in Tauren's hand. It instructed me to look under my pillow. There, I found another box. This one was larger than the one he sent to my house. I untied the black silken ribbon and lifted the lid to find a necklace nestled inside.

The word *necklace* didn't do it justice. This was a silver and black work of art. Two knocks came at my door before Mira pushed her way in, her arms full of gowns. She gasped as she peered around at the décor and then looked at my hands. "What is that?" she asked, her eyes lighting up. "Please tell me it's jewelry."

"It's jewelry," I deadpanned.

Mira squealed as she rushed toward me, throwing the gowns on the bed and grabbing the box from my hands. "It's exquisite."

A few of the gowns slid to the floor. I gathered them while she held the onyx gems up to the light.

It really was exquisite. And far too much. "Of course, I can't accept it."

Her mouth fell open. "You most certainly can. You are one of the invitees, a potential wife of Prince Tauren."

"I can't marry him."

"He doesn't know that yet, does he?"

I wasn't sure how to answer. I thought I'd made it clear that my acceptance of his invitation would be purely for the purpose of helping him determine who wanted him dead. But this necklace was too much. A gift like this was ridiculous.

"He probably gave one to every invitee," I hedged. Mira was too transfixed by the facets cut into the stone to push the issue further.

Fate had been oddly quiet. I called out for him in my mind. *Guide me to the one who's trying to hurt Tauren so I can go back home, please.*

I felt hollow. Fate, it seemed, wasn't ready to reveal the culprit. Perhaps they weren't in the palace… How long would I have to stay here?

"You can't refuse the Prince's gift," Mira said with finality, shoving the necklace toward me. "That necklace was meant to be yours."

It is *pretty…* I looped it around my forearm while she prattled on, hanging the dresses on a rack set up in the corner and chattering about how amazing the palace was.

Mira wondered if her sisters had seen her on the telecast as we arrived, or if they might later tonight. "Bay is going to let them watch nonstop while we're here! He has high hopes that your presence and participation will show the sectors how vital witches are to the Kingdom; that we are more than just conjurers and potion makers."

"How am I supposed to convince the people in the sectors that witches are good for it, when I don't even fit in among them? I'm afraid his faith in me might be misplaced." My grandmother's words had taken root in me, and I wanted to pluck them and leave them in the sun to wilt.

"What do you mean you don't fit in?" she asked, her hand stilling on a garment. "You're the one we all look up to."

I shook my head. "That's absurd. The Circle hates me."

"Ela does, though I'm not sure why…" she trailed off. I knew she was thinking about our bloodline and how easily Ela had come to hate my mother, and by extension, me. "The others don't hate you, they just don't understand your magic. And things we don't understand are scary. Right?"

"Sometimes," I admitted.

"I look up to you, and I'm not the only one, just so you know," she admitted. "Because *I'm* different, too. That's why Bay sent me to help you."

My brows kissed. "You're different in what way?"

She smiled and ticked her head toward the selection of gowns. "How do you think I made all of these for you so fast?"

"Wait – you *made* them? For me?"

"Of course. They fit you perfectly, right?"

They did. I opened my mouth to speak, but she continued. "In addition to a water affinity," she began, "I have an affinity for creating things. Well, I make helpers that actually bring my visions to life."

She reached into her pocket and pulled something out. Uncurling her fingers, she glanced up at me nervously. Two glass spiders sat in her palm. "They weave for me."

She whispered a spell and the spiders' legs uncurled. They crawled up her arm as she twisted it to see them.

"You have the power of animation," I marveled, watching the spiders skitter across her collarbone.

"We aren't the only witches who are different. There are a few others. You *are* the only diviner of Fate, though."

"You animate the spiders and command them to weave… gowns?"

Mira smiled proudly. "Among other articles."

Just then, someone knocked at my door.

Mira's eyes widened. "Do you think it's *him*?"

"It's probably Brecan." I crossed the large room and cracked the door open.

Prince Tauren greeted me with a lop-sided grin and a "Hello." Hands in his pockets, he rocked back on his heels. "I was hoping I could speak with you and your escorts before dinner."

My heart fluttered. "Sure. Mira's already here. I'll go get Brecan." I squeezed by the Prince and knocked on Brecan's door. He yanked it open, still sullen from our conversation. "The Prince would like to speak with us before dinner."

He narrowed his eyes and glanced over my shoulder at Tauren. "Very well."

We filed into my suite. Brecan made himself comfortable sitting on the arm of the couch. Mira sat in an adjacent chair, her leg bouncing wildly. I stood between them, and Tauren stood across the dark rug from me. He cleared his throat. "The other invitees don't know that a girl from Thirteen will be among them. I assume you've told your escorts why you're really here?" he asked me.

I shook my head. "I haven't, but now is as good a time as any." Brecan straightened his back, curious about the sudden turn in conversation. "Tauren came to The Gallows for the Equinox. I performed a reading for him, and it became apparent that someone—in the very near future—will try to kill him. He invited me here to try to determine who it is."

Mira's mouth gaped open. "The Circle doesn't know that..."

"No, they don't," Brecan seconded.

"They can't," I said pointedly. "No one outside this room can know."

"Why is that?" Brecan stood, crossing his arms over his chest.

I swallowed. He wasn't going to like what I had to say. "Because Fate hasn't revealed who the person is."

Brecan scoffed at the idea. "This is why we keep to ourselves. We don't get involved in kingdom politics." He brushed his long, pale hair over his shoulders and turned to me. "It's not a witch."

"You're probably right, but I want to be sure."

Tauren pinched his lips together. "I appreciate your help..." he paused, suddenly aware he didn't know my true name.

"Sable," I finished for him.

He smiled. "Sable. It suits you."

Brecan let out a mirthless laugh. "You didn't even know her name? That's rich. You send this invitation, pluck her from her home and cause a huge disturbance within our sector, and you didn't take the second it would require to learn her name?"

"I have it now," Tauren asserted. He turned to me, tension melting from his shoulders. "Everything happened so fast the night of the Equinox, I didn't know what to do. The next morning, I had the idea of inviting you to take part in our tradition, but I didn't mean to cause you trouble," he said, staring at me with eyes full of apology.

"So," Mira cut in, "the other girls have no idea a witch is crashing the party?" She grinned from ear to ear.

Tauren returned her smile. "None."

"This will be interesting to watch."

"My parents see your presence as an opportunity, for many reasons of which I'm sure my parents will bore you with very soon. Unless you can unravel the mystery quickly, I'll need you to stay until I make my final decision," Tauren apologized. "Which means you'll be among the last to leave the palace."

"Exactly how long does it take a prince to choose a wife?" Brecan asked.

I gave him a scathing look. *If he didn't want to escort me, he should've stayed home. As a matter of fact, he can go back there now, if he wants.*

"Usually the process takes a few months, but the given circumstances require a quicker decision. I hope to choose within a few weeks, at the most. My parents hope that by doing so, more people throughout the Kingdom will tune in and their interest won't fade so quickly.

When my father chose Mother, ratings were high in the beginning when the invitees were presented, but people soon stopped watching as it took him several months to decide amongst the women. Ratings peaked again when he announced his choice, and then fell away again until the wedding. In recent months, Father's addresses to the Kingdom have gone largely unwatched."

"Perhaps what he's saying is boring," Brecan suggested, looking from the Prince to me.

I ignored his snide grin. "I'll have to read a lot of fates in a very short period of time…"

Tauren nodded. "Does that adversely affect you? Reading that many so quickly?"

"Not exactly," I hedged, not wanting to explain the residual effect left by the reading of fates.

Brecan stood and strode toward Tauren, who met him in the center of the rug, standing toe-to-toe with him. Mira clutched her chest in alarm as they squared off.

"You *do* understand that she cannot marry you?" Brecan snapped, his eyes flashing.

Tauren looked at me over Brecan's shoulder, his golden eyes locking with mine. "I wasn't aware she was interested."

Brecan took a side-step, putting himself in front of me. "She isn't. And even if she were, she's bound by the Circle's rules. Witches do not marry. They hand-fast, and only to their own kind."

"Brecan," I said sternly. He turned to face me. "You have no right to speak for me." I turned my attention to Tauren, sighing. "But he's right. Hand-fasting is our custom, and I am bound by it."

The muscle in Tauren's jaw ticked as his eyes flicked between me and Brecan. "You mentioned the custom the night of the Equinox, Sable. And, of course, I will honor your traditions. But can you please keep that between us as well, at least for the time being? If the other ladies catch word of it, they'll question why you've been invited and why you're allowed to stay when your custom prevents us from marrying."

Soon, he would choose someone else, and I would be at his side to protect him, watching the happy couple embark on a life-long adventure with one another.

"We won't reveal it," I promised Tauren. Brecan would adhere to my vow, or I'd send him back to The Gallows. "Though I can't promise someone won't already know."

A clock chimed from outside the room, its weighty vibrations making the vase of roses by the entryway scoot across the tabletop. Tauren waited until it was finished. "Dinner will be served in one hour."

"Will I be meeting the other invitees?"

He shook his head. "Not tonight. Tonight, my parents would like to invite you and your escorts to dine with us privately."

I wouldn't meet his future bride tonight, but would dine with the King and Queen of Nautilus. At that moment, I wasn't sure which would be worse. Not that I got to choose. When the King and Queen asked for an audience, there was no option to politely decline.

"I'll leave you to get ready," he said, stepping around Brecan to get to me. Instead of shaking my hand, he placed his on my upper arms and leaned in, gently pressing a kiss to one cheek and then the other. My pulse quickened.

Brecan's eyes blazed from the intimate gesture, while Mira's eyes widened to the size of saucers.

Tauren gave me a wink before striding out of the room. When the door closed behind him, Mira squealed.

nine

My corset felt too tight. Likely because it was, despite Mira's repeated assurance to the contrary. I wasn't used to wearing them, but she insisted on it. The black silk gown she and her spiders had woven beautifully complemented the necklace Tauren gave me, which she insisted I wear as a gesture of gratitude. The dress was strapless and dramatic, and not at all what I imagined wearing while meeting the King and Queen of Nautilus.

I honestly hadn't given much thought to them at all before Tauren mentioned we'd be dining privately with the royal family. I'd only thought of the bleeding wishbone and a pair of curious golden eyes.

When I objected to showing too much skin, Mira balked, saying that the Queen herself would be showing more. "I want to look like me," I argued. "If I show up looking like all the other invitees, the King and Queen might assume I'm after the crown. We're walking a very delicate line, and I'd rather not be responsible for shattering whatever fragile understanding Thirteen has with the Kingdom."

Conceding to my wish, Mira spelled her glass spiders and whispered for them to weave a high neck and delicate sleeves out of sheer black fabric. After lifting my hair out of the way, they knit it quickly. In the time it took Mira to find a suitable pair of shoes, they'd completed their work and waited patiently for her on my shoulder. She whispered a spell that transformed them back to glass, and tucked them into her pocket before placing a pair of black heels on the floor. The heels were even higher than the last pair, the black as glossy as a beetle's back, but there was no dagger hidden along the backs.

"Just wear them," she chirped. "They'll look incredible. You'll even stand a few inches taller." After clasping the necklace and adding a few silver rings on my fingers, she held up a pair of gloves that would match the gown. "Do you want these?"

I shook my head, choosing to keep my hands bare.

"You don't think the King and Queen have anything to do with it, do you?" Mira asked, her eyes widening.

"I certainly hope not." *If a member of Tauren's own family wants him dead, how can I possibly prevent it? They have constant access to him.*

The clock began to chime, striking the hour of dinner, and Mira pushed me across the room and out the door, closing it behind us. She wore a simple, black cotton dress and Brecan emerged from his room in a black suit.

"Why aren't you wearing your House colors?" I asked them. Mira had the ability to weave anything; why did she choose something so plain?

"Because while we are here serving as your escorts, we represent you, not our Houses," Brecan replied primly. "And we can't look like your equals. We need to blend into the background, not steal the show."

"I'm sure Ela and Wayra will be thrilled when they see you," I deadpanned.

Mira giggled. "Bay won't be upset. It was his idea. Ethne will love it, too."

Fire and Water agreeing with one another? I was shocked to hear it.

But now it made sense why Wayra and Bay each sent an escort. The Houses were split. Water and Fire versus Earth and Air. The two opposing sides were equally represented with Brecan and Mira.

We walked together through the hallway to the stairs, taking them carefully down to the main floor, where we were met by a woman in white who asked us to follow her. She led us farther into the castle where everything was white and gold and shiny. The ceilings boasted immaculately painted frescoes with clouds and cherubs that looked so real, I thought they might swoop down and pinch our cheeks for sport.

The panels that lined the walls were inlaid with gold flake. The white marble floors shone like glass, pure and clean, in stark contrast to our dark apparel.

We finally arrived at a pair of tall double doors that parted when the woman knocked. The room held nothing but a blunt, rectangular table.

The royal family was already seated.

All conversation stopped when my heels clicked on the floor. Tauren stood and straightened his jacket, gesturing to the seats next to him. His father and mother stood, and I noticed that although they weren't wearing crowns, their clothing matched. Each wore deep teal suits, hers more femininely cut than his. The insignia of Nautilus had been sewn into their jackets, directly over each of their hearts.

Tauren was as tall as his father, but where his eyes were molten gold, the King's were the color of burnt toffee. There was kindness, but also something weary in their depths.

The King's eyes reminded me of Tauren's brother, whom I hadn't seen since the night of the Equinox. I hadn't seen him since I arrived or been formally introduced to him yet, and there was no setting at the table for him.

King Lucius and Queen Annalina returned the bow I gave. Her golden hair was the same hue as the eye color she'd passed to her son. Tauren stood proudly next to them as they greeted us.

"Miss Sable," the King hailed, holding out his hand for mine.

A flash of bitter pain shot through my middle just before he placed a kiss on the back of my hand. It disappeared as quickly as it pierced through me, but the feeling flustered me. When I regained my wits, I was still clinging to the King's hand. He'd kissed the back of mine, which I gathered was a custom here. I couldn't deny the fact that I had enjoyed the attention from the Prince, even though I knew Tauren hadn't meant anything by greeting me that way. He'd probably kissed the backs of a thousand ladies' hands.

I pushed the thought away and returned my hand awkwardly to my side. "King Lucius," I replied. His eyes shimmered kindly, but I didn't miss the worried glance he slid to his wife.

The Queen's eyes were sharper. She gave my hand a quick shake and offered a brief smile before dismissing me to greet Mira just as coolly. She barely even deigned to speak to Brecan.

My eyes unfocused as I looked at Queen Annalina's forced smile.

A feeling, not one of pain or shock, but one of wariness clung to my fingertips. The Queen cleared her throat and I blinked out of the daze of attempting to clasp onto the fleeting feeling. Though interrupted in my reading, I knew it would linger and I could further explore it privately, later.

Tauren placed another kiss on my hand and leaned in to whisper, "To erase my father's." I swallowed thickly as he guided me to the seat beside his. Shivers radiated from the spot where his hand warmed my lower back.

Brecan and Mira settled into the chairs situated across from us, while the King and Queen sat at either end.

With a nod of the King's royal head, the servants sprang into action, bustling to and from the kitchen. Ice water was poured into our glasses. Long stemmed glasses of wine were placed in front of us. Hors d'oeuvres were served, and once we were all satisfied, a calm fell over the table.

King Lucius regarded me for a long moment. I studied him just as shrewdly. His hair was as dark as Tauren's, but some strands had turned to salt, especially around his temples. Deep wrinkles bracketed his mouth and streaked across his forehead. As he opened his mouth, the worry lines deepened further. "I won't bother lying to you, my dear, as I'm sure you could see through any falsehood I attempted."

I inclined my head in thanks, waiting for him to continue.

"My son explained what happened on the night of the Equinox. In detail." I opened my mouth to defend my actions, but he stopped me. "Thank you for coming."

The scowl the Queen had fixed on me deepened, and she flinched with each of her husband's words.

I expected him to chastise me for hanging one of their citizens in front of hundreds of others. If I weren't seated, his words would have knocked me off balance.

The Queen spoke. "You truly believe someone wishes Tauren harm?"

"I don't simply believe it," I answered. "I know it to be true."

"Then I think," the King began, "that your visit couldn't have come at a more opportune time."

"What does that mean, exactly?" I asked, glancing at Tauren. He sat rigidly beside me, regarding his father.

"It means that your presence is crucial. Not only can you protect my son, you can help us in other ways. The Circle has been very... stubborn in the recent negotiations we've had with them. Perhaps, your being here and reporting back about the way you are welcomed and treated, would ease tensions somewhat."

If he thought my grandmother would listen to anything I had to say, he was sorely mistaken.

"Why have you spoken to the Circle at all? What were you negotiating?"

Queen Annalina took control of the conversation. "The Circle would like for us to find another way to send exiles to the wild lands, instead of routing them through Thirteen. But, you see, there simply is no other way. Thirteen is the final Sector, and the only one that completely encircles the Kingdom – with the exception of the area where the sea extends inland. Exiles must pass through somewhere."

"They always have. Why is there an issue now?" I asked.

"The Circle believes that many of the persons being exiled should be put to death. That their crimes are heinous enough to warrant execution instead of banishment," she said.

"Are they?"

"We don't believe in taking lives, though I know your stance on the matter is rather different." She daintily sipped from her wine glass.

"Why can't you sail them to the wild lands?"

Tauren asked, "Yes, Mother. Why *can't* we sail them to the wilds?"

Has he already suggested the same?

"Because it would be costly to do so," she snipped.

"Surely, there aren't *that* many people being banished each month."

"There have been recently," the King confirmed, his harsh tone effectively ending the conversation. A sheen of sweat broke out on his forehead. I almost asked if he was feeling well, but was interrupted when our entrees were served.

The gentleman who brought mine lifted the silver dome with a flourish. Roast beef, string beans, and carrots. A pale sauce lay over the meat. "Can you eat it?" Tauren whispered sheepishly. "I should have asked whether you had dietary restrictions."

"I have no restrictions, but thank you."

His eyes flicked to Brecan and Mira.

"They're fine, too."

Mira was already savoring a carrot while Brecan stared between me and Tauren.

"Why the shift?" Brecan asked bluntly, bringing up the sore subject again. "Why are there more being banished than ever?"

"Laws haven't changed, nor has our enforcement of them. However, it seems that more are choosing to break them than ever," Tauren gently explained.

"Because there isn't punishment severe enough to deter them," Brecan replied.

The King sat his utensils down and leveled Brecan with a glare. "Mr. Brecan, why exactly are you here? Who are you to Miss Sable?"

"Her escort," he answered shortly.

"And what would an escort and citizen from the Thirteenth Sector know about ruling the Kingdom from which they attempt to remain separate?" King Lucius asked.

Brecan surprised me by offering an apology. "Nothing, Sire. Pardon my interruption."

I knew he hated every second of being here. Of dining with the rulers of our kingdom, of even admitting we were part of it. But he was steadfastly playing the role for which he volunteered.

"Nautilus has enjoyed centuries of peace, but slowly, things are going awry – within the Kingdom, instead of without. There is a chasm between the upper and lower sectors, which widens by the day."

"They're too separate," I said quietly.

The King nodded. "And Thirteen has nearly cleaved itself from us entirely. In the past, the witches and non-magical always worked together. But now? It is becoming harder to even *speak* with the Circle members. The four of them walked out during our last meeting, and haven't replied to any correspondences I've sent since. I'm starting to believe they might secede from us altogether. Have you heard any talk of it?"

I hadn't, but I wondered if Brecan had and didn't mention it to me. "I am not a member of the Circle, and as such, am not privy to their conversations." I glanced at Brecan pointedly, but his expression gave nothing away.

My stomach began to churn. I had no idea there was such strife between the crown and the Circle. I smoothed my palms down the satin fabric covering my legs as everyone chewed in strained silence.

Queen Annalina sawed her carrots into tiny bites and chewed each bite thoroughly. I took this quiet moment to read the residue her touch left behind on my palm. It explained why each time her eyes met mine, disdain roiled within their depths. She and Tauren were close, and he never mentioned to her that he would extend an invitation to me. But it was also because I was from Thirteen. Because I was… different from the other witches with whom she'd come into contact, though she couldn't place how.

Her eyes snapped to mine as if she knew what I'd felt from her. I held them for a beat and looked to the King, calling on his residue. Lucius was firm, but not cruel like his father had been. He wondered if that was why there was a growing unrest within the Kingdom, and within his chest. He eased a palm over his heart and swallowed a wince. He was angry with Tauren for extending an invitation to me at first, but what was done, was done. Now, he planned to use it to his advantage.

There was something else about them both, an underlying apprehension. I wasn't sure what caused it. They'd seemed welcoming enough, considering the fact that my presence must have surprised them.

I ate slowly, focusing as much as possible at those around the table. Mira was in heaven with the unexpected flavors of the meal and the general splendor of the palace she'd seen from afar, but never close up.

Brecan… I didn't want to know what he was feeling.

Under the table, Tauren's fingers brushed over mine, igniting a fire over my skin. "Is the meal to your liking?"

"Yes," I said, after clearing my throat. "It's delicious."

He grinned. "Wait until you taste the dessert."

"There's dessert?" Mira excitedly gripped the table's edge.

"Your favorite," Queen Annamarie told Lucius. The two were obviously in love. The way he looked at her was more than a stiff *thank you*. There was appreciation, gratefulness – not for what she'd requested for him, but that she'd thought of him at all.

A tender look passed between them, and the Queen's smile lit the room. She was truly lovely. A ruler plucked from the sectors. From Five, according to Mira's chatter as she'd dressed me for dinner. Her family were renowned sculptors. Did she feel as comfortable with a hammer and chisel in her hands as she did holding a scepter? Was that why every time she looked at me, her face looked more like marble than skin and bone?

King Lucius's favorite dessert was decadent and delicious. Fit for a king, but simple. I wasn't sure if it was pudding, sweet bread, or a mixture of both, but the hard sugar crust was my favorite part. I hadn't eaten much of my dinner, but scraped the small dish that had held my dessert until no speck of the confection remained. With the last swipe of my spoon on the ceramic, I looked up to see that everyone was staring. Even Tauren, who wore a smile.

"You like sugar," he guessed.

"I don't eat it often, so this was a treat," I explained, my cheeks blazing under their attention.

When dinner was over, the King and Queen excused themselves, each promising to speak with me soon. *I just can't* wait *for those conversations*, I thought dryly.

Tauren leaned in to me. "The invitees are waiting in another room. I need to greet them briefly."

"How generous of you to spare a moment of your time for them," Brecan said derisively.

Tauren straightened. "If you cannot mind your tongue, Brecan, I will have you replaced."

Brecan fumed, but remained silent. I wondered how long he could hold his tongue, and if Tauren would follow through on the threat if pushed far enough.

"Tauren, go meet with them," I said, trying to smooth the tension Brecan's fat mouth had caused.

"That's the thing… I need you to accompany me," he replied apologetically.

"Do you fear them?" I asked.

"Not at all, but you are an invitee, technically, and this first informal meeting will be filmed."

"I need to be present," I said, finally understanding what he meant.

"I need you at my side," he corrected.

As Tauren and I left Brecan in the hallway and readied ourselves to step into an intimate sitting room, he took hold of my hand. Startled, I pulled away. "I'm not sure that's a very good idea, Prince. You'll be marrying one of these women."

"You're right." His face flushed, but he schooled his features and held the door open for me. I stepped inside, feeling his legs brush the skirt of my dress. His closeness was confusing, setting me at ease and on edge all at once.

Every woman in the room zoomed in on us, as did the cameras' wide lenses. I stepped away from him, walking to the side of the room and perching against a wall as he spoke to the group.

"Ladies, thank you very much for accepting my invitation," he began, sweeping his eyes across the room. "This year, I break with tradition. This year, I've extended an invitation to thirteen women, one from each of Nautilus's sectors. Miss Sable," inclining his head toward me, "is from Thirteen. And before you ask, yes, she is a witch." His smile gleamed as he looked at each of them in turn, then to me.

Must he state the obvious? I cringed, even as I plastered on a grateful smile and peered around the room of women who were not only beautiful, but ruthless. Some dismissed me at first glance. Others saw me as a threat.

Brecan silently slithered into the room, moving out of sight of the cameras, and many of the women nonchalantly glanced in his direction. They were in for a treat. Not only was Tauren handsome, but now they could ogle Brecan as well. The two couldn't be more different. And not just in the light and dark hues of their hair, but in their demeanors. They were from two different worlds that existed within the same kingdom.

Tauren stared at me, and when I caught the heat of his stare, he ticked his head toward the women. Each and every one was lovely. Each was beautiful and unique. Red hair and pale skin, dark skin and pale hair, freckles and those without a single freckle to be found. All of them, I realized, wore pastel colors.

Our party was the only one wearing a dark hue... with the exception of the Prince. He also wore black, though a crisp, white shirt peeked out from beneath his coat. His ensemble somehow bridged a gap between them and me.

Mira was right. All the women's dresses accentuated their breasts. I was shocked a few hadn't spilled out of their corsets entirely.

Before I knew it, Brecan stood beside me. "Let the game begin," he whispered, flashing me a look I couldn't read. He wasn't wrong, though I doubted any of these women were capable of murder.

With the official greeting concluded, everyone chatted together, most sticking with the familiar and conversing with their escorts. The cameramen looked bored.

Tauren made his way around the room, stopping on my right side when he reached me and keeping his distance from Brecan, whom he shot a dark look. "Didn't we agree you would remain in the hallway?"

Brecan smiled. "My duty is to Sable alone."

Tauren let it go. He leaned in close. "See anyone who looks suspicious?"

"Not in the least," I replied, looking at the women.

"That's what I thought. I'd like you to meet some of the staff after dinner, maybe shake a few hands?" he asked, brows raised.

"That's fine."

He nodded and cleared his throat, leaning back against the wall and surveying the room. He looked uncomfortable slouching and soon stood up straight again, striding back to the front of the room.

"I have a small gift for each of you. Well, it's a gift, but also a way to help me keep you all straight." The ladies tittered as if he'd told the funniest joke they'd ever heard. Thirteen servants, wearing stark-white uniforms, entered the room, each carrying a white box. Every box was tied with a white bow except for mine, which was tied with a black one. I couldn't help but smile.

"Untie them," Tauren encouraged with a broad smile.

Every girl tugged at her ribbon and removed the lid to her box, revealing a silver bracelet within each one. Mine was engraved with the number thirteen. "Our sectors," the redhead from Sector One flirted. "How clever."

While the women clamped the bracelets onto their tiny wrists, I placed mine back in the box and waited until they were finished stroking Tauren's ego. He stood and gave a bow. "I'd like to thank you all for accepting my invitation and formally welcome you to my home. For one of you, this will be your future home."

The girls sucked in a collective gasp as if they didn't already know this. I couldn't help but roll my eyes. When I looked back at Tauren, he was smiling at me.

"I look forward to spending time with each of you, getting to know you and seeing if there is a spark between us. For this evening, I'm sure you're tired. It's been a very long and exciting day. I'll send a staff member around tomorrow morning with a detailed schedule, so that you can plan for time with me and for your free time, of course. The palace has much to offer, and I hope you'll enjoy your stay, no matter how brief or long it may be." He gave a wave. "Good evening, ladies."

The girls filed out and met their escorts in the hallway, whispering about how handsome the Prince was and how he'd given them a special smile or pointed them out during introductions, most of which was complete garbage. He hadn't done anything overtly special for any of them, as far as I could tell.

Mira, who had obediently stayed in the hall, met my eyes. "You were more beautiful than any of them. I bet Prince Tauren is lamenting our customs right about now."

Brecan huffed.

"Did you see their dresses?" she asked, giving me an I-told-you-so look. "They were practically spilling out of them. You looked like a queen compared to those girls."

"I am no queen, and I'm not a slab of meat for sale. I'd prefer to be modest, even if it's unfashionable."

She nodded. "Then we make your fashion the talk of the Kingdom. We make your style exquisite. Everyone will be dressing like you by spring," she gushed.

I didn't think I would ever become a fashion icon, but I let her dream it was possible. I waved Brecan in. "I have to meet with some of the staff this evening. You're welcome to go back to your rooms and do... whatever it is you do. I can handle the readings by myself."

Mira let out a thankful breath. "I'm exhausted."

"I'm going with you," Brecan asserted.

"No, you aren't. Not after the way you acted earlier."

He snorted. "I was just informing *the Prince* of your predicament."

"All evening you've acted like a child."

Brecan grinned cruelly. "Is it childish to stand up for you? For our beliefs? Or have you forgotten them because the pretty prince extended a fake invitation so he could use you?"

My hand twitched at my side. For the first time in my life, I wanted to smack his face. To scream for him to take back his vile words. But how could I, when he was right?

Mira looked between me and Brecan and then let out a fake yawn. "I'm so sleepy. I'm turning in early." She grabbed my arm and leaned in to whisper, "If you need me, just knock. I'm not really going to sleep. I have work to do."

I nodded and glanced back at Brecan, who had crossed his arms. He looked so strange in black when I was used to seeing him in airy blue. Not only had his garments darkened, but so had his demeanor. Ever since I told him I wouldn't hand-fast to him, he'd been combative. And now he was jealous of Tauren when he had absolutely no reason to be. Tauren was using me, like Brecan said. Or rather, he was using my abilities. I couldn't blame him. If I were in his position, and I didn't want to die a painful, tragic death at a young age, I'd do everything in my power to stop it.

Mira walked away from us, heading in the direction of the staircase that led to our rooms.

"I am escorting you," Brecan insisted. "The Circle gave me very specific instructions, and I will follow them to the letter."

"Fine," I acquiesced.

His head ticked back. "I expected you to put up more of a fight."

"I don't want to fight with you, Brecan," I answered wearily. "I just want to figure out who wants the Prince dead and go home. I have so much work to do on the House, and I'll never get finished if I don't get started."

The tension in his muscles melted away after hearing my words.

"How do you know you can find this person?" he asked. "They obviously don't want to be found."

"It's not up to them. It's up to Fate."

He pinched his lips together. "What if Fate wants Tauren dead?"

I swallowed, refusing to let the visions of him dying surface... "He told me to come here. Why would he send me if he wanted the Prince to die? If he wanted Tauren dead, he would have given me the order while he was in Thirteen on the Equinox."

"Maybe he wants you to take the fall for it. Maybe you've lost his favor," he shrugged.

A deep breath flew from my lungs, deflating me. "Why are you being so cruel?"

He closed his eyes. "I'm not trying to be. I'm just trying to get you to see what's right in front of you."

Brecan was the only thing in front of me.

Just then, the door swung open and Tauren strode in, staring between me and Brecan. "Did I interrupt?"

I said *no* at the same time Brecan answered *yes*.

Rolling my eyes, I walked to Tauren. "I assume the staff is ready?"

"Yes, but they don't know what you can do. I asked a few of the other girls to greet them, so you don't stand out." He glanced at my chest where his necklace lay on my collarbone. "It looks beautiful on you."

"Thank you. I'm still not sure I should accept it. The other girls are actually competing for you. I'm just here to help."

He smiled and put his hands in his pockets. "Then you are the most deserving of all. Besides, I haven't given any of the other girls anything but the bracelets."

His admission sent moths aflutter in my stomach. I had to stop letting that happen. Somehow.

He looked to my wrist, his brows furrowing when he saw I wasn't wearing my bangle.

Brecan patted the pocket of his coat. "It's safe, Highness."

"Right." Tauren placed his hand on the small of my back, guiding me down the corridor. To the right, another pair of doors opened. The expanse of the space was only broken by the strategically placed, stark white columns that supported the ceiling.

The assembled staff stood in a large rectangle in the middle of the room. All of them wore starched white pants, and either button-up shirts or sweaters to match. The group was very diverse, made up of different ages and races. Most wore a smile, but you could tell in the way they stood up taller when Tauren entered the room that they were proud of what they did. It wasn't a fear response; it was a desire to please him and prove they were deserving of their positions.

Two of the other girls were making their way around the room, shaking hands with everyone and making polite, inane conversation. Their smiles were almost as fake as their feigned interest. Tauren lit up at the sight. Apparently, he was oblivious to the fact that these girls couldn't care less about his staff or being forced to shake their hands.

As he escorted me around the rectangle, Fate remained quiet.

I shook hand after hand and held on a few extra seconds to ask them questions about their duties or their family. Most were genuinely happy to work at the palace. Others, though they would never admit it aloud, weren't happy to work there, but enjoyed the life it provided their families. A few were dissatisfied. I clung to their hands the longest, but found that none of the unhappy staff members were disturbed enough to kill the Prince. And like I'd seen upon walking in the room, even if the person wasn't happy, they wanted Tauren to be King. They respected the royal family, even if they didn't particularly enjoy their assigned jobs.

As I finished shaking the last staff member's hand, I turned to Tauren, who was standing near the door with the other two invitees. His brows were raised in question, but I shook my head. No one I'd shaken hands with wanted him dead.

"Miss Sable," he called out. "I'd like for you to meet the ladies from Sectors One and Two, Rose and Leah."

Both women wore silk gloves. Palm to palm was the easiest way to read a person, but skin to skin worked well enough. Instead of taking their hands, I bent in to hug them, my hands clasping gently onto their upper arms.

"I'm Rose," the buxom redhead chirped.

"Sable," I answered.

On contact, images filled my mind.

Rose was famous. Her red hair was always twisted into bouncy, loose curls and she would touch them to draw attention to her face or breasts. It worked, most of the time. Through my mind I saw video cameras following her around, flashes from photographers' cameras, her pictures in the printed press.

She was a sensation. Very popular with the core four sectors, and she believed the public was behind her bid to be Princess. She often pictured herself as Queen, but she wasn't going to sit idly by and leave it to chance. She had her wardrobe planned. When she was given her schedule in the morning, she planned to use it to her advantage and not only make the most of her time with Tauren, but interrupt the time he spent with the other ladies—accidentally on purpose, of course.

She wanted the crown, but she didn't want Tauren dead. He was her way into the royal family.

"My name is Leah," the girl from Two stated. "Nice to meet you, Sable."

I shook Leah's hand and read from her touch… Leah from Two, with mocha skin and hair, was beautiful in a way that Rose wasn't, yet Leah was the girl who wanted to be like Rose. People in the Kingdom knew who she was. She had the occasional article written or telecast taped about her philanthropic projects, but in the end, she wasn't as outgoing as Rose. Her personality was dry, and though the Kingdom liked her, they didn't love her. She was jealous. A little bitter. But she wasn't upset with Tauren.

Rose? She hated Rose. She hated everyone who stood in her way. Even me, apparently. She smiled sweetly and shrugged my hand off, taking a step back.

"So nice to meet you," Rose said, flipping her fiery red locks over one creamy shoulder. Tauren's eyes caught the movement.

"Yes, so nice," Leah parroted with slightly less enthusiasm. "I'm glad they included Thirteen this year."

No, you aren't, sweetheart, but whatever you want to say to make the Prince like you…

"It truly is an honor," I replied obediently.

Tauren's eyes twinkled with orneriness. "I didn't think she would accept my invitation, to be honest."

Rose turned to him and put an arm on his chest. "A woman would have to be a *fool* to reject you."

He smiled at me. "Well then, I'm grateful that Sable isn't the least bit foolish."

Her hand curled away from his chest at the sound of my name.

Rose turned and gave me a half smile. "Absolutely."

Leah waited, her hands clasped meekly in front of her. "Thank you for introducing us to your staff, Prince Tauren."

"They are very important to me. Without them, the palace would crumble."

Rose scrunched her nose. "That's a bit dramatic."

"No," he said, "it isn't. Things run seamlessly because of their dedication. It would be important for any queen to not only know, but appreciate those who help support us every hour of the day."

Rose swallowed and pasted on another artificial smile.

Leah pounced. "A king is only as good as the people who lift him up."

Tauren grinned. "Well said, Leah."

Leah won that battle. I wondered who would ultimately win the war, and Tauren's hand in marriage.

Mira was right. The battle would be an entertaining one to watch. The minxes' claws had already come out.

"It's getting late, ladies," Tauren announced. "I'm sure your escorts are ready to relax a little."

In the corner of the room next to Brecan stood two middle-aged women, both dressed in pastel pantsuits that matched their charges' gowns. Neither had a hair out of place. Their posture was straight and tall, while Brecan slumped against the wall, hands in his pant pockets, watching me intently.

Rose and Leah said their goodbyes to the Prince, who kissed each of them on the back of their hand and promised to spend one-on-one time with each very soon. I thought the girls might fake a swoon, but they remained composed.

Rose paused at the doorway. "Do you want to walk with us, Sable?" she asked sweetly.

Her eyes flicked between me and Tauren, but he answered for me. "Actually, I have a question for Sable about Sector Thirteen. If you wouldn't mind offering another moment of your time to answer, that is," he added, bowing to me.

"I'd be happy to."

Rose's fake smile fell away. "Then have a good evening, Prince."

"You too," he threw over his shoulder, already dismissing her from his mind.

Leah and Rose whispered as they left the room. No doubt they'd spread a wildfire of rumors. By morning, the whole palace might be reduced to cinders.

"You felt nothing?" he asked.

"From those two? No. They want to be Princess, not ruin their chances by killing you."

"Then maybe it's not one of the invitees," he mused.

"It wouldn't be likely," Brecan interjected, pushing away from the wall and walking toward us. "I'm sure you have enemies outside these walls, though. Anyone you'd like for us to seek out?"

"None that would be safe for Sable to meet with."

"I assure you that Sable and I can handle her safety," Brecan asserted.

"I won't place her in harm's way. Besides, the groups of dissenters we know of have wanted my father and me dead for years. They want to bring democracy back to the Kingdom, and aren't shy about their desires. Their threats come weekly; sometimes we receive several a week."

"Then who's to say it isn't one of them?" Brecan argued.

Fate finally showed up to the party. A bitter, horrible taste filled my mouth. "It's someone closer..."

Tauren's brows furrowed. "That's what I was afraid of."

I fastened my attention on the flavor... "I don't know that it's an invitee, but it's someone within the palace. Do me a favor and let me smell anything you eat or drink."

Fate took the bitterness off my tongue. The person who wanted Tauren dead would strike soon. Perhaps with poison.

ten

Tauren turned pale. "You can't be with me all hours of the day or at every meal. And how are we supposed to be discreet if you need to taste or smell my food?"

"And drink," I added. "I can spell the room."

"Spell the room?" he asked.

"She would pause time," Brecan explained, giving Tauren a condescending look.

Hopefully, Fate's presence tonight meant he would help me find the person who would poison the Prince. Fate wanted me here. He hadn't yet called for Tauren's death, so Tauren was meant to survive this. I hoped.

The doors parted. A guard dressed in black with a large weapon slung over his shoulder stepped into the room. "Pardon me, Prince Tauren. Your father wishes to speak to Miss Sable."

His mouth parted. "I'll see her to him, then."

"He wishes to speak with her alone."

Brecan stepped forward. I knew he was about to insist that he accompany me.

"Thank you for a lovely evening," I said to Tauren. "Brecan, I'll let you know when I return to my room."

Neither Brecan nor Tauren was happy I'd dismissed them, but the two men stood back dutifully and watched as I followed the guard out of the room.

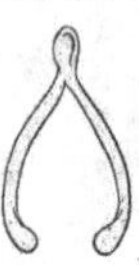

King Lucius looked as tired as he did frazzled, and nothing like the calm ruler he presented at dinner. He had dragged a chair to the window and was staring out at the night sky, but he turned around when I entered the room.

His suit jacket was unbuttoned as well as the top buttons of his crisp white shirt, and from the mussed look of his hair, he'd been raking his hands through it. The circles beneath his eyes were darker and the worry lines on his forehead were more pronounced.

The entire walk to his office, I'd dreaded what he might say. A hundred scenarios played through my mind, but none of them included the smile he graced me with now.

He smiled warmly, wrinkles forming at the corners of his eyes. "Miss Sable."

I wasn't sure how to greet him. "Your Highness."

He gestured to a plush chair sitting empty across from his enormous desk. Sitting down, I waited for him to roll his chair back to its normal position on the other side of the desk. Instead, he stiffly stood and gingerly walked across the room, sitting beside me in my chair's match.

"My wife and I have reasons to be distrustful of witches, reasons I don't feel apt to disclose at present, but I trust my son. I trust his instincts. He surprised me by offering you an invitation," he began. "I wanted to speak with you discreetly for a few reasons. The first is to get to know the young woman who caught his eye."

"With all due respect, that's not what happened."

He tilted his head and propped his ankle on his knee. "I'd say it is. I chose the other women for him. He dreaded turning eighteen, knowing this would be his invitation year. Yours is the only invitation he personally sent."

"He only sent it because I might be able to help him, sir."

"I don't envy you, Sable. I'm not sure how you do it."

"I don't have a choice."

He gave a half-smile. "Fate can make you quite uncomfortable. He did the same to your mother."

I tilted my head, surprised. "You knew her?"

"I did. Cyril was… I sought her advice often when I was younger and untested."

"I had no idea."

He shook his head. "Your grandmother hated that she read for me. She said that Cyril was more loyal to me than to her own kind. She thought we were lovers. We weren't, of course. Your mother was hand-fasted to another, and I was newly married as well. But people make assumptions and jump to incorrect conclusions sometimes. For the record, I love Annalina very much. I have never, and would never be unfaithful to her."

I narrowed my eyes. "Who was my mother handfasted to?" Fate called himself my father, but I was a child when he claimed me as his daughter. Someone else was my biological father, but who was he? My father's identity was a detail I'd asked for and never received. Everyone said it wasn't important, but it was important to me then, and it still was now.

"She never said, and I didn't ask. When we met, it was for a reading. We weren't friends, Sable, and thank God we weren't enemies. There were things Cyril could do that were frightening, frankly."

I swallowed, wondering if he suspected that I could likely do the same things.

"Is my son in love with you? I know that witches cannot marry. If he loves you, Sable, you should go back to Thirteen as quickly as possible. I don't want to see him hurt."

I pressed my lips closed. "I don't believe he does."

"If he develops feelings for you, I want you to leave."

"Before I determine who wants him dead?"

He inclined his head, though I could tell it was difficult for him to do so. The tendons in his neck were so taut, I thought they might snap.

"What would I state as the reason, when I've agreed to come and identify his murderer?"

Fate filled my mouth with bitterness again.

"While we appreciate it, we don't *need* your help, Sable. This palace is well guarded. No ruler of Nautilus has been slain in two hundred years."

"With all due respect, I don't believe you can defend him. Fate instructed me to accept his invitation. I've been sent here to protect Tauren. Fate wouldn't have sent me if he thought you or your guard could handle whomever plans to kill him. Besides, if you knew my mother, you know that I can't simply leave. That would defy *him*, and I would pay a very heavy price for doing so, a greater price than I already owe for coming to aid him."

"Then I suggest you work quickly, for I fear he's already too fond of you," the King replied, standing up and offering his hand.

If he knew my mother, he knew I could read him.

When my palm slid against his, there was a kaleidoscope of color. The King was genuine. He wanted what was best for his son, what was best for his people. He envisioned standing beside him, placing his crown on Tauren's head. Bouncing grandchildren on each knee. *He* wasn't trying to poison him…

A scene flashed into my mind. A woman with dark hair and silver eyes. She sat at a small table and waved her hand over a crystal ball, mist gnarling within. Across from her sat the young and untested King…

Beneath it all was a layer of anguish and fear.

He tugged his hand away and the scene vanished. "I'll speak with Tauren in the morning. Have a good night, Sable."

"Good night."

He sank into the chair as I slipped away from his study.

I retraced my steps down the corridor to the staircase. With two knuckles, I knocked on Brecan's door. He answered wearing nothing but a towel. His pale hair dripped water over his shoulders and rolled down his stomach and back. "That didn't take long."

"Long enough for you to make yourself at home," I quipped.

"Have you tried the shower? It's magical. Hot water. Jets everywhere. I think I might take another, just because I can."

I couldn't help but laugh, turning my head away from his bare chest and stomach.

"If anything could rid you of residues from so many readings, it's the jets along the wall," he offered, truly looking like he believed they might help. I wished it were so simple.

The residues from the staff assaulted my mind, making my head ache from front to back.

Hooking a thumb over my shoulder, I told him, "I'm going to check on Mira."

He stared at me like he wanted to say more, but in the end, simply said, "Good night, Sable."

I gave him a slight smile, realizing things between us had changed and might never be the same as they were before. I trudged to Mira's door.

She answered before I could even knock, grabbing my wrist and tugging me inside. "Wait until you see what we've made!"

Hanging on a rack was a nude-colored gown with intricate, black velvet patterns and slick beads all over it. The swirling patterns included candles. Tea cups. Crystal balls. Tarot cards. Palmistry. Wishbones. I lit up as I brushed my fingers down the fabric. "How did you do this?"

She shrugged. "It's what we do. Right, fellas?" She gingerly sat her glass spiders on a nearby table and breathed a spell over them. Obeying her command, they froze in place. Their legs curled in as if they were dead, and they tipped over onto their sides and rolled onto their bulbous backs, one scarlet, one cyan.

"You have jeans and a t-shirt in your room for tomorrow. During the day, you can dress casually."

"I've never worn jeans."

She winced. "They aren't nearly as comfortable as dresses, but they're all the rage in the lower twelve. Everyone wears them. The tighter, the better. And all your t-shirts have Thirteen stitched on them, so people can tell you ladies apart."

"Like they wouldn't know which sector I'm from?" I laughed, assuming she was joking.

"You have to wear them," she said gently. "You're supposed to wear the cuff he gave you, too."

"I'll do no such thing. It's appalling that the Prince of Nautilus cannot devote the time to learn thirteen names."

Her eyes widened. "What did the Prince say this evening?"

"Not much. But the King said plenty."

"King? You met with him again?"

I nodded. "He's worried about Tauren."

"He knows someone is out to…"

"No, he thinks Tauren might get his princely little heart broken if he likes me," I said disbelievingly. After pausing a brief moment, I decided to tell her the rest. "He knew my mother. He knows about handfasting."

Her lips formed a tiny o. "So, he knows you can't marry his son."

I scoffed, "He thinks his guards can thwart any attempt on Tauren's life. I'm supposed to leave if I think he's 'becoming too fond of me'."

"Should we pack our trunks now?" she asked, her eyes widening.

I shook my head. "He doesn't have feelings for me. There's nothing to worry about."

"Sable, I hate to be the one to reveal something obvious to you, but he had a room painted and decorated for you, he gave you a necklace from the crown jewel collection, and whenever you're in his presence, you're all he can look at."

He was all I could look at, too, if I admitted it to myself, but it didn't matter how he or I felt. We could never be. We were attracted to one another, but that was all it was or could ever be.

Mira yawned. "Sorry," she said, covering her mouth.

Happy for the change in subject, I replied, "Don't be. I'm tired, too. See you in the morning?"

"Your royal schedule should be delivered first thing tomorrow."

"Great."

"I'll trim any stray threads and bring the gown to you in the morning."

I walked to the door and stepped into the hall. "Thanks, Mira. For everything."

She fought another yawn as she closed the door behind me.

I pulled my key out of my dress pocket and slid it into the lock. Lying on the floor just inside the door was a slip of white paper.

I broke the familiar seal to read:

Sable,

Please meet me in the West Garden. I need to speak with you tonight.

With hope,
- Tauren

eleven

Skinny jeans were the devil's creation. I wasn't sure I was going to be able to get them over my hips, let alone button and zip them. But with some shimmying and hopping around the room, I finally tugged them on, lying flat on my back on the bed to get them fastened. *The tighter the better*, Mira said. But these were beyond tight. I turned the black t-shirt with Thirteen scrawled across the breast in white lettering inside out and ran a brush through my hair. I didn't bother with shoes. After a day prancing around in heels, my feet were killing me.

I quietly snuck out of my room, locking it behind me and tucking the key in my pocket. A staff member was kind enough to show me to the West Garden—somewhere I never would've found myself.

Tauren waited outside on a bench.

"I need a map," I grumped, sitting next to him.

"A map?"

"Of the palace, yes. This place is a labyrinth. I have no idea how to navigate it."

He gave a coy smile. "I should've left directions, but figured you were resourceful enough to find your way." He scanned my clothing, and in an odd tone said, "You look different in those clothes."

"You don't like them?" I glanced down, wondering if something was out of place.

"No, I... I like them." Tauren looked up at the sky, waiting a long moment before adding, "A lot."

We were silent for a moment, staring at the twinkling stars.

"Why is your shirt inside out?"

"About that..." I readied myself for a fight. "I will not be wearing shirts or bracelets for your convenience. I find it demeaning. You know my name and sector. Learn the names of the other girls... Highness," I added as an afterthought, to make sure he didn't throw me in a dungeon or something.

He answered with a smile. "I'll do that right away, *Sable*. The producers of the telecast thought it would be easier for the public to learn the girls that way at first. I actually *do* know all their names and sectors. I have voluminous files on each, thanks to my father's snoops."

"Each one but me," I added.

"Each one but you. You, I'd rather take the time to learn on my own."

The moths fluttered again. I tamped them down, reminding them that this attraction, if it could be called that, didn't and couldn't mean anything.

"Was my father cordial?" he asked.

"He was." I lowered my voice. "Did you know he knows quite a lot about witches? He knew my mother."

Tauren's brows furrowed. "When I was little, he used to tell me stories about the sectors. He knew a lot about Thirteen and I wondered how, since we never crossed the border. Throughout the years, we visited every sector except yours."

"Well, witches can be a little unwelcoming, except for when it benefits them. On Equinoxes and Solstices, we're happy to take money from whomever wants to give it to us."

"Do you use currency in Thirteen?" he asked, a curious glint in his eye.

"No, we trade – food, goods, or services – but some like to travel out of Thirteen, most often visiting Twelve to see new things. I've never left before today, though."

"And now that you have? What do you think of Nautilus as a whole?"

"From what I've seen, it's beautiful. Far more interesting and diverse than I realized. I'd like to visit each sector," I admitted, "and I'd like to see the ocean before I go back to The Gallows."

He glanced down at his clasped hands and leaned forward. I gazed at the familiar stars, comforted by their consistency.

"I wish I could see the world as you do," he said softly, watching me.

I blinked out of the daze I'd been in. "What do you mean?"

He shook his head. "Doesn't matter."

A brown and tan moth fluttered over the grass. I called her to me and she landed on my finger. "See?" Tauren said. "Whomever you choose when you arrive back home should cherish the year he'll have with you, for it will be the most memorable and magical time of his life."

I raised my finger and let the moth take flight again. "This is common for a witch." I shrugged. "It would seem boring for my hand-fasted."

"Nothing about you is mundane or common, Sable."

I swallowed, looking back to the sky to center myself. For a moment, it felt like I levitated. I may have.

"Do you want to know my first reason for extending you an invitation?" His hand crept across the cement bench and the tip of his pinky grazed my skin.

"Yes," I cautiously agreed.

"Because I've never met anyone I felt connected to so immediately, so... completely. I wanted you to accept, because I wanted you to consider me. Consider having me, that is. As your husband." His dark lashes fluttered the more flustered he became, and the sight made something in my chest ache.

As your husband. The words reverberated through my heart like the beat of a heavy drum.

"I can't," I told him regretfully.

He hung his head. "I know that now. You told me the night of the Equinox, but I thought there might be a chance that... never mind."

The two of us were on opposite sides of a very dangerous line, but when he said such things to me, it made me want to tread closer to him. But like Thirteen's boundary, this was a line we could never cross. There wasn't enough magic in the world to pierce it.

twelve

I left him in the garden and somehow backtracked to my room without becoming lost. I scrubbed my face in the pristine bathroom sink and stared into the mirror, repeatedly asking myself, and Fate, what I was doing there. Why wasn't he moving this along so I could return home?

Fate remained still, which was alarming since I could always feel him. Since I'd been chosen, he'd always hidden himself inside me. So, I wasn't sure why he wouldn't answer now. A simple, *Because it's not time* would have sufficed. At least it would leave me the satisfaction of knowing that the time to act was approaching.

Pushing away from the sink, I peeled the t-shirt and skin-tight jeans from me like a snake shedding skin, and slipped on a short, black silk nightgown Mira had laid out on the bed for me.

I slipped inside the plush, black sheets and pulled the soft blankets over me like a caress. For a moment, I even managed to close my eyes… only for them to pop open again to admire the room he'd appointed for me.

I chastised myself for going to the garden in the first place. I'd thought he was in danger, or maybe that he wanted to know what his father talked to me about. It never crossed my mind that he would say such things, and yet they were true. I felt an intense connection to him as well, before I even knew he was the Prince.

But a relationship between us, let alone marriage, was out of the question. I had to get to the bottom of this issue, find the would-be killer, and leave before my heart was shattered. The King was worried for his son, but no one would worry about me.

Restless, I flipped and flopped, tangling in the nightgown a few times before I finally drifted off to sleep.

I dreamed I was back in my House, staring at the mirror, dressed and ready to get in the carriage again. But this time, my reflection *did* move. It reached out to me and said… "The one who lies."

The one who lies? I panted as I woke, clutching my side. It was still dark. I panted through the pain. Fate whispered to me, *Go to him*.

I threw the covers back and ran out into the hallway. "Take me to him," I pleaded. My breath turned to mist and flowed in a dark ribbon that I followed down the corridor as I limped up another flight of stairs and took the hallway that bent to the right. At the end of the hallway was a door. His room – if this was it – was directly over the one in which I was staying.

The smoky ribbon drifted to the floor and slipped beneath the door.

I knocked, my hands still shaking with fear. The pain in my side sharpened. I gasped, holding tight just below the ribs on my right side. "Please be okay," I panted.

Tauren pulled the door open, blinking to clear his eyes. "Sable?"

I shoved my way around him, a cold sweat breaking out over my forehead. "Call for guards!" I shouted.

"Why? What's happening?"

Fate sent another sharp slice of pain through my side. "Tauren," I gasped, gripping my side. "Call for your guards."

He hit a red button on the wall just inside his door. "They'll be here in a moment. What's wrong with your side?"

"In a moment," I raged, tearing through his room, crying out as I bent to look under the bed, threw open the closet doors, and peeked behind every jacket and pair of slacks. I searched the washroom, under cabinets, outside each window. "Someone was about to stab you, and your guards will be here in a moment. Wonderful." I spun in a circle in the center of the room, looking for anywhere else they might be hiding. The curtains… His drapes were heavy and… I threw them back. There was no one lurking behind them.

A wave of pain rolled through me. I cried out and fell to my knees.

"What's happening?" he shouted, running toward me. He dropped to his knees, his eyes going to my side. "Sable, you're bleeding."

I brought my hand away and sure enough, my fingers were coated with sticky, warm blood.

"It'll go away. It's just a warning from Fate," I gritted.

He looked outraged. "I'd prefer him warn you without harming you, Sable." He put his hand over mine. "I'm calling for a medic."

A flash of a scene entered my mind. A dark figure, sliding through the shadows, around the room's perimeter. Footsteps from outside. A tendril of smoke curled under the door before someone knocked at the door… me.

"Someone was in here, before I knocked and woke you." I whispered to Fate, "Show me."

"Sable," Tauren rasped. "Look."

I opened my eyes to find a set of glittering, golden footprints shimmering across the floor. The steps crept close to the walls. Concealed by shadow…

Tauren's mouth hung open. "I don't believe this…"

He stood as six large men barged into the room. "Highness?" they questioned, weapons pointed at me. Their stunners could take down men twice their size or larger. I raised my hands so they didn't shoot, wincing through the pain. The men were taken aback by the blood all over my hands and the floor.

Tauren put himself between them and me. "Someone was in my room. Sable had a vision and came to help me. Those are the culprit's footprints," he told them, gesturing to the glittering patterns on the floor. The guards lowered their stunners.

"They wore boots," one of the guards said, crouching down to study the print. "Large ones."

The guard looked at my bare feet. "It wasn't me," I growled.

"Page the medic," Tauren ordered.

"That's not necessary," I argued, but Tauren insisted his physician look at me.

"Can you tell anything from the prints?" he asked his men.

"No, Sire. Did you see anyone? Could you tell if it was a man or woman?" one asked.

Tauren looked to me. I shook my head.

"I have no further information," he relayed, pinching the bridge of his nose. "Look, could you wait outside the door, please?"

His men complied reluctantly. Two went to search the perimeter and alert others about the intruder so heavier measures could be taken, while two remained outside the door, including the red headed fellow that was with Tauren the evening of the Equinox. He kept Tauren in sight, refusing to shut the door, and me inside alone with him. When Tauren barked at him, the guard barked back. I decided I liked him. He cared about Tauren's wellbeing, even if he was distrustful of me.

Tauren carefully picked me up and carried me to the bed. I hurt bad enough that I let him.

As I relaxed, the pain began to ebb. "I don't need a doctor. By the time he or she gets here, there will be no trace of blood or even a wound."

He knelt beside me. "I don't understand."

"It's real, but it's also not real." I shook my head, knowing my explanation left much to be desired. "How do I explain this? It's like Fate paints what he wants over reality so that it looks and feels like it's happening, but it isn't. Knowing that's what it is, keeps me from panicking."

"It doesn't help me at all," he said wearily. "I hate seeing you in pain. And the blood…"

I removed my hand from my side. It came away dry. My nightgown wasn't wet, and the fabric was intact.

"The threat is gone for now," I explained.

"What about next time?"

"Fate will warn me again. I'll get to you faster. I promise." I swung my feet over the side of the bed and Tauren's eyes caught on my bare legs. He swallowed thickly, keeping his hands on his thighs. I became aware of how close we were. How he was shirtless, his skin flawless, yet kissed by the sun, and of every muscle beneath that held him still as death.

It would be so easy for him to run his hand up my calf, then higher still. I pushed the thought away and refocused.

"You should keep your guards close at all times, even at night."

He nodded.

I wanted to rake a hand through his unruly hair, pull his face toward mine, and gaze into his golden eyes… and more. But I couldn't. "I should go back to my room."

His hand flinched toward me, but he schooled his features as the door opened, revealing the waddling form of a short, white-haired man.

"You called for me, Prince?" The man stared between us. "Is someone injured?"

"She had a pain in her side, but it's gone away now," he answered for me.

"May I check, dear?" the medic asked, pushing small spectacles up onto his nose.

"Please allow it," Tauren breathed.

At my nod, the doctor asked, "Could you give us a moment, Prince?"

Tauren stood, his eyes meeting mine. "I'll be just outside."

He would be safer in here. I opened my mouth to tell him so when he left me, striding across the room and ducking outside the door, pulling it closed.

The doctor opened a small bag and pulled out some sort of tube, the shape eerily reminiscent of a wishbone on one end. He stuck those ends in his ears and took hold of a piece of metal at the other. "May I listen?"

"Listen to what?" I asked, easing away from him.

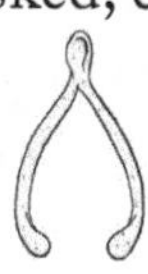

The doctor left, chuckling. "She's never seen a stethoscope," he told Tauren as he stepped outside, leaving the door wide open.

Glad to have provided his evening entertainment, I thought as I continued to eavesdrop.

"She's fine, Sire. If she has any more pain, she knows to come and find me."

"I need to give her the map she asked for so that she *can* find you."

The old man laughed and waddled back down the hallway. Tauren ducked back inside and leaned against the door. I'm so glad you're okay," he said, relieved.

"I told you I was."

"I know. I just… you scared me."

"I panicked because I thought you were in danger. I apologize for scaring you."

He shook his head. "You didn't scare me because you came, it scared me to see you hurt and bleeding. I don't want to see you suffer just for helping me, Sable."

I wanted to tell him it would hurt more for me to leave.

He pushed off the door and closed the distance between us, cupping my elbows and placing a gentle kiss on my temple. "You were right. You should go back to your room."

I nodded.

"May I see you in the morning?" he asked.

"That will depend on my schedule," I told him honestly. Someone had taken the time to fill the Prince's every waking hour with each of the invitees.

"What about checking my food at each meal? Is that still necessary?"

No bitter flavor slid over my tongue. "I'm not sure, but it would be wise. Brecan or Mira can also detect poisons, if my schedule is full."

He laughed. "Brecan wouldn't warn me if someone *did* attempt to poison me."

"He would," I defended. "He might feel threatened by you, but he wouldn't allow anyone to harm you."

Tauren sobered. "I'm sorry. He's not the only one who feels threatened, I suppose."

I didn't answer him, just turned on my heel and walked out of the room. His guards didn't budge when I walked past them, and that gave me some measure of peace. This wasn't a game. Someone wanted Tauren dead. Someone wanted to plant a dagger in his belly, to watch him bleed out, writhing in pain.

The person had entered the bedroom of the crown Prince of Nautilus.

And I didn't tell him, but I knew how they got away.

VI
THE LOVERS

PART TWO

WHEN WISHES ARE BURIED

thirteen

Whomever was in Tauren's room used magic to leave it. There was no other exit but his door, and I'd been on the other side of it. They made themselves invisible, and when I came to his aid, spirited themselves away entirely. Both abilities required a level of skill that only Elevated witches possessed.

Elevated witches were given the title when they showed mastery over their affinity. Only the priest or priestess of a House could Elevate someone and those who were honored with the title were permitted to practice more complicated and strenuous magic. It was a position that required a certain amount of trust – that the witch was ready to handle stronger magic and that they would not misuse it.

The only other witches in the palace were Brecan and Mira. Now, it seemed I couldn't trust them.

Was this why Fate wanted me here? To show me that I had no real friends, that everyone was an enemy, and that no one could be trusted?

In the morning, I didn't mention the night's excitement. Mira greeted me with a smile, carrying the nude and black gown she'd made me the night before. "My helpers made something special for today, since you don't want to wear the t-shirt provided." She hung up the gown and ran back across the hall.

I sat by the open window and sipped herbal tea while my hair dried in the breeze. "You shouldn't sit so close. There are no screens," she warned with a giggle.

"Why? Do you plan to shove me out?" I smiled, wondering if she might...

"Of course not! I want to see you in this," she said with a flourish, pulling out from behind her back a black sundress she had hidden. "Besides, you could simply spirit yourself someplace safe."

The dress gathered at the waist and flared at the hips, and would emphasize my figure without showing every inch of my skin. "It's lovely."

"It's perfect for your schedule."

"You've seen it?" I asked.

"They didn't leave one under your door? I found a stack downstairs on a table."

"I didn't receive one, but thank you for bringing one back."

"Are you feeling okay?" she asked carefully, sensing a change in my mood.

"I didn't sleep very well," I admitted.

She gave me an understanding nod. "It's an unfamiliar space."

I pretended to agree and looked around the room. "That must be it." She worried her hands. "What's the matter?" I asked.

"Your hair," she answered. "You can't just let it air dry and not style it."

I blew out a frustrated sigh. "Why not?"

"Because… it's beautiful and all, but you need to look like one of the invitees. Each of you will be filmed today. So, may I fix it?"

I nodded reluctantly. "You may."

She squealed and ran to my side, pulling me into the bathroom and assaulting my hair with dryers, hot irons that left curls in it, and spritzes and sprays that made my hair shine like silk, but not budge an inch.

"That's enough!" I coughed, waving the lingering sprays of hair product out of my face.

She smiled. "Perfect. I'll leave you to get dressed, and meet you in the hallway. Breakfast is a buffet and will be served in the north dining room," she announced. "Wherever that is."

Exactly, wherever that was.

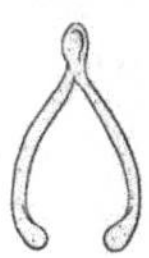

Brecan stepped out of his room the same moment I did. We locked our doors and turned to face one another, me still holding my room key, belatedly realizing I had no pockets. He held out his palm. "I'll hold it for you."

"Thanks." I gave him my key.

He straightened his back and cleared his throat. "You look beautiful, Sable."

"And you look handsome," I complimented honestly. He did. Wearing dark jeans and a matching t-shirt, in one way, he looked like he fit in here. Yet in another… he didn't. His blonde hair lay arrow-straight over his shoulders, and his lavender eyes clung to mine a beat too long before sliding away.

"Mira said we're scheduled to have breakfast with the others, but then the rest of our day is free," he said. "Tauren is spending an hour with seven of the invitees today, but you have no scheduled time with him."

It stung, to be honest, but it was for the best. The more time we spent together, the more I craved. And the more, it seemed, he wanted with me.

He had to choose a wife from this group of women, and that required getting to know them and spending ample time with each to make an informed decision. The time we shared would be focused on finding the one who wanted him dead, of course.

"What is there to do?" I asked.

Brecan smiled. "We'll have to explore and find out, but first… breakfast."

Just then, Mira walked out of her room. "Ready?"

"You'll have to spell the room to check his food," Brecan warned. "Is Fate still telling you he'll be poisoned?"

"Yes," I lied.

I tasted nothing bitter, but couldn't rule it out. Fate had given me the taste of poison just yesterday. My stomach still felt sour from it. Yet, today the bitterness was gone. It seemed as if the person who wanted Tauren dead hadn't quite made up their mind on how to go about it. Though they'd almost managed it last night.

With the staff's direction, we found the north dining hall, already filled with pastel-clothed young women and their escorts. Neither Rose nor Leah would even look in my direction. *Such well-mannered young women – but only in Tauren's presence.*

He stepped in moments after we did. "Will you check my meal?" he bent to whisper in my ear. His warm breath slid over the shell of my ear, making me shiver.

I nodded.

Brecan, Mira, and I sat at a table with four chairs while Tauren sat with two women I hadn't formally met. A girl from Nine and one from Eleven, per their tee shirts. Perhaps the shirts *did* help the viewers identify them more easily at first. They certainly helped me, as I only knew two of the ladies' names. Nine had olive skin, shiny, medium-brown hair, and a pretty smile. Eleven was the most muscular of the women in the room, but not overly so.

I watched as Brecan smiled and chatted with them. When platters of food were placed in front of them, I spelled the room and stood up from my seat, watching for anyone unaffected. Mira and Brecan were still. Brecan's mouth was open, stuck in the middle of guessing who'd been Elevated in the House of Air. Apparently, he was about to remark on one who had an unusual talent with water.

I removed the silver lid that covered Tauren's plate and inhaled the aromas stuck in the air. There was no poison. Even the odorless ones left the slightest flavor on the tongue. His water and orange juice were also untainted.

His food was fine. Fate confirmed it with a satisfied, full feeling in my belly. I replaced the lid, but couldn't resist dragging a knuckle down Tauren's cheek before walking away. I took my seat again and lifted the spell.

Brecan continued his story. Mira listened intently.

Tauren's eyes caught mine. He ran his fingers over his cheek, over the trail I'd left, and one side of his lips curled up. *Is it okay?* he mouthed.

I nodded once.

And somehow, I made it through breakfast, enduring scathing glances from women who considered me a threat, smiling my way through a conversation I didn't care about at all, and watching the one person I was beginning to care about very much break his fast with two other women.

Silently, I spent the meal begging Fate for a clue to help me quickly solve this mystery, to help me save him, and allow me to go home.

Fate remained stubbornly silent.

Mira promised she would join us later, but was in a tizzy because there was a heated indoor swimming pool here, and none of us brought swimsuits. She ran back to her room to remedy the situation, leaving Brecan and I to spend our "free" time together until she finished. Mira liked to swim and was determined to have us swim with her this evening.

We had no plan when we stepped outside, so when Brecan suggested, "Let's see what the palace has to offer," I eagerly nodded.

It took us half an hour to make our way around the palace, through beautifully manicured gardens and over to a lake where a gentleman sat alone under a tree.

"Hello," he greeted cheerfully, rushing to stand up. He pointed to three canoes large enough to each hold six people. "Care to paddle out onto the lake?"

Brecan waggled his eyebrows. "What do you say, Sable?"

I smiled. "I say yes."

I sat on one of the built-in benches and gripped the paddle while Brecan climbed in at the edge of the lake. The canoe bobbed back and forth until he sat down, and then the motion subsided.

The gentleman handed Brecan the other paddle and told us to come back whenever we were ready. There was no time limit.

"She'll have to mind her schedule," Brecan replied, giving me an ornery grin.

I felt like knocking him with my paddle, but refrained – only because I didn't want to rock the boat again. I could swim a little, but I'd never been in water that was deeper than I was tall.

Lily pads hugged the lake's edge. Brecan caught me admiring them and rowed close enough to pluck one of the only flowers left now that autumn was leaning further toward winter. He offered it to me with a tentative smile. I thanked him and cradled the pale pink bloom in my palm.

It was mid-morning, and warm sunshine yawned across the sky. "It would be horrible to have your entire life scheduled. It almost makes me feel sorry for our prince," Brecan mused.

"Almost?"

He smiled. "Well, he has everything else anyone could possibly want."

"No one has everything they want, Brecan."

"No, but you see, Tauren does. He has an army at his command, power, unimaginable wealth, the respect of his people, and the love of his parents. He's fully supported from every angle but one, and that deficit is about to be filled. He will literally have everything when he marries."

I had no response to offer him. Tauren was certainly very lucky. "Why would someone want him dead?"

"Any number of reasons," he said, resting his paddle on his thighs. I took mine out of the water too, and we floated contently in the calm, green-brown water, resting beneath the sun and the wispy clouds that attempted, but failed, to cover it. "He is to be King, so it could be to prevent him from taking the crown. He has a younger brother, if I recall correctly."

Yes, I'd seen him at the Equinox. "I wonder why he wasn't at dinner."

"Likely to protect him from the evil witches from Thirteen," Brecan replied, only half joking.

"No one here thinks that."

He guffawed. "Please, Sable. Look around you! Everyone is pleasant. *Too* pleasant. Their smiles are forced. They're glad to give us what we require so they can be excused from our presence. We frighten them."

"Only because they don't know us."

"I heard the redhead talking at breakfast. She plans to provoke you so that you'll retaliate with magic. She thinks you'll be dismissed from the palace if you use magic against any of the other invitees."

Rose, I thought. *Her parents should have named her Thorn.*

"I won't use magic against anyone."

"But you *have* used magic here. You spelled the room this morning."

"Discreetly," I pointed out. "*You* had no idea."

"True, though it's hardly the first time I've fallen under your spell," he teased, then glanced at me as if gauging my reaction.

"Brecan—"

"I was joking."

"I was going to ask you a question," I fired back. He waved for me to continue, so I did. "What do you know about Mira?"

"Not much. Water witch. Weaves clothing. Has weird glass spiders that completely make me shiver." He shivered dramatically.

"What about her magic?"

"I only know about animation and water." His eyes narrowed. "Why do you ask?"

"You only control air, right? What about spells?"

"I know a few, but in the Houses, we're mainly encouraged to master our affinities. The spells and incantations are performed by the Priests and Priestesses. Why so many questions?"

I swallowed uneasily. For the first time I could recall, I wasn't sure I could trust him.

Fate stirred within, and a cool breeze swept over my skin. Brecan was safe.

"Something happened last night," I started.

He straightened his spine. "What happened?"

"Fate sent a strong message that someone was going to attempt to kill him – by stabbing."

Brecan's brows furrowed. "Why didn't you wake me?" His tone wasn't angry, but concerned. Almost desperate.

"Whomever it was, disappeared when I showed up. Literally disappeared, Brecan."

"You thought it was me?" he asked, clasping his chest, stung by my accusation. "I volunteered to come here to protect *you*. I know what it means for you to have Fate pushing you, and what you go through if you don't do his bidding right away."

"You shouldn't—"

"Don't tell me I shouldn't speak it! It's true. He needs to understand that he doesn't have to hurt you to have you do his bidding. He needs only ask. You're one of the kindest, most loyal witches I know."

I pinched my lips together, thankful he thought so highly of me.

"But I want you to know that I could never – *would* never – hurt you. And right now, I know that hurting Tauren would do exactly that." He began to paddle again. "I see how you look at him."

A hard knot formed in the back of my throat.

"Besides," he paused. "You're my very best friend, Sable."

I'd hurt him by even considering that he might have been involved, and I felt terrible for it. "I'm sorry for even thinking it," I told him.

He nodded, but refused to look at me. "I don't know Mira well, but I don't think she would hurt him. Besides, you read his fate before we agreed to come. Whomever wanted him to die, was already close to him."

Fate filled my belly with warmth. Brecan was right.

"A witch was in his room, Brecan."

He shook his head and chuckled darkly. "Not every witch in the Kingdom chooses to live in The Gallows."

That was a possibly I'd never contemplated until he said it. I assumed all witches would want to live amongst our kind, but never considered there would be dissenters. And the King… he knew my mother. Which meant that when she was alive, there must have been more movement to and from Thirteen.

"You never knew?" he asked, a hint of wonder filling his voice.

"I never had the chance to know."

"The Circle emptied the House of Fate when your mother died, Sable. Those witches didn't die with her. If I was them, I wouldn't go into the Wilds; I'd head straight for the lower sectors. And anyway, there must be others who grew up in the Lowers. Witches aren't bound to pieces of earth or to their own kind. Not everyone wants to be ruled by the Circle, or by anyone, for that matter."

Brecan knew, but few others likely did. The Circle forbade me from leaving Thirteen for trade, afraid Fate would ask me to end the life of someone while I was outside our sector.

It was another reason I considered accepting the invitation. Only the royal family could overrule one of the Circle's mandates. With their permission, I could see the Kingdom, even if it was because the Prince needed my power.

Besides, every girl, witch or not, dreamed of becoming a princess. Not with crowns and gowns, but princess of the heart of someone she loved, and who loved her in return.

Witches only hoped to tolerate their hand-fasted for a year.

What would true love feel like? Love that knew no boundaries...

"I'll help you," he vowed. "We'll find the witch responsible, and then the three of us will go back home."

Home.

My House was there. Ready for me to finish cleaning it. Ready for me to paint. To revive and resurrect it.

Then I could figure out how to reclaim my position in the Circle.

That was all I wanted, until *he* sat down at my table for a reading of fate…

"You have to distance yourself from him, Sable."

"I'm not near him right now."

"Are you sure of that?" he asked gently.

Of course he knew I was thinking of Tauren while paddling with him. He knew me better than anyone.

"Hey," Brecan interrupted my thoughts. "Why don't we have some fun? My affinity may not be water, but… you should hold on."

I gripped the side of the canoe as he pointed a finger behind us. Wind whirred out of his fingertip, propelling us across the water so fast, the air stung my eyes. I closed them, unable to prevent the laughs that bubbled from my chest, followed by a squeal as we accelerated.

The sound of horse hoofs clomping to a stop made Brecan pause and the canoe skidded to a sudden stop, lurching us forward. Brecan caught me when I was flung into his lap. On the far bank of the lake, two horses had stopped.

Tauren sat atop a dark stallion while his date, none other than the scheming Rose, rode a glossy white mare. Its silky mane matched her off-white riding habit. Her escort had done her research and styled her accordingly.

Tauren's easy smile was missing as he took us in. I carefully scooted back into my seat. Brecan broke the tension by waving. "Sorry! Apparently we row quicker than either of us realized. Thank goodness we didn't roll the canoe."

"Can you swim?" Tauren asked.

"Of course, Highness," he answered.

"And you, Sable?"

I nodded once. "Yes." *Sort of.*

"Good," he answered, a muscle twitching in his jaw. He clutched the leather reins with his gloved hands. "Enjoy your day."

Before we could bid him the same, he'd kicked the horse and flicked the reins. Rose did her best to keep up.

fourteen

I made my way to the kitchens to check the Prince's picnic lunch, spelling the kitchen and staff before the basket was taken out for him and his date, and then Brecan and I spent the afternoon lounging in a pair of hammocks that swung between three large oaks that grew in a triangle. Mira joined us mid-afternoon, relaxing in the tall grasses and refusing to accept the hammock I offered to share with her.

That evening, I stopped to check Tauren's dinner before ordering plates for the three of us to eat in Mira's buttercup-colored suite. After which, she shoved swimsuits into both mine and Brecan's hands and ordered us to get ready. She wanted to go to the water.

I imagined that it called to her much like Fate called to me at times.

Brecan's suit consisted of soft, black shorts that stretched from just below his navel to the top of his knee. Mine? Mine was more revealing than anything I'd ever worn. The bottoms were skimpy; I was certain my underwear covered more than they did. The top was a halter, comprised of little more than a scrap of criss-crossed black fabric that tied behind my neck and back. She'd given me a loose, but structured dress to cover up with on the way to the pool. I considered wearing it *into* the pool instead.

Of course, on the way through the palace, we bumped into Tauren and his latest date. The girl was pretty, all wide eyes and innocence. A farmer from Ten, according to her t-shirt.

He stepped in front of us as we tried to pass by them quietly.

"Hello," he said, looking down at me. I hated that he was taller, especially when I was barefooted.

A strand of dark hair hung into his golden eyes. My fingers twitched to brush it away. Brecan cleared his throat behind me.

"Hello," I returned.

Tauren stood up taller and glanced at each of us, his eyes settling back on me. "Have you enjoyed your free time today?"

"We have."

"Undoubtedly," he replied, a sharp edge to his voice.

I looked at his date, who looked confused and a little lost. She crossed her arms, then relaxed them and let them hang at her side.

"Well, have a good evening," I dismissed him.

A wicked gleam appeared in his eyes as he looked me over. My skin warmed under his gaze. "Going swimming?"

"Yes."

He nodded. "Enjoy the amenities."

He moved toward his date and I eased past him, Brecan following directly behind. He had to grab Mira's hand and pull her along with us. She was still mooning over Tauren.

Oh, what it must be like to be him. Every girl swooning in his presence, tittering over his every word, constantly stroking his ego. It turned my stomach.

I led the others through the palace, stopping when I realized I had no idea where I was going. Thankfully, the water called to Mira, and after a couple more wrong turns, we found the door leading into the pool area.

I'd expected to find a small pond, but should have realized a small pool would've been lost in a palace so big. The pool we found was an enormous, rectangular lake that faded from shallow to deep, the water transforming from light blue to cobalt as the depth increased.

Brecan walked to the edge and dipped his toe in. "It's not hot," he grumped.

Mira swatted him. "It's not cold, either."

"How would you know? You haven't even touched it," he challenged.

She smiled fiercely, then sent a wave of water over his body. He stood still for a moment, obviously in shock, then let out a dark, warning laugh.

"You should run," I told her.

She made it two feet before he caught her and tossed her in the water. Then he turned to me.

I held my hands out. "No."

"Oh, yes," he teased, inching closer.

I backed away, ready to run. "Your fight was with Mira, not me!" I squeaked.

His eyes glittered. "I don't care. You're the only one still dry."

I whispered a spell and spirited to the other side of the pool before he could catch me. "Not fair!" he yelled, diving in gracefully.

Though I could swim, my movements could never be considered graceful, so I sat on the edge of the pool and dangled my legs in the water, letting them get used to the temperature. I slid in slowly when Mira threatened to soak me like she'd done Brecan.

The water felt glorious, neither too hot nor too cold. I sloppily made my way to the shallower side where my toes could easily touch the bottom. Mira and Brecan splashed one another playfully on the other side of the pool. She sent small bursts of water arcing from one side of the pool to the other and back. I smiled, then laughed as I tried to catch them in my hands. Then she crafted a herd of Pegasus from the water. They whinnied, swooped, and dove over us, splashing when they rejoined the water.

When the door opened, she released her magic and all the effects rained down on us. I wiped a splash from my face and blinked up to see Tauren dive into the deep end. He swam beneath the surface, breaching right in front of me, rising from the water with a triumphant smile.

"The other girls are too afraid to get their hair wet," he panted, raking his dark hair back.

"I think they're nervous for you to see them in a swimsuit," Mira told him, moving into deeper water so that she was concealed from the neck down. She shot me an anxious smile, gawking at the prince standing in front of me.

Brecan swam to the deep end and back, which made me feel as if he were pacing. His white-blonde hair streaked through the water like angry ribbons.

Mira faked a yawn. "Wow, I'm really tired. We did so much today. I think it's time I head back to my room."

She looked at Brecan. For a moment, he didn't budge or reply. For a moment, I didn't want him to go with her.

That moment evaporated when Tauren took my hand under the water and tugged me ever so slightly closer.

"Will you check in when you go upstairs?" Brecan finally asked, looking between the two of us.

I discreetly pulled my hand from Tauren's and used both to slick my hair back. "I won't be much longer."

Brecan walked to the nearest ladder, climbed up, and escorted Mira to the towel rack. They wrapped themselves and left the pool area, but not before Brecan shot us a look of warning.

"We are scheduled to spend an hour together tomorrow," Tauren said, his voice echoing over the empty space.

"Aren't you supposed to be spending this evening with someone else?"

"This is my free hour," he answered, swimming around me with ease. His muscles rippled with every movement.

"Do you swim every day?"

"No. I don't swim very often at all."

"Then why are you here now?"

Tauren grinned and my knees weakened. "Because you're in my pool."

"So?" I said, crossing my arms. The movement drew his attention to my body. A fire ignited in his eyes.

"So, I was jealous."

"Of your pool?" I said incredulously. "How can anyone be jealous of a *thing*?"

"I'm jealous of lots of things," he said with a half-smile. "And people. You and Brecan looked like you were enjoying yourselves on the lake."

"I imagine just as much as you enjoyed your romantic horseback ride with Rose."

"You're at ease with him," he noted.

"He's my best friend," I volleyed.

He swam faster around me. I spun faster to keep up. Then he stopped and stood at full height, and I was mesmerized by the water sluicing from his skin.

"What am I to you?" he asked softly.

"You are my prince."

He took a step forward, then another, until our bodies almost touched. "I am the Prince of every subject in the Kingdom. What am I to *you*, Sable?"

"The boy with the golden eyes, and heart to match," I admitted before I lost the nerve to say it aloud.

"Is that how you thought of me? Before you knew who I was?"

He moved a step closer, pressing his front to mine. This time, I didn't retreat. I did swallow nervously. Brecan had been just as close before, but this was different. As much as Brecan thought he wanted me, it had never felt as intense as this. Tauren definitely wanted me in this moment.

He raked a knuckle down my cheek. "I don't understand."

My brows furrowed in confusion.

"Have you cast a spell on me?"

"I would never do that," I answered, shaking my head.

"Then what is this?"

Fate, I wanted to say, as a warm sensation filled my stomach. *This is fate.*

When the heavy door opened, Tauren and I stepped away from one another guiltily, the tether between us slackening. "Sire," a guard announced. "Your father needs you. He's quite shaken."

"Of course. I was just enjoying an evening swim." Tauren climbed out of the pool, grabbed a towel, and strode out of the room behind the guard.

His father wasn't the only one who was shaken. Just then, a vision popped into my mind of Tauren's dead body, floating face-down in this very pool.

fifteen

I knocked on Brecan's door to tell him I was back, and when he was satisfied with my whereabouts, rushed to my room. I'd tried to dry off while at the pool, but despite the towel wrapped around me, I was still dripping water all over the floors. A warm shower did nothing to ease the ache in my chest, or the unsettled feeling in my stomach.

Does the mystery witch know we were swimming? Is he watching us?

The boot prints in Tauren's room were large, too large for Mira's tiny feet and much larger than mine, which led me to believe they were made by a male witch. But it couldn't have been Brecan. He was sincere when he said he wasn't involved, and Fate confirmed it. Fate had never lied to me, and now I knew Brecan hadn't, either.

Showered and restless, I knew there was no way I could sleep. I dressed in a sleeping set of shorts and a camisole that Mira had laid out for me made of soft, black cotton, lined with matching lace. Exiting my room, I headed out to find solace in one of the gardens that dotted the perimeter of the palace. A guard nodded as I passed by and opened the door to one of the gardens.

I regretted stepping foot in it the moment I looked up. Tauren was on a balcony with his back to me, his arms wrapped around Leah, the exotic beauty from Sector Two. She pushed up onto the tips of her toes and placed a lingering kiss on his lips. Her slender fingers raked through his dark hair.

He returned the kiss with matching fervor, pulling her closer until not even a sliver of light could pass between them.

I swallowed the knot that formed in my throat. *What a stupid girl I am!* I was no better than the murdered witch I tried to warn away from Twelve. She was blind to what was right in front of her face, and I was the same.

I edged back to the door and opened it to head back inside, startling the guard positioned at it. "Miss Sable, is there anything I can do for you?" He waited patiently, brows raised.

"No. It… it's colder than I realized."

He averted his eyes and I walked back toward the staircase, rushing down the hallway and falling against my door when I closed it behind me, chastising myself for being such a fool. Somehow, I'd believed Tauren and I were fated, which wasn't even possible. We were from different worlds, different beliefs, upbringings, and values.

He must marry one of these women, I reminded myself. I silently thanked Tauren for the reminder of the purpose of this contest: the prize of a wife.

Two taps sounded on the door. "Sable?" Tauren suddenly said from behind my door where he stood in the hallway, as if conjured by my thoughts.

Tears pricked at my eyes. *Oh, Goddess, no.* He must have seen me in the garden. He probably thought I was spying on him, or worse. Perhaps he would ask for my discretion. Mortified didn't begin to describe how I felt.

He knocked again and I watched the brass door handle turn slowly to the right. I waved my hand and whispered a spell to seal it shut.

"I'm tired, Tauren. Could we speak tomorrow?" I asked softly.

I just couldn't face him. Not after he was with her.

I had no claim to him. Nor would I ever. It was a stark reminder that I needed to distance myself. Brecan was right. This was getting out of hand.

"Sure." he answered. Disappointment hung heavy in his tone, but I couldn't dwell on his feelings and ignore mine. Not tonight. "Goodnight, Sable."

Goodnight, Tauren.

I must have looked awful when I opened my door the following morning. Mira gasped and then turned me around and pushed me back inside. "You have time scheduled with Tauren today. We need to get rid of those dark circles. We have to detangle your hair!"

"My hair is fine," I grouched. "And *what* dark circ—" She shoved me into the bathroom where the mirror showed me what she meant. "Oh."

"What happened to you? Late night with the Prince?" she asked with one brow raised.

"No, I'm afraid he was busy with an invitee."

Her brows kissed. "But he came down just to swim with you."

"And promptly left, right after you and Brecan did."

She puffed her bottom lip out in a pout. "I'm sorry. Well, at least you get to spend time with him today." She blew out a tense breath. "What should you wear?"

I didn't want to see him today. At all. "What's scheduled?" I sighed.

Her eyes grew to the size of saucers. "You haven't read your schedule yet?"

I didn't even hear the paper slide under the door, and frankly, Mira should have expected it. It took her five solid minutes of knocking for me to stir, according to her.

"I have an idea!" she chirped, pulling out her eight-legged spinners. She gave them their knitting instructions, and then began tearing the tangles from my hair. "How do you feel about braids?"

"Does it matter?"

She rolled her eyes at me via the mirror. "I want you to feel comfortable. You'll need to keep your hair back for today's activity, though."

"What is it we're doing again?"

She smiled. "Archery."

"Archery? I've never used a bow in my life."

"Then I'm sure Tauren will be happy to instruct you, Sable."

That's what I was dreading.

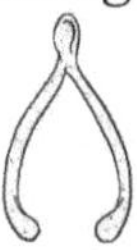

Skin-tight, black trousers hugged my lower half. My upper half was somewhat less binding. A loose white shirt hid beneath a close-fitting black leather vest with matching gauntlets. Mira had braided my hair and then wrapped and secured the long end into a bun at the nape of my neck.

"You look ready for war." She glowed with pride, once I pulled on a pair of boots she'd plucked for the occasion.

Good.

"The cameras will be on, and this will be telecast to the entire Kingdom. The witches, including the Circle, will see your every move. They'll cling to and analyze every word, so choose wisely, Sable," she warned. "You're in a strange mood today. I'd hate for you to…"

"Do or say something I shouldn't?"

"Bay is convinced you can show the Kingdom that witches shouldn't be feared."

I didn't look at her when I answered, "But they should." Instead, I stared in the mirror at the warrior Mira had conjured, hoping I had the strength of one.

She pursed her lips. "Are you alright?"

"I'm fine."

I could tell by her expression that she didn't believe me, but it didn't matter. My appointment with Tauren was just before lunch, which meant that I could check his meal before returning to my room.

I'd slept most of the morning away, and eleven A. M. – my scheduled time with Tauren –approached too quickly. When I emerged, Brecan was already waiting in the hall for me and escorted me down the steps. "You don't have to come. There will be cameras and crew scattered all over the place."

He grinned. "I don't want to miss out on the nonstop entertainment your nonexistent archery skills will provide."

Guards let us out the front doors and instructed us toward the archery range. It was on the southern grounds and apparently, we'd passed it in the carriage when we first arrived. I didn't recall it, so it was either unremarkable, or I was too busy looking at something else.

Brecan wore his dark suit. The wind stirred his fair hair. "What is it?" he asked, catching me looking.

"I'm just not used to seeing you in black."

"If you resurrect your House the way I believe you will, perhaps you'll allow me to wear it permanently."

I stopped abruptly, gasping. There was no way. "You would never leave the House of Air."

He raised a brow in response.

"You love your affinity," I argued.

"Would you bar me from practicing it?"

"Of course not, but –"

"Then it's settled. Here we are," he announced, waving toward a grassy area where two targets were being erected.

Tauren waited patiently, surrounded by guards and cameramen who were readying their equipment. My palms began to sweat at the thought of being telecast, especially to the Circle and to my peers.

"Calm down," Brecan whispered.

My heart thundered in response. I felt so out of sorts, almost like my body was screaming for me to run. Was it Fate or nerves? I couldn't tell.

I sucked in a shallow breath. Then another. "I can't do this."

"Just be you. It'll be fine."

He'd obviously forgotten about the small fact that everyone in my own sector hated me. There was no way that being myself would win the hearts of anyone in the Lowers. But I couldn't bear to be anyone else, or even attempt to pretend to be something I wasn't.

Then there was the fact that Tauren was obviously playing some silly, boyish game with me. He knew I was attracted to him and used that fact to his advantage, it seemed. He certainly had no problem kissing Leah last night.

I steeled my spine. "I can do this."

"That's the spirit," Brecan encouraged. "And if you legitimately can't do it, use magic."

"On telecast..." I deadpanned.

"Yes. I mean, don't use all your powers and soar the arrow all the way to the Thirteenth Sector, but you know... hit the target."

I could do that. It would take just a slight shift in trajectory.

Tauren's eyes darted between me and Brecan. A cameraman clipped a small black device to his lapel, handing Tauren a black, rectangular box. The cameraman strode to me, holding an identical device.

"What is that?" I asked as he got close.

"A microphone, Miss Sable. No one will be able to hear your words without it."

I was okay with that, to be honest. More than okay.

Tauren appeared behind the man, who still held the device as if he wasn't sure what to do with it. "May I have a moment with Miss Sable, John?"

"Of course," the cameraman answered. Tauren deftly took the microphone from John and walked with me a few paces away.

"Are you okay?" he asked. "You seem shaken."

"I'm nervous about being telecast."

He smiled warmly. "This is just you and me."

"And everyone else in the Kingdom..." I groaned.

He looked all around us. "No one else is here."

"*They* are." I motioned to the guards, the crew, and Brecan.

"Then we'll ask them to step back. They can film from a distance."

"That would be better," I said, relaxing a little. It would also likely be safer for them. I had no idea what I was doing, and wasn't likely to be an archery prodigy.

He raised the microphone. "Can I put this on you?"

I nodded, waiting for him to move.

"Before I do. Last night. Why didn't you open your door? I wanted to speak with you about something."

"I think it's best we don't," I said abruptly. "I have to leave here soon, Tauren. Your life with your future wife is about to begin, and I don't want to tarnish it in any way. What you do with the other invitees, of course, is your business."

His brows kissed. "What do you mean, 'what I do with the other invitees'?"

"Highness?" John called out. "We really need to hurry. The telecast will be live in two minutes."

Two minutes?

Tauren gently clipped the microphone to my vest and clicked a small button on the box. "Your mic is on," he warned. "Tuck this into a pocket, or clip it somewhere."

I nodded and clipped it to the waistband of my pants.

"Just shoot with me," he whispered. His soft, golden eyes wandered over my hair, my face, and traced the shape of my lips. Tauren had more magic in his person that I had learned in all my years. He was like an undine, luring me into troubled waters and coaxing me to take his hand, only to drag me into the depths, never aware that I was slowly drowning, never caring if I ever tasted the air I desperately needed again.

"I don't know how."

He pursed his lips. "Then let me show you." He held out his hand for me.

I took it for John and his crew, for the witches in Thirteen, and for Bay and Ethne who elected to give me the chance to come here. And… I took it for me.

John announced that we would go live in five, four, three… he mouthed the two and one.

Tauren's fingers closed around mine and he gently tugged me forward to a spot where a metal cylinder had been driven into the earth. It was filled with arrows, their multi-colored feathers fanning out from around the end of the shafts.

"So, you've never shot a bow and arrow?" Tauren asked conversationally, letting my hand go as we parted, each taking up a bow that had been laid on the ground for us.

"Never."

The bow was extraordinary. Almost as tall as I, it was carved from cherry wood and polished to a glistening shine. I could see every vein and striation in the glossy arc. The bow string was taut, but easy for me to pull back when I tested it.

"Looks easy, doesn't it?" he asked.

"I'm sure it's harder than it seems," I answered warily.

"Grab an arrow. Let's see how well you can shoot."

I wouldn't use magic just yet. I wanted to see how well I shot without it. I fumbled with the arrow and string, and again when I tried to hold it still while pulling the string back. The arrow swung to the side, so I had to start over. "There. Got it," I announced, when I finally held the arrow on the string and drew it back.

The target had a nautilus shell on it. No, not a shell… a map of the kingdom. I hoped he'd brought a spare for me. I found Thirteen. My eyes traced the spiral of the Kingdom to its heart, where the palace lay. "Strike true," Tauren encouraged.

I squinted, trying to align the tip with the tiny square palace on the map… and then I let go.

The arrow did not strike true. It soared wildly over the target and embedded into a nearby cedar. I straightened my back. "It appears I need some practice."

"The tree doesn't mind," he answered with a wink.

"Let's see how well *you* can shoot," I challenged.

"If you insist."

"I do."

His motions could only be described as effortlessly fluid. He took an arrow, nocked it on the string, and pulled back and fired, all in one movement. The arrow struck the map, clinging to his target. It didn't pierce the palace; it was embedded into the target in the exact spot where we stood.

I stared at him, mouth agape.

"I can show you how, if you'd like," he offered.

I could tell he wasn't boasting, and his demeanor was humble, not haughty. I wasn't sure if I should accept, but had to admit I wanted to learn. I wasn't sure I'd get another chance with a teacher as skilled as Tauren.

"That would be lovely. Thank you."

He searched the arrows for one he felt was suitable. I wasn't sure what the difference was or why it mattered. If you could fire one arrow, couldn't you fire any of them?

Sensing the question in my eyes, he offered, "This arrow's shaft is straight and its feathers are perfectly spaced, which means it's well balanced." He let the shaft balance on his finger, the tip and feathered end teetering for a moment before going still. "Take up your bow," he instructed.

He showed me how to nock the arrow. I repeated it clumsily a few times, but managed to copy his motions.

"When you aim..." he started, sliding up behind me. He positioned my arm and shoulder that held the string back. Then with his foot, he eased my legs farther apart. "Relax your muscles. You're too tense."

I smiled, biting back a smart remark.

He was so close his chest brushed my back, and if he thought I was tense before, I wondered if he could feel how rigid my body was as he leaned against me.

"Now," he said, putting his hand over mine on the bow, "you want to aim just below where you want the arrow to land." His stubble grazed my cheek and his scent surrounded me. Masculine. Clean. Completely, uniquely his. I swallowed thickly. "Because when you aimed the last time, you overshot."

"Won't I undershoot if I aim lower?"

He smiled. "Try it." As he stepped away, I missed the warmth his body provided.

I aimed just below the palace and let go of the string. The arrow wobbled through the air, embedding into the target stand's wooden leg.

"Better," Tauren said proudly.

"Your turn." I motioned to his target, wondering if his next shot would be better than the last.

He took up his bow, selected an arrow, and fired it… and the arrow landed on the map, striking the palace itself.

I laughed. "You can't do that again."

It was too perfect.

"What would you wager that I could?"

"What would a prince want from a witch?" I teased with a grin.

"A kiss," he answered confidently, as if he knew exactly what he wanted.

I studied his target. The shot was impossible. His arrow stood in the way of his goal. "You'd have to split your arrow."

"I've done it before."

"Under the constraint of time? We only have…" I looked to John, who mouthed the word thirty to me. "Thirty minutes left to spend together."

"We'll just have to see," he answered, determination glittering in his eyes.

He could probably do it. His princely self had probably taken lessons from the greatest archers in the Kingdom. He could probably hit the target blindfolded. But could he hit it if I interfered just a tad? He hadn't forbidden it…

"You have a deal," I answered.

A glance at Brecan revealed his displeasure, so I looked back to Tauren. "Good luck," I said sweetly, moving behind him to get a better view.

He gave me a small, somewhat wary smile, chose an arrow, and positioned himself in front of the target. He nocked the arrow and let it fly. I flipped my fingers to the right, manipulating the arrow's trajectory, then quickly tucked my hands behind my back. The arrow soared far right of the target.

His mouth gaped open, watching the shaft wobble from the tree trunk it had struck. He shook his head and glanced over his shoulder at me.

I smiled at Tauren's frustration, but he regrouped. "I'll choose a better arrow this time," he promised with a wink.

I nodded encouragingly, and as he searched for one, stifled a laugh.

Brecan smirked approvingly from afar. John lifted his fist to his mouth, covering his smile.

Tauren shot the second arrow. I waved my hand to the left, guiding the arrow into a bush. Tauren looked flustered, but was determined to try again. He flashed a determined smile at me. "This might take a while."

"You have twenty-six minutes," I teased, estimating the time left.

I sent his next two arrows into the ground, and the third into the cypress beside mine. "I don't understand," he said, grabbing two more arrows and testing their weights on his fingers.

He fired again. I nudged it just a bit. It hit the target, but didn't strike the map. "That's better," he said, breathing a little easier. A sheen of sweat glistened on his forehead. The pleasant, mild morning was becoming hotter as we moved toward midday.

Tauren fired again. This time, it struck the map, but in the area of the swimming pool. The next arrow, I directed to strike in the location I estimated Leah's room to be in.

After that, I sent arrow after arrow to different points on the map, but never allowed him the chance to strike his target again. The moments ticked by and Tauren quickly ran out of time. I couldn't let him win.

A kiss? A kiss might completely unravel me, and on live telecast, no less. Finally, he lowered his bow.

John gave us a two-minute warning.

Tauren stared at the map and shook his head. "I don't understand."

I stifled a grin. "What's the matter, Prince? You started out by hitting the very heart of Nautilus, and now you can't strike anywhere near it." I couldn't help but smile.

The tele-crew began to chuckle at the bewildered look on Tauren's face. He narrowed his eyes. "What?" he asked the group who'd gathered to watch.

I stifled a giggle.

"What is going on?" he asked again. Then he tilted his head and turned to me. "Oh, I see. You've been using a little magic to sway the odds, huh?"

My eyes widened as he crossed the space between us. He clutched my waist, his hands tightening when they found bare skin under the seams. "I think I won the battle."

"You didn't," I argued, breathless from the look of utter longing in his eyes. "You didn't split your arrow."

"Only because you kept me from it."

"If you were truly skilled –"

He put his finger over my lips and my throat dried up, along with whatever it was I was about to say.

"A kiss," he whispered, eyes glittering. "I think I deserve it after you made me the laughing stock of the Kingdom." He wasn't angry, but he wanted his payment.

"I'll repay you. I swear it," I told him, deftly spinning out of his grip. Those were the same words he'd spoken as he ran away from my House the night we met. I could see he remembered.

He grinned playfully. "I'll see that you do. With interest."

John yelled, "Cut!" and ran to Tauren to remove his microphone. As the three of us stood in a circle, a familiar sound cut through the commotion – the sound of an arrow's point and shaft splitting the air. I turned to see a sharp, deadly tip spiraling toward Tauren.

Shoving him out of the way, I stepped in front of the arrow and held a palm out, shouting a spell to stop it. The tip bit into my palm, then the arrow fell harmlessly to the grass at my feet. I clenched my hand into a ball, concealing the stinging wound left by the arrow's tip.

My heart pounded as I searched for the person who'd shot at the Prince.

"Sable!" he shouted, leaping to his feet. "You could've been killed."

I closed my eyes and listened. Footfalls. In the woods. "That way," I pointed. His guards were already running. They shifted to the direction I'd shouted in pursuit of the would-be murderer.

"I can find him," I said, closing my eyes and focusing on their every sound. All of a sudden, I was the forest. I felt him trample me. I heard his harsh breath and tasted his fear.

"NO!" Brecan screamed. "Sable, don't!"

Tauren's hand found mine. It was shaking. "Sable," he said quietly. "Please, don't. My men will find him." My eyes snapped open, only to be met with molten gold ones. The Prince was frightened. His hands shook as he clasped my upper arms. "You're okay," he said.

I wasn't sure if he was speaking to himself or to me. I was terrified. For a split-second, I'd worried I was too late to get him out of harm's way.

Tauren looked above us where dark, low-flying clouds raced across the sky, then he glanced back at me with bright eyes. I made the change. I'd called on a darker magic and he knew it.

"Your men won't find him," I rasped. "He's already gone."

I eased my hand out of Tauren's and ignored the frightened stares and worried whispers of the tele-crew.

I unclipped the box from my waistband and was searching for a way to turn the device off when it was torn away, the microphone's clip snapping from my vest.

Brecan took the device and threw it at John. "We should be going," he angrily announced. "The Prince is busy the rest of the day with *other* invitees."

Tauren shouted for us to wait, but Brecan whispered a spell and spirited us away. We reappeared in his room. "Dark magic? What if they caught it on telecast, Sable?" he shouted, raking his hands through his hair.

"They didn't. The cameras were off," I answered feebly.

"What about the telecast itself?" he demanded. "The Circle saw you promise him a kiss."

Clothes were strewn about his room like he'd created a twister and thrown them into the core of it. "No," I argued. "They saw me win a bet using a small amount of magic, thereby *evading* a kiss. You were the one who suggested I use magic in the first place."

"To give yourself an advantage, not to flirt with him! Have you lost your mind? How do you think Ela and Wayra will respond to this? They'll call for you to come home." He threw his hands in the air before continuing, "Maybe that's for the best. You're obviously getting too close to him."

I'm not nearly close enough! I wanted to shout. "I'm not arguing with you about this right now. I was just having fun, Brecan."

"It was reckless! Your silly crush almost got you killed. Someone shot an arrow at your heads." Brecan grabbed my arm, his fingers leaving indentions in my skin.

"Take your hand off me *now*," I warned, the taste of smoke filling my lungs.

"Or what?"

"Or I will send you back to The Gallows."

"You can't send me away."

My eyes glittered. "I can. And I can bind you from returning."

A fire blazed in his eyes, and for a moment, I wondered if he'd developed a new affinity. A knock at the door interrupted us. "Come in!" I yelled, wrenching my arm away from Brecan.

"Oh…my…goddess!" Mira squealed. "That was amazing, Sable. Bay is pleased."

So, no one back home saw the assassination attempt, or the dark magic I almost conjured. I leveled Brecan with an I-told-you-so glare, which he answered with a snarl.

"How do you know how Bay felt about it?" Brecan snapped.

Her smile fell away. "Because I communicate with him. Through water. Don't you talk to Wayra through the wind?" I could almost see her hair blowing in her own personal breeze as Brecan dutifully reported to her that I'd called on a darker source. Interestingly, Brecan didn't answer Mira.

The fact they communicated through their affinities was news to me. If they were reporting back, what else had they said? And who else overheard their conversations about me and my time here? If Mira called on Bay, could any other Water witch listen in?

I walked out the door. "Where are you going?" Mira called after me as I strode down the hallway.

"To check Tauren's food."

And to get away from them for a while. Especially Brecan. He had no right to spirit me away. I wasn't a child and he wasn't my keeper. Or my hand-fasted. He was supposed to be my friend, but apparently couldn't accept that I had no feelings for him. He was obviously unable to control his own feelings.

I wondered if I could either, as I fought back tears of frustration and humiliation.

And now I would have to face Tauren again. I would have to spell a room to make sure his lunch wasn't tainted.

I waited outside the dining room between two hulking guards. They were stationed at every door, shadowing Tauren's every move now, thank goodness. Inside, a girl from Five with colorful swatches in her hair and wearing a bright pink dress waited for Tauren. He walked in using another door and kissed her hand as he seated himself next to her. He'd changed into a smart, sapphire suit and pressed white shirt. His hair was still damp from his archery exertions in the burning hot sun, as well as from the fright he had.

When the staff brought their plates, I spelled the room, checked for traces of poison, and walked out of it, removing the charm and making sure he saw me slip out the door. That was code for 'your food is fine.'

He apparently didn't want to accept a simple explanation this afternoon. Moments after I left the room, the door swung open behind me. "Sable?" he said tentatively.

I turned to face him.

"Are you okay?" he asked.

"Yes, are you?"

He affirmed that he was, and I could see he was no longer shaken. "Brecan was furious," he noted.

"I used magic on the telecast. He was worried I'd upset the Circle."

He nodded once, like he didn't entirely believe me. "And did you?"

"I upset two members, but the other two weren't concerned." This experience might at least convince them they needed a fifth, to settle disputes among them and to avoid such divisive stand-offs in the future.

"My men didn't find the culprit."

I told him they wouldn't. The witch had fled, then disappeared altogether.

He hooked his thumb over his shoulder. "I have to get back to lunch."

"I know."

"Can I see you tonight?" he whispered. "Please?"

I swallowed, then nodded my assent.

"Thank you, Sable, for everything."

sixteen

I avoided Brecan the remainder of the day, though he checked periodically to be certain I was in my room. Mira came by to chat, but I wasn't in the mood. Thankfully, she left me alone with my thoughts.

I was sure the person who'd shot at Tauren was a male witch. Fate confirmed with a warm feeling in the pit of my stomach, but it wasn't a pleasant or reassuring feeling. It was a warning.

The witch was dangerous. But something darker, more ominous settled into my bones. My fingers and lips began to chill. My teeth chattered uncontrollably.

If I hadn't sensed the arrow, Tauren would be dead.

That was far too close. I had to find the witch, and soon. Before he struck again.

There was one way to ensure that if the witch managed to slip past me and succeeded in harming the Prince, Tauren wouldn't die.

It would require a dangerous spell, one I was happy to work if left no other choice. And unfortunately, my choices were being whittled away by the moment. This way, I might be able to find the witch if he returned to the palace to make another attempt.

I rummaged through my trunk and pulled out my pendulum, cursing for not having a map of this place. Then I remembered the map of the Kingdom on the targets.

Outside, the sky was gray and solemn. The first sprinkles of a rainstorm splattered the land. Droplets fell onto my arms and splashed the crown of my head as I hurried through the manicured yard.

"Please be there," I whispered under my breath.

Thankfully, no one had taken the targets down. Tauren's map was pierced in several places, but mine was pristine, thanks to my non-existent archery skills, as Brecan referred to them. I plucked the map from the bale of hay and quickly folded it to keep it dry.

Before I reached the palace again, the sky began to weep.

The door I'd exited from was locked. I ran to another to find it locked, too. No one was posted at it. I decided to run for the front door. I wound through garden paths and rushed down the sidewalk. When I turned the curve, I ran into someone, both of us falling backward from the impact. I landed hard on my hip.

Rain saturated the young man's dark hair, and when he looked up at me, I gasped. It was Tauren's brother. I hadn't seen him since the Equinox.

"You must be Sable," he said with an easy smile, chuckling as he winced, clutching his knee. "Tauren's told me all about you."

I doubted that, but still. "What did he say?" I asked, standing and offering him a hand.

"That you were the most beautiful thing he'd ever seen in his life. I thought he was being dramatic, but I see that if anything, he understated your beauty."

Tauren's brother flashed a confident, roguish smile and clasped my hand. "Why are you outside in the rain?" he asked, water sluicing off his face in rivulets.

"I could ask you the same thing," I challenged.

He gave a lop-sided grin. "I was headed out to meet someone, but the weather… it's getting rather nasty. I doubt they would have ventured outside. I think I'll head back in."

The two of us jogged to the front of the palace, up the stairs, and to the enormous doors. They were unlocked, thankfully. Two servants scurried away to fetch towels as we stood awkwardly, dripping puddles on the pristine foyer tiles.

"My name is Knox. I'm sure Tauren's told you all about me as well," he hinted. I wasn't sure what to say back, but didn't have to worry long. Knox enjoyed dominating the conversation. "My brother is stuck with one of the women he's not fond of at all. He'll be sour after this hour is over."

"Why does he bother?" I blurted.

Knox's brows furrowed. "What do you mean?"

"I mean, at some point, he'll have to cull the invitees. Why bother spending time with the women he doesn't really like?"

Knox smiled. "Strictly for the viewing public's entertainment. Every sector cheers to see their invitee. Plus, they like to see him with each woman. They place bets on who he ends up with, who he sends back to their sector… they pretty much bet on everything, actually."

When the servants returned with fluffy, warm towels, I wrapped mine around me and thanked them, apologizing for the mess I'd made. Knox thanked them as well, then waltzed into the palace like he owned the place. I suppose in a way he did.

Where has he been during the first two days of filming? I wondered.

As I approached my room, I saw Mira pacing outside, biting her thumbnail while Brecan pounded on the door of my room. "What are you doing?"

Brecan snapped his head toward me and blew out a tense breath. He was upset. His pale hair blew in a breeze that I couldn't feel or see affecting anything else. I thought Wayra was the only one who had that ability, but maybe I'd just never seen Brecan this upset.

"Thank the goddess," he breathed, the wind quieting instantly.

"What's the matter?" I asked.

Mira rushed to me. She looked immaculate in a sharp, black suit with a nude camisole peeking out from under the jacket. Her hair was arrow straight, the blue-gray tones shimmering in the hallway light. "We thought something had happened to you! You didn't tell us you were going out." Her eyes darted over me appraisingly. "You look like a drowned rat."

"Thank you, Mira," I teased.

"You have less than an hour before tonight's festivities begin."

"What festivities?" I asked, trying to suppress the shivers running over my body.

The palace had cool air pumped in somehow, but that wasn't why I was cold. Fate's warning was getting stronger. Did the would-be killer plan to strike again so soon? Tonight? Fate was quiet. He neither confirmed nor denied. Perhaps the plan hadn't been decided upon yet.

Mira snapped her fingers in front of my face. "Dinner and then the play. Did you hear anything I said?"

I raised my brows. "Play?"

"Yes, play," she chastised. "Haven't you looked at your schedule?"

"I went to archery..." I hedged, but even then I hadn't looked beyond the afternoon, and evening was closing in.

Mira stuck her hand in my vest pocket and plucked out my room key. "Let's get you dry and dressed," she said kindly but impatiently. "The rain storm should ease shortly and be gone by dinner. Hopefully the seating dries before the play starts."

Brecan brooded, keeping his arms crossed and leaning against the wall outside my room. His eyes looked dark purple instead of the calming lavender to which I was accustomed. "Come get me when she's ready," he said to Mira, even though I was right there.

Mira closed the door behind us. "Don't pay any attention to his moodiness," she said softly.

"What did I do this time?"

"I think you scared him, or..."

"Or what?"

She winced. "He thought you were with Tauren. He thinks Tauren is toying with you to see how far he can push your boundaries."

"Why would he think that?"

She shrugged.

"Do you agree with him?"

She shook her head. "I don't. Tauren looks at you like... Well, I shouldn't say anything else."

"How does he look at me, Mira?"

"Like you're the one thing he wants and can't have," she finished. She guided me to the bathroom. "You could take a warm shower if you do it very quickly. I'll get your things ready. It's a formal event. Would you like to wear the gown we made for you the other day?" Her eyes glittered with anticipation.

"Would it be appropriate?"

"Indeed it would. And I promise that if you wear that gown tonight, you'll see what I and everyone else does when Tauren looks at you, Sable."

I'd seen it, or thought I had. Then again, he must see something in Leah. He may have wagered with me for a kiss, but he actually gave her one. How many of the other invitees had he kissed? Or gone even further with?

I scrubbed myself in the scalding water, leaving the safety and security of the shower before my shivers eased. Mira dried my hair and asked whether I wanted to straighten or curl it. I felt sharp, like the edge of a knife. "Make it straight."

"We'll match," she chirped, her eyes twinkling excitedly. She ran to her bag on my bed and pulled out her straightener. Slowly, she ironed each piece until it was arrow straight and shone like dark silk, and every trace of the slight natural wave disappeared.

My hair was longer than I realized.

Mira seemed lost in thought as she worked a few drops of coconut oil into the strands to make it glisten before applying my makeup. I didn't enjoy wearing it, but had to admit that when she was finished, I looked fierce. With dramatically dark eyes, pale, glistening lips, and contoured cheekbones, I could wear her creation with pride. If Bay wanted me to represent our sector, this dress was the perfect accessory.

Tauren asked to see me tonight, and I knew he meant privately. Which meant late, because this dinner and play were going to take forever.

I pushed the thought away as I slipped into the gown, the nude-colored silk slip softly whispering over my skin. Would Tauren truly look at me tonight the way Mira said he did? I would be lying if I said I didn't want him to. Even though it could lead nowhere, if he truly had feelings for me, this dress would draw them to the surface. Then again, the other girls would be dressed in fine gowns, too; though I doubted any would be as intricate and personal as this one.

I didn't know how Mira's helpers managed to spin the black overlay so perfectly, with symbols of our heritage and those uniquely Fate's scattered throughout. Wishbones lined the modest V-neck. There was a crystal ball, tea cups, lit candles, a human palm, the Lovers card, various bones, gemstones, herbs and flowers, and around my waist coiled an embroidered rope.

Mira, who'd stepped out of the washroom to give me privacy to change, gasped when she came back in. "It's perfect."

Her eyes became glassy as she took in her creation. I spun in a slow circle so she could see all of it. The back was gathered at the small of my back and spilled to the floor in a short train.

Her eyes caught on my feet. "I'll get your shoes."

"Do you have any that match with daggers in the heel?" I asked as she hurried away.

She glanced at me over her shoulder. "Of course I do."

She returned with nude-colored heels that shone like glass, placing them on the floor in front of me.

They were like the black ones I'd worn here, with a small, silver dagger built into the heel. I slid one out, the metal raking against its sheath. "Perfect."

She worried her hands as I pulled on each shoe, casting wary eyes around the room.

"What's the matter, Mira?"

"What exactly are you conjuring?" she asked, pushing her blue-gray hair out of her eyelashes. "I noticed your things are set up in the corner."

"Nothing. I was just searching for something in my trunk," I lied.

The crease between her brows didn't fade.

"The necklace… the black necklace Tauren gave me. Would it look good with this gown?" I asked, attempting to change the subject.

She smiled. "It would! I'll get it," she whispered and ran to the bed, sliding her hand beneath the mattress where I'd hidden the box to prevent anyone from stealing it.

"How's Brecan? Has he calmed down?" I asked as she clasped the heavy necklace around my throat.

"As much as he's going to," Mira said, a hint of warning in her voice. "He loves you, you know."

"He thinks he does, but what does he know about love? Sneaking off behind the House of Air with any willing witch doesn't make him an expert on the subject."

"Nor does isolating oneself from peers..." she added gently.

"I didn't isolate myself. I was told not to go near you. Any of you." She opened her mouth as if to argue, but I cut her off. "I wasn't even welcomed into the House of Fire to pay my last respects to Harmony."

Just thinking about it made me furious. How dare the Priestesses and Priest pretend that I'd *chosen* not to be part of my own people? *They* were the ones who placed me in the woods, in a cabin, as a young girl. A child. They'd forbidden me from joining the others, from even speaking to other witches. Some defied them when they wanted their fate read, but many more were too afraid to step foot anywhere near me. They came to fear me.

Over time, I became like the House of Fate... something to hide from and peek at from a distance. To run from, squealing and shivering from adrenaline and fright. I became a thing, not a person, and certainly not a peer. While they honed their affinities, cheered on by those in their House, I had no one but Fate on which to rely.

Fate – who had begun to writhe in my stomach.

I clasped a hand over my middle. "What's the matter?" Mira asked, her eyes flicking from my hand to my face.

"Something is stirring, and I don't know what." I did know that it was bigger than anything I'd felt from Fate before. This wasn't some small nudge or even a warning. This was something darker. More urgent.

"Sable," Mira gasped. "Your fingertips."

I expected them to be blue from cold, for my lips to match them. But the tips of my fingers weren't frosted. They were black. As if I'd dipped each into an ink pot and let the ichor dry on my skin.

My eyes met Mira's frightened ones. "What does that mean?"

A shiver ran up my spine. "I'm not sure."

I stared at my skin, watching the inky stain spread ever-so-slowly.

Two quick knocks at the door announced Brecan's arrival. "I need gloves," I whispered to Mira.

She nodded and pulled her glass spiders out, shoving the washroom door closed and sealing us in. The spiders knit black silky gloves over my hands, spinning them to my elbows. When they were finished, she whispered them to sleep again and tucked them away. "There," she said, making sure they were situated correctly.

Fate's voice filled my mind. *From death, springs life.*

My heart thundered as I pulled the washroom door open and ran across the room. Brecan caught me. "What is it?"

"I don't know, but I want to check on him. Now."

He flung the door open and took hold of my hand. "We go together," he asserted.

I whispered a spell that spirited us to him in seconds, and Tauren was surprised to see us on the other side of his bedroom door. We'd arrived just as he opened it. I was just glad to see him alive. I pushed past him and checked every square inch of his room.

"What's wrong?" Tauren asked.

Brecan told him to give me a minute.

I didn't smell poison. No one lurked in the shadows. There were no weapons. No threat. "Where on earth are your guards?" I asked.

"They're just outside..."

"No, Tauren. They aren't."

He was surprised to find his door unguarded. His muscles rippled beneath his starched, black jacket. The collar of his white shirt was a stark contrast to his dark hair. Pieces of it hung over his forehead. "I didn't give them an order to leave."

"Someone spelled them," Brecan said, crouching down outside his door. "Black salt." Particles of it clung to the pad of his finger. Traces littered the carpet.

Someone had used the dark crystals to form a barrier at the door. The guards wouldn't have been able to cross it. Mentally, the spell and salt would've made them feel wrong for stepping across the salt line. And after a few moments, it would have repelled them altogether, which explained why the guards were nowhere to be found. They'd made their way as far from the salt crystals as possible. We might find them in another Sector if the witch who spelled them is strong enough.

Brecan's pale hair hung over his jacket. He stood and brushed it off his shoulders, staring at me with a look I couldn't decipher.

"This is getting dangerous," he finally said. "I am afraid for you, Sable."

"Me? I'm not the one being targeted."

He pinched his lips together. "Are you sure of that?"

"What do you mean?" Tauren interjected.

"What better way to turn the Kingdom against Thirteen than to accuse a witch of murdering the Prince?"

My stomach turned at the thought, and then Fate confirmed Brecan's suspicion.

"Even if that's true, what else can I do? Fate wants me here. He wants me to protect Tauren."

"*Protect* him? He usually sends you to redirect people or take their lives, not to *save* them," Brecan argued. "Are you sure this isn't what *you* want?"

"Why can't it be both?" Tauren asked, glancing toward me.

Brecan growled. "This is becoming too dangerous for her," he told Tauren. "Can't you see that?"

Tauren threw up his hands. "What can I do?"

"Send her home."

Fate sent fire up my throat. As I opened my mouth to argue, plumes of smoke erupted. "I can't go," I said around the ashy taste.

Brecan's eyes widened in shock. "I'm so sorry. Sable, I'm sorry. I understand now that it's Fate urging you to stay." Brecan's hand found my upper arm. "It's okay. Calm down."

Tauren took a deep breath. "Fate did this?"

I nodded, still unable to speak.

"He gives you wounds that aren't real, but are. He singes you from the inside out... What else does he do?"

"Worse," Brecan answered snappishly. His lavender eyes drilled into mine. "Much worse."

Brecan had seen what Fate was capable of, but he still didn't understand. No one did but me. Fate never did anything to hurt me; he did it to direct me. If he wanted something done, it was my duty as his daughter to do as he said. I knew there were reasons for everything he asked of me. Some of it was for my benefit, some for his.

Fate eased his grip on me and the fire in my belly was extinguished. I could breathe again, even as the acrid scent of smoke lingered in the air and in my nostrils.

Tauren nodded his head. "I'm narrowing my choice tonight. Five women will remain. I'll have to ask you to be one of them, if you're still agreeable, but I'll hurry this process along. It's the least I can do."

Tauren's golden eyes met mine, a torrent of emotion swirling through them. I wondered if mine roiled to match. Because as much as I appreciated the gesture, it meant my time with him would be cut short.

"Thank you," Brecan answered. I couldn't bring myself to say the words.

"Would the two of you like to go ahead to the dining room?" Tauren offered.

"We should stay together," I croaked. "You're unguarded."

He pursed his lips. He wasn't sure he was truly unsafe in his home, I could tell, but he'd been shot at on these grounds today and his guards had disappeared. The danger was clear and present. It couldn't be ignored or balked at anymore.

As we exited his room, Tauren locked his door as Brecan started down the hall. Tauren slid his key into my hand. The golden metal gleamed against the black silk of my glove. I was about to ask why he'd done it when he leaned in. "You promised to meet me later, after all this. Return it then."

The metal warmed in the palm of my hand. He closed my gloved hand around the key and I tucked it into the small, right-side pocket Mira had sewn into the gown. In the left-side pocket was a thinly folded map and my pendulum. If the murderer struck again, I would go to him. I would find him and make him pay. The embroidered noose tightened around my stomach, comforting instead of painful.

When Brecan turned the corner ahead of us, Tauren grabbed my hand and pulled me to a stop. "Thank you for once again coming to help me."

"It's what I agreed to," I replied.

"It's more than that to me."

I nodded once. "You're welcome."

His eyes raked over me. "My God, you're stunning."

There it was. The look Mira described. Part pain. Part longing. Part lust.

My skin heated under his gaze.

"You're wearing the necklace."

The fingers of my free hand drifted to the facets of the largest center stone.

I slipped my fingers out of his. "Let's catch back up with Brecan."

He opened his mouth as if he wanted to say something, but I jogged ahead. Brecan waited impatiently at the bottom of the stairs.

The worst part was seeing Brecan wear the same look that Tauren had given me as he watched me descend the staircase with our prince.

Mira eased out from behind Brecan, her hair slick and shiny, grazing her shoulder. She wore a simple, but elegant black dress. As I passed, she bent her mouth to my ear. "My spiders are uneasy. Please be careful tonight."

In that moment, a vision overtook me. I grabbed Mira's arm to steady myself as I entered the mind of someone else. It was Rose, the redhead from Sector One. She stood in front of a mirror, applying more lipstick, pursing her lips again and again to even out the pigment. Then she turned her attention to her hair, even though there wasn't a strand of it out of place.

She was talking with someone. In the mirror, I could see the girl from Sector Five with colorfully streaked hair. Her cuticles had been scrubbed, but vibrant splashes of paint still clung to them, refusing to budge because the hues were part of her. She was a painter, and a brilliant one at that. Rose suspected it was why she'd been invited.

"How was your lunch with the Prince?" Rose asked. Her eyes cut sharply to the girl. I didn't know her name, but Rose looked at her as if she were nothing more than a sheep being cornered by Rose, a wolf.

"It was nice."

Rose gave the girl a pout. "Oh, that's too bad," she said pitifully.

The girl's brows kissed. "What do you mean?"

"At this point, the date must be stellar. I bet you'll be sent home soon."

"Mind your own business and I'll mind mine." The girl made a crude gesture toward Rose and stormed out the door. The girl was certainly no sheep. She had teeth, too. I decided I liked her.

"Sable," Tauren said. When I blinked again, I was back at the bottom of the steps.

"What?"

"Thank goodness," he breathed.

Brecan snorted. "I told you she was fine. It may happen periodically, so you should get used to it. Just make sure you stay with her if it happens when we aren't here."

"What did you just experience? What was that?" the Prince asked.

"It was nothing."

He shook his head. "That wasn't nothing."

"It's the residue. That's all."

"Residue?"

"That's why she usually wears gloves in crowds," Brecan explained. "When she reads people through touch, sometimes the effect lingers for Sable."

"Until the residue wears off," I added quietly.

"Which will be when?"

"I'm never sure," I answered.

He paled. "I've asked you to read so many."

"It's nothing," I brushed it off.

"I've asked too much of you," Tauren realized, concern creasing his forehead.

A servant rushed down the hall. "Prince Tauren, your parents are waiting for you." The man waved the Prince forward, and we followed him down the hall and into a dining room I'd never seen. The walls were silver, trimmed in white, and each shimmered beneath the chandeliers that were positioned in a spiral that expanded across the ceiling.

A cluster of round tables was arranged around the space in a curling pattern. The royal family would sit at the center table, where the Kingdom's palace was located. From there, each girl and her escorts were positioned at the table representing the location of her sector. We made our way to the farthest table, representing Sector Thirteen.

Brecan pulled my chair out and then Mira's. She sat to my left and he sat to my right. "Why such large tables?" he grumped.

Mira evaluated each girl's gown, hairstyle, and accessories, as if each one was my competition. Each wore a different color, some still clinging to the pastels they'd been wearing, while some donned bolder hues. She ultimately dismissed each one as inferior, and when she'd finished her perusal, gave me a satisfied smirk.

The room went quiet as the royal family was announced.

Tauren entered the room behind his father and mother, Knox walking a step behind him. Tauren's eyes found mine, holding them for a beat too long before looking around at the swirl of tables and the women they held.

My cheeks stung as if reality had backhanded me. He was the Prince and I was a witch from The Gallows. Not even Fate could change that.

The women would be culled, just as I suggested, but now I hated myself for doing so because it brought him closer to choosing one of them; one step closer to marriage and binding himself to one of these women until death parted them.

Like his father, he would love the one he married. He would give her his heart, his life, and his energy. I didn't know who she would be, but couldn't help but hate her for it. Tauren had claimed to be jealous, but he hadn't seen the bold shade of green my envy bore.

The royals encircled their table. Everyone in the room stood as they took their seats and sat again once the King gave a nod. Tauren didn't touch the drinks poured for him, but when his meal was brought out, his eyes found mine. Brecan's hand found my arm and I spelled the room, slipping away from his touch and moving toward the Prince.

Bitterness filled my mouth and cascaded down into the pit of my stomach, which began to spasm. *Poison,* Fate whispered.

A cold sweat pebbled across my skin, along with a blanket of goosebumps.

I sniffed his plate. It was untainted, but his wine was not. Someone had slipped nightshade into it. The sickening flavor was almost able to hide within the woodsy aroma.

I took his wine glass and glanced around, catching movement in my periphery. A girl with sandy hair pushed out the door. I removed the pendulum from my pocket, along with the map, and ran after her down hallways, through doors, until I spilled into one of the gardens where nightshade grew.

She'd disappeared.

There was no way she had worn the boots that left the prints in the Prince's bedroom.

She was petite like Mira, but she was lithe and fast.

I let the pendulum swing over the map, the wind rattling the paper. It turned circle after circle, searching for her as I commanded, but never found her. If she wasn't in the Kingdom, where was she? The Wilds?

Or did she perform a blocking spell to conceal her whereabouts, so I couldn't drag her and her little friend back by their throats?

seventeen

These witches were powerful. No one had ever evaded me before, not for this long. And certainly not two of them. Fate rumbled inside me, making his aggravation about the matter clear. But if he couldn't use me to catch them, what would happen? Would Tauren suffer the consequences?

My stomach dropped.

The witches were somehow immune to my spell, and I'd left him frozen. Unguarded.

I whispered an incantation and spirited to him.

He was fine. I blew out a pent-up breath and scanned the room. Brecan and Mira were still in the same positions. Everyone else was, too. Nothing was out of place.

Though I only smelled the bitter poison in Tauren's glass, I refused to take the chance that the witch might have poisoned an entire bottle.

I took all the wine glasses away. Someone would notice, but I couldn't risk anyone drinking from them. Nightshade would kill anyone who consumed it. The poison was potent, and whomever drank it would wish themselves dead long before they actually died. It would tear through even the largest man's system and leave nothing untouched. Every organ would suffer before it finished the person off. I knew, because I'd used it before. I'd watched someone die from it because Fate commanded it.

I removed glass after glass from the room, carrying them to the kitchen just down the hall. I emptied the glasses into the sink, leaving them for someone to wash. When no wine bottles or glasses remained, I reentered the room and made my way around the frozen party, taking my seat once again.

I took a steadying breath before un-spelling it.

Brecan's hand fell through the air where my arm had been. Confusion marred his face for a moment. "You could warn me before you— what's wrong?"

I locked eyes with Tauren. He took one look at me and stood up. I spelled the room again. How was I going to admit to him that I'd once again let the witch who wanted him dead get away? His parents were right. I couldn't protect him.

Un-spelling only him, I stood as he approached, his mouth gaping as he took everyone and everything in. "This is..."

"Time is stopped. When I ask it to begin again, no one will feel the loss of the moments I've stolen."

His mouth parted slightly as he surveyed the room. Then he focused back on me. "What happened?"

"A witch. She poisoned the wine with nightshade – which I learned you grow in abundance in your gardens, just outside."

"She got away?"

I nodded, again berating myself for not being fast enough.

"Thank goodness you weren't hurt."

I wasn't physically hurt, but my pride stung badly. It made my alternate plan more crucial to execute, though I'd have to be careful. A spell that powerful required a heavy concentration of magic. I'd worked them before, but not with so much at stake. It had to be performed perfectly, and it had to be done quickly.

Tonight.

After dinner and the play, I would meet him privately and work it.

"I removed the wine and glasses. People will notice."

"How long until time resumes?" he asked.

"Until I command it to."

"Would you help me? We could open new bottles and pour new glasses. Then no one would be the wiser."

I nodded. "Of course I'll help." I'd been too upset to consider pouring new glasses for everyone.

He wanted to split up, but I refused to leave his side. "The witches who are behind this, and there are two – a male and female – have somehow warded themselves against my spell. It's how I found the girl. If she'd kept still, I wouldn't have known she was there at all."

"What was she wearing?"

"White servant attire."

We retrieved several bottles of wine from a nearby storage room and then fetched fresh glasses for everyone. Tauren was quiet as we placed them and began to pour, a pensive look on his face.

When he was finished, he turned to me. "Thank you again. You saved my life."

"I did no such thing," I scoffed, shaking my head. "I almost got you killed. I should never have left you alone and unguarded. I should've woken Brecan and Mira. I'm messing this up. I thought it would be easy to find the person who wanted you dead when I left The Gallows, but I also expected the person who wanted you dead to be human, not a witch. And certainly not *two* of them."

I paced the floor as I ranted, tears pricking at my eyes. Fate intervened, a feeling of cool serenity flooding over me. I took a deep breath and apologized again.

"Sable, no one else could have detected the poison. You saved me. You've saved me in more ways than one. I'm just not sure how to repay you for your services this time."

"This isn't about my services. I don't want payment, Tauren. I want to make you safe. I want to make the witches behind this pay for what they've tried to do to you."

He approached slowly and reached out, as if asking permission to take my hand. I slid mine into his waiting one. "You're trembling."

More than my hands were trembling. I was quivering from head to toe.

He pulled me to him and held me against his body, wrapping me in his arms, infusing me with his warmth, steadiness, and strength.

"We can't –"

"Shhh." Tauren's eyes searched mine. The corner of his lip curled upward. "I believe you owe me a kiss." I was about to protest, but then the tip of his nose brushed my cheek and his lips raked across mine, completely undoing me. I pushed forward, pressing my lips to his, a shuddering breath escaping as I pulled away.

I kissed him.

I kissed Tauren.

The trembling born of fear transformed into shivers of need, and his chest swelled against mine as he fought to regain his composure. I was glad I wasn't the only one affected. This… whatever this was, it was as glorious as it was dangerous – for both of us.

He held me for a long moment and finally relaxed his hold on me. The room's cool air rushed around me, chilling what he'd made warm. Then I remembered where we were and what had transpired, and the weight of the world returned all too suddenly. Tauren walked me to my chair and held it out for me, pushing it in as I sat down. He silently walked to his own and took his seat. We both looked around to make sure everything looked right. As far as I remembered, it did. When he nodded, I un-spelled the room.

Brecan's eyes raced over to me. "Something happened."

"I'll tell you later," I said, a warning lacing my tone.

Mira straightened in her seat, then nodded to the Prince. From his seat, Tauren stood and held his wine glass up. The room went quiet.

"Ladies, again, I'd like to thank you for traveling to the palace." Rose beamed at him, playing with her hair. She didn't catch his eye, though. "I know it's customary that the first pick come much later, after every lady has been here a while and has spent ample time with me, but it seems very clear to me after the past few days that there are only a few with whom I feel I would be compatible, and who I feel would perform the duties as Queen in a way befitting the title."

Murmurs rumbled through the room, but Tauren continued his speech. "Tonight, I will narrow the choice to five so that I can focus on the women I've felt a spark with, and see which of those sparks might produce a flame." His eyes locked on mine for a beat. My face heated and I looked away, noticing Brecan stiffen beside me.

"After tonight, only five ladies will be invited to remain at the palace. I appreciate each and every one of you taking time out of your lives and spending it with me. That being said, if you find a raspberry on your dessert plate, you are welcome to stay. I'd like to get to know you better in the coming days."

Mira grabbed my hand. "You are *so* getting a raspberry."

I rolled my eyes and bent to whisper in her ear. "You know I'm staying. He already said he needed me here."

Her gray eyes met mine and she gave my hand a squeeze through the glove. "You can't believe it's the only reason, Sable."

It was.

It had to be.

I stared at my fingers and pictured the stain that lurked beneath the silken gloves, feeling pinpricks of pain from the contact with her. Mira sucked in a breath. "Did I make it worse?"

"I don't know."

"Did I hurt you?"

I shook my head. "It tingles."

"What does?" Brecan asked. He looked to my fisted hands. "You're defying Fate, Sable?" His voice was loud enough to draw attention from the group from Twelve.

I swatted him. "Shut. Up. I'm not defying him. I'll explain later."

His eyes narrowed on my lips, but I stared him down. They weren't blue. I wasn't sure what this was, but it was no punishment from Fate.

Dinner was served. My stomach still roiled over the details of the evening. What if the witch had poisoned the whole bottle, and someone else drank from the bitter wine? What if they blamed illness or death on me, or on Brecan and Mira?

"Are you well?" Brecan asked. "You're suddenly pale."

"I'm always pale."

"Paler than usual, then," he corrected with a smirk that didn't meet his pale purple eyes. The girl from Eight caught his eye, blushing and looking away when Brecan didn't avert his.

I stifled a laugh. "You're popular with the invitees, I see."

"Unfortunately," he replied, straightening his back and toying with his silverware.

The conversations from the surrounding tables were about the girls' chances of receiving a raspberry. I wondered who came up with the idea to use such a tart fruit to indicate who was staying, and a dessert devoid of it for those who would spend tomorrow morning packing their things and leaving the palace behind them.

The girl from Twelve was literally in tears. She trembled, unable to control her nerves. Her eyes caught mine and she scowled before turning to her escorts for comfort.

I couldn't help but wonder what was so bad about her life in Twelve that she would have this sort of reaction about returning to it. Tauren saw that she was in distress. And while I could tell he felt empathy for her, he was right not to have chosen her. If this miniscule amount of pressure was more than she could handle, she would never handle the decisions that being a Queen required.

Steaming plates of food were unveiled in front of us. The three of us checked our plates by inhaling the aromas lifting off them. Mira clutched my forearm, staring into the steam. "What is it?"

She shook her head. "A message. I need a clearer picture. Excuse me," she stood, the backs of her knees scooting her chair out. Mira hurried from the room, returning with a troubled and grim expression – one I'd never seen on her normally cheerful face.

"What's the matter?" I asked.

Mira looked from Brecan, who was leaning forward to listen to what she said, to me. "Priestess Ela is dying."

My brows furrowed, and a tumult of emotions washed over me. The woman's unabashed hatred of me, the way she opposed my trip here, and how she'd aged so much in hours the day of the Equinox all flooded my mind.

"How is that possible?" Brecan softly whispered. "I mean, I know what Wayra said, about her power waning when yours came to its fullness, but why would it kill her?"

"It isn't killing her. It's just her time. How long has she held time's hands? Witches aren't immortal," I replied.

"I know that, but Ela – she seemed youthful until…"

Mira and I answered at the same time, "The Equinox." The Equinox, a moment no one who witnessed would ever forget. *And my birthday…*

"Who will be Elevated to Priestess?" he asked Mira.

She shrugged, her sleek hair sliding toward her pointed chin. "The House will nominate witches for the position, and the Goddess will reveal her choice to the Circle."

"How?" I asked.

She blew out a tense breath. "I'm not sure how it all works."

"Sable," Brecan said tentatively, "do you want to see her before she passes?"

I swallowed, twisting my napkin into a tight coil. "She wouldn't allow it."

"She may be too weak to prevent it," he mused.

What would happen to the House of Earth in the meantime? Would they place her in the hallway and usher the witches from the other Houses through before she was buried in the soil she loved, or were the rites of Priestesses altogether different?

My plate was removed before I could savor and chew even one bite of the decadent pasta. The tension in the room thickened as dishes were cleared and the dessert plates were carted into the room.

While everyone watched the cart roll toward the royal table, I spelled the room and checked all the plates just in case the witch attempted to poison him or anyone else again. She would suspect I would check, but would she think I assumed the danger had passed? I couldn't take the chance.

Staring at Tauren, I realized how tense he was. His back was a rigid line. His lips were pressed tightly together, and I'd frozen him while tugging on his collar. The room was cold, but nervousness raised a person's body temperature a few degrees.

I wanted to touch him, to take my silk-covered finger and trail it down the back of his hand, just to offer a small measure of comfort, but I couldn't do that to him. With things on the brink of a drastic change in Thirteen, I had to stop this – whatever it was – and focus on finding the witches behind this and getting back to my House. This might be my chance to claim a position on the Circle.

It might be my only chance for years to come. Bay, Ethne, and Wayra were all relatively young. Ela was the eldest, the shrewdest, and some would argue the wisest among them. While she was staunch in her views, they had preserved our way of life amidst an ever-changing Kingdom. No one could fault her for that.

I made my way back to my seat and listened to squeals of delight from Rose and Leah, a girl from Five named Estelle, one from Six named Tessa, and finally… a server placed a raspberry punctuated plate in front of me. I smiled and pretended to be as surprised and overwhelmed as the other ladies, but tried to remain graceful. Surrounding each of us were ladies who didn't make the cut, and their emotions ranged from disappointment to heartbreak to devastation. The girl from Twelve sobbed openly beside us.

Surely there was a kinder way to have done this, cameras and telecast be damned.

Tauren glanced around at each of the invitees and gave them a nod, pursing his lips. Did he also disagree with the way this was handled, or had he chosen the method himself?

"You haven't eaten a bite," Brecan noticed beside me.

"I'm not the slightest bit hungry."

He glanced around the room. "This is cruel."

"Very."

Hand-fasting, to the Kingdom, was an archaic and strange custom. But it was kind. A witch asked another if they would be loyal to them for a year. If they agreed, they were fasted. If not, there was no ill will. Other than the two involved, it was rare that anyone even knew one had approached the other, though sometimes it was obvious.

"They think witches are vile creatures," he snorted. "But have they even thought of how this makes those involved feel, or does it matter to them at all, as long as telecast ratings stay high?"

Even Mira was uncomfortable, and none of the three of us lifted a spoon to eat the confections before us.

I needed a minute.

"I have to use the restroom. Will the two of you watch Tauren while I'm gone?"

Brecan stood when I did. "I can go alone."

He eased my chair out, ignoring me, and placed his hand on the small of my back as I walked around the table.

I could feel Tauren's eyes on me as I left the dining room in search of the washroom. I didn't have two minutes of peace before the door opened and Rose sashayed in. Did she enjoy spending time in these rooms? She'd blathered cruel words to one of the other girls through the guise of applying makeup.

My plan was to ignore her entirely. I knew she wanted to rile me in an attempt to prove that witches were easily provoked, and that one seated on the throne of Nautilus would be dangerous to all its citizens.

The only problem was her scent.

She plucked a small vial from her purse and dabbed a clear liquid onto her throat and at each pulse point on the inside of her wrists.

"The only way you can attract Tauren is with a love potion?" I snapped.

"Please," she said, rolling her eyes and tucking the vial away. "Everyone knows you've bewitched him. I'm just evening the playing field."

"Where'd you get it?"

"Tauren wasn't the only one to travel into Thirteen on the Equinox."

My ribcage tightened.

"That's right. I saw what you did. I know what you are. And I am absolutely positive you've used magic to lure the Prince into your tidy little web. Well, I'm going to free him," Rose exclaimed, a victorious glint in her eyes.

"I haven't used magic on Tauren."

She quirked an eyebrow, tousling the red waves in her hair and pursing her lips, watching her reflection closely. "Then I guess the crown will be mine after all."

I stared straight ahead, gripping the edge of the stone countertop, all the while telling myself not to hex her.

"I know you can't marry him," she said, her tone darkening. "So why are you here?"

When I refused to speak, she narrowed her eyes. "Your custom is to hand-fast. You're not even allowed to marry, especially to a non-witch."

"Maybe I'm breaking with custom."

"Maybe… but then again, maybe not. I bet the producers would be interested in that little tidbit."

I finally smiled, reveling in the sight of her confidence seeping out of her like a sponge wrung until no water could even drip from it. "If you say one word about me to the producers, or to anyone else, I'll know…and I will make sure you never in your lifetime utter another."

"You can't do that."

I grinned. "Then go ahead and try it."

She walked out the door, her heels clicking hurriedly along the polished tile.

eighteen

I sealed the door, unable to take another second of Rose or anyone else's presence at that point. For years, the only company I had was Brecan when he could steal away, the occasional witch who sought a reading of their fate, usually around Elevation time, and the occasional squirrel who liked to chomp on the wood of my cabin. I realized I'd come to appreciate the calm solitude of a lonely existence.

Tugging the gloves off, I looked at my necrotic fingertips. I was pleased to see the ichor hadn't spread, and stretching them out didn't hurt. They didn't ache. My lips weren't frozen. Whatever the warning was, I wasn't sure what it meant.

Someone knocked. *That's probably Brecan…* I tugged the gloves back on, but couldn't bring myself to whisper the spell to unseal the door.

"Sable?" Tauren's voice penetrated the air.

I unsealed the door. "It's unlocked."

He inspected the knob on the inside of the door when he stepped inside. "There are no locks on the powder rooms, as there is more than one facility."

"I can stop time, Tauren. Sealing a door – locks or none – is child's play."

"Right," he said with a cough.

"I'm sorry. I'm just having a…" I didn't know what type of moment I was having. There were no words to describe my roiling emotions.

"Do you want to leave?" he asked sincerely.

"My grandmother is dying."

His brows kissed in concern. "How do you know?"

"Mira can communicate with those in Thirteen." I didn't tell him how or divulge anything further, but I could see the question painted across his face.

"Go to her," he quietly urged, crossing the room and taking hold of my elbows. I couldn't look at him. When I tried to pull away, his grip tightened. "Sable, if you need to leave, I understand."

"No you don't. My grandmother hated me."

"That's not possible."

He finally let me go when I took a step back. "She hated me. She told me once that it was *I* who killed my mother; that Fate turned on her because he chose me instead. And now that I am of age and my power has matured, hers has faded, along with her life."

Fate rumbled in my bones. An unhappy, roiling displeasure sank in deeper than ever before, but I begged him to calm down and just leave me be for a little while.

"Did she hate your mother?" Tauren finally asked, his golden eyes swirling with concern and what I hoped wasn't pity.

"She did."

I glanced at the door. Someone would walk into this powder room eventually, and I was sure it would cause quite a scandal for the Prince to be found inside with a witch.

"It doesn't matter," I told him woodenly.

"It upsets you, so of course it matters."

I nodded toward the door. "You should go before someone sees you with me."

"They'll be seeing the two of us together much more often now, Sable," he warned.

"Not in powder rooms."

"I don't care what any of them think," he swore.

I could tell he believed the words he spewed, but he didn't understand their importance. "What about your father and mother? What about the citizens? *They* will care, Tauren." I didn't give him a chance to argue further, walking quickly to the door.

He didn't follow, standing rooted in the same place. "There's more. You aren't telling me everything."

I glanced at him over my shoulder. *No, I'm not. But you'll find out soon enough.* On the tip of my tongue sat the truth about Rose and the sweetly magical scent she was using against him, but maybe her using the potion was for the best. One of the girls had to ensnare him. Rose was one of the four left that Tauren wanted, and I hadn't smelled the love potion until tonight. He must have seen something in her before now.

"Can I still meet you tonight?" he asked, standing up straighter as if his body was a shield for his heart.

It would be best to tell him no, to deny the Prince his request, but everything inside me screamed yes. I needed to work the spell, which was the only way I could absolutely ensure his protection. So that was the answer I whispered before leaving him in the powder room and returning to my seat.

The dessert plates had thankfully been cleared by the time I returned. Brecan's countenance had darkened. "Both you and our fair prince have been absent for a long while."

"I couldn't breathe," I told him. He studied my face. Surely, he could see that my lip gloss wasn't messy, that every strand of my hair was in place, that my face wasn't flushed from passion.

Brecan looked away. Mira nudged me softly with her elbow. "The play will take place outside. There's a small amphitheater to the north."

"What sort of play is it?"

"A tragedy," she said wistfully.

At one time, I had wondered why anyone romanticized such terrible circumstances as love, loss, and death... Then I saw the play that evening, and all the pieces slid into place.

Outside, the air was humid, thanks to the earlier rain storm. Mira remarked on each woman's hair, noting how those who'd curled theirs were wishing they hadn't. The curls hung heavier and lower, eventually falling away altogether

The amphitheater was small, but large enough for our party. Four wide rows had been hewn into the bedrock in front of a smoothly polished, matching stage. A plush, teal curtain had been hung across the stage to hide the actors and scenery lurking behind. Golden columns streaked up either side of the curtain rod, slowly being consumed by creeping ivy from the ground up.

I could imagine being here in early summer with fireflies lighting the paths down into the hewn earth, cricket song on the gentle breeze, the sky streaked with gold to match the gilded columns.

"This is amazing," Mira remarked, awestruck by the beauty of such a simple place. "We need one of these in Thirteen."

I nodded emphatically. "Completely agree."

"It could be done. The House of Earth could make one."

I smiled, hoping one day this small dream might come true.

The sky faded to a dark sapphire and diamond stars began to show themselves, the largest boldly sparkling overhead. Seating wasn't assigned in this place, but we took up a corner of the last row. Tauren sat in the center middle of the bottom row with his parents and brother. He stood and turned to the left and right, peering out over the crowd. When his eyes hooked on Rose, he waved for her to come forward and sit next to him.

My fingernail tips bit into my palm.

Mira made a choked sound. "I thought he was looking for you."

"He can't."

"Why?" she asked, mouth still agape.

"Because I can't marry him, and he has to choose a wife – soon."

Brecan nodded. "Glad the two of you finally came to your senses before things went too far. Assuming they didn't."

I felt like clawing him. "They did not."

"Good," he said, extending his long legs and leaning back on his palms.

Sometimes, I loved Brecan's friendship. Sometimes, I didn't. This was one of the latter times.

"She's wearing a love potion," I whispered.

Mira slapped my arm. "I knew it!"

I shushed her when the people in front of us turned around to gawk.

"I knew it was something," she said quieter.

Brecan sat forward, elbows on his knees. "Where'd she get it?"

"She says she was at the Equinox and bought it in Thirteen."

"Maybe it'll help Tauren make up his mind." It was the cruelest thing Brecan had ever said to me. Not the words he uttered, but the fact he said them at all, knowing how I felt.

Mira leaned closer. "What if she's bad for him? Bad for the Kingdom, I mean."

"Right," he said sarcastically. "Then shame on him for allowing this disgusting pageant in the first place."

I couldn't say I disagreed with his logic, but I understood all too well about being bound by customs in which you didn't want to partake. I agreed to handfast when I stepped back inside my sector, knowing full well there wasn't a single witch to whom I wanted to bind myself.

A gentleman stepped onto the stage and the murmuring of our small crowd ceased. He teased us with the story they were about to unveil; a tale of love which caused strife, and strife which caused death, and death which caused woe.

The actors were skilled. They projected their voices and emotion into the night, and the enraptured crowd soaked up every syllable, every feeling. The story was of a girl, a pauper, who wanted nothing more than to be loved. She met a prince who gave her his heart, but his parents wouldn't allow them to wed. They wed in secret, bribing a priest to join them despite his parents' wishes, but the priest had already been bribed by the King and Queen to poison the girl. He disposed of her in a lake, and two days later, the grief-stricken Prince waded into the dark water, never to be seen again.

A shiver scuttled up my spine when Tauren turned to look at me over his shoulder.

Rose followed his gaze to me. One side of her upper lip rose in disgust, but hatred was what shone so brightly in her pretty blue eyes. Realizing her hold on him was failing, she reapplied the love potion, and with it, regained the Prince's attention. I hoped she'd bought gallons of it. She would need every ounce.

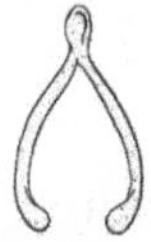

Knox sat on the other side of Rose. Rose's escorts had squeezed into the second row, sitting directly behind her.

What was strange was that Rose was literally sandwiched between two Nautilus brothers, yet only one of them paid her attention. The love potion should draw any male to her, but Knox... Knox seemed immune. Brecan had been watching, too.

"An Elevated witch made that potion," he surmised.

I nodded in agreement. "But whom?"

He shrugged. "A few had tables set up along the periphery that evening, if she's being honest about purchasing it then."

Most of the witches in The Gallows who bothered to sell potions during our celebrations charged a mint for them. They were easy to make. Even the least gifted among us could make a basic love potion, and those attracted anyone within a fifty-foot radius. The whole party should be fawning over her; the women telling her how pretty she was and how they wished they could be her, and the men falling over one another to do favors for her. But this potion was specifically concocted for Tauren alone, and a spell *that* concentrated reeked of an Elevated witch.

Once the play concluded, the King and Queen stood, escorted by several guards as they took the rough steps to the soil above us. The Queen's eyes darted to mine as she passed our row, holding them until she stepped above us. The last of her residue evaporated, but I felt the warning she'd meant to transfer. She wanted me to hurry up. She wanted me to leave her son alone...and then leave the palace.

How did the Queen of Nautilus know how the residue worked? Did my mother teach her?

Knox jogged up the steps next, then came Tauren and Rose. Her arm twisted around his like a vine. She held her shoulders back and her head high, Rose posing like the queen she wanted so desperately to one day be.

Once the royal guards surrounded their charges, we were free to leave. Sector by sector, people filed out of the amphitheater. We were the last to leave. The players busied themselves behind and on stage, disassembling the scenery and taking down the curtain. They loaded everything into hand carts and rushed away, leaving the stage barren.

For a moment, I saw the stage in a different light. Cracks running through the smooth surface, filled with weeds and crushed bits of leaves. Creeping vines covering half of it, threatening to swallow it whole. The place was forgotten.

Fate was upset. He squeezed my middle until I stood from the discomfort. "We should get back," I said to cover up why I'd risen so abruptly.

Brecan's eyes glowed brightly in the moonlight, like amethyst. Mira yawned and stretched her arms out wide. "I'm tired."

"Did you stay up late last night?" I asked as we ascended onto the soil.

"I had to make a few things for you," she replied.

"Hopefully, this will all be over with soon and you'll be able to rest, Mira. I appreciate all you've done to help me."

She inclined her head. "Don't apologize. It's been the best experience of my life."

As we walked to our rooms, the cries of those who weren't invited to remain spilled into the hallways and down the staircase. Mira unlocked her door and said goodnight. Brecan waited in the hall until I'd unlocked mine. He lingered, twisting his key in his hand. "What is it?"

"If you need anything, if Fate tells you Tauren needs you, I want you to wake me."

I opened my mouth to agree, but he strode across the hall and put a finger to my lips.

"I know you don't want to hear this, but I need to say it. So, please, allow me to get this off my chest." He closed his eyes and then opened them again. "I know you have feelings for Tauren. I recognize it, because I feel the same for you. And I know that you're trying your best to keep him safe, but I want to keep *you* safe. If something happened to you –" His voice shattered.

I clasped his hand for a moment, squeezing it. "I'll wake you," I rasped.

He pursed his lips, then asked, "Swear it?"

"I swear. If there is danger, I'll come to you."

He nodded, satisfied with the vow I'd made. I felt like a cockroach, scuttling away from the light that was the truth, terrified to be caught even for a second in the open honesty of a lie. The moment he went into his room, I planned to change and sneak out to see if Tauren remembered that he'd asked to see me, or if Rose's potion was still affecting him.

I hoped it wasn't affecting him too much.

Brecan tipped his chin toward my room. "Good night, Sable."

"Good night."

I slipped inside and locked the door behind me, taking a deep breath. The shoes were the first things I shed. I liked them. They were beautiful. They were also hard to walk in on grass, and my ankles throbbed.

Instead of skinny jeans and the ridiculous numbered t-shirt, I gently pulled my gown over my head and laid it at the bottom of the bed, then fished one of my dresses out of my trunk. The familiar, worn velvet settled over me like a comfortable blanket. I unclasped the necklace Tauren had given me and laid it next to the gown. My stomach growled. No wonder. I hadn't eaten a bite since midday.

Leaving my gloves on, I slipped out my door and quickly locked it, heading downstairs. My footsteps didn't make a sound on the cold, marble floors. Guards stood at each door leading to and from the palace, but their numbers had increased since dinner. Had Tauren told his father about the attempted poisoning?

Tauren wasn't waiting in any of the gardens I could find. Rose's potion must have done the trick.

I pushed through the kitchen's heavy swinging steel doors and almost ran into Knox again. He laughed, holding up two glasses and a bottle of Champagne. "We have to stop meeting like this, Sable."

I stared at the twin glasses. *Did Tauren send his brother to retrieve them for him and Rose?*

"He's not with her," Knox supplied, reading my thoughts. "He's in his room, but will be down soon."

"I wasn't looking for him."

"Liar," he whispered, a knowing smirk on his lips. A long, silent moment stretched between us. Knox bent forward, whispering, "For the record, I'm all for shaking things up in the Kingdom."

"What's that supposed to mean?"

"A witch and a prince? What an interesting match."

Didn't he tell Knox that I couldn't marry him?

"You seem upset," he mused, watching me carefully. His eyes were sharp, like his mother's.

"I'm starving."

He gave me a look like he didn't believe me, but then used the Champagne bottle to point toward the back of the room. "The refrigerators are right there. Help yourself."

"Thank you."

He nodded once, gave me another quizzical look, and then bid me goodnight, pushing his way through the door.

On the center of one of the cutting board counters was a basket of fruit. I found a napkin and filled it with a bunch of grapes and a green apple, then left the kitchen to return to my room. I met Tauren in the hallway.

"How did you know where to find me?" I asked.

"I bumped into Knox."

He stood in front of me, close enough that I could smell his cologne. Something spicy and rich. He didn't smell like Champagne or rose hips, thank the goddess. Tauren studied my dress. "You look beautiful, Sable."

"There's nothing beautiful about this old rag."

"You wore it the night of the Equinox, didn't you?"

I nodded. That night would be permanently etched into his memory, and no matter what I did from this point forward, I would always be the Daughter of Fate to him, the girl who hung a criminal in front of a crowd of his people. The girl who told him he was going to die.

I might as well have been wearing my noose as a belt.

Silently, he brushed my gloved hand. "Too much residue?" he asked.

"Yes." I nearly choked on the lie, but allowing him to see my necrotic fingers was not something I was willing to do. Not until I knew why Fate had altered them.

"Will you come outside with me?"

"Of course."

He led me to a garden I hadn't seen before, one that was partially enclosed with glass. Pale white moonflowers bloomed all around us, their musky fragrance perfuming the air. There was a small pond with a fountain in the center, its surface covered with pink waterlilies that craned their delicate necks toward the moon. "This is the Night Garden," he told me once we were inside.

A simple, wooden plank swing hung in the corner. Tauren gave an encouraging nod. "You can swing if you'd like."

I made my way to the swing and unwrapped the food I'd smuggled away. "Are you hungry?"

"No, thank you."

I plucked a grape from the stem and popped it into my mouth.

"How are you?" I asked him.

Stress lines creased his forehead. He relaxed his expression, but answered honestly. "I feel horrible for sending so many home, but it had to be done. I hated hearing how upset some of them were, and I don't understand why I couldn't have just told them individually. Some were humiliated. Their family and friends were no doubt watching, hoping they would receive a raspberry. The producers insisted it was tradition, but it didn't sit right with me. And I didn't want to upset my father by asking him to change it. He has much on his mind."

"I think some traditions should be broken."

His eyes searched mine. "What do you think of the four who remain?"

Should I tell him Rose was manipulating him, or keep quiet? The sound of laughter – male and female – slid into the garden seconds before Knox and Leah popped through the door. He was still carrying the glasses and Champagne, and her arm was wrapped around his as if she'd gotten quite comfortable with Tauren's younger brother.

Noticing us, she quickly recoiled her arm and stood up straight.

"Relax, Leah," Knox said. "Tauren knows."

My brows rose. *Was it* Knox *who was kissing Leah like she was the air in his lungs the night I saw the shadow I thought was Tauren in her room?*

"It's why he extended your visit. Relax," Knox soothed. His eyes slid from his brother to me. "It seems a little crowded in here. What do you say we find another garden to haunt, Leah?"

"That would be best," she agreed, tugging him back out of the garden.

I breathed a sigh of relief. "How long have they been…?"

"Since the second night she was here. Knox is typically very casual with women, but he seems to really like Leah. I think the feeling is mutual, too."

"It must have been uncomfortable having to pretend-date her on telecast, then." I'd eaten half my grapes.

"You have no idea. I mean, she's nice enough, but I knew she and Knox were getting serious fast."

"What about the others?" I led, giving him a sideways glance. "Which one do you like the most?"

He hesitated. "You want to know who I want to marry?"

"I'm a citizen of this Kingdom. As such, I'm as curious as any about who my queen might be." *Please don't let it be Rose.* I didn't know much about Estelle or Tessa, as they were quieter and kept to themselves, but I would blindly choose either of them before knowingly wishing for the she-devil.

"Tessa is nice. She's a sculptor, like my mother was, so my mother loves her."

I nodded. "It's good that they get along."

"Estelle is a painter, and she's incredibly talented."

"What do you like about her? What attracts you to her? The skill of painting is admirable, but what draws you to Tessa or Estelle?"

He ignored the question. "Then there's Rose."

My heart skipped a beat.

"I'm confused about her. One minute, I feel like maybe she could be the one I choose. The next, I'm not sure why I even thought it."

I made the mistake of smiling.

"What?"

"Nothing. I was just thinking about how confusing feelings can be," I lied. Love potions could have that effect on their targets.

Tauren nodded toward the green apple I'd taken. "It's a Sugarvein. Very sweet. You'll love it."

I took a bite and it was delicious. Like an explosion of sugar on my tongue, yet with a hint of tartness to counter the flavor. The Prince laughed as I greedily took another bite.

"Why didn't you eat dinner, or dessert?"

"How do you know I didn't?"

He studied me for a long moment. "Because I watched you."

"Why?"

"I can't seem to stop, Sable."

I swallowed thickly as he approached. I let the napkin fall from my hands, gripping the coarse strands of rope on either side of the swing.

He stepped around me and gave me a push, swinging me toward the pond, then stepped away, toward a sliding door that had been left open. I stopped myself and twisted the swing to look at him.

"I'm afraid," I croaked.

"Of me?"

I shook my head. "*For* you."

"Has Fate sent a message to you again?"

"Nothing specific, but there's this unsettled, almost writhing feeling within me, and I don't know what to make of it. I've never felt anything like this before. It's not pleasant."

He walked over to me as the swing's ropes untwisted. He took my hand and waited while I stood. The flecks in his golden irises flickered in the moonlight. I brushed a dark strand of hair out of his eye.

"Today was busy. The coming week will be worse. I'll get to spend time with you, but it'll be while cameras are watching," he said softly.

"You mean, while the Kingdom watches."

Tauren nodded. "Sable, I need to propose to someone soon –"

I knew what he was going to tell me, but didn't want to hear it. Not here. Not now.

I tugged my gloves off. Tauren's eyes widened at the sight of my fingertips. "What is this?" He touched them, and a rush of warmth spread through my veins. I expected him to recoil, to curl his upper lip and back away. But I needed to touch him to perform this spell, and Fate's answering warmth urged me to do it quickly. A violent magic churned in my bones. Fate was not only going to bless the spell, he would solidify it until it was unbreakable.

"I owe you a kiss," I said, watching as his pupils dilated.

"Yes, I believe you do."

"With interest."

He smiled. "With interest."

"Would you like to claim it now?"

Tauren didn't hesitate. He brought his lips so close they brushed mine. "I've never wanted anything so desperately."

Neither have I.

I took his hands in mine and held tight, then pushed my lips to his. I expected a tentative, exploratory kiss. What I received was an explosion of passion, want, and need.

One of Tauren's hands found the small of my back and brought me forward until the front of me was plastered to the front of him. He threaded the other into my hair. The kiss was magnetic. He moved his lips over mine, waiting until I parted them. To complete a soul-binding spell was dangerous for both of us, but the witches were becoming bolder. They wanted Tauren dead, and if something happened that made it so I couldn't be with him when they came…

And Fate... Fate was on my side.

I pushed the negative, invasive thoughts away and focused on the spell, letting it wrap around us while I enjoyed Tauren's lips, the feel of his muscles flexing against me, and the silkiness of his hair. And then, when I could sense with every cell in my body that the magic was ready for the final ingredient, I leaned back and bit my lip until it stung, the coppery tang of blood seeping into my mouth. Then, while he was still dazed, I captured his bottom lip between my teeth and nipped. Tauren's eyes popped open. Our blood mixed and the magic shimmered gold around us, the color of his eyes but brighter, too bright to look at for very long.

He withdrew, putting several feet between us, running his thumb over his injured lip. But the spell had been cast. He was protected now. "What was that?"

Just then, the door burst open and Brecan ran to me, nearly knocking Tauren over. "What did you do?" He wrapped his hands around my upper arms and shook, hard. "Do you have any idea how dangerous that was?"

"How did you know?" I asked, my eyes open in shock.

He didn't have the opportunity to answer, because Tauren grabbed the back of Brecan's shirt, hauled him backward, and punched him, the blow rendering him unconscious. It seemed to happen in slow motion. Brecan's lavender eyes rolled back in his head as he fell slowly to the ground, as heavily as a tree would tip in the forest. His pale hair splayed around him in the rich, dark soil. For a moment, all I could do was cover my wide-open mouth. Then, I realized what happened. Tauren knocked Brecan out.

"Why did you hit him?" I growled, falling to my knees, unsure what to do next.

"You're actually defending him? He put his hands on you, Sable. A man should never put his hands on a woman – not like that."

He was right. Brecan crossed a line. But I knew my friend was also right to worry about the spell.

"What was he talking about? What did you do, Sable?"

Unable to meet Tauren's eyes, I tried to downplay my actions. "It wasn't dangerous. I just bound our souls."

"Bound our souls?" he breathed. "What does that mean, exactly?"

Tears pricked my eyes. "I can't let you die. Not when I have the means to prevent it. And I'm afraid I'm not strong enough to stop them. I had to do something," I tried to explain, my rambling emotions getting the better of me.

"How does the spell prevent it?" Tauren swiped his thumb over his bottom lip again. The blood had stopped pooling, but if he didn't leave it alone, it would start bleeding again.

Brecan groaned from his place on the ground, blinking his eyes a few times.

"How does the spell prevent my death?" Tauren demanded.

Brecan answered him, clutching what would be a very sore cheek. "If someone gravely injures you, Sable will forfeit her life for yours."

Tauren's mouth gaped open. I'd never seen the sea, never seen a ship when the wind left its sails, but I imagined it would look much the same way Tauren did. "Sable, no. Undo it."

There was so much fear, so much desperation in the plea.

I couldn't bring myself to answer him, so Brecan did it for me. "She can't. Soul binding cannot be undone."

Tauren shook his head. "Why would you do something so foolish?"

"Foolish? You are the crown Prince of Nautilus! *You* are the next King. *That* is your fate. And besides that, my actions weren't chivalrous. Any citizen would do the same if they could. They would protect you, Tauren."

"Just a common citizen doing her duty, huh?" he spat.

"Tauren, I can't be with –"

He stormed away before I could finish my sentence. Brecan jumped to his feet, cutting me with his stare. "Why on earth would you do that? Bind yourself to him? He's not one of us. Someone will likely always want him dead, Sable, which means you've forfeited your life. When he wears the crown, there will be no shortage of people who want to take it. It's the fate of all kingdoms, of all Monarchs, to be replaced. There will always be strife and upheaval somewhere."

"Don't talk to me about fate, Brecan," I seethed. "Nautilus has been ruled by the same family for thousands of years."

"Apparently, someone thinks it's been far too long," he growled, stiffly standing to face me.

A frigid wind whistled through the garden and the night-blooming flowers began to sag. "What was that?" he asked.

I swallowed. "I think we both know what's happening."

He closed his eyes tightly, pinching the bridge of his nose. "Ela. She's weakening."

She was the Priestess and protector of the Earth, its source of power and energy while she lived. Now, that source was evaporating quicker than a drop of water in a desert. I wondered if the soil would turn to sand once she faded away. Would the Circle be able to appoint a new priestess before the earth itself died?

Brecan left me in the garden without another word. I still wasn't sure how he knew I'd bound my soul to Tauren's, but asking him now would just cause another eruption of anger, and I didn't want to endure more.

I sat on the swing, rocking back and forth, watching the flowers as their leaves and stems slowly withered.

nineteen

Many hours later, as the sun began to creep over the horizon, Brecan returned, sporting dark circles and a bruised cheek that no doubt matched his injured pride. A muscle flickered in his jaw. "Mira is worried sick. She needs to get you ready for the day."

I wasn't ready to face the day, or to return to my room.

"Ready for what?" There was no way Tauren wanted to see me.

"You're traveling to Sector Three, to a children's medical ward."

Witches rarely fell ill. Until their time on earth drew to an end, they barely even aged. But I'd never considered the people in the Lowers. I'd never given any thought to children falling ill or dying.

Silently, I stood, watching the garden for any other signs that Ela was gone. The leaves drooped on their stems, the edges curling slightly in on themselves, but they hadn't fallen. "Is every garden like this?" I rasped.

Brecan nodded. "The trees and grass, too. Most are saying it's just an early fall, but you know who they'll look to once everything dies."

"*If* it does. A new Priestess can replenish the earth and stop the death spreading across it."

Brecan didn't respond, he just waited as I walked toward him, and then he did what he came to do. He escorted me to my room and lurked in the hallway while Mira flitted around me like a crazed moth.

Finally she went still, her lips pinched tightly together. She stuck her dainty, ebony finger in my face and squinted at me. "You… you *love* him," she whispered accusingly. "You can pretend not to, but now I *know* the truth."

"I barely know him."

"You bound your soul to his, Sable. Even the best of friends would never do that."

She was right. I wasn't sure how it happened, or how he slipped so easily through the walls I'd erected around my heart, but I loved Tauren. Did it happen the moment he stumbled up to my table, or even before that, when I thought he might have been the boy I was meant to hang? Or did it blossom when I received his invitation, or the subsequent profession that he was sincere about his reason for sending it? All I knew was that something in him was mine, and something in me belonged to him. I couldn't let anyone snuff that out. That was all I could think of. All that mattered.

I showered quickly, the steam clouding the mirror. Mira was frozen, staring into it when I stepped out, wrapping myself in a towel. "What do you see?"

Her braided hair trembled. "Sable?"

"Yes?" I replied, grabbing a towel and wrapping it around my body.

"We are being recalled to The Gallows. The Circle demands that we return immediately."

Fate roared in response. My skin turned molten and flushed bright red. My hair grew several inches at once. I expected ashy scales to erupt on my flesh and for fire to pour out of my mouth and nose.

Mira moved away, putting her hands out in defense. "I'm sorry."

"I wouldn't hurt you. This is Fate," I gritted. "I can't leave."

She gulped. "Brecan!"

The door to my room burst open and Brecan ran into the washroom. He looked from Mira to me and sucked in a deep breath. "It's getting worse."

The dark stain had spread from my fingers, up my arms, and over to my collarbone. Inching up from my toes, it had spread to mid-thigh.

And I was hot. So hot.

"Stop hurting her!" Brecan shouted.

Mira started chattering about the message she received and what she'd seen from me afterward.

He cursed. "Mira, tell them that Sable is unable to leave. Fate forbids it. She cannot physically leave the Prince."

Fate began to ease his grip on me.

But Brecan wasn't finished. "And tell them that I refuse to leave Sable. You should go back so you don't get in trouble."

"I'm not leaving," she said, balling her fists. A handle blew off the sink's faucet and sprayed water across the room, catching us all off guard. Mira regained her composure and quickly raised her hand, using her affinity to stop the fountain, promising to repair the handle.

She stood up straight and spoke into the still-steamy mirror. "Fate won't allow Sable to leave the Prince at this time, and Brecan and I wish to stay with her."

Suddenly, a blurry image emerged on the steam-coated surface. "Bay?"

He tilted his head. "Can you see me, Sable?"

"Yes."

"You truly *can't* leave?"

"*I* can't."

Mira chimed in, "Fate was furious when I gave her your message."

Bay looked at me with concern in his dark blue eyes. "Were you injured?"

"No, but if I attempted to leave Tauren, I would be."

He took in a deep breath. His wavy gray hair undulated like surface water. His dark blue eyes speared mine. "We need you here, but it's too dangerous to bring the Prince to Thirteen now."

"Why do you need me?" I asked, ticking my head back in surprise. "Why is it dangerous for him to enter our sector?"

"Has Mira told you that Ela is dying?"

"Yes."

He seemed to be choosing his words carefully. "Sable, if Ela dies, Cyril – your mother – will wake."

"What?" I could feel my brows touch.

"If Ela dies, Cyril will wake," he said again, sterner and louder than before. I'd heard his words, but didn't understand what he was saying.

"My mother is dead."

He shook his head. "No one could kill her. Not even the four of us together. So, we did the only thing we could."

"What did you do?" I whispered.

"Ela bound her in the soil."

My throat constricted. I could almost feel particles of dirt inside my nostrils. Caked in my throat. The taste of a grave in my mouth.

They buried her alive. She'd been under the earth for seventeen years.

I wrapped my arms around my ribs, unable to breathe. No wonder they were frightened. If someone buried me and held me in the soil for even a moment, I'd claw my way out and make them pay for every suffocating, agonizing second.

Bay was still talking, but the cool air from my room was thinning the steam. Bay began to fade. "Brecan, turn the hot water on again," Mira instructed, closing the washroom door and stuffing a towel into the space at the bottom of the door. We waited as the steam built and for Bay's face to grow bolder again.

The first words he spoke were, "Sable, you need to be on constant guard."

"Why? She is no longer Fate's chosen. Why are you frightened?" I asked.

Bay shook his head. "Even without Fate, she's one of the strongest witches to have ever lived."

My mother no longer required Fate's powers, and that was a terrifying thing to consider. Could she really be as big a threat as they believed her to be?

"Witches are trying to kill the Prince," Mira blurted.

Bay went still. "You know this for certain?"

Mira looked to me. "Yes," I answered.

"Likely cast-outs from the House of Fate."

That's what Brecan suspected, but hearing it confirmed by a Priest sent goosebumps over my skin. Brecan stood a few inches taller beside me.

"How will you contain her?" I asked.

He shook his head. "Without your help, Sable, we can't."

"*My* help? I have no affinity."

"Only a witch of Fate can end her. And if you can't bring yourself to do that, you could use the power of your blood connection to bind her once more. Though you won't be able to do it in the earth."

Fate confirmed his statement with a gentle warmth, but soon that warmth turned hotter, scorching my marrow. He wanted my mother to burn.

But if I couldn't leave Tauren, how did he expect me to end her? How could I get close enough to? Unless she was coming here, for him. The thought made me welcome Fate's flame.

If I finally saw my mother face-to-face, would I be strong enough to do what Fate or the Circle required? I had so many questions. "What did she do to deserve the punishment meted out?"

My grandmother lied to me – to everyone – about her death, but hadn't the foresight to see she would escape her prison of roots and soil. I wanted to know what she'd done to garner such a harsh punishment.

Suddenly, Bay was gone.

Mira called his name, but it was no use. Brecan turned the shower off.

"Do either of you know anything about my mother?"

Mira shook her head, but Brecan refused to look me in the eye.

"You know something."

He put a finger to his lips. "I won't speak of it here."

A knock at the door startled all three of us.

Mira let out a pent-up breath. "It's just your schedule. I wonder what time you'll leave with Tauren today?" She was trying her best to remain cheerful, but the morning's revelation had set us all on edge. Brecan and I waited as Mira went to retrieve the paper.

He still wouldn't look me in the eye. "I have to shower. I'll be back soon."

Clutching my towel tighter, I nodded and watched as he left the washroom.

Mira returned a moment later, looking pale. "You leave just after breakfast and will return this evening. Sable…"

"What?"

"Escorts are not allowed to go with you on this outing."

A key turned in the lock to my door. Mira and I stepped into the bedroom and watched as the Queen and her guards stepped in. "You're dismissed," she said to Mira in a cold tone.

Quiet as a ghost, Mira slipped through the small entourage and out the door.

Rage roiled in the Queen's eyes. I called on her residue to find that it was gone. Her guards, four hulking men whose arms were larger than my waist, looked straight ahead at nothing at all.

The Queen's golden eyes locked onto my stained fingertips, tracking the ichor up my arms and across my chest.

I clutched my towel tighter to my body.

"Your grandmother is dying," she said slowly.

"I know." But I wondered how she'd learned of it.

"I know what she did to your mother."

I hadn't known until moments ago. The thought of being trapped in the soil made a shudder roll through me. "My earliest memory was of my grandmother telling me my mother was dead." I didn't elaborate on how Ela told me she'd died. "I just learned of her lie."

The Queen stalked forward and didn't mince words. "After we were married, your mother came to the castle often. Lucius said it was for readings, and I believe him when he said he wasn't unfaithful. Cyril didn't want him... she wanted his crown."

I pursed my lips. It was painted all over her face that she thought I was no better than my scheming, manipulative mother.

"I'm sure that when she rises, it and you will be the first things she comes for. She's powerful, Sable."

"I know that."

"Are you being honest when you say you want to protect my son? Because he's a good man. He doesn't deserve to be hurt. He certainly doesn't deserve to be killed."

"I bound my soul to his, Queen Annalina. If anything happens to him, if anyone mortally injures him, my soul will guard his. He will live."

"And you?"

"I will accept his fate."

"You would die for Tauren?" Her face blanched. A tear rolled from the corner of one eye. "Truly?"

I'd seen the Queen plenty of times since arriving at the palace. Never was a hair out of place. She remained poised, showed grace, and most of all, was the strong anchor on which the King depended. You could see the love between them as they presented themselves as a united front. This was the first time I'd seen her the least bit undone.

I should've expected nothing less from a mother who loved her son.

"Tauren isn't very happy about the spell I used to bind us, but yes." I took a deep breath before continuing, "I may not know very much about my mother, but I know without a doubt that I'm not like her."

Her brows furrowed. "Do you care for Tauren?"

I swallowed. I couldn't tell her how I felt when I hadn't even told Tauren.

She nodded, straightening her spine and her suit jacket. "Thank you, Sable. I just pray that you are stronger than Cyril, and that you never give in to the darkness that consumed her." Again, her eyes caught on my stained flesh.

Did she see the same spread over my mother's skin?

Queen Annalina left as quickly as she'd come, her brawny guards trailing behind.

A moment later, Mira slipped back into the room. "Are you okay?" she asked, concern shining in her eyes.

"She knows about Ela's failing health."

"How?" she gasped, clutching her chest.

"Someone from Thirteen must have told her."

"If the Circle knew someone was reporting to the King and Queen…"

"It could be a Circle member, for all we know."

Mira was holding a black garment in her hand. "We made this for you to wear today."

"Do you know what the other women will be wearing?"

"They'll all be in pastels, of course," she said disgustedly. "All of them are wearing their hair up in twists and braids."

"I'd like to wear mine down." Not only would it set me apart, it might conceal the stain if it spread farther up my neck.

She nodded. "Straight or curled?"

"You decide." I didn't care, but knew she did. Mira reveled in the details.

She'd made me a pair of dark trousers and a turtleneck to match. I held the shirt up. "It should hide the stain," she suggested.

"Thank you," I said, clutching the shirt to my chest and wondering how long anything would conceal it.

"You still don't know what it is or why it's spreading?"

I shook my head. "I wish I did."

"There must be a reason," she reassured. "I'll get the hair iron ready while you dress."

In the end, she ironed my hair and applied my makeup lightly; slight, dusky brown shimmering eyelids and peach cheeks with kohl-rimmed eyes. She motioned to a pair of sleek black witch boots near the door, complete with pointed toes and a broad heel. I grinned as I went to tie them on. "They're perfect."

I finished the look with a short pair of matching gloves.

Brecan brooded in the hallway. "I want you to see if Tauren will make an exception and allow me to go."

"I'm not asking him for that."

"Why not?" he asked, his pale brow rising.

"I'm not sure if you noticed how angry he was, but I'm probably the last person he wants to speak to today."

"The cameras will be rolling. He'll have to speak to you," Brecan argued, crossing his arms over his chest. "You're leaving the palace, traveling into a sector you've never visited. There are a thousand places for a would-be assassin witch or witches to hide. His guards cannot keep him safe if you have to go after them. But I can."

"I know you can, but I need you and Mira to do something for me while I'm gone."

He stood up straighter. "What?"

Mira's brows furrowed. "Name it."

"Protect the King and Queen."

Mira's eyes grew wide. "Are they in danger?"

"If someone wants Tauren dead, if they want the crown, they'll have to remove his parents first."

Brecan shifted his weight on his feet. "Then I want you to promise me something in return."

"What?"

"If an attack occurs, protect Tauren, but do not leave his side. Don't go after the witches. They'll eventually plan an ambush for you if they know you'll run after them. And if you leave Tauren unprotected, they'll strike. We know there are at least two, but many more were cast out of the House of Fate when Cyril was buried. Who knows how many are involved in this scheme?"

I nodded. He was right. "I promise."

Seeming satisfied, he and Mira vowed to keep a close eye on Lucius and Annalina.

twenty

Four carriages waited outside the Palace's entrance. A small camera crew hovered outside one of them, stuffing their equipment into a large trunk compartment. The weather was gloomy, the wind as turbulent as I felt. Rose, in a pastel pink day dress, climbed onto the step of the lead carriage, glancing over her shoulder and pinning me with a glare. "Come on, Leah."

Leah followed Rose's look and found me walking down the palace steps. Her mocha skin looked lovely, accentuated by a mint green, tea-length dress that swayed when she walked. She climbed into the white carriage and sat across from Rose. "Tauren will want to ride with us," Rose assured her loudly. "He'd never travel with the artists. The sculptor has the most disgusting hands. They're calloused and rough like a man's. And the painter? Has she ever scrubbed her cuticles a day in her life? There's dried paint all over her, I bet."

The artists, Estelle the painter and Tessa the sculptor, wilted as they waited outside the second carriage. "Don't listen to her," I told them.

"What would you know about it?" Estelle snapped. Her blonde hair was streaked with neon pink and slashes of green. Her pant suit wasn't pastel, but rather a surprisingly bold shade of egg yolk yellow.

"I know you were invited here among thousands of other women, personally by the Prince. The same as Rose was. He was obviously drawn to you, and he knows you're a painter. He admires your work. He told me so himself."

Her brow quirked, but she relaxed.

"He likes your sculptures, too," I told Tessa. Tessa was as petite as Mira, with hair the color of ash. I wondered if the hue was passed down from generations, absorbed into their familial lines from the ashen stones they worked. Her nose and cheeks were smattered with freckles and her smile was genuine and beautiful.

"Thank you," she said. Tessa hooked her thumb over her shoulder. "Would you like to ride with us?"

"I'd love to."

Suddenly, their eyes widened behind me and each of them stood a little straighter. The Prince was standing behind me. I could feel it. I turned slowly to face him. He was so close, his head blocked out the bright morning sun to the east.

"Sable," he greeted coolly.

"Prince Tauren."

He looked over at Estelle and Tessa. "Good morning, ladies."

"Good morning," they said in unison, Tessa's soprano voice colliding with Estelle's huskier tone.

Tauren pardoned himself to check with the camera crew, and when they assured him they were ready and would require two of the four carriages for crew and equipment, he strode to the lead carriage and climbed the steps, settling next to Rose.

"Other than you, Sable, she's his favorite," Tessa said disappointedly.

"I'm not his favorite." *As a matter of fact, right now I'm his* least *favorite.*

Besides, Tauren had spent the entire play with Rose by his side. She was from the most affluent sector, and was as popular as she was because her father was one of the Kingdom's most decorated generals. The Kingdom already loved her. Maybe Tauren could as well. Rose may have started using the love potion yesterday, but she probably didn't even need the edge it gave her.

Estelle climbed into the second carriage, followed by Tessa. They sat together on a bench, smoothing their dresses. Silver bracelets with their sectors engraved on the smooth surface adorned their wrists. I slid across the carriage and sat next to the far window so I could see out. A few moments later, our carriage lurched forward and rumbled along the long road, spiraling away from the palace at the center of Nautilus.

I was quiet as we bumped along the road. "Have you ever been to Sector Three, Sable?" Tessa asked, finally breaking the uncomfortable silence that had settled in.

"Only on my way from Thirteen to the palace. I've never actually visited any other sectors. In passing, your sectors were the loveliest. I'd like to visit them one day."

Both women smiled proudly.

"Can I be honest?" Estelle asked, glancing between us. "I'm shocked to be here. I'd never met the Prince, so I don't know how he even knew I existed. My mother is a well-known portrait painter, and the King recently commissioned her to paint Queen Annalina's likeness."

"Is that her painting in the main hallway?"

"It is," she beamed.

I raised a brow. "I thought it was a picture at first glance, before I saw the brush strokes. She's very talented. Do you paint portraits?"

"No," she answered. "I prefer landscapes, or more correctly, seascapes."

"I want to visit the sea," I told her wistfully.

"The Kingdom only has a sliver that citizens can access, located at the outer borders of Ten and Eleven. The rich soil ends and becomes sandy, like the earth is ending, and then it does. Tall cliffs drop straight to the deep, blue sea, but there's a tiny beach at the bottom you can climb down to at low tide." Estelle's eyes took on a faraway look, as if she were painting the scene in her mind. "It's worth it. The tide pools hold a vast array of sea life, and the water in summer is glorious. But you can't linger. The tides are always sweeping in and out, and you don't want to get caught unaware and have to scramble up the side of the cliff. Rough steps have been hewn along the cliff face, but they're slick as an eel's back from the constant sea spray. The best beaches are reserved for the naval fleet, of course."

"Have you been?" I asked Tessa.

She wrinkled her nose. "Only once, and only to look at the rocks along the cliff. None of them were good for chiseling. Too porous from the constant battering of wind and sea water."

The tension broken, we enjoyed the ride in silence as we traveled over hills dotted with small purple flowers. A short time later, we ambled through the palace's divisive wall and entered Sector One. "What is the purpose of the walls between sectors?"

Estelle answered first. "Each sector is like a small city-state, with elected officials and a city structure unlike the others. Citizens pay taxes within their sectors."

"Which means the most densely populated are the nicest," Tessa added.

"Our sectors don't have the amount of people the Core Four do, but we have enough, and our finished art earns a hefty wage. People from the Four decorate and redecorate to stay on top of trends we tell them about," Estelle explained with a knowing smile.

"And the trends always change somewhat." Tessa grinned to her new friend.

The countryside of Sector One was like that of the palace, with soft, rolling hills that were meticulously cared for. The enormous brick houses with wide, white columns weren't palatial, but were certainly large and stately enough to be built around the palace. We passed a yard separated from the others dotting the land, trimmed with a small, white-picket fence. The house was immense, at least five stories tall. There were romantic gazebos and immaculate gardens filled with roses in every shade, scattered with lily pad-laden ponds with fountains of water gurgling and arcing from their centers.

"That," Estelle said, sliding closer to the window we shared, "is Rose's house."

I knew she was from Sector One, but I was startled that she lived just a short ride from the palace.

Tessa snorted. "And unlike us, she *knows* Tauren. She's known him since they were little."

"They didn't seem that close," I argued.

Tessa nodded. "I wouldn't say they were close. Not friends, perhaps. But certainly, she's attended balls at the palace with her father. Tauren was definitely acquainted with her before he extended an invitation."

Estelle shrugged. "It's his right to invite whomever he likes."

"Do you want to be Queen?" I asked, waiting for her answer.

Estelle looked me up and down, her eyes catching on my turtleneck, then on my gloves. "Do you?"

Tessa started laughing. "It won't be me. I'm absolutely sure of that."

"Why?" Estelle asked, sliding back toward Tessa, her eyes glittering with interest. She wanted to hear all the juicy gossip.

"Rose is right. I have calloused, manly hands. If I became Queen, I would never be able to do what Annalina did and leave my passion behind."

"You would have to, if that's what the Kingdom required," Estelle said gently.

"Would *you* be able to give it up so easily? Never hold a brush in your hand? Never mix a new shade, or a familiar one? Never visit family or the sea again without a guard with you?" Tessa challenged.

"I really like Tauren, so I don't know what I'd be willing to leave behind," she mused. For the first time, Estelle stared out the window and was quiet.

"I don't understand why you'd have to give up your passions just to wear a crown," I gently observed.

The other two shared a look, but remained quiet.

We passed into Sector Two, where the buildings rose to hold the blossoming population. And then into Three, which to me, looked identical to Two. If it hadn't been for the wall dividing them, I wouldn't have known we had crossed over.

The carriages ambled through the streets, eventually stopping in front of a large, stone and metal building. "Do sculptors make these smooth stones?" I asked Tessa as we climbed out and stood beside the Sector Three Children's Medical Ward.

She nodded. "Those who love the feel of working rock but who can't sculpt, shape stone for the Kingdom. They make a decent wage."

Tessa's hand drifted along one of the stones as we walked forward to meet Tauren, Rose, and Leah. The crew unpacked the carriages behind us.

Tauren left Rose and Leah to speak with Estelle and Tessa, while I stepped closer to the crew, studying the faces of the three men and two women. They were rushing, gathering their things and preparing their recording devices. Each of them who met my eye looked away, as did Tauren when our gazes met.

He was still angry. I didn't regret binding my soul to his, so we were at an impasse.

Tauren led Estelle and Tessa up the short set of stone steps and held the door of the Medical Ward open for them to pass through. Leah filed in next and then Rose, who touched Tauren's arm as she thanked him for holding the door for her. The camera crew caught every movement. Every word.

I climbed the steps, prepared for him to leave me behind and get my own door. Instead, Tauren waited. Our eyes collided as I passed him, and though we never spoke a word, a thousand passed between us.

The crew followed us inside. Tauren shook the hand of a middle-aged woman with tawny hair, streaked gray around her face. She fawned over the Prince, thanking him for bringing us. The woman knew him well enough that I couldn't help but wonder how often Tauren came to visit the ill children in his kingdom.

"This is Doctor Kingston," Tauren said. "She will be giving you all a tour of the ward. Some of the children are very ill. You'll be able to see them and wave at them, but you cannot get near them for their own safety. Each of us carry germs that could harm them. She will let you know if and when to approach or stay in the hall."

Doctor Kingston wore a sturdy white coat that swished as she walked down the hall and up a set of steps to the second floor. At the landing, she smiled kindly at each of us. "The children on this floor are almost ready to go home. I'd ask each of you to wash your hands before touching them, but you are free to speak with or approach any child."

She glanced at my gloved hands. "Miss Sable, are you comfortable removing your gloves?"

The ichor on my skin began to tingle, as if it were coming alive. "Yes, Doctor."

She inclined her head and waited as the ladies washed in a nearby washroom. I was the last to wash my hands. When I removed my gloves, Estelle's mouth dropped open. She looked from my face to my hands, then to my throat. In the mirror, I could see that the stain had spread beyond the tall neck of my shirt. Like a dark flame, it now licked at my jawline.

Fate sent a calming wave of energy through me just when I needed it. Tauren was concerned. I could see it in the tension between his shoulder blades as he bent to wash his hands beside me. He was probably embarrassed of me. Most likely wanted me to return to Thirteen and never set eyes on me again.

He insisted that the crew wash their hands as well. Once they set their cameras down, he took the opportunity to come to me. "Why is it spreading?"

"It's not a disease; I won't harm the children. Witchcraft isn't an illness to be caught."

"That's not what I meant," he gritted, eyes boring into mine. "Is it because of what you did?"

The accusation stung. "No, it was already here. It's Fate's doing, and he will reveal the purpose in his own time."

"Does it hurt?" he whispered.

"No. It doesn't hurt."

Tauren slowly nodded.

Doctor Kingston waved her hand toward the hall. "Enjoy the children. They're a little rambunctious, as they're anxious to be discharged."

The children had been gathered into a large playroom for our visit. The room was painted a cheerful shade of pale yellow, decorated with bright posters and furniture. Some of the smaller ones pushed toy cars and rocked dolls in their arms. Older children read or chatted, sprawled across the many plush couches and chairs that peppered the space.

Their attention snapped to us as soon as Doctor Kingston came into view. The youngest children scampered over and wrapped themselves around her legs. She laughed and plucked them off one at a time before walking farther into the room and introducing us to them.

I was surprised to see they already knew Tauren. As he knelt, several ran to him, throwing their arms around his neck. The timbre of his deep chuckle filled the room, and he called them each by name as they reluctantly let him go.

One small boy with beautiful dark chocolate skin and short hair with yellow lightning bolts painted on his cheeks grinned. "I've missed you," he told Tauren.

The Prince patted his shoulder. "And I've missed you, Wes. Has your leg healed?"

The boy nodded.

Rose forced a smile as Wes beamed up at her. "She's pretty," he told Tauren. Then he looked at Leah, Estelle, and Tessa. "They're all pretty."

When his eyes found me, they grew as wide as saucers. "I've seen you on the telecasts!" he chirped and ran to me, stopping before he reached me. "I've never met a witch before."

I pulled a small wooden chair over and sat in it. "Well, now's your chance to ask me anything." I grinned.

"Truly?"

I laughed. "Truly, Wes."

"What is your talent? Water? Wind? Fire?" he asked so fast I could barely keep up.

"I have a unique affinity," I told him. "I divine fates."

"You know the future?"

"The future is fluid, but yes."

Tears flooded his eyes. "Can you visit my sister? She's on the fourth floor."

I glanced at Tauren, who swallowed thickly. Doctor Kingston pushed her lips together.

Wes put his small hand in mine. "Please, Miss Sable?"

When Doctor Kingston inclined her head, I squeezed his hand. "I will visit her."

"Thank you."

"That doesn't mean I can help her, Wes. Do you understand?" He sniffled and nodded his head. The boy looked like he needed someone, anyone to hold him. I extended my arms and he ran into them, crying fat tears as I gently rocked him. My chest became tight, and a knot the size of the palace formed in my throat. Eventually, the boy calmed down.

Doctor Kingston introduced the rest of the children. There were eleven, ranging in age from fourteen to four. Wes was seven. His sister, Belle was ten. I learned that the apartment below theirs had caught fire, sending plumes of flames and smoke upward. Their parents weren't home when it happened, and the two small children couldn't get the window unlocked and opened to escape. Luckily, a neighbor heard their pleas for help and came up the fire escape to get them out. He used an axe to break the glass and helped them to safety, but Wes's leg was burned. Belle's burns were more extensive, and her lungs were damaged from the smoke and flame.

While the other women politely shook hands with the other children, Wes and I sat in the chair together and talked.

"I get to go home soon," he said in a quivering voice. "But I wish Belle could come home with me."

"I hope she gets to go home soon, as well."

"Thanks for sitting with me, Miss Sable."

I smiled. "Thank you for telling me about Belle."

Something happened while I listened to Wes tell his sister's story. Fate called me to visit the girl. "Can you excuse me?" I asked Wes, standing up and following the pull of Fate. Doctor Kingston chased me into the hallway, followed closely by Tauren. The other girls looked awkwardly at one another, unsure what to do.

"What's the matter?" Tauren asked, waving off the cameramen.

"I need to see the girl. Belle."

"You can't," Doctor Kingston said regretfully. "I only nodded to keep Wes from going into hysterics. She's in no shape for visitors."

I looked to Tauren for help. "Fate requires it."

He nodded understandingly. "Please, Doctor Kingston," he pleaded. "I give you my word that Sable will heed your every precaution."

She pinched her lips together. "No cameras," she ordered.

Tauren gave a relieved smile. "I'll give the order."

While he did, Doctor Kingston turned her attention to me. "I don't envy your affinity, Sable, but if Belle is about to die, I want to know it."

Fate didn't confirm or deny the girl's status. "I will let you know after I see her."

She inclined her head, and when Tauren emerged from the room, the three of us jogged to the fourth floor. Half of the rooms were empty, the curtains pulled back to allow a clear view of the sterile rooms. The other half's curtains were drawn, concealing the ill from light and intrusive stares.

Belle's room was at the very end of the hall on the left. Doctor Kingston made us wash our hands again and don a plastic gown and mask. Then we were permitted inside.

Belle was hooked to several machines that emitted different-sounding beeps. I followed a vast array of cords and tubes to the girl. Her eyes danced beneath their lids. Her lungs expanded harshly and then deflated with a hiss. At my quizzical stare, the doctor supplied, "She's on a ventilator."

"What's that?" I asked.

"A machine that breathes for her. Her lungs were badly singed in the fire."

I could only imagine what she'd experienced, and at such a young age. The fingers of my right hand began to tingle, and I started to reach for her. "May I hold her hand?"

The doctor nodded and watched carefully as I took the girl's limp hand in mine, clasping my other on top. As I closed my eyes, a scene emerged.

One of terror. Of distorted, super-heated air, of clawing at a windowsill, tears and fear for Wes. Belle tried to break the window, but she wasn't strong enough. She even tried hitting the glass with a chair, but the wooden legs bounced harmlessly off the window before splintering to pieces in her hands. She managed to crack the window a little, but the glass was still too strong for her to break, and the fire spread so fast. She covered Wes and shoved his nose and mouth toward the crack in the window so he could drag what little fresh air was available into his scorched lungs. He screamed for help, and she screamed as the flames spread closer.

Fate stirred. He showed me how this girl was destined to help others. To learn to be a healer like Doctor Kingston, and to wear her own white coat. But first, she had to heal. She had to wake up.

I had no power to affect these things. There was no spell I knew to regenerate her lungs, or to erase the burns marring her head, face, arms, legs, and trunk.

But Fate could intervene. He could take it all away and make her whole again.

I clasped both of her hands, lending Fate my lips. He whispered over her, an incantation as ancient as he and nearly as powerful. The ichor that had stained my hands seeped slowly into the girl, healing every raw wound. Every puckered inch of flesh became new. Where the hair had burned away, it grew in soft and fuzzy.

Fate used me, whispering over her until she looked perfect and not even a scar remained. She sacrificed herself to save her brother, and Fate rewarded valor.

He rewarded selflessness.

Her healing complete, Fate brought Belle out of the deep sleep in which she'd been entombed. The girl's eyes blinked open drowsily. I smiled at her. "Hello, Belle. Please be calm."

Doctor Kingston, her hands covering her mouth and her eyes swollen with tears, burst into action. She called for a team to help her, and they worked to remove the tube from Belle's lungs.

Suddenly aware of the unnatural obstruction lodged within her throat, Belle began to panic.

I held tight to her hand, sending calming thoughts to her and settling her back into a light sleep. "She will wake in an hour," I told the doctor.

"Thank you," she cried, swiping tears from her cheeks.

I stepped away toward the door where Tauren waited, still as death.

"The magic in your skin was meant for her," he marveled.

I nodded. That was how Fate worked sometimes. I'd learned not to question it. He always revealed himself in his time, not mine. Flexing my hands in front of me, I saw that all the ichor was gone.

Tauren took my hand in his. "Thank you, Sable."

"It wasn't me, but you would have done the same. You'd do the same for every child in this ward, if you could."

"Can you?" he asked hopefully.

I shook my head. "Belle is who I was supposed to help. I can visit anyone you'd like, but…"

"You can't heal them."

"I didn't heal Belle. Fate did. She's going to do great things when she gets older."

His brows furrowed. "You can see that?"

I nodded.

"We should tell Wes," he breathed.

Doctor Kingston raised her head. "Tell him he'll be able to visit within the next few hours. The two might be discharged together, after all."

As another team of medics rushed into the room, Tauren and I slipped out into the hall. We walked slowly past the other doors. "How often do you visit here, Tauren?"

"At least weekly," he answered.

"These children love you."

"It took me weeks to get to know many of them, but when you walked in, they gravitated toward you. You'll make a great mother one day, Sable."

I swallowed. Thirteen wasn't like the Lowers. Once a child was weaned, he or she was given to the House of their affinity to raise. Most never remembered their parents. My lineage was unique, because my mother was the Daughter of Fate before me. And also because her mother hated her for it, and was very vocal with her disdain.

Suddenly, remembering how standoffish he'd been since our encounter in the garden, the blood in my veins heated. *He was angry with me? Fine. Now, I'm angry with him.* I rushed away, but he caught my arm.

"What did I say?"

"You know what, Prince? You were right. Why don't you focus on the other four women waiting in the room on the second floor?"

A bewildered look washed across Tauren's face. "What happened? I just complimented you on how comfortable you are with children."

"Do you know how children are raised in Thirteen?"

He shook his head. "I have no idea."

"You assume that everything that happens in this Kingdom is as it is in the Core Four. Well, it isn't. Thirteen is vastly different, Prince. So much more different than you even realize."

"How are children raised?" he asked. "Educate me, Sable. Don't get angry with me because I don't know your traditions. Teach me."

"Children rarely know their parents. They're raised by their Houses."

"You don't approve?" he surmised.

"Whether I approve or not doesn't matter." I wanted him to drop it.

"That's how I felt last night when I learned you'd worked that spell."

With one sentence, he cleaved me in two. I deserved to be split down the middle. With my actions, no matter how well intentioned, I took away any say he had in the matter.

"Does the spell work both ways?" he asked.

"I don't know what you mean."

"If something happens to you, will my soul save your life?"

I shook my head. "I did it to protect you, Tauren. Let Fate worry about me."

He reeled me in against his body. "I can't do that."

"Why?" I breathed as his nose brushed against mine.

"Because I care for you, Sable. So much."

"Too much," I added.

"Too much," he agreed. "And yet, not nearly enough. Do you have any idea how –?" His words dried in his throat and his eyes searched mine, begging for permission.

In the dark, abandoned corridor, I lifted my chin and positioned my lips just shy of his. If he wanted a kiss, he would have to claim it.

And then... he did.

His hands gripped my waist and then slid around to press against the small of my back. A kiss that was tentative at first quickly became all-consuming, and for a long moment, we lost ourselves in each other.

Someone cleared their throat behind us. We parted guiltily, looking over at Doctor Kingston, who smiled behind us. "A very wise choice, Tauren." Tauren looked to me and then opened his mouth, but Kingston was walking away. "Your secret is safe with me," she tossed over her shoulder.

Tauren linked his pinky with mine as we followed the doctor down the stairwell, but I pulled away when the first camerawoman panned in on us as we approached the second-floor common room once again.

Rose looked uncomfortable, sitting on a bright orange couch with a small girl who was showing her how to care for her baby doll.

Leah was in deep discussion with the oldest girl in the room about a book she'd read. Estelle had found finger paints and an easel with paper and was having a blast with two young boys, and Tessa was playing cards with Wes. His eyes lit up when we entered the room.

"Did you see Belle?" he asked excitedly. I looked to Doctor Kingston.

"Belle is doing much better, Wes," the doctor answered. "You'll even be able to visit her later today."

"Today?" he asked, mouth agape, swiveling his head toward me. "Did you save her, Miss Sable?"

"No, Wes. I'm afraid *I* didn't, but your sister is as strong as she is brave. Fate has wonderful plans for her."

He nodded emphatically. "She sure is brave."

I crouched down to hug him again, my heart much lighter this time.

Doctor Kingston told the children it was time to continue our tour, and the invitees filed out of the room. Rose lingered by the door for Tauren, who met her with a kind smile.

I'd be lying if I said I didn't mind.

twenty-one

"How was Sector Three?" Mira asked when I knocked on her door after we returned to the palace.

"It was one of the best, most humbling experiences of my life." *Thanks to Fate.*

He nearly purred within me.

The heat of Tauren's forgiveness was still branded on my lips.

"Do tell," Brecan said sarcastically, exiting his room and joining us as we strode across the hall to mine.

"The children were wonderful," I answered sharply.

"And has Tauren magically forgiven you?" he asked. "I noticed he left in Rose and Leah's carriage, but rode back with you."

"And Tessa and Estelle," I added.

Mira's eyes bounced back and forth between us as we argued. Attempting to quell the tension, she blurted, "The King and Queen are fine. We checked their meals, kept an eye on them as best we could, and when they retired to their rooms, came back here. They have several guards watching over them now."

"What's on the schedule for tonight?" I asked.

"Your evening is free," Brecan chirped. "The Prince will plan a special evening with each of you this week, beginning with Rose."

The thought of Rose and Tauren enjoying a romantic dinner made me burn with envy. But I would feel the same if he were dining with Estelle or even Tessa, who wasn't sure she wanted to give up her life for a royal one – even if it meant being with Tauren. Leah, I knew, was only granted the chance to stay so she could spend more time with Knox.

Footsteps came from down the hallway. Brecan, Mira, and I turned to find Knox waltzing down the hall. *Speak of the devil, and he shall appear.* The same must apply to thoughts.

"Sable? Could I have a moment of your time?"

"Of course," I replied, straightening my back.

Knox nodded to Brecan and Mira. "Privately, if you don't mind."

I certainly wasn't inviting him into my room unchaperoned. If he mentioned anything to Leah, she would blab to Rose, and Rose would make sure to mention it on camera.

I followed Knox up another flight of steps, down a hall, and up a spiral staircase that emptied into a solarium. If it weren't so overcast, the sun would spill through the glass panes and dapple the potted plants, all of which were wilted, the color leached almost entirely from their leaves and petals.

Knox leaned his hip against the cushioned arm of a plush blue chair. "My brother told me what you did today."

I quirked a brow.

"He said you couldn't heal just anyone, but I couldn't help but wonder if you could make a plea on our behalf."

"A plea for what?"

"Not what, *whom*. Our father, Sable. No one but he, my mother, Tauren and I know, but he is ill."

The tone of his words and the soft pain they held told me it was grave. "That's why he wants Tauren to marry so quickly," I surmised. "It's why he didn't protest when Tauren sent most of the women home early."

Knox nodded. "He hopes to live long enough to watch him marry."

It was strange how much he resembled his older brother. I wondered just how many years separated them, or if maybe there were only minutes between the brothers. They looked like twins, except for the bridge of their noses – Knox's had been broken – and their hair – Knox's was longer, wilder.

"What does he suffer from?"

"A cancer."

Fate coiled tightly around my middle. "The stomach?"

"Stomach. Intestines. It's everywhere."

I silently asked Fate if he would intervene. He remained with me, but silently refused the request.

"I'm sorry," I croaked. "I cannot help him."

Knox's face had held a tiny sliver of hope until the words left my mouth. Once they did, his head fell to his hands. "I was afraid you'd say that."

"But if he is in pain, I can ease it," I offered.

Knox's eyes flicked to me. "Truly?"

I nodded. "Truly."

"Could you come now? He's... this has been a hard day for him. He pretends well enough most of the time, but... Well, you'll see."

Knox led me through the castle to the King and Queen's chambers. The guards posted outside their rooms announced us and we were granted entry.

We walked into a sitting room appointed with plush furniture, accented by wooden tables and leather chairs positioned in front of a hearth. Knox gestured to a doorway and I walked into a bedroom with walls painted a shade of deep teal that I imagined was possessed only by the ocean herself. The King lay in his bed, propped up on a stack of pillows. The Queen sat at his side, spooning broth into his mouth. She took one look at me and dropped the spoon into the bowl with a clatter. A servant retrieved it from her.

The King tried to sit up, but panted from the exertion. His face was beet red, a sure sign of the pain lancing him from the inside out.

"How long have you suffered?" I asked.

"Only a few months," he answered breathlessly.

A question sat on the tip of my tongue, but I didn't utter it. *How long did he believe he had left?*

"I know I'm dying. Some days, the pain releases me and I feel fine. I feel like myself. Other days, I can barely leave this bed, let alone the room."

Knox stiffened behind me.

"May I?" I held my hand out for him.

His eyes filled with unshed tears, but the King placed his large hand in mine. I closed my eyes and whispered a spell to quench his fiery pain. Within moments, his grip relaxed and he sighed, letting his head sink back onto the pillows. "Thank you, Sable."

"It's the least I can do."

He breathed deeply, effortlessly. Queen Annalina put her hand over her mouth, stifling the sobs that threatened. Her eyes met mine and she took her hand away, mouthing the words *Thank you.*

"You should rest," I told him, but he was already half asleep.

The Queen gently rose and led me and Knox to the sitting room. "The palace physician told us he has three months to live."

I wanted to give her better news, but Fate told me otherwise. "He will pass sooner than that, I'm afraid."

The Queen's lips began to quiver, and a suppressed cry escaped them.

"How much sooner?" Knox asked for her.

"He will pass on the eve of the next full moon."

Knox uttered a curse. The Queen let out a quiet sob, falling into her son's comforting arms. "I'm sorry, Mother."

I was sorry, too. King Lucius seemed strong when I arrived at the palace. Strong but kind, despite how intimidating it was to speak with the King of Nautilus. But now I knew what had caused the underlying tension and worry that I picked up from both of them. Yes, the King and Queen had concealed this secret well, but I berated myself for not delving further into their residues while I could. I could've helped him sooner.

I slipped out the door and was walking down the hall, retracing the steps to my room when Knox caught up with me. "How long will the spell last?"

"Until he…" I couldn't say it. "He will not feel pain again, Knox."

He swallowed thickly. "Good."

"I'm sorry."

He stuffed his hands in the pockets of his dark trousers and rocked back on his heels. "No sorrier than I am." He was quiet for a long moment. "I'll tell Tauren. I imagine he'll want to move things along so our father can attend his wedding."

I swallowed thickly. "I imagine he will."

"I need to get back," he said regretfully, hooking a thumb over his shoulder.

We parted ways and I walked back to my room with leaden feet.

Brecan was waiting in the hall. He smirked, no doubt ready to fire a smart remark in my direction, but stopped when he saw my face. "What happened?"

"Where is Mira?"

"She went to the pool to swim for a while."

And to speak with Bay, I assumed. I wondered how much longer Ela could hold on. From the look of the potted flowers, not much longer at all.

The need for fresh air consumed me, and Brecan dutifully followed me outside. Estelle sat on one of the garden benches, studying the intricately shaped hedges and the floral tufts and vines rising from the soil. She invited us to sit with her, but we thanked her and kept walking. I wasn't sure where I was going, but my feet led me to the amphitheater. Jogging down the hewn steps, I pulled myself up to sit on the stage.

Brecan followed and settled beside me, a troubled look on his face ushered in by gusting winds that scuttled dark clouds across the sky.

"Can you contact Wayra?" I asked.

"I've been trying."

Whether it was Fate revealing it to me or some tether within me being severed, I felt the very moment Ela died. The earth trembled beneath us. I closed my eyes.

Brecan cursed as the ivy that had been creeping up the columns to either side of us shriveled, tumbling off their vines and littering the smooth stage behind us. The wind quickly blew it away.

"I hope they hurry. The Earth is parched and already craves a new Priestess," he said.

"It won't matter," I told him. Just then, a darkness slid through me; a tendril of something I thought was dead and gone. A link to my mother. "She's free."

Brecan's brow furrowed.

My thoughts went to Tauren. How could I keep him safe now that my mother had broken free of her earthen tomb?

"What do you know about Cyril, Brecan?"

He took a deep breath, resigned to his task. "I overheard Bay speaking to Mira just before they assigned us to be your escorts. From what I could glean, when you were still a toddler, Cyril threatened the King and was driven away by Annalina, who had gone to the Circle for help when she became leery of Cyril's intrusion into their affairs. When the Circle confronted her about it, Cyril flew into a rage and attempted a powerful spell to siphon the magic out of the Priest and Priestesses. The Circle fought her, and in the battle, both Wayra and Cyril were injured. Bay and Ethne helped Wayra, while Ela followed Cyril as she retreated into the House of Fate." He swallowed. "Cyril called on dark magic to evict Fate from your body, but when that didn't work, she attempted to kill you…to force him out."

My mouth fell open in shock.

"Bay said you were tiny, but that you knew exactly what was happening and what to do."

Fate must have guided me.

Brecan clasped my elbow. "You stopped her, Sable. You, with Fate's help, held Cyril until Ela was able to lure her onto the soil in the center of the Circle, where she bound her."

How many times had I walked directly on top of her?

"Why don't I remember anything?"

"You were very young."

As a toddler, I still would have been old enough to have memories. At least I thought I would. The first memory I could recall was one of fear – of being led to the cabin behind the House of Fate and told it was my home now, and that I had to live there alone. Ethne had escorted me because my grandmother refused. I wondered if it was because whatever she saw occur in the House that day frightened her, or if she was afraid of getting close to me only to have me tear her heart to shreds like my mother had.

Brecan continued, "The pentagram in the center magnified Ela's spell and contained her, until now – if you're right and she's escaped."

"She has. I can feel it, just as I can feel that Ela's spirit is with the Goddess."

"Sable!" someone yelled from the palace. I jumped down from the stage and ran, knowing within my heart it was Tauren who was calling.

"Tauren!"

Please, let him be okay. Fate protect him.

We met in the yard. His eyes searched over me. "Your mother…"

"I know."

"I was scared she'd come for you," he admitted.

Brecan stopped alongside us, drawing Tauren's eye. "I didn't realize you were busy," Tauren said, his princely manner smoothly clicking back into place. "I… I have to meet Rose for dinner." Tauren was out of sorts.

"Did you speak with Knox?"

He nodded, and it was then that I saw the redness that had settled into the whites of his eyes. Tauren had been crying.

Brecan's eyes pierced me, waiting for clarification, but I didn't want to speak about his father's failing health in front of him, or anyone for that matter.

"I would be happy to check your meal and drinks," I offered.

"Thank you. Just don't let Rose see you, please."

Ouch. "Of course."

"I didn't mean it like that. I just meant that –"

"It's fine. It doesn't matter. I'll check your food and then enjoy my free time. Right, Brecan?"

I felt horrible the moment I said it, but Brecan backed me up as he always had. "Right."

Following Tauren into the palace, I watched the way his muscles flowed beneath his tailored suit. He strode through the rooms and halls confidently, yet inside he was breaking. I knew he didn't mean to use his dinner with Rose against me. I shouldn't have used Brecan as ammunition against him in return.

I felt like a worm.

Tauren walked into the intimate dining room, where the table was lit by flickering candles and a trio of musicians were assembled in the corner, lightly tuning their instruments. Rose absolutely bloomed when he entered the room, rising from her chair and sticking her hand out for him to kiss. The smell of rose hips wafted through the air, not that she needed the love potion anymore. Tauren enjoyed her company.

I spelled the room, checked their meals and the wine and water glasses arranged on the table, and quickly took my leave.

Again, Brecan waited for me. I unlocked my room and he silently followed me in. "Don't use me like that again," he seethed once the door closed behind him.

Only one other time had I seen him so angry, which reminded me…

"How did you know I'd worked the binding spell?"

"The magic, Sable. It was so powerful, it woke me from a dead sleep and led me straight to you. I could smell it. I could taste and feel it. Even the air bent to you. Did you know that?" He stalked toward me with each proclamation, and I stepped back until my shoulder blades hit the wall and I could retreat no further.

"Why didn't it wake Mira?"

"Mira?" He laughed mirthlessly. "Mira's only known you since the day we left The Gallows. *I* know you, Sable. Better than anyone. I know the unique feel of your magic."

He braced his hands on the wall, caging me in. "Do you know how easy this would be?"

"What?" I croaked.

"*This*. You and me, Sable."

His lavender eyes glistened with something unspeakable. Something I'd seen again and again. He slowly leaned in, letting his arms hold his weight.

I wished it were as simple as Brecan thought it was, but nothing was simple now that Tauren was in my world. He was the only one I wanted, and at the same time was the fruit from which I was forbidden to eat.

"Would it truly be such a hardship to spend a year with me?" he asked, his lips a breath away from mine.

Brecan didn't want to hear the truth; he wanted me to accept him. To admit that spending a year together would be perfectly fine. But any year spent with another witch while yearning for Tauren would be a hardship.

"Brecan –"

He leaned in to press a kiss to my lips, but I put a hand between us and whispered a spell to move him away. Apparently, I put a lot of emphasis on the *away* part, because he was dragged across the room and far away from me.

The look on his face said that I'd hurt his pride. He tugged at his collar and strode to the door. "I'll be across the hall if you need me," he said, composing himself.

"I can't think about this now, Brecan. Not with Ela's death, my mother being set free, and trying to protect Tauren."

His shoulders tensed upon hearing Tauren's name. "I understand."

He left.

I changed into a comfortable pair of knit pants and a slouchy shirt that was thicker and hung off my shoulders, kicked my shoes off, and headed to the Night Garden. I felt like swinging.

Downstairs, I met Mira in the hall. She nearly bumped into me, startling when I caught her shoulders. "Are you alright?"

Her teeth were chattering and she hugged herself around the middle, trembling violently.

"Mira?" I looked closer to see that strands of her hair were frozen. "Who did this to you?"

"I did," she answered. "I wanted the water to be cooler. I guess I took the spell a touch too far." Mira smiled, but it wasn't genuine. "I'm going to run a hot shower. Don't worry, Sable."

"Do you want me to go with you?"

She shook her frozen hair and thanked me. "There's no need, really. I'm tired. I think I'll turn in early."

I decided I would give her time to shower and then go check on her.

Mira made her way up the steps and I peeked in the pool room, shocked to find the entire pool of water frozen. The once humid air was frigid. I closed the door behind me and made my way to the Night Garden.

Soft, lush tufts of grass tickled the bottoms of my feet as I walked over to the swing. I leaned my head back as

I swung, watching dark clouds race across the sky. Only a few panels of the glass enclosure were left open to the elements tonight, and the scent of something enigmatic and heady wafted on the breeze. There was something familiar in the smell. It pricked at my memory.

The earth looked sad. All the flowers that were merely sagging yesterday were now dead. Did the Circle fail to Elevate a new Priestess of the House of Earth? How could they?

Unless… unless my mother prevented it somehow.

Tauren cleared his throat as he walked into the garden. "Am I interrupting?"

"Interrupting my swinging? Yes, I suppose you are."

"Then by all means, carry on. Don't let me stop you," he teased.

"How was your dinner?"

Tauren leveled me with a ponderous look. "Why do you ask?"

"Curiosity."

"You know what they say about that."

I tried to laugh, gripping the ropes of the swing tighter.

Tauren sighed. "Dinner was good. No poison, so that's something," he finally said, settling on a stone bench nearby. The garden's narrow stone pathways were exposed now that its flora was dead. He stretched his legs out and leaned back on his palms.

"Good."

"And your time with Brecan?" He watched me intently.

"My evening was good as well," I said, re-using his bland description.

"Good," he muttered.

A long moment of silence stretched between us.

"I hate it," he finally said, tearing at his hair.

"Hate what?"

"Seeing you with him."

I took a deep breath. "Well, I hate seeing you with Rose. And Leah. And Estelle. And Tessa."

He looked up at me. "Thank you for helping my father. I didn't get a chance to tell you earlier. He's resting more soundly than he has in months."

"I wish I could do more for him," I admitted. I wished I could heal the King the way Fate allowed me to heal Belle today. But it was time for the King to pass, just as it was time for Tauren to take his place as the ruler of Nautilus.

Tauren leaned forward, placing his elbows on his knees and scrubbing his face with his hands. "This is so hard. He's been sick for a while, but we didn't realize it was this grave. For months, he brushed everything off as stomach upset or indigestion, and we let him," he scoffed. "We didn't ask questions. I never sent for a doctor until the day he collapsed."

"You didn't know," I tried to comfort.

"He's my *father*. I should've done *something*."

"His illness was not your doing, and you can't blame yourself for something completely out of your control." No more than my mother or her actions were my fault. I hated that he blamed himself. He shouldered too much. Far too much.

"For the record," he said, sitting up straighter, "I hate dining with Rose, or Leah, or Estelle, or Tessa."

"Why do you say such things?"

He shrugged. “Like you, I’m just being honest. There’s only one woman I want to have dinner with every evening, lunch with every afternoon, and breakfast with each morning.”

“We’re impossible,” I breathed.

“I’m not so sure about that.”

“I thought you were still angry with me.” I watched him out of the corner of my eye.

He blew out a tense breath and looked to the heavens. “I wish you hadn’t worked the spell, but now that you have, I’ll just have to work doubly hard to protect you,” he vowed.

He is ridiculously stubborn. “You should worry about protecting yourself, not about me.”

“No, now that we’re bound, you’ll be my shield, but I will also be yours. We’ll keep each other safe – and alive.”

I smiled. “We’ll defend one another?”

“Back to back.”

“It might come to that,” I told him. “My mother has been freed.”

“I had a lengthy discussion with my own mother after we returned from Sector Three, and she told me all she knew. Now I’d like to ask...how do *you* feel about Cyril?”

“I always felt cheated out of knowing her, out of being raised by her. If she were alive, I would have been a member of her House, not handed off to another Priestess. But now that I’ve heard more about her and the way people speak about her... they’re frightened. Not just afraid enough to avoid her, but terrified of her. And now I can’t help but be frightened, too.” Plus, there was the little tidbit Brecan had overheard about her threatening to kill Lucius, and then trying to kill me.

Fate woke inside me. His comfort curled all around me.

To those who were worried because there could only be one witch of Fate, I felt it down to the dust of me that I was his choice.

Not my mother.

Never her again.

A dark smoke curled through the open glass doors and flooded the garden, despite the wind swirling through it. I leapt from the swing and crossed through the dead foliage to stand beside Tauren.

His eyes were alarmed. "What is it?"

"I'm not sure," I answered, on edge.

The smoke continued to gather, building in height and width until the shape of a human formed. Out of the plume stepped a male witch with shaggy, midnight-blue hair and pale skin. Silver slitted eyes twinkled as he smiled at me and stepped forward.

"You," I breathed, finally recognizing his face. He was the boy who clung to the tree outside my cabin, the boy who chose the tea leaves… with the slitted eyes and indecision. "Who are you?"

"Daughter of Fate," he greeted so much more confidently than he had seemed in my home.

"Come no closer," I warned, raising a hand to defend Tauren and me. Tauren unsheathed a dagger, the biting sound of metal raking metal filling the air until he held it out in front of him.

"I am not here for a fight, Daughter of Fate," the male witch proclaimed.

With sharp features that highlighted his nature, he was beautiful – darkness embodied. Without the red cloak hiding his face, he was a sight to behold. Gone was the angst that rolled off him in waves while I read his tea leaves. In its place was boldness.

He's made his decision.

"What do you want, then?"

"To deliver a parcel."

I ticked my head back. "A parcel?"

"Yes, Sable. A parcel," he confirmed, hissing each *s* sound.

From a leather satchel at his side, he gingerly plucked a small, rectangular package, wrapped in brown paper and tied with a matching string. "Who are you?"

"I am the Son of Night," he answered.

"And do you often deliver parcels, Son of Night?"

He grinned like a panther. "When it benefits me, yes."

"Who sent it?"

"Your mother." The words sent a chill up my spine.

He tossed the package to me and I caught it, holding it against my chest. The witch strode back into the cloud of smoke and let it swallow him. A second later, not even a wisp remained.

"You're not opening that," Tauren ordered.

"I am, but not here," I amended.

"Sable, anything sent by your mother is unsafe for you."

"She didn't come here," I reasoned, "and he didn't threaten me. Perhaps this is an olive branch. In any event, I can't open it here. I need Brecan and Mira with me in case I'm wrong."

Tauren stared at the parcel like it might turn into a scorpion and strike at him with its bulbous, barbed tail. I was about to dismiss him when he speared me with an intensely determined look. "I'm coming with you."

"It's too dangerous for you."

"When you open it, I will be there, Sable." He sheathed his blade, never taking his eyes off me. Then he offered his arm, leaving no room for argument. I accepted it and together, we walked quickly upstairs.

Mira had showered, but was still shaken when she entered my room. "My mother froze the pool, didn't she?" I surmised.

Mira nodded, her eyes wide as she looked between the Prince and me. "What's that?" she asked, pointing to the package I held securely in my arms.

"I need you and Brecan here in case something happens when I open it."

"Is it from her?" she rasped. "You don't want to open it, Sable. She's... she's... she took over Thirteen."

"What?"

Mira nodded. "That's what she said. At the pool, I was trying to reach Bay when *she* appeared instead."

Brecan slipped into the room, catching the last of our conversation. "I can't reach Wayra, either. And it's obvious that no Priestess of the House of Earth has been Elevated, since everything remains dead." Brecan pushed off the wall. "It'll stay that way if an Earthen Priestess isn't Elevated soon. If Cyril is strong enough to block the Circle, irreparable damage might be done."

"Nothing is irreparable," I whispered.

"Let's go see what your mother sent you." Brecan gestured to my door, then looked at Tauren. "Are you sure he should be here?"

"No," I grumped. "But I'm not sure he shouldn't, either."

Tauren stiffened beside me, but I took his hand and pulled him into my room. Mira followed us.

Sending an anxious glance to Brecan and Mira, they extended their hands and readied themselves for battle as I untied the string and unwrapped the parcel. Inside was a simple, hand-held mirror. The handle and frame were ornately carved from jade, and ivy tendrils crawled up each side of the oval frame.

The mirror smelled of rich soil.

It also smelled like my grandmother's rosemary hand lotion.

I looked in the smooth glass. My reflection was quickly replaced by another, but the one looking through the mirror smiled. The way her lips moved, the dark shade of her eyes… They were the same as mine, yet there was a rage, barely restrained, contained within.

"Stop reading me, Sable," she snapped.

Blinking, I snapped out of the lazy haze and focused on her. "What do you want?"

"What do I want? Is that any way to greet your mother after seventeen years of absence?"

I remained still, careful to keep the mirror trained on my face and not allow her to see Tauren, Brecan, or Mira.

"How is your little Water witch friend?" Cyril grinned.

"She is well. Why would you ask?"

Her eyes narrowed fractionally, and then she began to pace in front of the purple couch in my House. "I've resurrected the House of Fate. Thank you for attempting to clean it before you were plucked away."

Number one, it was my House now. And she was thanking me? "I wasn't *plucked*. I chose to leave."

"Chose... it's such an interesting word. As if Fate ever offers a choice."

Fate growled within me, a rumble resonating through my bones.

Her eyes speared me like a fish on the end of a trident. "I could offer you one, though. I can break his hold on you, the way I broke his hold on me. I could set you free, once and for all," she offered. "No more fire inside, no more orders to follow, or frigid hands and lips. No more answering to anyone."

"Except you, I wager." And I bet she would try to lure Fate back into herself as well...

She smiled. "I am the Priestess now."

"Where are Wayra, Ethne, and Bay?"

Her eyes narrowed, and her lip curled into a snarl. "I do not answer to you, *child*."

Her eyes caught on something over my left shoulder. I'd shifted and revealed Tauren to her. "I see..." she said. "You're as handsome as your father was in his youth," Cyril said slowly, calculatingly. "You've done well, Sable. Luring him in, weaving a strong enough web to hold him there. Now that you have his heart, the crown is as good as yours."

As a dark, glittering ribbon slid out of the smooth glass and slithered toward Tauren, I flung the mirror across the room. The glass shattered on impact, skittering shards of mirrored glass across the floor.

Had her magic reached him?

I spun around to find him looking at me as if he didn't know me at all. As if my mother's words had poisoned his heart instead of his food.

"Tauren?" I said softly, approaching slowly. "Please tell me you don't believe her."

"Is it true? Do you only want the crown? The power?" he asked.

His words stung. "Surely you know that isn't what I want, Tauren."

He braced his hands on his hips. "I honestly don't know what to think anymore." Pinching the bridge of his nose, he let out a growl and threw the door open, striding out into the hall.

I wondered if he would come to his senses. I didn't want his crown, the Kingdom, or any of the trappings that went with it. I just wanted him safe, and for my meddling mother to stop manipulating his thoughts. With one sentence, she'd muddied his feelings for me. And the worst part was that he let her.

I stared out the empty door, willing him to return and say he believed me over Cyril, but he didn't.

Brecan leveled me with a glare. "Let him go. He doesn't deserve you if he so easily dismisses your feelings."

Ugh. I didn't want to deal with Brecan or his feelings, either. Not now.

Mira finally let out a breath. "I should've told you, Sable. About the water. I was just so scared."

"I understand."

"What can we do to help Bay?" she asked. "And Ethne and Wayra, too."

I didn't know what to do. Fate was still clinging to Tauren, but the witches in Thirteen needed help. If I left,

Fate would tear me apart for defying him; if I stayed, I'd rend myself for not going to help them. Not that I'd stand a chance against Cyril if Fate wasn't with me.

Brecan knelt and gathered the slivers of glass. "I'm getting rid of this. She could still use the shards to spy on you. There are a hundred tiny mirrors she could use now, all still enchanted. I can smell the spell on them."

"I need to know Tauren is okay," I said under my breath.

Mira's hand found my elbow. "I can help."

She removed a brooch from my trunk. "I snooped a little," she admitted. The trinket was old and tarnished, one I found along the trail on the path to my cabin one day, but I liked it so much I took it home with me. It was silver, a death moth so intricately carved, it looked as if it might flutter its wings and take flight. When Mira breathed on it, that's exactly what it did. The moth peeled away from the pin back and took flight. She went to the door and whispered for it to find Prince Tauren. Her eyes glazed over as she eased into a chair near the window.

"You can see through its eyes?" I asked.

Mira nodded. "It will find him." A handful of precious seconds passed before she spoke. "It's flying up… up the stairs. Up again. A twist, and then… down a long hallway. It flutters near a door that is closed."

"His bedroom?"

"No… it's crawling under the crack at the bottom of the door. It's inside. Oh my goddess – it's the King's bedroom. Tauren is sitting on the bed. The King looks sick! Something's wrong."

"He's dying," I entrusted.

Brecan paused in his cleaning and glanced up at me. "How long does he have?"

"Until the next full moon." Brecan's lips pressed into a thin line.

"I can hear them," Mira said. "Shhhh."

She listened for a long while. I settled into a chair beside her and waited while she eavesdropped.

"He thinks you tricked him," she whispered.

"I didn't."

"I know," she answered. "He thinks you only pretended to love him. He's telling the King about what your mother said in the mirror."

I balled my hands into fists.

Mira continued, "But the King doesn't believe it. He said that Cyril loves to play games, and that Tauren should never take her word over yours."

I threw my hands up. *Exactly!*

"The King told him to listen *here*," Mira relays, clapping her hand over her heart. "He doesn't believe you would lie to him. He thinks you love Tauren."

Brecan stiffened as he walked to the window and opened it. The shards of glass turned to dust in his hand, and with his breath, he sent a violent gust to scatter the particles.

"Awww," Mira sighed. "He says you look at Tauren the way Annalina looks at him. He says the other girls are nice enough. They'd enjoy being Queen. They might even be a good partner. They'd enjoy the title, the prestige, and the privilege that comes with it. But he says they don't have hearts to lead; hearts strong enough to weather storms and withstand battles and all that comes with them, yet be soft enough to show mercy. He says you have that." She smiled. "The King likes you, Sable."

Her smile faded slowly away.

"What's happening?"

"Tauren said you can't be with him, but the King said he thinks Tauren's being foolish. He says… rules can be rewritten. New traditions made. Compromises forged. He doesn't think there's anything you and Tauren couldn't figure out and withstand… together."

Brecan stood stock-still, his arms folded tightly over his chest. I noticed he didn't close the window.

"Tauren…" she began.

"Tauren, what?" I asked.

She shook her head. "He's leaving the room. He patted his father's hand and told him to get some rest, that he's sorry to have bothered him." Mira's eyes refocused. She turned her head to me, giving me a look that was part sorrow, part pity. "The moth is returning."

A knock came at my door, and the three of us stared at it for a moment before I stood to answer it. Tauren stood on the other side. "I'm sorry," he said, glancing into the room to see Brecan and Mira were still inside.

"We were just leaving," Mira chirped, standing up and grabbing Brecan's arm. She had to pry him from the wall beside the window, but he left the room with her and they returned to their own. I searched the walls for moths, just in case.

Tauren hovered outside, his forearm braced against the door frame.

"Come inside."

"I shouldn't."

"Yes, you should," I said softly, taking hold of his free hand and pulling him in.

He looked to the ceiling, but I could see tears glistening on his long lashes. "It's so hard to see him weakening. Day by day. Hour by hour. Knox is with Leah. I didn't know where else to go."

"I'm glad you came to me."

He glanced toward my trunks. "Did you bring your wishbones?"

"I would never leave them behind."

"Would you read mine again?"

A sliver of fear coiled in my middle. "I don't think that's a good idea."

"Why not? What could possibly be worse than my first reading?"

"Don't tempt fate, Prince. Things can always be worse."

He walked toward my trunks. "May I?"

I nodded and waited as he gingerly lifted the silver bowl of bones from the trunk. Settling on the bed, he approached from the other side and placed the bowl between us. "Are you ready?"

Resigned to his wish, I sat down on the bed. "I am. Choose a wishbone."

The corners of his lips turned downward as his hand hovered over the bowl. He plucked one out and waited until my eyes locked on his.

"Break it," I guided.

He snapped the wishbone.

It did not bleed. It burst into flame.

VI
THE LOVERS

PART THREE

WHEN WISHES BURN

twenty-two

Tauren dropped both ends of the wishbone into the silver dish amongst the other bones. I expected the pieces to flicker out and die down. Instead, they burned hot and bright, quickly igniting the entire dish.

I raised my hand and called on water. A puddle floated out of a nearby vase of red roses and doused the flame before it could spread to my bed clothes.

Smoke filled my bedroom, mouth, and nose. Tauren's haunted stare focused on the charred pile of bones.

"What does this mean?" he dared ask.

I opened my mouth, but no answer left it. My mind raced to make sense of what just happened.

Fate whispered to me. *This is not only* his *fate, daughter. This is yours.*

How can that be? I thought. No one's fate could transfer to another.

Your fates are one, he answered.

One prince.

One witch.

One fate.

I closed my eyes, but all I could see were flames. Walls of them. One right after another. They weren't concentric like those painted on a target, these flames swirled… igniting far away and gathering power as they twisted in on themselves.

My eyes snapped open.

They begin in Thirteen and end at the palace.

It was a warning from Fate. My mother was coming.

I closed my eyes again, and a vision of flames licking the sky and a full moon floating helplessly above filled my mind. The scent of smoke lingered in my hair, making it feel too real. *But it's from the bones, the reading*, I told myself. *It's not real. Not yet.*

There was still time to stop it from happening.

"Sable?" Tauren said after a long moment.

"That fate wasn't yours," I croaked. His brows kissed. A dark strand of hair fell into his eyes and I brushed it away. "Tauren, the fate was ours."

"Ours?"

I nodded. "We share the same fate now."

"Because of the binding spell?"

The two of you have always shared the same fate.

"No. The spell has nothing to do with it."

"Does this mean we'll die in a fire?" he asked, worry painting his face.

"I'm not sure. The fire could be metaphorical," I hedged. But I knew it wasn't. My face still stung from the heat of the flames in my vision. The fire was very real.

"The bone actually caught fire, Sable. I don't think that's a metaphor."

"I need to think." I leapt from the bed and began to pace, biting the inside of my cheek as I concentrated on deciphering the vision.

"Is the Kingdom in peril?" he asked abruptly, standing up.

"I believe so. My mother has taken over Thirteen. She hasn't killed the Priest and Priestesses yet, but I think she'll try. She'll kill them or bind them the way they bound her, and then... I think she'll come for the Kingdom and crown." *And then for me.*

"My father won't survive an attack, Sable."

"He won't have to," I vowed, my voice a growl.

"I need to talk to him. We need to discuss whether to continue the telecasts, or if it's safer to send the girls home. Then we need to figure out how to defend our sectors against your mother, if it comes down to it."

It would. I was sure of that much.

"I'll talk with Mira and Brecan."

"Can I come back later? I know it's late."

"I won't be able to sleep anyway, Tauren. Come back any time."

Watching him stride out the door, I wanted several things at once. To kiss him before he took another step; to tell him I would defend him and his family, his people, against my mother; and to somehow summon her and extract every particle of magic that lay inside her.

Brecan and Mira were ready when I knocked. "What happened?" Brecan snapped. "I felt your magic again."

I looked to Mira. She confirmed the same with a nod, adding, "So did I."

I took them to my room and showed them the bowl with the charred remains of dust and bone. Most of the pieces were so brittle, they fell apart when I lifted the silver bowl from the bed.

"It looks like there are no more fates for you to read, Sable. What does this mean?" Mira asked quietly.

Brecan's mouth gaped. "Has this ever happened before?"

"No."

Brecan was terrified, and for good reason. "We need to leave. *Now*," he ordered.

"And then what? We need a plan. If we waltz back into Thirteen, my mother might bind us the same way she has the others."

We talked in circles for hours, but in the end, we agreed it was too risky to spirit away to Thirteen. We had to try to reach someone there and find out what exactly was happening, who was helping Cyril, if anyone, and where the witches and members of the Circle were being held.

Tauren returned near daybreak, just as light from the sun began to yawn across the sky. The whites of his eyes were red and his clothing was rumpled, his hair disheveled.

"We think it's best to tell the invitees what's happening," he announced. "If they want to return home, so be it. For now, we need to figure out what's happening in Thirteen, while acting as if all is well on the telecast."

"I can send something to spy on Cyril," Mira offered. "How attached are you to your garden statues, Prince?" she grinned.

"I'm not nearly as attached to them as I am my own head."

Brecan snorted, pushing away from where he leaned against the wall. He, Tauren, and I followed Mira to the north garden where a statue stood in the center of a small pond. It was of a woman, so detailed that even her tears tugged at my heart. The draping gown she wore showed every crease and fold as it hung from her ample body. She poured water from a clay pot into the pond below. A concrete dove with outstretched wings was perched on her shoulder.

Mira walked on the water's surface and called on her affinity for water, reaching up and using her other ability on the stony dove. A wing twitched. Then the other. The fowl's head craned from side to side, then its smooth stone faded, transforming to pale gray feathers. Bits of rock sprinkled into the fountain, pebbling the surface.

My breath caught in my throat when the dove cooed. Mira held out her hand and brought the dove close, whispering instructions as her free hand slid down its soft, downy feathers. She raised her hand and the dove flapped its wings and took flight, heading toward Thirteen.

The sculpted woman haunted me. The artist had chiseled the dove as a comfort to her, and without it she looked inconsolable.

The sky lightened as we waited with Mira, who watched the world through the eyes of the dove she brought to life. Tension settled among the rest of us, thick enough that even the light morning breeze couldn't disperse it.

Tauren looked at me. "My father wants to have an emergency meeting with the invitees this morning. After that, he will consult his generals and we'll make a plan."

I didn't have the heart to tell him that my mother would undoubtedly dash his plans, no matter how masterful they were laid out.

Even though she hadn't raised me, the longer my mother breathed above the soil, the more I felt I knew her. She would strike hard and fast, and likely first. And if I was right, she wasn't a patient woman. Cyril would use dark magic to give her the edge, which meant that we needed to be ready for her, and I would need to use my darkness against hers. Brecan would oppose. I glanced at him to find he was already watching me.

"She's getting close. I can feel the magic from the wall," Mira suddenly reported, her chest rising and falling rapidly. Her breathing became erratic.

"What's wrong?" I asked, fingertips biting into my palms.

"She's across it, but something isn't right. This doesn't feel right," she said slowly, eyes darting in every direction.

"Is the bird just spooked? Some animals don't like the feel of magic," Brecan offered.

"No," Mira said sharply. Her eyes widened. "No, fly away!" she screamed, then clutched her chest in pain. She squeezed her eyes tightly closed and let out a guttural scream. If I didn't know better, I'd think she'd been run through. "The dove is mortally wounded, but I saw..."

"What did you see?" I asked, placing a hand on her shoulder to steady her, and waiting until she took several deep breaths to compose herself. "What happened to the dove?"

"Someone shot an arrow through her heart; a male witch with long, stringy dark hair. I've never seen him before. He's not from Thirteen." She rubbed her chest over her heart, feeling the residual pain of the animal. "The dove… her spirit is almost gone, now. She's on the ground, staring up at the canopy."

The witch was the same one who shot the arrow at Tauren. I was sure of it. Loyal to my mother and willing to do her bidding, he was also on my short list of people to hang. He and the girl who'd attempted to poison my prince.

Mira couldn't take a deep breath until the dove died. When it did, a tear fell from her eyes, making her look more like the statue of the woman in the pond than my friend for a moment. She wiped the tear away. "She's trapped all the witches in the Center."

"How is that possible?" Brecan breathed.

"Dark magic," Mira and I answered at the same time.

"You felt it the moment the dove crossed the border," I whispered. "Didn't you?"

Mira shuddered. "Yes. It's powerful… like nothing I've felt before."

Fate came alive inside me, bringing forth an image of the Son of Night. Was he involved somehow?

A muscle ticked in Tauren's jaw. "We have to free them."

"Why do *you* care?" Brecan challenged.

"They are my people." Tauren slid a look in Brecan's direction that left no room for argument. The witches in The Gallows might separate themselves from the rest of the Kingdom, but it didn't mean the monarchy felt they were any less citizens of Nautilus. And like a good prince, a good king, Tauren cared for his people.

"And how do you propose we set them free?" Brecan asked, part challenge and part curiosity.

He had no idea how to challenge my mother, but I did.

"The only way to fight her dark magic is with something darker," I replied flatly.

"No," he said immediately, standing from the bench he'd sprawled out on. "You can't do it, Sable."

Fate disagreed. He slithered warmly in my stomach. "Yes, I can."

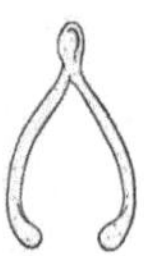

The King wasn't well, but Annalina had hidden his exhaustion beneath a layer of fine, translucent powder. She'd washed his hair and helped him dress. The fact that he wasn't in pain relieved him tremendously, but the cancer ravaging his body couldn't be stopped. Its insidious effects were visible as the final five invitees joined the royal family in the King's private study.

Brecan and Mira slid into the room while the other escorts waited outside. No doubt they'd try to eavesdrop. I discretely poured a silencing spell from my hand. What was said in this room would stay within it. The other ladies gasped as the shimmery silver magic formed a solid bubble that spread out until it hit the corners of the room. It was the same spell the Circle used to protect their conversations.

The King sat forward, resting his elbows on the top of his tidy desk, another reminder that he'd been unable to perform many of his duties over the past few days. "You're probably wondering what the emergency is, and I'll quell your worries soon enough, but what is discussed within this room will *not* be discussed with anyone outside it, under penalty of treason. Is that understood? Not even with your escorts." The King's burnt toffee eyes were hard as they met each invitee's, but they softened when he found mine.

The ladies assured their full cooperation and understanding with nods and affirmations. Rose stood up straighter, giving the King her undivided attention. Leah stood tall beside her while Estelle and Tessa clutched hands, standing together to the right of them. The party from Thirteen settled against the wall. Even though I was lined up with the other women, I was separate.

The King explained how I came to be part of the invitation. Rose flicked a disgusted look my way, then turned it on Mira and Brecan. She quickly pressed her lips into an expectant smile and flashed it at the King. Annalina, who stood behind her husband, speared Rose with a look so severe, she should've cowered.

I wanted to claw the smug look off Rose's face, but refrained. Barely.

He told them of the threat against his son.

Then he told them of Cyril, never mentioning that she was my mother, and informed them that she had caused a disturbance in our sector that might spread across the Kingdom if not extinguished.

Tauren, standing at his father's right hand, spoke next. "If you want to return to your sectors, families, and lives, I completely understand. I would never keep you here against your will."

Tessa straightened, glancing at Estelle.

"If you want to stay, we will film scenes to make the Kingdom believe all is well – including the traditional journey to the coast."

"To distract them?" Leah asked. "Why would you do that? The Kingdom's citizens can fight."

"They can't fight Cyril and win," I interrupted.

Rose crossed her arms over her chest. "And I suppose *you* can defeat her?" she scoffed.

I remained silent.

"Arguing will get us nowhere," Annalina told everyone. "You've been informed of the situation. Now, you must choose to stay or go."

"What does this mean for you, Tauren? Will you choose one of us now?" Rose asked, her eagerness hidden beneath a curious expression.

Tauren opened his mouth to speak, but the King beat him to it. "Tauren has more important matters to think about than this silly contest. Personally, I think it's time that we think of a more appropriate way for a prince to find the one he wants to spend the rest of his life with. This invitation system is the way it's been done for five hundred years, and while I was able to find my true love through it, who's to say Tauren can? I say, if the answer isn't crystal clear by now, then he's not ready to make the decision. I also say he can wear a crown and rule, if need be, without a wife by his side."

Rose's mouth gaped.

"I want to go home," Tessa said in a quiet voice, looking at Tauren. "I really like you, but I don't love you and I don't want to be Queen. I love my family and I love working stone. I didn't realize how much it meant to me until I came here."

He inclined his head. "Completely understandable, and I respect your decision. I've enjoyed spending time with you. I hope we can remain friends."

Tessa curtsied, pulling her day dress's skirt wide. "As do I."

Tauren looked to Estelle. She tucked her colorfully streaked blonde hair over her shoulder. "I'd like to stay. If I can help, I will."

Leah smiled. "I'll stay to help, but at the first sign of trouble, I'm out. I have family, too."

"Not to mention that you're actually into Knox," Rose muttered snidely under her breath.

Leah nodded. "I *am* into Knox," she confidently confirmed, "and Tauren knows that. As do his parents. And all of them approve, Rose."

Rose's mouth gaped open again, then snapped shut. I enjoyed watching Leah put her in her place more than I should have.

"Rose?" Tauren asked. "Have you decided?"

"I'll stay, of course," she confirmed with a nod.

Decisions made, we learned Tessa would leave us that afternoon, pretending that Tauren had dismissed her and giving the viewing public the impression that this competition was still light-hearted, and that we were oblivious to what was transpiring in Thirteen. Rose would throw a tea party, as it was already scheduled, and then we would travel to the coast. Tradition decreed that if the sea blessed our prince, it would offer up a nautilus shell, which would pave his path to the crown with luck and prosperity.

"That's awfully close to Thirteen," Brecan noted. "I'm not sure that's safe."

"Don't film it live. You can film it and then air it later, once everyone is back here and safe, right?" Estelle suggested.

"You have a few hours to rest," the King announced, ignoring the suggestion but staring at me intently. "I suggest you take advantage of it."

Brecan used his magic to pop the bubble enclosing us and led our party outside, down the long corridor to the main staircase. Mira made me promise to wake her if anything happened. With the exertions of the morning, she needed a few hours of sleep. So did Brecan and I. We trudged to our hallway and Mira closed the door behind her, giving a weak wave.

I pulled out my key and unlocked my room, catching the barest trace of sage and black salt swirling in the air. After quickly scanning the room, I couldn't see anything out of place.

"What's the matter?" Brecan said, his chest suddenly against my back.

"Someone was in here – a witch."

"There." He pointed to a small table just inside the door. "Someone delivered a letter."

The letter was sealed in midnight blue wax, a symbol of a moon and stars stamped into its glossy surface. I hesitated to even touch it.

Breaking the seal, pieces of wax sprinkled my boots and bounced onto the floor.

Dearest Sable,

With great discretion, there are urgent matters I'd like to discuss with you – and you alone. Meet me in my favorite garden when you can. I'll be watching.

Best Regards,
Arron, Son of Night

Brecan fumed. "You are *not* going alone."

I wished he hadn't been watching out for me just this once, because I knew I needed to meet Arron alone. He wouldn't speak to me otherwise. I remembered his silver, slitted eyes – reptilian, yet eerily beautiful. They somehow fit him, just as he belonged to the dark smoke that was a harbinger of his arrival.

Tossing the letter onto the table, I scrubbed my hands down my face. "Let's rest. Then we'll discuss."

"We *will* discuss it," he warned.

I walked to the bed and flung myself on it, barely registering his 'sleep well,' or the moment he locked the door and closed it behind him.

I try to blink, but something thick blankets me. Something heavy. It presses all around me. I can't shift or move even a fraction of an inch.

The weight keeps me still, silent. My heart thunders.

There is dirt in my mouth. In my nostrils. In my ears. But I can't move my hands to dig it out. Not even a finger will flinch. I can move my tongue, but not my lips. The pressure holds them shut.

I remember that the Circle, led by Grandmother Ela, captured and encapsulated me with magic. The four of them together are too powerful to fight against.

"Daughter of Fate, you are bound to the soil, and there will remain until I no longer draw breath," she said.

No, they did this to my mother. Not me.

Not me!

Soil in my mouth.

It crushes me.

They buried me…

I can't breathe.

The sound of splintering wood woke me. Brecan fell into my room just as I sat up, desperate for air. I clutched my chest and crawled to the edge of my bed. Strands of saliva fell from my mouth as I retched. Brecan grabbed a nearby garbage can and positioned it under me, scooping my hair away from my face and holding it back.

"Talk to me, Sable."

But I couldn't. The taste of earth still coated my tongue.

I coughed, and clumps of dark soil erupted from my mouth.

"What's happening?" he breathed.

I gagged and coughed until nothing else came out. "I'm okay," I finally croaked.

He ran to the bathroom to retrieve a damp cloth as Mira cautiously entered the room. "What happened to your door?" she asked as Brecan returned.

"I broke it down to get inside," he answered. He handed me the towel, but my hands were shaking so violently, I couldn't get them to work.

Brecan took the towel from me and cleaned my face. "Why were you vomiting dirt?" he asked gently as he wiped beneath my eyes.

"I dreamed I was her. Cyril."

Mira clapped her hands over her mouth. "Buried alive?"

I nodded.

Brecan looked at the pile of earth in the trash can and back at me. "How?"

"I don't know." I took a moment to draw in as much air as I could, settling myself.

"Your mother did this," Brecan growled. "She or that devil, the Son of Night."

"What time is it?"

"An hour before the tea party," Mira answered shakily. "You need to get ready, Sable. I'm so sorry you don't have more time to compose yourself." Mira shifted her weight on her feet, worrying her hands.

"I need a shower. I need to rinse the dirt out of my mouth, and…" I raised a strand of damp hair. "It's even in my hair."

Mira gave us a worried look before helping me off the bed and into the washroom.

twenty-three

The tea party took place in a small sitting room with walls the color of blushing primroses. A round table sat in the center of the room, topped with a white cloth and surrounded by elegant, matching chairs with long, silk ribbons tied around the backs. Tauren was seated at the far side, and a guard stood in each corner of the room. The soldiers were so still, they nearly faded into the décor. If they'd been wearing pink, they would have.

Rose sat to the left of the Prince in a rather revealing, dusty pink day dress. Leah sat to his right, and Knox sat beside her. Estelle sat next to Knox, and the only empty seat put me between Estelle and Rose – almost as far away from Tauren as possible, I noted.

Well played, Rose.

Tauren had already bidden farewell to Tessa in front of the cameras. She boarded a carriage outside the palace, waved goodbye, and didn't look back. Mira watched the telecast while I showered, reporting every detail as she braided my dark hair and applied my makeup. I think she was trying to get my mind off the terrible nightmare I had.

Rose cringed at the sight of my raven-colored dress as I walked closer. Two cameramen were preoccupied, checking the angles of their cameras to make sure the entire table was captured, when she stood and rounded the table, stopping to whisper, "Would it *kill* you to wear something other than black?"

"Yes," I replied sweetly.

"I sent instructions to your escort for you to wear something... brighter."

"Well, my escorts and I don't answer to you, and I prefer to wear this color. So, I politely decline."

If Rose were a tea kettle, she'd whistle. The fake mask she'd worn since waltzing into the palace, expecting to win a crown and a prince, had begun to crack.

"Fine," she recovered, smoothing her hands down her dress just as three kettles of hot water were brought in. Rose moved to place them on the table as the crew raised their hands to indicate the live feed would begin in five, four, three... they counted down with their fingers.

Rose flashed her famous megawatt smile, a dimple popping in her cheek. She toyed with her beautiful red hair and stared into the nearest camera. "Thank you all for coming. Afternoon tea is an important tradition in my family. It allows us to step away from all the important work we do and take a breath, recharge, and reconnect with one another."

She lay tea bags into our empty floral cups, smiling as she made her way around the table, serving Tauren last, only so she could fill his cup with steaming water first. He thanked her and waited as the tea steeped. I could still smell the love potion on her skin, but Tauren wasn't affected. That was the down side to using them. The target often became immune if actual feelings weren't present.

A sense of relief loosened my ribs, although the fact that he didn't love Rose tormented me. I was beyond happy that he didn't. But would he marry her anyway and enter a loveless marriage for the sake of Nautilus?

Estelle wrinkled her nose at the smell. She obviously wasn't a tea fan.

I loved the taste, but better than that were the leaves that foretold.

Ripples spread across the surface of Leah's tea. She took a sip. Knox whispered something in her ear, then clinked her cup with his. The two might as well have been in their own world, and now the entire Kingdom knew they were interested in one another.

Tauren grinned at them both, then motioned for a cameraman to come closer. "In case you haven't noticed, my brother and Leah have hit it off. Leah declined my invitation, but I have hopes she might receive another."

Knox never took his eyes off Leah. "Actually, that's rather perfect timing, brother." He stood up and pushed his chair out, kneeling in front of Leah. She clutched her chest, awestruck by Knox as he pulled an enormous gold and emerald ring from his pocket. "Green is your favorite color, and it reminds me of every fleck of the shade in your eyes. We haven't known each other long, but the thought of you leaving tears my heart to shreds. Will you stay? And will you consider being my wife?"

My brows raised at the tender question. I knew they enjoyed one another's company, but marriage? Marriage, to everyone but witches, was for life. Marriages were rarely dissolved, and only under the direst of circumstances. The King himself had to counsel anyone seeking divorce.

Leah silently cried, even as she smiled. She nodded her head and threw her arms around Knox's neck. "Yes!"

Estelle started clapping beside me, and soon, applause filled the room as everyone rose from their seats. The cameras whirred, panning in and out on Leah, Knox, and the ring. I imagined Mira squealing at the sight as she watched the events unfold upstairs.

Tauren's eyes met mine, glittering happily as his hearty claps and wide smile filled the room. Once Knox rose and kissed his future bride, his brother was there to greet him with a hug.

Rose watched them both with a plastered-on, saccharine smile. She made sure to catch the eye of a cameraman as she pretended to swoon over the engagement, but when they focused on the rest of the party, Rose continued to stare at the brothers with a calculating eye. I wondered if she saw them as men, or simply as a means to a queenly end.

After everyone settled back at the table and the congratulations had ended, Rose suggested everyone drink their tea before it got too cold. She was *not* happy she wasn't the center of attention, like she'd undoubtedly planned.

"So, can witches read tea leaves, or what?" Estelle asked after sipping hers again.

"I can," I answered.

"How? I want a reading!" she pressed.

"Now is really not the time," Rose snipped, sharp as a thorn.

Knox nodded his head. "That would actually be really interesting to watch."

Instead of responding, Rose passed everyone what she called biscuits, though they were actually cookies. Hard cookies. They nearly broke my teeth when I tried to bite one.

I put the cookie down and hoped everyone would let the tea leaf thing go.

They didn't.

Instead, they tore open their tea bags and emptied their leaves into the water. "Will you at least read for *one* of us?" Tauren pleaded. His voice was hopeful and worried at the same time.

I inclined my head. "Very well. Estelle, since you asked first, would you like the reading?"

She grinned. "Absolutely. What do I do?"

I told her to drink as much of the tea as possible, letting the leaves settle where they wished. Estelle sipped hers until the remaining water barely covered the leaves, then placed it on her saucer as I instructed. She scooted it toward me, careful not to disturb the cup. I waved my hand over it, erasing all the pastel pink roses. A web of black threaded around the inside, forming the familiar pattern required to read her fate. "Turn the cup over," I told her.

She quickly flipped it, and the little bit of remaining tea emptied into the saucer. The pattern of leaves left a story. It always did.

I inhaled, closed my eyes, and recalled the pattern from memory, watching as Fate gave me visions of Estelle's future. "You… you will attend a wedding very soon. I see you in the audience, watching the couple…"

Hearing Knox and Leah laugh, I kept reading. "Everything is about to change."

She made a *wooo* sound, wiggling her fingers to tease me.

"Smoke," I breathed. And then tasted it on my tongue, smelled it in the air. "So much smoke."

"What's on fire?" she asked.

"Everything," I answered.

"Okay," Rose chirped with a clap. "That's enough darkness and despair from The Gallows, don't you think?" She tucked her scarlet hair behind her ears as everyone around the table gawked at her.

"Witches have senses of humor," I said to lighten the mood. "We aren't *all* darkness and despair."

"I've yet to see it," she smarted. "The only thing you know how to do is wear black and be creepy."

I quirked a brow. *Creepy? She hasn't seen creepy from me yet.*

As she took a dainty sip from her cup. I whispered a transformation spell and darkness descended over the room. The walls began to bleed coal black paint from the ceilings to the floors, until each was evenly coated. "What are you doing?" she cried.

Tauren gave an approving laugh and Knox watched in awe, though Estelle seemed a little unsure of how to react.

The rosettes that lined the rim of Rose's cup turned black, and when she looked from me to them, her eyes grew wide. "There are words at the bottom of my cup," she said, squinting until she made them out. "You've been poisoned." Her wide eyes turned to mine, questioning.

Does she actually think I would hurt her?

"Have I?" she shrieked, dropping the cup and saucer. As soon as the porcelain hit the table, the spell broke and everything was pink and perfect again.

I smiled at her aghast indignation. "Of course not. It was only a joke. I told you we witches have senses of humor."

"Dark, *creepy* humor," she jabbed, trying to cover the fact that she was shaken.

I shrugged. She wasn't wrong.

"I like her sense of humor," Tauren announced, winking at me as he took another sip.

Estelle began to laugh, shaking her head. "That was awesome. I wish I could do things like that. My mother would never rest."

Rose guffawed. "Well I, for one, pity her future husband."

Her pretty feathers ruffled, Rose pretended I wasn't in the room for the remainder of the tea party – which thankfully was nearly over. At which time, she sweetly thanked everyone but me for attending. The moment the cameras were off, she strode from the room with her shoulders back and her chin up.

"That was hilarious," Estelle whispered as we stood.

Admittedly, I may have taken it a bit too far. Rose was already on edge, and even though she was prickly, I shouldn't have teased her, even if I only meant it in jest.

"Ladies," Tauren declared as he stood, "we leave for the coast in half an hour." With that, he excused himself and rushed from the room, jogging in the direction Rose had stormed.

"Looks like he's made his mind up. Guess you're riding with me," Estelle said playfully, nudging me with an elbow.

Brecan glanced into the room from the hallway. I walked to him. "Mira is getting something ready for you to wear." I nodded and thanked him, and then we headed to our rooms. "I don't like this," he finally admitted. "I have a bad feeling."

"As do I."

"Then why are you going?"

"To protect him." It really was as simple as that. "Besides, it's not *him* I'm worried about; it's something else. I just can't put my finger on it yet."

Brecan paused outside my door. "I'll wait here. Scream if you need me."

I took in the splintered door frame, thankful he'd felt magic erupt from me earlier and came to help. "I will." My eyes drifted to his lavender ones. "Thank you, Brecan."

He pursed his lips together and inclined his head. I could tell he wanted to say more on the matter of leaving, but he wisely held his tongue.

I slipped into my room where Mira was waiting. She sat in a chair with a garment folded over her arms. "I don't know if you'll like it or not," she said nervously, standing and clutching the fabric to her chest.

"I'm sure I will."

She slowly unfolded it, revealing a gauzy, strapless dress that was black around the bust and waist, fading to deep teal around mid-thigh, lightening to a lighter shade around calf-length, and morphing to white at the bottom hem that grazed my bare ankles.

"It's beautiful," I marveled.

"I wasn't sure if you'd like that it wasn't all black."

"It'll look like I melted into the sea."

She grinned, handing me the dress. "That's what I envisioned." When I gave her a bone-crushing hug and thanked her, she pulled back, surprised at the contact, but beamed. "I have the perfect sandals, too!"

I quickly changed and emerged from the washroom to find her ready with the shoes. They were made of white leather that had been stitched into a tangle of pale thorns. They wound around my foot to the ankle, and like everything she'd made, fit perfectly.

"What about my hair?"

She fingered a wavy strand. "It's perfect the way it is."

"Are you excited to visit the sea?" I asked.

Her eyes welled up. "I've seen it once, but it wasn't enough. Besides, I wonder if I might be able to contact Bay through the power of the ocean."

I hadn't thought of that, but Mira was a genius. "Brecan might be able to reach Wayra, as well. The sea breeze should be strong."

Mira's eyes met mine as she gently gripped my elbows. "Let's hope it's strong enough."

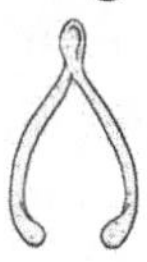

Brecan sat beside me in our carriage and Mira settled across from us. I glanced out the window as the road twisted and curved, watching the lead carriage ramble through the countryside. Estelle, Rose, and Tauren were inside, and the dark teal carriage was large enough that two cameramen traveled with them as well.

An unsettled feeling pricked at me. I would meet with Arron, Son of Night when I returned. Would he be able to tell me more about what was happening in The Gallows, or why the witches couldn't break free of Cyril's hold and exit the Center? The pentagram was the source of their power, but all witches could harness it; it shouldn't bind them. Then again, it was where Ela had bound Cyril in the earth, and her connection to it was probably stronger than most.

Our carriage ambled through Sector One and we passed Rose's house again. I couldn't help but feel a stab of jealousy, even though I knew Tauren didn't want to choose a wife at this point. Between what was happening in Thirteen and his father slowly dying, he had enough to worry about. But once we resolved the issue in The Gallows, and after King Lucius passed, Tauren would need someone to comfort him.

Rose would be there. She lived close to the palace anyway, and her life would meld seamlessly with Tauren's. She'd practically been raised as royalty.

Through Sectors Two and Three, Brecan began to fidget.

Mira noticed and shot me a concerned glance.

We traveled a simple spiral through Four, Five, Six, Seven, and Eight, but the trip still took hours. I expected the long travel duration, but I didn't anticipate the feelings that came with it. It felt like time wasted. We should be doing something to help our kind, not going to the beach to look for some 'blessing' from the sea. If Tauren found a nautilus shell it would either be a miracle, or it was planted beforehand.

Brecan sat on the edge of his seat through Nine.

"What's the matter?" I finally asked.

"Don't you feel it?" he grimaced, raking clenched hands through his pale hair.

I did. In the pit of my stomach, insidious ropes of dread had coiled. "I do."

"Me too," Mira admitted.

We left the main road and took a smaller one through Ten, all the way across it. The feeling in my stomach never eased and Brecan never relaxed, even when the air became thick and humid, with a briny taste.

Mira's eyes glazed over. "Do you smell the sea?"

I had to smile. "I do. How long has it been since you've visited the sea?"

"Years. I was just a little girl. Bay took a small group of us to see it. We'd just displayed our affinity and been accepted into his House."

"Bay seems kind," I said quietly.

"He is. He's the kindest person I know. That's why I'm so worried."

"Do you think we should send another animal to spy on them?" I asked.

She nodded. "I will as soon as we stop. If I send a sea bird, Bay will know it's from me. I want him to see it and know we're aware of what's happening."

Fate flared in my stomach. He approved of sending a message, but not of me leaving Tauren.

"How do we help them? I can't leave Tauren."

"We could bring him with us," Brecan said with a poor attempt at a smile.

Fate whispered to me... *You will save them.*

But how? I asked. *If you won't let me go to them, how can I possibly save them?*

Fate did not answer.

As the carriage lurched to a stop, Mira was the first to climb from the vehicle. The ocean glittered in the distance, sparkling like diamonds across a vast, undulating terrain.

"I thought it was only accessible by cliffs?" I asked, remembering the lesson I received during my initial journey to the palace.

Tauren strode toward me. "This is the Kingdom's port. The cliffs are that way." He pointed in the direction I'd been staring, toward Sector Eleven. "They want to film me with each invitee near the sea. Would you honor me by being the first?"

My lashes fluttered, along with the moth wings taking flight in my stomach. "Of course."

He offered his arm and I took it, noting the downward slant of Brecan's mouth and the way his eyes latched onto the place where my hand met Tauren's arm. As we walked toward the ocean, I was mesmerized by the undulating motion of it, the ebb and flow. A few ships were moored in the distant waters, bobbing with the tide. Rowboats had been dragged far up onto the shore and temporarily abandoned.

"It's beautiful."

"It definitely is," he said. But when I glanced at him, he was staring at me, not the sea.

With each step we took to the shore, the soil underfoot lost its vegetation and turned completely to sand. Warm grains sifted through my sandals. I stopped and removed them, happy to feel the warm sand between my toes. Tauren tugged his shoes and socks off and rolled the legs of his pants up, revealing the lower half of his muscled calves. He rolled his sleeves up to match, and when he offered his arm a second time, my fingers curled around his soft skin.

I wasn't sure if the cameras were rolling.

In truth, I didn't care.

Tauren led me through large puddles that he called tide pools. "There's a starfish!" I exclaimed, dragging him to go look at it. He threaded his fingers with mine and let me tug him from pool to pool to examine the treasures nestled inside. Some were empty, whereas others had shells as large as my head. An urchin, sharp and spiny, crept across one pool.

"Careful of those," Tauren warned.

The sun was bright and beautiful overhead, warming my shoulders as we walked toward the water. Frothy waves lapped at our feet and I was mesmerized by the sight. The water wasn't frigid, like I expected. Something so vast and deep… I didn't think it could ever be warmed. Tauren's fingers tightened around mine for a second. "You look like you belong here."

"The earth belongs to all of us. We're a part of it; not just bodies dwelling on it."

Farther down the shore, Estelle was gathering shells into a pile, chattering to Rose about grinding them for iridescent paint. Rose, ignoring the cheery words pouring from Estelle's mouth, glared at Tauren and me.

Mira was waist deep in the water, staring into the surface and whispering spells in an attempt to connect with Bay. When we made eye contact, she shook her head. Brecan's hair thrashed in the wind, but from the strained look on his face, he couldn't reach Wayra, either.

I stared at the sand for a moment, noticing a nautilus shell lying only a few feet away, half buried in wet, smoothed sand. I was about to discreetly point it out when Tauren pulled me close so that I faced him. "Sable –" he began.

In that moment, the sun suddenly disappeared and dark clouds rolled over the sky. "What is this?" I blinked at the intrusion, confused by the sudden change in weather.

Searching the shore for Brecan, I found him running toward us, gesturing wildly. The wind gusted fiercely, lashing my hair across my face in painful welts. "Go! Sable, get back!" Brecan yelled.

I faced the sea, only to find that it had reared back and was charging toward us.

Rose and Estelle, Mira and Brecan, Tauren and I… we would be crushed by the wave. There was no time to spirit everyone away. Mira thrust her hands out, but she needed help.

"Go!" I screamed to Tauren, whispering a spell that dragged him far away from the shore. He kicked and fought the entire way, but I had to keep him safe. His guards, who'd been standing back a discrete distance, surrounded him in a flash.

Brecan whispered a similar spell for Rose and Estelle, but unlike the Prince, they went willingly. Working with Mira, he directed his wind to hold back the sea; instead of stopping its tumultuous force, it built higher and higher, frothing and churning, anxious to consume everything in its path.

"Recede," I commanded.

The wave resisted. Something – or someone – was pushing it toward us.

Fate urged me toward the vertical wall of water, so I obeyed, taking careful steps toward it. Brecan growled as he poured more wind against the water. Mira's face was strained. "We can't keep this up, Sable. You need to go."

I couldn't run from danger. Not when Fate demanded I walk toward it.

"Sable, no!" Tauren screamed. Fighting against his guards, he somehow freed himself and raced toward me.

I thrust my hand into the ocean and all the water fell, crashing straight down instead of over our heads. Whatever force had been pushing it, suddenly let go. The force knocked me off my feet and soaked me from head to toe, but we were all alive. The Prince, the invitees, the camera crew, Mira, Brecan.

Brecan rushed to me. "Are you okay?"

Mira, visibly frightened, shook as she threw her arms around my neck.

Fate whispered one name… *Cyril.*

"Mira, send the gull to Thirteen. That was a message from my mother. Let's send Bay one in return."

"Are you sure? What if it upsets her?" she asked.

"Let her come for me." *I'll be ready for her.* I could feel Fate nearly purring at the thought. He would give me the strength I required. He would guide me and together, we would win.

Brecan and Mira stepped away as she called for a sea bird. One landed on her arm and she whispered to it, sending it wheeling toward Thirteen. The gull shrieked as it flew away from us, disappearing within seconds.

Tauren was livid. "You could've been killed!" he seethed.

"But I wasn't," I argued, turning my attention back to him.

"You shoved me away," he accused, his voice rising with each word.

"Of course I did!"

"Why would you do that?"

"I had to protect you."

"Why, Sable?" he angrily demanded.

"You're my prince," I offered weakly.

"*Why*, Sable?" he growled.

He was insufferable. He knew why.

"Why, Sable?" he repeated, softer this time.

I threw my hands in the air. "Because I couldn't live with myself if something happened to you!"

I couldn't. If he died, the weight of my soul would bring his back. But still, the thought didn't just sour my stomach. It ripped my heart to slivers.

The anger melted from his face and he pulled me into his chest and wrapped me in a hug. I held tightly to his back, fighting tears that threatened to spill.

Cyril could have killed us all.

"I love you, too," he whispered, sliding his hand over my hair. He took a shuddering breath. "I'm sorry I yelled. I was scared out of my mind. I couldn't live with myself if something happened to you, either."

"Look," Mira said from nearby. She bent at the waist and plucked something off the sand. "A nautilus shell."

"What is happening?" Rose demanded.

In the blink of an eye, the wind died and the ocean stopped roaring.

Everything went completely still.

Mira covered her gasp with her hands. "Bay," she whispered, dropping to her knees.

Brecan knelt beside her, his face full of despair. "Wayra, too."

"Are they dead?" I asked, dreading the answer but feeling the truth in my bones.

Fate stirred within me.

Mira sobbed, head in her hands, rocking back and forth in front of the still sea. The nautilus shell lay forgotten in front of her.

The camera crew caught the entire thing.

"We're returning to the palace. Everyone to the carriages!" Tauren shouted.

Brecan grabbed the shell Mira found and stuffed it in his pocket, then he and I helped her stand and walked with her to the carriage. I wrapped my arms around her and let her cry on my shoulder.

Tauren would have to explain what happened, as best he could, to Rose and Estelle.

"Are you sure they're gone?" I rasped when the carriage lurched forward and we rolled away from the dead sea.

"I'm sure. Remember how everything in the soil died with Ela? It's the same with Wayra and the wind, and Bay and the sea," Brecan explained.

Even without their confirmation, I felt the loss of them.

"At this point, it's safe to assume that Ethne is also gone. We can't wait any longer. We must return to Thirteen before she kills all the witches." Brecan's knuckles turned white as he clutched the nautilus shell, turning it around and around in his fingers.

The sun began to set as we raced through the countryside at a much faster pace than we'd set on our way toward the shore.

Mira's eyes glazed over as we passed into Sector Six. "The gull has crossed the border."

A tear fell from her eye. Her message to Bay arrived too late.

Within moments, she began to shriek, flailing around and patting herself down. Brecan took her face in his. "Mira. Look at me."

She snapped out of the daze she'd been in, panting until she could speak. "Fire. It… someone set the gull on fire," she choked out as the scent of singed hair flooded the carriage.

If fire still existed, then Ethne still drew breath. I hoped I was right.

Brecan sat down on the other side of Mira and the three of us discussed what to do. We had no idea how Cyril was holding the witches or how to break the spell she'd cast, but if we didn't figure it out soon, more witches would die.

But we couldn't waltz back into The Gallows without knowing what we were up against, either.

twenty-four

We led Mira to her room. Part of her crumbled when Bay passed, and I wasn't sure how to help ease her pain, other than to ensure Cyril hurt no one else.

After checking my room for any unusual mail and deeming it safe, Brecan promised to find me after he changed clothes. All three of us were salty, sandy, and still damp.

I heard his door close across the hall.

As soon as his door clicked, the scent of smoke immediately filled my nose. I followed it out of my room, down the hallway and outside. After a thorough examination, I was relieved to find the palace wasn't on fire, although I alerted the guards to make sure all the rooms were cleared. Word quickly spread, but the smoky scent's origin couldn't be traced.

I found myself standing in the Night Garden. In the distance, Brecan called my name. Before I could answer him, the Son of Night's billowing smoke appeared beside me. I raised my palms, ready to defend myself, and Arron's slitted eyes narrowed on mine.

"I take it you know about the Priest and Priestesses."

"Are you my mother's pawn?" I asked pointedly.

"I'm no one's pawn."

I narrowed my eyes at his answer. "Are you bound to her?"

"No," he asserted. Arron sat on the swing, backing up a few feet and then soaring forward as if he didn't have a care in the world. "But she believes I am."

"Why does she think that?"

He blinked slowly, tilting his head to the side as if to size me up. "Because I didn't correct her. I never, however, pledged myself to her. I'm always careful to avoid such unfortunate entanglements."

Enough semantics. "Why did you write to me? What did you want to discuss?"

"She wanted me to bring another message. She wants to meet with you, and she also wanted to warn you never to trust Fate. She did, and ended up being bound because of it. She says that you can trust her, though. She is your mother and wants you to come home."

Did Fate help the Priestesses and Priest bind my mother in the soil? Had he somehow weakened her from within? Or was she bound after she cast him out of her – or so she claimed?

"And if I can't return home?"

"Can't, or won't?" he asked curiously, abruptly stopping the swing and standing up, still clinging to the ropes.

"Take your pick."

He stepped toward me, flicked his midnight-blue hair out of his face, and shoved his hands in his pockets. "You must defy Fate or defy your mother. Either way, you will face consequences. The choice is yours."

"How is she holding the witches in the Center?"

"An ancient spell. One that can be broken only by another Fate witch..." he offered. *Which is why my mother wants me to visit so badly,* I surmised. *She wants to bind me so I can't break the spell.*

"Are you saying I can break it?"

"Easily." He looked into my eyes, unblinking. If he was lying, I couldn't tell. "With a brush of your hand, the spell would be extinguished."

"Can I kill her?" I boldly asked.

Arron pursed his lips. "I'm not entirely sure you could, unless you used dark magic. That's how she killed Bay, Ethne, and Wayra. But, if you choose not to go down that path, you may be able to bind her with your power."

I didn't want to bind her; I needed Cyril dead. I wouldn't unleash her on an unwitting generation once my power faded with my death unless it was the only way, and I could hold her in stasis until I figured out a way to end her for good.

"There's more to her message..." the Son of Night dangled, like a carrot.

"What else is there?"

"She plans to burn a witch every hour on the hour until you and your entourage return to Thirteen."

With his words, the smoky scent that hung in the air turned to ashes in my mouth.

"What you're smelling is the burning of the Priestesses and Priest right now. The stench will only become stronger, the smoke more invasive, as time passes. Ethne whispered some sort of protection spell before Cyril lit them on fire, so the flames haven't consumed their bodies yet, but I suggest you hurry."

There was no hope. I felt the wind die and saw the stillness of the sea.

The thought of the horrors they'd endured turned my stomach.

"Tell me how to sneak back into the Sector. I have to enter without her knowing."

"Spirit yourself in. I think she believes you'll arrive in a royal carriage. She's hoping for cameras and fanfare. Spoil her plans."

"You could be lying," I accused him.

He gave a half-smile. "I can show you, if you'd like."

I swallowed. "Show me what?"

"What's happening in the Center."

I wasn't sure I wanted to see it. Things might be as bad as I imagine them, or they might be worse.

"What *is* happening in the Center?" Brecan asked as he appeared behind me, Mira standing opposite him, flanking me.

Arron swiped his hand across the air, making dark clouds form. Within them, a murky scene emerged. Ethne, Bay, and Wayra were burning. Their arms were wrenched behind their backs and their chins drooped against their chests. More stakes were being erected surrounding the three to which they were tied.

"They're clearly dead – why keep the fire going?" Brecan fumed.

"At first I thought Cyril was preserving them to inflict fear, or to manipulate and deter those who might challenge her authority," Arron mused. "But, as I told Sable, Bay and Wayra were unable to fight back using their affinities once Cyril used fire and dark magic to nullify their gifts. However, she could not prevent Ethne from using hers, and Ethne whispered an incantation before the flame took hold of her. It was her last stand against Cyril."

Ethne's incantation was a final stand, all they could do before she killed them. I could almost imagine Ethne trying to keep the flames away from Bay and Wayra. Used to the flame, she would've been the last to die. But the horror of being alive but powerless to stop someone from harming the people you loved, and the horror of knowing you would die by your own affinity, was too much.

"Why are the witches huddled in the middle of the Center?" I asked.

"Cyril won't step near it. She hovers on the Circle's borders, afraid to get too close to the spot of soil that bound her for so long. She literally shudders at the sight of it."

"We could use that fear to our advantage," Mira suggested, iron resolve in her tone.

Brecan shifted his weight. "We need the element of surprise. If we try to stroll into Thirteen, we'll end up like the dove or the gull."

"I could get you in," Arron offered casually.

Brecan answered quickly and without hesitation. "No."

"Who are you to speak for the Daughter of Fate?" Arron inquired, as if he actually wanted to know. Brecan was my best friend in The Gallows, and here, he was more than an escort. He was the voice of reason.

"You don't know him any better than you do your mother, Sable," Brecan proposed sagely. "This could be a trap. We'll find another way in."

Could we find a *better* way, though?

As I called on Fate to help me choose, I closed my eyes. *Can I trust Arron, Son of Night?*

A warm feeling filled my belly.

"Fate says I can trust him," I confirmed. Brecan uttered a curse. "Fate wouldn't lead me into danger, Brecan. If he says Arron can be trusted, I believe him." That much I was certain of.

Mira's attention was fixed on the image still projecting in the smoke cloud behind Arron. Tears welled in her eyes. Without warning, she let loose a guttural cry and stomped out of the garden, straight to the lake far across the lawn.

We followed closely.

She kicked her shoes off and removed her pants and shirt. Wearing only her bra and underwear, she stepped onto the water's surface, chanting something I'd never heard before. She commanded the water, called it her own, and demanded that it obey.

And suddenly, it did.

It lifted her high into the evening sky and swirled around her, an inverse whirlpool encasing her body in a watery gown. It crowned her its own, and when she commanded, the water sat her gently down again. Arron grinned at my side, and then knelt and put his fist over his heart.

"Priestess of the House of Water," he said proudly.

Mira strode from the lake, robed in a glittery, watery gown.

"Brecan," I muttered. "The position for the Priest of the House of Air is open."

"I don't know how to claim it."

Mira's eyes snapped to him. "You have to *want* it. You must make the wind understand that it needs you. And it does, Brecan. Right now, it really does. Don't give it a choice to cast you aside and claim another. You are its choice. Its only choice."

Having claimed its new Priestess, the lake sprang to life. The water that had laid stagnant, coated with leaves and scum, cleared and became like a sheet of crystal glass. Frogs began to croak, and water spiders skidded across the calm surface. Even the vibrant backs of gliding goldfish were highlighted by the rising moon.

Brecan wanted to claim his place, but was unsure of his right. I saw it in the lines that formed around his mouth. So, I decided he needed a little push.

I called on the dark magic he hated so much, calling for storm clouds to race toward me, knowing they would drag the wind with them.

"Sable, stop," he gritted.

My lips trembled from the energy I was pulling. "Claim it."

My eyes closed, and I felt the earth beneath my feet shift. I sensed the life force of every tree around me, where the roots plunged into the deep, loamy earth. I recognized the energy of the lake, the cloak of the midnight sky, and every star that twinkled overhead. I filled the air with turbulent clouds and drew them toward the opposite ends of the magnet I'd become.

The turbulence from the clouds streaking across the sky created wind. It filled the valley and poured over the land like a whispering caress.

Brecan sighed when the wall of air hit him, and like Mira, something in him shifted.

"Remember what she did to Wayra," Mira demanded.

Brecan's lavender eyes filled with rage, desiring revenge and the power to make Cyril pay for what she did to his Priestess. He spread his arms wide and called the wind to him. It poured around and through him, a violent tunnel that knocked me flat on my back. I had to shield my eyes to see him, but what a sight he was.

Brecan's wind pulled the night clouds from Arron and took them swirling to the sky, and then gentled and soared in wisps as delicate as thin, spun sugar.

He took in the air, becoming it. And when he commanded it to calm, it listened.

Arron again knelt and held his fist over his chest. "Priest of the House of Air." He shifted his attention to me. "Guardian of the House of Fate."

"Why isn't she considered a Priestess?" Mira asked, almost outraged at the title he'd spoken on my behalf.

"The House of Fate belongs to Fate, and she is his daughter. She is charged with guarding it now that she is of age. And right now, she needs to be its defender and champion." Arron extended his hand and I clasped it. "I pledge myself to your service, Daughter of Fate,

Guardian of the House of Fate." He squeezed my hand tightly. "You told me to make a decision, and I have. I know now it is the right one."

He hadn't given my mother a vow, but offered it to me instead.

"Why are you pledging yourself to me? I thought you avoided such *unfortunate entanglements*."

"Because you are the only one worthy, as well as the only one who can save our kind from your mother."

Brecan stood behind him, and Mira beside Brecan. Something had changed in them. There was a spark in their eyes that wasn't there before; the magic that poured off them was visceral and potent.

"Tell us what you need, Sable. Name it, and it will be done," Arron promised.

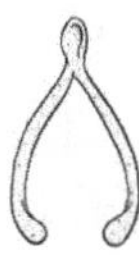

"Miss Sable?" a guard shouted across the Night Garden.

The urgency of his voice told me the guard needed me. I ran toward him, leaving my friends behind.

"Here!" I cried out.

A look of relief slid over his face when he caught sight of me. "The King needs you."

"Is he okay?" I asked as I reached him.

"Yes, Miss. He said he needed to speak with you about an urgent matter."

I followed the guard to the King's bedroom. Four other guards stood outside, ensuring the safety of their king.

Stepping into the room, I took him in. The effort of just walking to his study this morning had depleted his energy. He slumped in his bed, the pillows stuffed behind him unable to prop him up. "King Lucius," I greeted.

"You must go," he rasped. "Tauren told me that the witches are in trouble. You have to go to them and help them."

"Who will protect Tauren if I leave?"

"He agreed to double or triple his guard – whatever you think is best. Name it, and it will be done."

Those were the same words Arron had just spoken outside.

Fate straightened my shoulders. *It is almost time to defend my House.*

I blinked rapidly. "Quadruple his guard, but I'll send someone to watch over the palace. And Tauren."

The King blinked tiredly, weakly gripping the edge of his blanket. "Thank you. For all you've done."

My muscles went rigid, fingernails biting half-moons into my palms. I shook my head in frustration. "I haven't done enough. I wasn't able to find the ones who tried to hurt him."

The King offered a weak smile. "You did something far more important, Sable. You kept him safe, and you showed him true love in the process."

A knot formed in the back of my throat.

"I'll always watch over him."

This was it. I knew when I left the palace, I wouldn't return. Either Cyril would win, or I would take my rightful place among my people. But I couldn't stay here.

The King offered a sympathetic smile and reached for my hand. I placed it in his and he brought it to his lips, placing a kiss on the back of it. "I know you will.

Now, go. Save my people. Save *your* people." His grip tightened with each word.

I strode from the room and headed for mine. I shrugged on a pair of black-as-night pants, the white shirt and leather vest I'd worn during my archery lesson with Tauren, and filled my pockets with black salt.

Walking back to the Night Garden, I was shocked to see Tauren there.

"Where are Brecan, Mira, and Arron?" I asked, breaking the awkward silence.

"Were you going to leave without telling me?"

"I have to go."

His Adam's apple bobbed in his throat. "Brecan filled me in on what was happening in Thirteen. The smoke..."

"That's why I have to leave."

Fate was antsy. I could tell, because suddenly I couldn't stop fidgeting. He hadn't given me the order to leave yet; he'd said it was *almost* time. So why was he writhing beneath my skin?

"What's the matter?"

"Fate. He's uncomfortable."

"Do you trust him?" Tauren asked, watching me carefully.

"Implicitly."

"Arron said something about your mother warning you not to give yourself over to him. That he longed to remain corporeal, and that you would be trapped within, unable to resurface."

"My mother is burning my brothers and sisters. Forgive me for not trusting her advice."

He steeled his shoulders. "I want to come with you."

"No." He tilted his head and got that look like he might order me to do it anyway. "No, Tauren. I cannot keep you safe if she is near."

A throaty laugh came from behind me. "You're right about that much," a woman said, slipping out of the shadows.

I looked so much like her it was frightening. From my long, dark hair and straight nose, to the almond shape of my eyes. We even had the same build and height. But there was something deranged about her. Her appearance was harried, the glimmer in her dark eyes wild.

I put myself between her and Tauren.

Slowly, she stalked toward me. With each step, I backed Tauren away. He pulled his dagger from its sheath, ready to battle her with me. But this was a battle he shouldn't fight, and couldn't win.

It was mine. And Fate's.

Cyril never let me out of her sight, approaching carefully. Was she afraid of me?

"I want you to come home, Sable. We have much to discuss."

Fate roared inside me, gnashing to be released.

Cyril didn't look *at* me as much as she looked *through* me, as if she could see Fate himself. She didn't fear me. She feared him.

Brecan, Mira, and Arron appeared behind my mother. Cyril's eyes flashed with anger. She glanced from Tauren to me. "You will hear me out before choosing sides."

"I'll never let you harm him," I warned. *Tauren is mine.*

Fast as a viper, she spirited to Tauren and grabbed his wrist. Then she grabbed mine, and together, we vanished. I barely registered Brecan's anguished roar as we faded away.

I stood alone in the House of Fate.

Where was Tauren?

I turned in a tight circle. My heart thundered, pounding as I searched for him in every direction. Cyril had hung an enormous mirror in front of the purple couch. The dappled, aged glass stretched from floor to ceiling, casting a hazy reflection back to me. Fate urged for me to watch.

A scene emerged, a moment I lived but was too young to recall.

I hid behind Mother's skirts. Grandmother Ela's face was pinched tight as a fist. "Who is responsible for this?" Ela demanded, pointing to a circle of smoking, split trees behind the House of Earth.

I looked up into Mother's proud face. Mother smiled at me and smoothed her hand over my hair. "She was responsible."

"You are teaching her dark magic?" Ela blustered. Her hair was the color of a fawn's, tawny and thick. Grandmother was beautiful. Her beauty was natural, not sharp like Mother's or mine.

"I will teach her many things, Priestess. All of which she has a right to know."

"Fate bade you introduce her to the darkness?"

Cyril smiled. "Fate no longer controls me. I cast him out."

"You couldn't," Ela argued, but her voice wavered.

"I told you I would be stronger than he, stronger than you all one day," Cyril said sweetly, but there was something in her tone that made the hair on my arms raise. My belly started to burn. I clutched it with my hand.

A voice inside my head spoke gently. "Be still, little one."

Grandmother's eyes snapped to mine. She stared at me until her eyes went blank. "He lives in Sable," she whispered, her fingers raising until they covered her mouth.

"What?" Mother asked. Her brows kissed as she crouched down and looked into my eyes – the way Grandmother had.

"She is only a child, Cyril. How could you?"

"Have you been keeping secrets, Sable?" I cowered from the look Mother gave me. "I didn't send Fate to her, Priestess. I would never have wished such a future for her, but perhaps it is fortuitous."

"Fate will do nothing but twist her, as he's twisted you. The Circle will not allow that to happen. We must protect our home, our Houses, and the witches within them – from Fate, from you, and now from Sable."

"Do as you must, Priestess, but know that I will protect my daughter from you as well."

Mother called upon the sky. It turned dark, much darker than I had made it. The ground shook underfoot, vibrating the smooth pebbles beneath my pointed boots. I didn't understand all her words, but knew what she'd done. Her spell had created a divide between the Priest, Priestesses, and me. A magical circle was rooted around me, preventing their magic from being used to harm or influence me. I could feel the dark power radiating from it.

My grandmother looked horrified. "Recant the spell," she demanded.

"Never," Mother snapped. "I will protect her from you. I will protect her from this kingdom, and I will find a way to cast Fate out of her as well. I've found that I might need his favor again to achieve the goals I have in mind..."

The voice in my mind spoke up. "Do not fear her, little one. She cannot force me away."

Fate was speaking. Grandmother said he was inside me, and now I could hear his voice. I felt the knot of him in my stomach.

"Cyril, if you continue down this path, you will be banished. Both of you."

Mother threw a laugh over her shoulder as she took my tiny hand in hers and began to lead me back to the House of Fate. "And which among you is strong enough to cast us out?"

My mother was the one who drove the wedge between my grandmother and me. Grandmother feared Fate, and Cyril driving him out only sent him looking for a new witch to inhabit. For some unknown reason, he chose me.

She lived in terror of me because of his influence, combined with that of my mother's. She knew that even though she bound her own daughter, she would never be able to bind me.

And now Tauren was at the mercy of my mother, a woman who didn't know the meaning of the word.

Fate clawed at my insides. "Where is he?" I begged him. "Tell me where Tauren is."

Focusing, I heard voices. Many distressed, quiet voices. I walked to the front door and threw it open, my eyes landing on the witches gathered in the Center. They huddled together away from their priest and priestesses, who still burned. I looked for his tall figure, but couldn't see him among the crowd.

"Tauren!" I called out, searching for him among the hundreds of familiar faces. When the witches saw me, they began to shout, begging for help.

I would help them, but first I had to find Tauren. She hadn't killed him yet, or else I wouldn't be here.

My stomach sank the moment I found him.

He was bound and gagged, a noose cinched tightly around his neck, standing on the trap door of the gallows.

Cyril suddenly appeared in front of me, stopping me on my way to him. I sucked in a startled breath. My heart began to thunder. I wasn't afraid of her, but I was terrified she would hurt Tauren. For a long moment she stared at me in silence, taking me in from hair to pointed heel. And if I wasn't mistaken, she found me lacking. The feeling was mutual. She was beautiful at first glance, but at second, I could see the hatred she harbored, clinging to her like a parasite.

I looked back to Tauren, hoping I was strong enough to save him, and that if I couldn't, the spell I'd used to bind us would save his life and Brecan and Mira would arrive in time to spirit him away and hide him from my mother. That somehow the two of them could bind her, in water or in the sky, so she couldn't hurt anyone else.

The trapped witches' cries grew louder.

Cyril threw a glance their way. "Do not pity them, Sable. They are what is wrong with The Gallows. The Houses are divisive. The Priestesses and Priest clamored for power they didn't deserve."

"And you deserve it?" I asked, raising my brow.

She stabbed a pointed nail in the direction of a clump of disturbed soil in the Center. "I spent seventeen long years being trodden upon. I deserve every ounce of power that's due me, and I will make sure nothing like that happens to me again. I know how you've been treated, Sable. Like a castoff. Like nothing. How can you even stand to look in their direction? They mean nothing to you, because you meant nothing to them."

"*You* are the reason they treated me as they did. You turned my own grandmother against me."

"I protected you!" she roared, taking a threatening step forward.

I matched her step. "I didn't need you to protect me from them. The only one I've ever needed protection from is you. *You* are the only one who has ever managed to hurt me."

She shook her head. "The only reason you weren't bound with me was because of my protection spell, but even it didn't cast Fate away from you as I'd hoped."

"For that, I'm grateful," I snapped.

She bared her teeth. "Fate hurts you every day, just by inhabiting you. He poisons your thoughts, makes you do things you otherwise wouldn't, makes it hard to look at yourself in the mirror. He hurts you just by existing inside you. If he loved you, he would leave you alone. He would respect *your* wishes. He would honor *your* choices."

Fate had never treated me like I didn't matter. He came to me. He protected me. And he wanted to protect me now.

A frustrated, heavy tear fell from my eye. "And if *you* loved me, you wouldn't be doing this to those I love."

Before she could respond, I spirited myself to the Circle and reached out to touch the barrier – to shatter it as I had the mirror she'd sent. Arron said that only a Fate witch could break her spell. I didn't care how I'd been treated in the past or how divisive the Houses were, my mother was wrong.

Something lashed around my neck and tightened, jerking me quickly away and abruptly cutting off my air supply. Cyril held the other end of the whip.

"I, too, was Fate's daughter. Don't try that again, or I'll hang you myself – on the gallows that *I* built."

I tried to speak and couldn't. My vocal chords wouldn't allow even a squeak.

Mother let go of the whip's handle and I collapsed to the ground, my fingers digging into the parched grass. I unwound the whip's sharp leather from my flesh, gasping for breath.

Mira and Brecan appeared near the Center. A fierce wind blew across the pentagram, but even the gusts couldn't extinguish the flames attempting to consume Ethne, Bay, and Wayra. Cyril started toward them.

I called on Fate, rising to my feet again. As I did, Cyril felt the shift.

"Don't," Cyril snapped, shoving me so hard I landed on my back.

It was strange seeing her hovering above me, because it was like looking in a mirror. She hadn't aged during her internment beneath the soil, and now that I was of age, we looked like sisters, almost like twins. She grabbed my arms and shook me. Hard.

"Don't unleash him. You will regret it."

"I'd never regret ridding the world of you," I spat.

She stiffened, her mouth gaping as if she'd been slapped. "I thought you would at least listen to reason."

"If you were reasonable, I might have."

Her expression closed off. "You have a choice," she said coldly. "Save the witches, or save your prince." Cyril glanced over her shoulder, her eyes narrowing at Tauren.

"If you hurt him..." I warned.

Tauren thrashed, trying to break free of his bindings, but they were likely spelled, and even if they weren't, it was nearly impossible to do.

Brecan spirited himself across the lawn to stand in front of the gallows and our prince. He nodded once to me, then called on his wind to push upward against the trap doors beneath Tauren, while Arron appeared beside him, loosening his noose.

Cyril was livid. Her plans were slowly unraveling, and she did the only thing she could. She called upon the darkness. Murky shadows slid over the earth, cooling the grass beneath me and spreading frost across the dried blades of grass. My bones rattled within my skin from the power of their mist. Black fire burst from the ground, quickly spreading, outlining the pentagram and slicing through the worn trails. The witches enclosed within the Center screamed, huddling together in groups to keep away from the dark flames slicing between them.

If only I'd reached a little farther, and had broken Cyril's holding spell.

Once Arron freed him, Tauren jerked the gag from his mouth. "Sable, get away from her!" Tauren yelled. He stalked forward, his golden eyes aimed at Cyril. "My father doesn't believe in putting criminals to death, but

I am not as good a man as he," Tauren warned. "You will die for the terror you've inflicted."

My mother smiled maliciously. "Will I?"

Everything that followed seemed to happen in slow motion.

Cyril spirited to Tauren before I could reach him. Arron was suddenly behind my prince, clamping a hand on his shoulder and preparing to flee.

I appeared behind my mother a second too late.

She screeched as she dragged a dagger from within the folds of her dress and stabbed at Tauren's middle. The resulting tumult was concealed by the dark shimmers of clouds left in Arron's wake. Tauren's roar of pain was swallowed up as the two disappeared.

A sudden, blinding pain made me buckle. The bottom of my shirt was soaked crimson as the coppery scent of blood filled the air. I pressed a hand to my flesh, but it didn't ease the pain or stanch the bleeding. I sucked in a sharp breath.

"Sable!" Brecan screamed from somewhere off to the right. He sounded far away. Everything did. Sounds were muffled. I blinked heavily, wanting nothing more than to tell Tauren I loved him before my life restored his.

I called upon Fate to help me, feeling his comforting darkness unfurl inside. His legs steeled mine. He stretched my fingers and then curled them into tight fists. His eyes saw through mine. My stomach stopped hurting and I floated somewhere inside myself, letting Fate consume me from within.

We started toward her.

Cyril.

The one who betrays.
The one who destroys.
The one who covets.
The one who kills.

Fate's thoughts jumbled with mine. They slid over and around until I couldn't tell whether they came from him or me.

Cyril was not concerned for me, but she was shaken, obviously struggling to make sense of what she was seeing. "I stabbed *him*, not you!"

"She bound her soul to his," Brecan spat, approaching her from the other side, herding her closer to us.

"Sable, come back while you still can," Cyril warned, reaching out to me while maintaining her distance. "You need help. Your body is dying."

Fate chuckled darkly. His voice overshadowed mine, then I couldn't hear mine at all. All that remained was his warning.

"No," Cyril growled. She knew she couldn't stand against Fate because she knew intimately how powerful he was. She'd had it inside her but foolishly cast him away; she regretted it every moment since. She pretended it was what she'd wanted all along, right up until the moment she tried to kill me to get it back.

She called on the dark magic she knew so well, the atmosphere trembling with magic so terrible, so powerful, even the earth itself vibrated underfoot. She lashed out with a powerful blow. The writhing darkness should've knocked me off my feet, but with Fate steeling me, it was no more than an annoying flick. Fear flashed through her eyes a split second before she lashed out again.

"Sable, he will not leave you if you don't come back right now. Trust me, daughter."

The one who lies.

Fate marched me toward her. He thrust his hand out and oozing darkness poured from his palm, knitting an otherworldly length of rope. The strand glittered as he used my hands to knot the end with practiced ease. It was almost as if he'd somehow stolen the dark umbilical cord of the universe itself and hidden it away until this precise moment, like it was the cord's fate to protect me, to protect us all.

The rope ached and rejoiced in its freedom, encircling her neck and reeling her in until my steely fingers gripped her jaw. She thrashed and fought to free herself, panting and cursing and attempting every spell she could think of as she clawed at my arms. She tried to call forth more dark magic, but Fate would not allow it.

Fate roared in her face and then, as if she weighed no more than an acorn, he threw Cyril toward the Center. The witches trapped inside jumped to avoid her and Cyril landed in the middle, sprawled on the heap of earth from which she'd recently clawed her way out. The instant she realized she was coated in the soil, she jumped up, screaming and rubbing her skin where it lay as crumbling dust. Bits of earth flew from her skin as she hurried to rid herself of it.

Her eyes glittering with malice and rage, Cyril lodged a burst of darkness toward me. It shattered against my chest, but didn't break me. Fate again sent out his dark, viscous tendril. It coiled around her like a twister, tightening like a serpent who delighted in squeezing its prey until its bones snapped and it went slack.

Cyril grunted as her magic escaped her.

Fate used my body to march toward the Center, breaking through the magical barrier Cyril had erected. His presence alone extinguished the black fire, breaking the spell and setting the witches free. They spilled onto the lawns in mystified disarray. Some panicked, running into their Houses for cover. Others hovered, unsure what to do or how to help. Brecan and Mira shouted to them, but I couldn't hear what they said. I could only feel Fate.

In this moment, he embodied the feeling he gave me when I stalked someone he wanted dead.

It was terrifying. It was wonderful.

Cyril saw his intention to kill her.

Her body deflated before she regrouped. Her eyes darted from side to side. She was going to make a run for it.

"Keep her in the Center!" I managed to fight past Fate to scream to Brecan.

He cast wind around the circle that spun faster and faster around us until everything beyond it was a blur.

"Sable. Take back control of your body," he gritted. "I can't keep this up forever." His wind began to weaken, the tight funnel loosening like the strings of a corset.

Tauren fought his way through the fleeing witches and fell through the weakening wall of wind, calling my name, unaware of the tiger in his midst. Cyril grabbed Tauren, using him as a shield. His defiant golden eyes met mine as he screamed for me to run.

Deep within, I struggled with Fate, trying to thrust him out. He wanted revenge. He wanted Cyril to suffer. But his ire, his uncontrolled anger, blinded him to

Tauren's presence. And I would protect him, even from Fate.

"You promised," I reminded him. "Let me do this. I trusted you; now you must trust me! I have to save him. I love him."

Tauren needed me. I took in the small blood stain on his shirt, then looked at the crimson dripping from the white fabric of my own. "Please," I begged again.

Fate paused, then slowly receded, tucking himself somewhere deep within me.

Cyril laughed. "You actually did it."

The wound on my stomach pulsed. My legs faltered as I clung to Fate's rope, whispering an incantation he fed me. As my lifeblood dribbled from me, in penance, her magic would bleed away from her. When Tauren and I locked eyes, I flicked mine to the side and he dipped his head in understanding. When I threw the rope, he dove sideways and the loop of Fate's rope fell over Cyril's neck. "Let's see how *you* like it, Mother." I jerked the cord. Hard. She lost her footing, clawing at the strand that I'd transformed into a slick, black serpent.

She croaked a spell, desperation lacing her voice as she repeated the incantation again and again to no avail. Her magic was nearly depleted, as was the strength in my legs.

As I dragged her into the Center to one of the empty stakes, Brecan appeared next to me, his wind dying down. The snake coiled around Cyril, wrapping around her quicker than she could move.

Cyril's eyes snapped to Arron, who sauntered over as if he had nothing better to do. "You betrayed me," she accused.

"I was never bound to you," he informed her nonchalantly. "I am bound only to the Daughter of Fate."

"I should have killed your father when I had the chance," she grunted to Tauren as the serpent coiled tighter around her, squeezing the air from her lungs. Her eyes bulged from the snake's insistent pressure. Her face mottled and contorted grotesquely.

I stumbled forward, falling to my knees. With a flick of my fingertips I conjured fire, reaching out and lighting the wood piled at her feet.

twenty-five

I could hear my name being shouted as the light began to fade.

It was on Tauren's tongue, on Brecan's lips. I could feel Mira's hand clutch mine, and taste the brine of Fate's sorrow from within. But all those sensations drifted into nothingness as I slipped into a pale gray void somewhere between this world – this life – and the next.

In death, time was meaningless. Only life gave it shape. I realized this fact within the span of a few moments as I died, and as Fate tugged me from Death's cold clutches, gifting me a second chance and breathing life back into my lungs. He squeezed my heart until the rhythm suited him, and then bade me open my eyes once more.

I woke feeling numb, only to find that I wasn't the *only* one who had danced with Death and returned to the living.

The instant Cyril died, the flames surrounding Ethne, Bay, and Wayra winked out. When Mira began to cry, the sky cried with her. Torrents of rain soaked the earth and everything on it. The droplets hissed as they evaporated off the charred wood beneath Cyril's victims. Tauren gathered me in his arms. "You're okay," he breathed.

"So are you." I couldn't have been more thankful.

"I was so scared," he admitted.

"I was terrified for you, too." *Terrified* was too soft a word for what I felt when my mother whisked him from the Night Garden, or the events that unfolded afterward.

Dry coughing startled everyone… because it came from Ethne. Mira rushed to her. "Oh, my goddess. You're alive."

She untied the Priestess and helped her out of the pile of charred logs stacked around the base of the stake. Ethne blinked, took in Bay and Wayra's still forms, and let out a shrill, keening sound I never wanted to hear again.

She fell to her knees with heaving sobs. "I thought I could protect them!" she cried, her hands trembling violently. Mira knelt at her side, offering what comfort she could. Ethne's sorrow and rage were difficult to endure, but the Priestess gathered her wits and calmed herself to the best of her ability. Moments later, she stood with Mira's help and the two of them assisted Brecan as he took Bay's body down. Brecan hefted the Priest's weight as the ladies unbound him.

Brecan lay Bay on the earth for a moment while he helped free Wayra, and then he carried her to his House. All the lingering Wind witches trailed behind their new Priest, mourning the loss of their former Priestess.

Mira made her way to Bay. Water flowed over her palms, forming an aquatic stretcher, and she carried him to her House.

Ethne stood in the pouring rain, staring at Cyril's charred body. "You did it," she whispered.

I swallowed thickly. Tauren grasped my hand and squeezed.

"You saved us," she said.

"I'm sorry I was too late to save Bay and Wayra," I rasped.

The flame in Ethne's eyes had nearly been put out, but within their depths, it flickered. Her once vibrant, red robes were charred and stiff, but even they had survived. "Their deaths were not your doing. You shouldn't blame yourself for someone else's acts, Sable." It was the first time Ethne had ever used my name, and the kindest words she'd spoken to me.

The Fire Priestess looked at Cyril again, raised her hand, and incinerated my mother's body. It burned white-hot and was consumed within seconds. The second she was gone, I could breathe easier.

The Center's pentagram paths were scorched, and the lawn was a mess of mud and clumps of thick grass.

"I think I'll go home and rest, if you don't mind," Ethne finally said, exhaustion filling her voice.

She stiffly walked toward the House of Fire, her witches surrounding her with love and flame as they guided her inside. She met my eye before entering the door and inclined her head respectfully. I nodded back in silent understanding.

Tauren was still holding my hand. "Thirteen suffered great losses, but much more was saved, thanks to you."

"When Cyril made me choose – you or them – I chose you, Tauren. I'm not sure how the witches will feel about my divided loyalty once the shock of everything that happened wears off."

Tauren and I slept in the House of Fate in the room I claimed before he sent the invitation, wrapped in each other's arms, both too afraid to let go. But dawn broke and with it, the responsibilities of the world returned and settled on our shoulders again.

Standing awkwardly on the steps of my House, we joined hands. Tauren's golden eyes searched mine the same way they had when I first read his fate.

"I have to go to him. He's probably worried sick, and that's the last thing he needs," he softly explained.

"I know. I'll take you to him."

"You won't stay?" he asked, clasping my hands a little tighter.

I shook my head. "I can't. There's so much to do now that they're gone. The important thing is that you're safe, and that's all that matters. The witches my mother used to strike at you will be swiftly dealt with."

"How will you find them?"

Fate conjured an image in my mind. He had inscribed his sigil in their foreheads. They would be easy to identify now. I silently thanked him – again.

"Fate marked them. I will find them and see that they pay for their attempts on your life."

He bent down and placed a lingering kiss at the corner of my mouth, then I closed my eyes and spirited him to the palace. In a blink we were standing outside his father's bedroom, our sudden appearance startling the guards from their posts.

At the sound of the commotion, the King's chamber door opened and Annalina rushed to her son, hugging him tight and crying into his neck. Her tears made my throat feel tight.

Tauren did his best to comfort his mother. He promised to tell her everything and assured her that Thirteen was safe – thanks to me. She dragged him into the room where the King waited, propped up on his pile of pillows. I met his eye and gave a small wave, which he returned. But I didn't step foot inside.

When Tauren turned to wave me in, I gave him a small smile and hooked my thumb over my shoulder. "I'm needed in The Gallows."

"Now?" he asked, sadness arcing through his eyes. "I thought you might stay for a few hours, at least."

"Now." I nodded, affirming the most difficult lie I'd ever spoken. While no one had called for me to return, my friends needed me. Tomorrow would be a day of mourning. The day after would be the first of many we would spend attempting to restore what had been destroyed. Though it was a noble enough excuse, it wasn't the only reason I needed to leave his side. I couldn't stay there a second longer or I knew I would never leave.

Tauren needed the following days with his father, for they would be his last.

"I wish you well, my prince," I whispered, disappearing from the palace.

His glittering golden eyes and the look of longing mixed with disappointment marring his beautiful features burned into my mind.

I landed back on my cold, rain-soaked steps and opened the door to the House of Fate, wondering if I'd just made the biggest mistake of my life and feeling sure I had by the time I reached my bedroom.

I changed out of my sodden dress with trembling hands and laid down. When the tension finally flooded from my muscles, I let myself cry.

Lightning lit the room in fiery bursts as booming thunder cracked across the sky.

twenty-six

I didn't sleep.

I watched the night fade away as dawn stretched pink fingers across the sky. A knock at the front door dragged me out of my bed, and I found Brecan waiting on the landing. I squinted against the early morning sunlight and waved him inside.

"Are you okay?" he asked tenderly.

I nodded, afraid that if I spoke, my voice would crack.

"She was your mother…" he started.

"I do not mourn her, Brecan. She was no mother to me."

I mourned Bay and Wayra. I even mourned Ela. I mourned for the witches who would have nightmares of Cyril – who my dark looks unfortunately favored – for years to come. But most of all, I mourned the loss o Tauren. Nothing would ever fill the hole of his absence in my life.

Fate attempted to comfort me, but I wouldn't allow it.

"Tomorrow, a new Priestess of the House of Earth will be anointed."

"Who will it be?"

"A few have indicated their interest. One seems to be more powerful than the rest, though."

I nodded and looked out the back door. Not a single living leaf hung from the branches of the deciduous trees. They'd all turned brown and brittle, curling in on themselves. Even the evergreens had dried from the root up, their deep green color nowhere to be seen. The earth needed to be revived. A new Priestess could bring life to what was now dead.

"Did you take Tauren home?" he asked, looking out over the Center, studiously ignoring my face.

"Yes."

"Is he expecting you back soon?"

I swallowed. "No."

He closed his eyes for a long beat. "I will urge the Circle to ignore the mandate placed on you before you left."

Hand-fasting. I hadn't thought of their forced decree since I returned. Decrees, typically, were sealed with magic. If Brecan didn't succeed in persuading them, I would have to honor my word.

A tear fell from my eye. He saw it before I swiped it away. "I know it was hard for you to leave him there."

It was the hardest thing I'd ever done.

"I just hope you know that things will be different for you here in Thirteen from now on. Mira and I, and even Ethne, will not tolerate anyone showing you disrespect. Not after all you've done."

"I didn't do anything, Brecan."

"The hell you haven't!" he whispered angrily. "I *know* what you did, what you sacrificed for us, and I'll make sure that you're not only respected, but treated like the Guardian of the House of Fate."

"Thank you," I told him. What more was there to say? "I want to help," I said, taking a deep breath and straightening my back. "I want to help set this mess right."

"Come with me," he urged, clasping my hand and pulling me toward the door. "There's something you need to see."

He threw open my front door and tugged me onto the landing, where I gasped at the sight of every witch in the Gallows staring back at me. "What is this?" I whispered, inching backward.

Brecan was the first to bow, then everyone did. Ethne, Mira, and every witch from every House. "Thank you for saving us, Sable," Ethne's voice rang out over the crowd as she straightened.

Tears clogged my throat.

I didn't do enough. I hadn't saved Bay or Wayra. I was too late to help them.

My fingers trembled as the assembled witches bowed again and then meandered back to their chores.

Brecan hugged me from the side. "You are *revered*."

A strange laugh bubbled out of me. I didn't deserve it, but for the first time in my life, it felt good not to be looked upon as a pariah.

That evening I washed my hair, scrubbed the soil from my cuticles, and donned the best dress I had left. Arron waited patiently downstairs near the door, peeking out the window across the lawn. "I'm not sure I'll be welcome," he said with a wince.

"You are a member of the House of Fate, and we have been invited to mourn. You are as welcome as I, Arron."

He inclined his head, but I could see he thought we might be in for a fight.

As the stars began to wink, the two of us walked across the lawn side by side, our strides falling in sync. Brecan waited on the landing, greeting each witch as they entered his home. Each wore the colors indicative of their Houses, a kaleidoscope of red, blues, and green. Arron and I added black to the hues.

Brecan had cleaned up, too. He donned new, pale blue robes that somehow made his lavender eyes brighter. I was absolutely certain Mira had helped with those.

Two Fire witches climbed the steps, pausing to greet Brecan. They bowed to him, expressed their condolences, and entered the House of Air on silent slippers.

Brecan took a deep breath and let it out when he saw me. "I'm glad you came." When I tried to bow like the other witches, he wouldn't allow it and instead pulled me in for a hug. "Thank you, Sable."

I squeezed him tight and stepped away. Brecan accepted Arron's brief bow and waved us inside.

Every wall was painted sky blue, and on every ceiling was painted a different type of cloud. It was light and airy, just the way the witches of the Wind would want it. The furniture was painted white, accented with silver candlesticks and pale tapers. Even the soft-spun drapes looked like airy extensions of the sky.

In a large, open room where rows of witches lined the walls, Wayra's body hovered in the air beneath a constant torrent of wind that held her upright and still, as if there was a slab of marble beneath her. Her long, white hair stretched to the creaking floor boards. Once all had mourned her, she would be offered to the sky. Brecan would float her up until she vanished from sight, and the goddess would receive her body.

Wayra wasn't as young as most of the witches in The Gallows, but you'd never know that by looking at her. She didn't have a single wrinkle. Her skin was as flawless in death as it was in life.

Arron and I paused in front of her for a long moment and then moved further into the House to allow others to pay their respects, before exiting out the back and making our way to the House of Water.

Mira's dark blue robes swirled around her like a whirlpool, wrapping around her legs. A tear fell from her eye when she saw us in Bay's line. She took a moment to usher in three Earth witches and then threw her arms around me. I cried into her soft hair.

"I'm sorry," I sobbed.

Her body shook with the sorrow that tore through her.

Arron waited on the step, giving us a moment to grieve together. When we parted, I pulled him up onto the landing to stand beside me. "You remember Arron," I said politely, desperately trying to regain my composure.

"I do. Thank you for helping us. At first, I wasn't sure we could trust you," Mira said honestly.

His cheeks turned scarlet and he stared at his feet. "It was nothing."

"Do you know where the witches who helped your mother are hiding?" she asked.

I gave a nod. "In the Wilds."

"I want to hunt them with you." A calculating chill took over her demeanor. Mira wanted them to pay. In addition to the witches, they killed the animals she'd brought to life and sent to Thirteen.

"I plan to leave at midnight."

She grinned wickedly. "Count me in."

Arron's silver, slitted eyes narrowed at her. "You hunt?"

"I do now," she sassed with a quirked brow that dared him to question her again.

With our plans settled, we turned our attention back to the somber processional. Inside the House of Water, everything was painted in varying shades of blue and teal. Some faded from pale to dark, reminding me of the graduated pool in the palace.

Bay rested on a column of water rising from an indoor fountain. The tips of his wavy gray hair were tugged along with the current. We stood in front of him for a moment and stepped away to allow others to pay their respects.

Ethne waited in the hallway, standing straighter when Arron and I approached. "May I speak to you for a moment?" she asked quietly. "Alone."

Arron told me he would be nearby but stepped away, making small talk as he walked further into the House with a small boy. The child showed Arron a small twister that he swirled between his palms and Arron pretended to be most impressed.

I turned my attention back to Ethne. She swallowed thickly. "I felt you should know that Bay was your father. He was hand-fasted to Cyril in the months you were conceived. He wanted to tell you, but Ela forbid it and I seconded her. Even Wayra believed it unwise."

The revelation knocked the breath out of me.

It was why he was kind. Why he tried to empathize with me. Why he supported me in accepting the invitation and sent Mira to help me.

My eyes began to water. "Thank you for telling me."

She inclined her head, her fiery hair falling over her shoulders. "I am so sorry, Sable, for how I treated you. We thought Cyril had twisted you. We were afraid of you, but that doesn't excuse how we treated you. If I could take it all back, I would."

"Thank you," I whispered despite the knot in my throat.

I stared at Bay again as Ethne took her leave, patting my arm as she passed me by. Bay – *my father* –loved me. He was bound by a duty I didn't fully appreciate or understand, but he did what he could for me when he was able.

And now he was gone.

A tear fell from my eye. Standing in the middle of the House of Water, I cried for Bay, for all he did for me, for his sacrifice, and for all the wonderful moments life would offer that he wouldn't see come to fruition.

Arron came to stand at my side, silent but present. I appreciated it more than he knew.

Soon, Mira would take Bay's body to the lake, situated in the wood far beyond the Center. She would place him in the water, where the Goddess would absorb him. Then, she would come find me. Together, we would hunt down the witches who tried to kill Tauren.

Who sided with my mother.

The witches who deserved to die.

Using a concealing spell, Fate led me into the Wilds, where the undergrowth was thick and thorny for many miles before the forest thinned in a quaint valley. A brook babbled nearby. The witches had warded the area. Charms made of bent, woven wood swung in the breeze.

If it weren't for the spell I'd conjured, the charms would have alerted them to our presence. We passed charm after charm, and as the trees became scarce, the charms thickened. Three hung from the branches of larger pines. We were close.

Fate gave me a vision of his sigil, a mark that darkened the closer we came to our targets. We found the male witch sleeping in a dilapidated cabin. The only part of the roof not covered in a thick carpet of moss had caved in. He never saw us coming.

Mira kicked the door open. The witch threw his blankets off and siced his pet on us. The large canine had been dead a very long time, from the looks of the rotten bits of flesh and fur dangling from his underbelly. I ordered the dog to sit and he obeyed.

Arron appeared in front of the witch. "Is that any way to welcome guests?" he teased.

The witch flung spell after spell, but Fate's sigil pulsed on his head. I used my hands to bat the desperate attempts away like pests until finally, the witch relented. He begged me not to take the life of his lover, which enraged me.

"You tried to kill the man I love and you're asking me to spare your lover? I don't think so."

Rope in hand, I started toward him, but Mira reached him first.

Mira, thick tears clinging to her eyes, let out a roar and drowned him with a torrent of water so strong, it plastered him to the wall, holding him in place until his lungs filled with fluid. Once she was sure he was dead, she let him fall bonelessly to the ground. Arron strode toward the body, his heavy boots bowing the floorboards. Clouds poured from his hands, swallowing the male witch whole. When they dissipated, the witch's body was gone.

"Where is the female?" Mira asked, glancing around the filthy space with wild eyes.

"Farther… she is near the sea," I answered. Grabbing each of their hands, I spirited us to his accomplice. She wasn't just *near* the sea, she was in it; standing knee deep, looking out at the incoming tide. The waves rose and crashed into her legs with a ferocity that heralded Mira's rising anger.

When the woman sensed us, she turned, Fate's mark emblazoned on her forehead. "You found him, didn't you? We knew you'd come for us eventually. Since Cyril's death, we've been almost powerless. We can't even spirit ourselves away from harm." She sniffed, wiping her tears away.

"Your lover is dead," Mira informed her coldly, watching as the witch deflated. "Just as you will be."

The witch's smile wobbled. Her auburn hair thrashed in the wind. Moonlight turned the tears in her eyes to glitter as she gritted out, "Then I shall be reunited with him and the goddess on this night."

The girl didn't fight back. She didn't whisper a single spell. She steeled her spine and faced us as Mira strode toward her on steps fueled by purpose, never sinking into the sea. The girl turned around just in time to see Mira grab her hair. She dragged the girl far beyond the line of breakers and disappeared beneath the surface with her.

When the girl had drowned, Mira dragged her body back to the shore for Arron to dispose of.

"They deserved it," he said with finality as the doomed witch's body disappeared.

I didn't feel bad about claiming them. Fate may not have ordered it, but he guided us to them.

"Were they the only two helping Cyril?" Mira asked, waiting as I felt for Fate's answer. He'd been strangely quiet since Cyril's death. I could still feel him, but things between us were different.

He confirmed my suspicion with a warm flutter. "Yes. There was only the two of them."

I was grateful there weren't more. Given the size of the House of Fate, there must have been many more, but most chose not to remain loyal to my mother. Most were wise enough to cut ties with her and move on with their lives.

And now, we had to do the same. We had to move forward, one minute, one day, and one choice at a time…

"So, who is Night, and does he speak to you?" Mira asked Arron as we walked away from the shore.

He nodded towards me. "Yes, but not in the same way Fate speaks to Sable. Night – darkness – is a vital part of nature. That said, Night is a separate natural affinity – not like Fate, who is very much alive."

Grasping their hands yet again, together we spirited to the Center where Mira lingered. It was obvious that she wanted to talk to me…alone. Luckily, Arron was very good at taking hints. He hooked a thumb over his shoulder and pointed back to our House. "I, uh, have… There are things I should do."

Mira giggled. "Then by all means, go and do them."

He strode to our House and disappeared behind the door.

"He has the biggest crush on you," I told her when we were alone.

"He does not."

"Yes, he does. Since you told the water who was boss, he hasn't stopped staring at you."

Mira smiled, but the smile soon fell away. "Sable," she began, "the moon is almost full."

I looked to the dark sky above and wished I had the power to drag the shadow back again, to hold it in place so the moon would never be full. I wished Fate would ask me to heal the King, ensuring that Tauren's heart wouldn't break from the sight of his father drawing his last breath. That he wouldn't have to hear his mother's cries.

"You should go to him."

"I left him."

"If anyone could understand, he would, Sable. He understands duty and responsibility better than anyone." She squeezed my arm. "Thank you for letting me tag along tonight."

I appreciated her help, but was sad it came to this. To death. But with death would come rebirth. That was the cycle of life.

"You might be interested to know," Mira started, "that Tauren sent Rose and Estelle home. He was very nice about it, but told them neither one was his match."

My heart leapt, trying vainly to escape via my throat. I couldn't speak, couldn't find the words to tell her how glad I was to hear this news. I thought he might just choose one at random and hope for the best, just so his father could attend his wedding. Truthfully, I liked Estelle, and I knew she liked Tauren, too. But *like* wasn't *love*, and that was what Tauren deserved more than anything.

"I still say you should go to him. Arron can stay in your House, and I'll watch over him and it while you're gone," she offered. "Think about it."

I nodded.

Mira waited until I looked at her. "Promise me you'll think about it."

Sighing, I replied, "I promise."

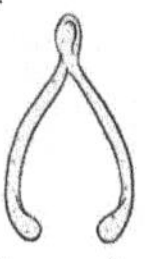

The next morning when I woke, the din of conversation grew in the Center as witches from every House gathered. I woke Arron and we went out to join them. An Air witch excitedly informed us that the new Earth Priestess was about to be introduced.

As soon as she said it, Ethne, Brecan, and Mira emerged from the wood with a fourth witch. Ivy, from the House of Earth, had been anointed as the new Priestess. She was lovely, with hair and freckles the same dark, earthy shade of pine bark. Her kind, evergreen eyes fell on everyone who came out to applaud her, including Arron and me.

I felt the pull of her power from where I stood. Tender grass shoots flourished beneath her feet as every step she took brought life. Every tree she touched regained its color, and while leaves wouldn't come until spring, she promised they would return. That all would be as it once was.

With regard to nature, all would be restored. With regard to life? Nothing would be as it was.

Ethne stepped forward, a rare smile on her face. "Witches, I give you Ivy, Priestess of the House of Earth."

Ivy bowed as Ethne crowned her with a wreath made of twisted vines. As soon as the dry vine touched her head it came alive, small flowers budding and then blooming around the circlet.

"We have much to do to set things right," Ivy said in a sweet-sounding voice. "But, as soon as the balance has returned, the Circle wants to celebrate with an Affinity Battle, which will take place on All Hallow's Eve."

The witches gasped collectively and then cheered.

There hadn't been a battle in at least five years, but from what I remembered from watching the last one, it was something the witches enjoyed. They challenged one another to retrieve a specific crystal from the porch of each House. No spiriting was allowed; only Earth, Air, Fire, Water, sweat, and determination.

"This year, we'd like to invite the House of Fate to join us as well."

My mouth gaped for a moment before I recovered. "We accept." I smiled and nudged Arron, who seemed confused. I whispered to him, "I'll explain later."

Mira explained that we would divide into our Houses and receive further instructions. Everything that had been marred would require replenishment, and since much had been affected, there was a lot of work to be done between now and All Hallow's Eve.

Arron and I would help, too. We hovered in the Center to see where we could best assist.

Brecan found us first. "You ready?" he asked.

Arron glanced at me and answered, "We were wondering what was taking so long."

Brecan laughed and waved for us to join his House.

It was strange to feel welcome here, but it gave me a sense of relief. I didn't realize how tense and uncomfortable I'd been in my own sector until I left it.

Having a purpose made the hard days pass quickly, but I watched the moon in my empty moments, even during the day when the sky was clear. Tomorrow, she would be full. I was restless. Fate was so quiet, at times I forgot he was there.

"Does Tauren need me?" I asked him into my mirror while towel-drying my damp hair. "Should I go to him?"

Fate did not answer. But my heart did.

I threw the towel to the floor and jogged down the steps. "Arron, I need to go –"

Arron was in the sitting room, standing awkwardly beside Courier Stewart as he worried his hat. "Miss Sable," he greeted with relief.

My eyes filled with tears. "Is he okay?"

"He'd like you to come to the palace, if you're not too busy."

I nodded. "I'll go to him now."

The Courier inclined his head. "Thank you, Miss."

I glanced at Arron, who nodded in understanding. Without further thought or conversation needed, I raced to the door, flung it open, and spirited to the palace steps, surprising the two guards who were stationed there. Once they saw my face, they relaxed. "I need to see Tauren," I demanded breathlessly.

They opened the doors and I slipped inside, scurrying on feather-light steps to the King's chamber. The guards standing sentinel outside the door waved me inside without complaint. I entered and almost gasped at the heart-wrenching tableau spread out before me. Tauren sat on one side of his father and the Queen sat on the other, each grasping one of the King's limp hands. King Lucius lay almost flat, his head elevated with a pillow. His skin was yellow and sagged on his bones. The thick blankets covering him could not conceal his swollen middle.

Tears pricked my eyes.

Tauren glanced up as the door opened, and I saw his face crumble when he saw me. Dropping his head with a trembling sigh, his dark hair and shoulders shook with every tear he tried to hold in.

With his free hand, he reached for me. I rushed to him and grasped him as tightly as I could, attempting to infuse every ounce of my love through my embrace. His arm wrapped around me and he fisted the fabric of the back of my dress. With every sob he let out, fissures spread through the wall I'd erected around my heart.

Annalina watched us with tears streaming down her face. "Thank you," she mouthed. I nodded once, focusing again on Tauren.

I stayed for minutes, hours, holding the man I loved. Lucius's breaths faded until they were shallow and spread far apart, and then, just after dusk, they stopped and the King faded away. His soul rose up into the room, regarding his loved ones. I whispered a blessing to him and urged him to follow the light. It would guide him to his next destination.

In all my years of dealing with death, I knew there was a moment of numb shock that hit each person after they lost a loved one. Even though they knew death was inevitable, in that moment it suddenly became real. The fact that their loved one was truly gone would pierce them like an arrow to the heart.

I was there the moment it hit Annalina. As if sensing the separation of her beloved's spirit, she let out a wail that made the marrow nestled within my bones ache. I wished there was some way I could comfort her, but without speaking, Tauren went to her. He held his mother, rocking her until she calmed.

When she was exhausted and depleted, Annalina looked up and gingerly stood. "We need to admit the physician to prepare him for burial." She squeezed Tauren's hand tight and reached for me with trembling fingers. I walked around the bed to her and slid my hand into hers, and the three of us walked from the room.

Annalina might have been grieving, but she was still Queen, and it showed with the way she held her head up despite her tears. The way she straightened her back and put one foot in front of the other when I knew all she felt like doing was falling to her knees.

Tauren and I walked with her to a set of rooms she'd occupied temporarily during Lucius's illness. When Tauren offered to stay with her, she shook her head dismissively and hugged her son.

"I need some time alone," she said, her voice cracking.

Once she shut her door, Tauren turned to me, his chin quivering as he held back more tears. "I know it isn't exactly proper, but would you come to my room? It's private, and I just want–"

"Of course I will," I answered.

We walked together to his room. He didn't say a word; he tugged me toward the enormous bed, where we lay on the covers and eventually gave in to exhaustion together, falling asleep cradled within each other's arms.

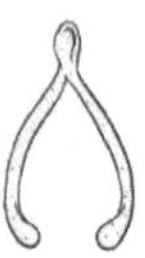

I woke before he did. It was hard to tell the exact time, as the sun was hidden behind the clouds, but I knew it was late afternoon. Tauren began to stir when I brushed away a strand of hair that had fallen across his eyelid.

When his golden eyes slowly opened, I saw the bloodshot veins that spoke of gallons of shed tears. "You stayed," he rasped.

"I wouldn't leave you," I answered.

"You did, though."

"I had to, then." Maybe he didn't understand, and maybe I should have explained my departure better, but I had a duty to my home and to find the witches still loyal to my mother's cause, and he had a duty to spend every remaining minute with his father.

"I missed you," he breathed, placing a sweet, chaste kiss on my forehead and wrapping his arms around me.

"I missed you, too," I breathed, holding him tight.

"My father's funeral will take place tomorrow. Will you stay for it and attend with me?"

I wanted to, but wasn't sure if…

"What is it?" he asked.

"Am I welcome at his service? Witchcraft is considered evil by most religions."

He smoothed the worry line between my eyes. "You are welcome anywhere in this kingdom, Sable. Nothing about you is evil. Everyone knows that now."

"Then, yes. I'll attend with you."

He swallowed. "Do you need to return to your House?"

"Not yet," I told him. I could only help so much with the rebuilding of Thirteen without a nature affinity, but even so, there was nowhere else I'd rather be than with him.

Someone knocked at the door. While Tauren went to answer it, I stood and walked to the window to see black pennants flapping on the rooftops. The Kingdom was already mourning its King.

Tauren had a brief conversation with someone and then closed the door. "Would you care to dine in here tonight?"

"Of course."

He walked to the window and looked out, his eyes locking on the flags. He stared at them for several long moments, his hands folded behind his back. "I'm afraid I have nothing planned for us."

"Tauren, you and I don't need fanfare or constant entertainment. We just need one another."

He swallowed thickly, then nodded several times, pursing his lips tightly together.

There were no words to express how sorry I was, how I wished I could have saved his father, or how I wanted so badly to ease his pain. But I wouldn't take even an ounce of grief away from him, because I knew more than most how he needed to feel his way through and emerge from it stronger and more resilient. If I took his feelings away, he wouldn't be Tauren.

We had to process death with emotion, and experiencing death, and mourning the loss of someone you loved, was not only inevitable for all of us, it was something that transformed us into a stronger version of ourselves. Tauren would be stronger in time, I reminded myself.

For now, I would be strong for him.

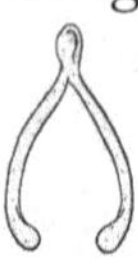

Later that evening, someone knocked on Tauren's door to wake him for dinner. He groggily rose and stumbled to the door on leaden feet, offering a soft *Thank you*. I sat up on the bed as he walked back across the room and sat beside me. His eyes were heavy-lidded and dark circles ringed underneath. "Thank you for staying with me."

Instead of telling him 'you're welcome,' I took his hand in mine, brushing my thumb over the back of it. I wanted to be here with him. "I was about to come anyway," I confessed. "Before Courier Stewart arrived, I had already decided I was going to show up uninvited."

"I invited you. Remember?" He tried to smile. "The invitation was never rescinded."

"So I can just waltz back in here whenever I'd like?"

"Yes, and I hope you do so often." He watched my thumb move back and forth in lazy circles. "Your things are still in your room. I started to have them sent to you a dozen times, but never did."

"You've had a lot on your mind."

"It wasn't that," he admitted. "I just kept thinking if I left them there, you might come back for them. Selfishly, I wanted to see you."

My heart cracked. "I thought about leaving you a token, spelling something so you could use it to reach me if you needed to."

"I wish you had," he said, his voice breaking. "How am I supposed to get through this day?"

"One minute at a time," I answered.

He nodded and wiped a tear from his cheek. "It just might be possible with you here."

The crack in the wall around my heart widened.

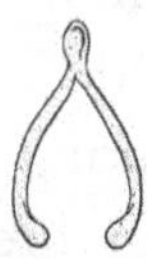

Folded neatly in my trunk was a dress I'd never seen before, but the moment I saw it, I knew Mira had made it. She either knew I'd come back here for him to mourn his father, or had spirited it here. I wasn't sure which.

I brushed my teeth and showered quickly, towel-drying my hair before combing it and twisting it into a bun at the nape of my neck. The dress's fabric felt like silk, but slightly thicker, with a pebbled surface. It fastened at the back of my neck, was sleeveless and fitted at the top, and flared slightly from the waist. The dress was black until it hit my knee, where it bled into the Kingdom's signature dark teal. Lying in the trunk beneath the dress were matching teal heels and the box containing the necklace Tauren had given me.

I slid the heels on and secured the necklace, skipping the makeup still arranged on the bathroom counter, then walked back to Tauren's room. I knocked twice and waited until he eased the door open.

He stepped out, locked his room, and slid the key into his pocket, offering me his arm. Ever the gentleman, and not because it was proper, but because he was just a good man. We met his mother, Knox, and Leah at the bottom of the staircase.

Annalina wore a simple black dress with a matching sheer veil draped over her head beneath her golden crown. Knox was dressed in a crisp black suit and Leah wore a simple black pencil dress. The couple held hands and stood closely together. The Queen handed Tauren his father's thicker, matching crown. "Would you place it on his casket?" she asked.

Tauren nodded, accepting the golden circlet. Knox pulled away from Leah and threw an arm around Tauren's shoulders and tugged their mother close, the three sharing a hug before taking a moment to compose themselves.

It was time for the service to begin.

Guards pulled the main doors open when the Queen gave a nod. When they parted, it looked like the entire Kingdom sat on the lawn outside. The rows of chairs situated on the grass were filled, but mourners flooded the palace lawn in every direction as far as I could see. Dressed in black, those who had been sitting stood to honor the Queen and Princes.

Lucius's teal casket sat on a golden stand at the bottom of the stairs with a spray of roses in every color arranged on the glossy wood. I could smell Ivy's magic mixing with their floral scent.

Tauren escorted his mother as Knox ushered Leah and me down the steps. The Queen paused at her husband's casket, taking mine and Leah's hands as Tauren and Knox stepped forward. Tauren placed Lucius's crown on top of the floral spray.

The crowd was silent, but I could feel the weight of every breath being held.

Annalina gave me a wobbly smile and let go of my hand. "Go to him," she whispered, before walking to one of five reserved chairs situated just in front of the casket.

I walked to Tauren, who stood in front of his father. His shoulders began to shake as he cried. I slid my hand into his and he gripped it tight as he fought the desperate sadness that death left in its wake.

Knox's silent tears were just as heartbreaking. Leah stood at his side, her arm around his shoulders.

When the two princes were ready, the four of us took our seats beside their mother.

The service was beautiful; the sermon delivered was poignant. And at the end, Tauren, Knox, and four of the King's personal guards hefted his casket on their shoulders and carried him far across the lawn to a small cemetery. There, amongst the Kings and Queens who came before him, Lucius was laid to rest.

I stood with Tauren as the casket was lowered into the ground, and as it was covered with earth. I stood with Tauren as the crowd thinned until only he, Knox, Leah, and Annalina remained. When they were ready, the five of us walked back to the palace.

I stayed with Tauren that night. As we held each other, I told him what Ethne had revealed about Bay. Together, we cried for the loss of our fathers. We cried until we were exhausted, and then we fell asleep in one another's arms.

Mira came for me the next morning. I was needed in The Gallows.

twenty-seven

Mira and I were sitting in my room as she helped me pack the trunks. "You could stay," she suggested half-heartedly. But we both knew that wasn't an option. I couldn't live in the palace indefinitely. Not only would it bring shame to our sector, it would cause the Kingdom to whisper about Tauren. If they didn't already believe it, they might think we were lovers.

"The longer I'm here, the less I want to go home," I admitted.

"If he placed a crown on your head, you could."

I closed the lid on the trunk I'd been situating. "He can't do that."

Mira regarded me for a long moment. "I'll wait on the palace steps while you say goodbye."

I thanked her and watched her walk out of the room, then I peered around at the stack of locked, packed trunks by the door. Tauren promised to have the Courier deliver them soon. I could've spirited them home, but he insisted.

Tauren stood just outside my room. He pushed off the wall when he saw me exit. I walked to him and returned my key.

"Thank you for staying, Sable."

"You would've done the same for me."

He inclined his head in acknowledgement.

Tauren stared at me for a long moment, ponderous words lying just beyond his lips. I brushed a dark strand of hair out of his eyes. He gently caught my wrist, bringing my hand to his lips for a parting kiss that made the moths flutter in my stomach, despite the dread I felt from leaving him again.

"I left something on the bed for you. If you need me, you can reach me."

His eyes flicked to my door. "Thank you."

Tauren walked me down the hallway, down the staircase, and out the door where Mira was waiting patiently. He thanked her for coming and she hugged his neck, expressing her condolences.

She grabbed my hand. With one last look at my prince, we disappeared.

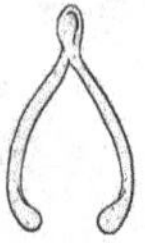

Much had been done to rectify the damage to the earth Ela's absence had caused, and the Gallows was abuzz with excitement when we returned. At the week's end, our fallen Priestess and Priest, and the new Priest and Priestesses, along with Ethne, who had survived the unthinkable, would be honored in an Affinity Battle that promised to be both entertaining and poignant, a celebration of endings and beginnings. And while it was refreshing to think that life was still moving along despite all that had happened, it was also a bit jarring. I'd just watched Tauren bury his father. Then I left him… again.

Brecan asked me to take part in the hand-fasting ceremony that would take place after the Affinity Battle – but as the Guardian only. The Circle had agreed to release me from the mandate that I hand-fast to someone this year, or any other year. The decision to do so would be mine to make when, or if, I chose. Like Brecan had promised, I was now revered.

That, too, was jarring at times, though it wasn't at all unpleasant.

Arron was increasingly enamored with Mira and made excuses to visit her House at every opportunity. He was shedding his nervousness like a too tight layer of skin. If she needed something, he volunteered before anyone in her House had the chance. He was a full-fledged resident of the House of Fate now, but was hardly ever there, thanks to his crush on my friend. I had the House mostly to myself… again.

Watching him pine over her was sweet.

It also made my chest hurt.

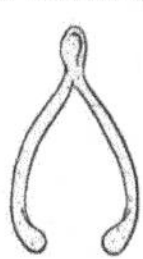

The morning of the Affinity Battle, Arron and I dressed in black pants and shirts. The two of us couldn't fight with water, air, fire, or earth, but we had other tricks up our sleeves.

There were no rules, other than to gather as many crystals from the steps of the other Houses as possible – by any means possible, except for spiriting. No spiriting was allowed. That would be too easy, and the battle would be over as quickly as it began.

I tied my hair back and Arron bounced on the balls of his feet nervously, peering out the door in the direction of the House of Water. "I'm not a good loser, Sable. Do we need a plan?"

"A plan? There is an endless amount of possibilities to consider all the moves the other witches might throw at us."

"What good is it being a fate diviner if you can't cheat?" he teased.

Ignoring his taunt, I asked, "Is Mira ready?"

"Everyone is in the Center but us and Brecan's House."

That was odd. Brecan was always punctual, if not early.

I checked my reflection and walked outside with Arron. He seemed unusually antsy as his slitted eyes narrowed on our competition. We were vastly outnumbered, but had skills no natural witch possessed. "This will be intense."

"But we're going to win," I vowed. "I never thought I'd have a chance to participate. We have to show them we're equals."

"So, no pressure?" he asked sarcastically.

I suddenly noticed he'd shaved off his midnight black hair. "I like your hair."

He quirked a brow. "I didn't want my vision to be obscured today."

I stifled a laugh.

"What? This is a battle, right? Battles are fought to be won."

"It's only a game," I advised with a grin. He could've tied it back or worn a hat, but the short hair suited him somehow. Mira certainly thought so. From across the lawn, she kept Arron trained in her sights. She'd smile or address whomever asked a question, but then her eyes inevitably drifted to him.

Ethne, Ivy, and Mira met in the Center. I searched for Brecan among the crowd, but he was nowhere to be found.

The witches gave their Priestesses the honor they deserved by quieting immediately. Ethne smiled. "Brecan is placing crystals on each step." I turned to find him behind me, placing obsidian on the top step of the House of Fate.

His footsteps were silent as he rushed around the circle of houses placing the crystals, and then slipped through the crowd to join his counterparts.

"To your Houses!" Ethne announced.

Arron and I returned to our lawn and watched the other lawns fill with witches. The Air witches were the most populous, the lawn barely visible beneath their feet. The Fire witches looked like they were ready to do battle. They stared across the Center, their plan of attack probably running through their minds.

"So, do we have a plan?" Arron asked.

"Yep. Steal the crystals from the other Houses while guarding our own."

"Inspiring, Guardian," he smarted.

"Let the Affinity Battle begin!" roared Ethne. She threw her arm down and the battle began.

It was slow at first, each House tentative in their strikes. We were outnumbered, so the House of Fate couldn't afford to be tentative. Arron poured his clouds into the Center as he ran toward the House of Fire. Brecan's Air witches quickly used their affinity to form a funnel from Arron's clouds, a second too soon. My cover blown, the Fire witches caught me on their step.

They realized I was there too late, though. I clutched their hematite stone in my palm and ran as fast as I could, but not before I felt the heat of a hundred flames on my back.

"Fate has the Fire stone!" Brecan yelled.

The stone shot out of my hand, flying into the sky and bursting into a thousand tiny cinders that rained down over the Center. The smell of burning wood filled the air and the lingering smoke hovering overhead formed the shape of a flame, sigil of the House of Fire.

The contest was not over. It had only just begun, but it felt good that Arron and I had made the first strike.

Mira used her power to dehydrate everyone but her charges. Earth, Air, and Fire witches flopped on the ground uncomfortably, like a pond of fishes with too little water. Familiar with Mira's talents, I'd blocked myself and Arron against the onslaught. With bubbles around us, he tried to distract Mira by catching her eye and luring her into a chase. She laughed as she chased after him, forgetting her dehydration spell, while I crept toward Air.

"Oh, no. I don't think so, Sable," Brecan warned. He recovered from Mira's magic quickly and sent me flying into the air. Suddenly, the light of day disappeared and all became night as Arron's clouds lassoed me and brought me to the ground.

"No one messes with my Guardian," he teased Brecan.

Brecan hopped a ride on a jet stream and landed in front of Arron.

The Fire witches claimed the Water witches' crystal, celebrating as they jogged safely back to their lawns. Mira was livid.

A fountain of water exploded overhead, raining down onto the lawn and everyone on it. The briny scent of the sea hit me and immediately jolted a memory of Tauren holding me in the sand, moments before the world fell apart at the seams. In the air, vapor hung in the shape of a single cresting wave, the sigil of the House of Water.

Arron held out his hands, unsure what else to do as Brecan advanced on him. Whispering a spell to blur reality, everything began to melt. People, our Houses, the trees, the fountain in front of the House of Water. The world oozed like ice cream on a scorching hot day.

Brecan held his hand out in front of him, watching it drip to the ground. "What is this?"

"I didn't know you could do that," I marveled.

"I have a few new tricks up my sleeve," Arron said with a friendly wink.

Sensing Brecan's discomfiture, Ivy took over. All the witches grew tall, stretching toward the sky like peeling, knobby birches. My nose sprouted into a long, skinny branch and my fingers became trees. The Earth witches turned into lumbering stone soldiers, marched to the House of Air, and snagged their crystal.

Brecan roared at their blatant thievery as his Air witches fought to free themselves, but they remained helplessly rooted to the soil.

A fierce wind tore through the Center, the fresh scent cleansing our sweat-soaked skin. Dried leaves were torn from branches, rushing into a pattern that formed three distinct waved lines over the Center, the sigil of the House of Air.

The wind blew Ivy's timber curse away as well. The witches gasped to be free and immediately began to fight with torrents of air, torrential rain, walls of fire, and metal called from deep within the earth by the Earth witches. It bubbled up from fissures, cooling and solidifying once again.

Arron locked eyes with Mira and the two of them teamed up. She called forth a dense fog and Arron made the light of day fade into total darkness. The combination made it impossible to see. "Arron, guard our obsidian!"

"I've got it," he promised.

I sprinted through the dark fog to the steps of the House of Earth and scooped up their emerald. Just then, the fog and darkness faded and daylight pierced everyone's eyes. Pine needles formed the shape of the tree that bore them before falling to the ground, their astringent scent permeating the air. Arron let out a hoot and announced, "Fate takes the Earth crystal!"

He was still celebrating when he realized, too late, that our obsidian was in jeopardy. He tried to fight Brecan off, but my best friend managed to grab our crystal and held it aloft victoriously.

Brecan let out a victory roar and threw our stone into the sky where it exploded into millions of sharp, black wishbones. They covered the lawn in a thick layer before Ivy instructed the earth to absorb them so everyone could walk comfortably.

"All the crystals have been stolen," Ethne announced, soot and a sheen of sweat covering her face.

Brecan laughed, clapping Arron on the back. "You are a warrior, friend." He took Arron's hand and held it up high. "The House of Fate is victorious!"

Witches from every House applauded. Arron bowed as I strode across the Center to join him on our lawn. My hair was a damp, snarled mess thanks to the Water and Wind witches. I was sooty and somewhat singed, thanks to the Fire witches, and pine needles littered my hair, thanks to the Earth witches. But I couldn't stop smiling. I grinned until my cheeks ached.

"The Memoriam celebration will begin at sundown," Ivy announced. "Ready yourselves, and we will feast and enjoy this reverent day. Then, as we wait on the winter season to approach, we will finally rest. Come spring, all will be set right."

In my bedroom, a magnificent velvet gown hung from a hook on the washroom door. I twisted it around on the hanger to get a better look. The back was open to my waist, the front high enough to conceal my collarbones. I vowed to thank Mira for making it.

"Someone put a suit in my room!" Arron hollered from the room he'd claimed upstairs.

"I have a dress!" I yelled back.

"Goddess, she is wonderful," he marveled. Mira truly was.

He drew a bath and when he was finished, I drew mine. We had been working on upgrading the aged plumbing, and now had running water in every washroom. The pressure wasn't as forceful as the palace's, but it was a million times better than washing with a tub and pitcher.

I scrubbed myself until the water dissolved the dirt and soot etched on my skin and in my hair. A strange feeling unfurled in my stomach. No matter what I did, nothing eased it.

Fate was finally stirring.

Please don't ask me to hang anyone tonight. Not tonight. Please, I begged. Ivy had promised we would be able to rest for a season, and I felt tired enough to hibernate all the way to spring.

Someone knocked at the front door. Wrapped in a thick robe, I went to open it, startled to see Brecan standing on the step. "Mira told me to come over and dry your hair. She's coming over to style it. You might want to close your eyes and hold onto your robe," he warned with a grin.

He pointed a finger at me. Wind gusted from it and almost instantly, my hair was dry and fluffy. I thanked him, but told him to let Mira know she didn't have to worry about me. "You know her. She'll be over in a few minutes." He winked over his shoulder and hovered down the steps, across the Center, and to his House.

I barely made it back to the washroom before Mira entered the House. "Sable?" she yelled. "Did Brecan dry your hair yet?"

"He did, but honestly, I'm fine," I told her, puzzled about why they suddenly felt I needed help grooming myself.

She waved me off. "You are *not* wearing the gown we made you with hair like that."

"Like what?" I scoffed.

"It looks like it's detecting a nearby lightning storm!" she giggled.

"Thanks a lot, Mira."

She shrugged. "You asked."

She marched me to the washroom and then left it, returning a moment later with a kitchen chair. "Sit."

I sat.

She brushed and twisted and pinned my hair until it resembled a beautiful, sleek mass of coiling serpents on my head. "It's beautiful," she whispered, popping in the final pin.

"Thank you, Mira. For everything."

She kissed my cheek. "What are best friends for?" When someone outside shouted her name, she blew out a long breath. "I need to go make sure my witches are ready."

"Me too," I pretended to worry. "Arron, are you ready?" I yelled.

"Almost."

Mira laughed.

"He likes you, you know."

Mira's face turned red. "Good."

"Good?" I asked. My brows arched, and I giggled as her blush deepened to crimson.

She nodded. "Could I speak to him for a moment?"

"Absolutely. I have to get dressed anyway."

Her footsteps creaked up the stairs.

I could hear her speaking with Arron, but wasn't sure about what. I wanted so badly to eavesdrop, but refrained.

He walked with her down the steps, his eyes on her instead of the staircase. I was afraid he'd tumble down them or worse, that his suit would be stained with drool. I hid my smile behind my hand.

"Ready?" he asked, more chipper than I'd ever heard him.

Mira promised to meet us at the Memoriam celebration and walked to her House to ensure all was in order, herding a small flock of Water witches back with her. They disappeared behind the main door.

The Fire witches, bedecked in blazing red, orange, and yellow gowns made their way into the Center. Ivy and her Earth witches were next, garbed in every shade from emerald to jade. Then emerged the witches of Air, arrayed in complementing shades of white and sky blue. Last, Mira led the witches of Water to join the others, their kaleidoscope of deep blue hues completing the colorful rainbow.

Arron nudged me. "Our turn."

He offered his arm and I wrapped mine around it, wistfully wondering where Tauren was on this night, and with whom he might be enjoying it.

The Gallows had been decorated with pine boughs from the House of Earth and icicles from the House of Water. The frozen pillars glittered like glass in the fading daylight.

Ethne and her Fire witches unfurled white paper lanterns, lit the wicks, and lifted them gently into the air where they hovered, casting a warm glow over the crowd. She cleared her throat as she ascended the steps.

Ethne congratulated Ivy, Mira, and Brecan on claiming dominion of their respective elements, thereby Elevating to Priestesses and Priest. She asked everyone to raise their hands in honor of our sisters and brothers who had passed, including my grandmother Ela, Bay, Wayra, and even Harmony. She did not mention my mother's name.

Ivy stepped forward and announced the names of the witches who would graduate from their novice positions in the House of Earth and become Elevated among their peers. Normally, such promotions were awarded at the Equinox, but this year they'd been postponed, and if things had turned out differently, they would have been forgotten entirely.

I was thankful all was finally settling.

The Earth witches she called by name formed a line, and as they took the steps and greeted their Priestess, floral crowns threaded around their heads, tightening to a perfectly comfortable fit.

Ethne announced the Elevated from her House, each one awarded a crown of flame that did not burn their hair or skin, but crackled and flickered like the wicks of the lanterns hovering above.

Next, Mira stepped onto the platform. Her eyes found Arron at my side. His Adam's apple bobbed as he watched her. She congratulated the Elevated from her House one at a time, crowning them with a band of churning water.

Brecan took his turn last. He smiled over the crowd as he listed the Elevated among the Air witches, a swirling swath of wind churning the hair of the promoted.

He fastened his eyes on me. "Now, Guardian Sable will announce the hand-fasted."

I made my way to the platform and stared out at those gathered. I cleared my throat and tried to expel the nervousness from my stomach that had settled into my hands, causing them to quiver. "As we've learned, life and time are precious. While we want to honor custom and tradition, sometimes, exceptions must be made in order to heal. Much was taken from us, and as the Priestesses and Priest have promised, much will be restored."

I paused, gathering my thoughts and trying to remember the words Brecan had suggested, when I noticed a tall gentleman in a dark hooded cloak, standing at the fringes of the crowd of witches. My pulse quickened. *Did Fate fail to reveal one of Cyril's loyal witches?*

I glanced from him to Brecan, who motioned for me to continue.

"To honor our fallen, would those who would like to begin a new year together come forward?"

Mira nudged Brecan and whispered to him behind her hand as Ethne announced several couples. Brecan watched the hooded man as eager couples stepped forward, standing at the base of the platform and raising their clasped hands in the air. Brecan used his affinity to send red ribbons swirling through the air, deftly knotting them around the couples' wrists and symbolically sealing their year-long commitments to one another, while Ethne charged them to be respectful, faithful, and to honor their fasted above all others, save the Goddess, of course.

"Are there any other couples who would like to come forward to be hand-fasted?" Brecan asked, his voice echoing over the hushed crowd.

A commotion came from somewhere at the back of the mass of witches, and colorful cloaks and gowns began to shuffle and part as the stranger made his way toward the gallows. When he was close, he removed his hood.

His golden eyes were the first things I saw.

"Tauren?" I jogged down the steps, heedless of the audience in my joy to see him. "What are you doing here?" I asked when he reached me.

He glanced nervously at Brecan. "I don't know the proper way to ask this, but..." He got down on one knee, just as I'd seen Knox do to Leah, and took my hands in his. "Sable, will you hand-fast to me?"

"You're about to be crowned the King of Nautilus. Your coronation is tomorrow," I told him dumbly, still not believing he was there. I'd planned to watch it with Mira on their telecaster.

"I know I'm to be crowned tomorrow, but I can't do it without you by my side." He reached into his pocket and pulled out a small box.

"I can't marry you, Tauren. It isn't our custom." I glanced to Brecan and then to Mira, noticing the small smiles of... approval on their faces. Sucking in a breath, I turned back to Tauren. A strand of dark hair fell into his eyes. He smiled nervously.

I brushed his hair back in a habit I'd come to adore, and he continued. "I want to spend the rest of my life with you, and if we have to hand-fast one year at a time, so be it. We'll come back to this spot next year and the year after that, and so on. If this is what it takes to make you mine, I will hand-fast to you again and again and again. I love you."

The moths in my stomach took flight. My lashes fluttered. I pressed my hand to his cheek. "I love you, too."

Fate stirred for the first time in so many days, weeks. *You must choose.*

Choose? I asked silently.

You can only be bound to one of us.

A tear slid from my eye. *Why?* I silently asked as my lips began to wobble.

That is simply the way. I will always look out for you, Sable. You are my daughter, not by blood, but something much stronger.

I love him, I told Fate.

As I conveyed the words, I felt warm inside. Comfortable. Like a sip of hot tea on a chilly, winter evening. And when he left me, he left gently, soft as an expelled breath.

My mother lied about him. He didn't refuse to concede control when I asked for it to be returned, and he wasn't spiteful or filled with hatred. I realized that he chose me to protect me from her, and that he knew what path she would choose all along.

I clasped my hand over my heart, already feeling his loss. I wasn't sure who Fate would choose next to be his, but I was certain of one thing: I was Tauren's and Tauren was mine.

And Fate had known all along that this moment would come.

Tauren swallowed thickly, waiting patiently, still kneeling in front of me.

I pulled him to his feet and threw my arms around his neck.

"Is that a yes?" he asked. I heard the grin in his voice even though his mouth was at my ear.

I looked to Brecan, Mira, Ethne, and Ivy. All four nodded their approval.

"Yes!" I laughed.

He twirled me around, and when he moved to set me back down, my feet didn't touch the ground. I hovered a few inches above, as light as I felt inside.

He lifted the hinged lid on the small, black velvet box and pulled out a black silken ribbon to act as our hand-fasting symbol.

My breath caught. "I love it. As I love you."

He grinned and kissed me. We could only peck, really, both smiling too widely to do anything more.

The witches of every House began to applaud. Whistles, cheers, and claps surrounded us. I looked all around at the smiling, genuinely happy faces. Even Brecan clapped, a small smile playing on his lips. Mira was giddy, of course.

This was happening.

This was actually happening.

I felt like pinching myself to be sure I wasn't dreaming. But when Tauren kissed me again and I felt his soft lips on mine, I knew this was real. We'd survived so much. And now? Now, we could begin anew.

King Lucius was right. There wasn't anything we couldn't figure out – together.

Tauren clasped my hand in his. We held our arms up and watched as Brecan used his wind to capture the ribbon and bind our wrists, knotting the ends of the silk together.

And just like that, Tauren and I were hand-fasted.

twenty-eight

Tauren spent the night in my House. Well, in the House of Fate. I wasn't even sure I was still the Guardian, as a new witch hadn't come forward yet. Was I the interim Guardian? Could I ask Arron to become the interim Guardian of Fate's House? I wasn't sure how this worked. How any of it would work.

Stress cinched my rib cage as dawn broke. Tauren stretched as he slowly woke, scrubbing a hand down his face. He felt for me beside him and found me near the window, a lazy smile spreading over his lips. At my expression, the smile faded.

"What's the matter?"

"What if the people of Nautilus don't want a witch for their Queen – even if it's only for a year?"

"Number one," he said, sitting up and swinging his legs over the side of the mattress. I tried to ignore the V-shape of his shoulders and how the sinew of his muscles slid down to his taut waist, how he wore no shirt and grinned unapologetically at my reaction to him. "It doesn't have to be for just a year. We can hand-fast again at the next Solstice. Sable, we can be together for as long as you'll have me."

I grinned playfully. "I'll consider it, as long as you deserve me."

Tauren stood and crossed the room, locking eyes with me. "Then I will work to do so every day," he breathed. "The people love you, Sable. Witch or not. Daughter of Fate or not. Don't worry about their reaction."

If I was being honest, I wasn't sure who I was without Fate. I wasn't sure what, if any, ability I might have on my own. I'd always read the futures and fates of others. Could I even do that now, or would I have to conjure love spells for the rest of my life to eke out a living?

Would I have to work magic at all if I was with Tauren?

Would I be the queen? Would the people even want to call me 'Queen' if I didn't marry Tauren permanently, instead of hand-fasting each year?

My chest felt tighter and tighter, and my breaths became more labored as I thought through the myriad of intricacies our irreverent union would reveal.

This will be more difficult than he realizes. This might not work at all. If the people fear me, then no amount of Tauren's reassuring words will persuade them.

"Hey." He ran the pad of his thumb over the crease between my brows. "Stop worrying."

"I can't."

I couldn't stop worrying or running scenarios through my mind, wondering what was to become of me or my House now that Fate had left me in search of someone else.

Tauren pulled me in and hugged me tight. I finally relaxed a little, able to breathe for the first time in hours. "There is nothing we can't figure out together." When he pulled back, I clung to him. "What does Fate say about our future?" he asked softly.

Tears pricked the backs of my eyes. "He left me."

Tauren tilted his head to the side. "What do you mean?"

I took a deep breath. "He said that I couldn't be with you and serve him at the same time…and when I chose *you*, he left me. He's gone. I can't feel him at all."

"Who is the new Daughter – or Son – of Fate?" he questioned, pure curiosity lacing his features.

I shook my head. "I don't know."

"No wonder you're so unsettled," he said tenderly. "You've had him to lean on since you were a child."

A knot the size of a wishbone formed in my throat. I was thankful he understood my unease, but pained to hear him say it aloud.

"Sable, I don't want to seem unsympathetic, but he was right. He was right to give you a choice and to honor it. It would have been very difficult for you to perform your duties to him, and be hand-fasted to me. I'm glad he understood that. But I want you to know that it would be the greatest honor of my life if you would now lean on me in his stead."

I nodded, one of the many knots curled in my midsection beginning to unravel. "I will. And I want you to promise to do the same." He once had a father, a King, to turn to, and now that Lucius was gone, I wanted nothing more than to be the confidant Tauren needed.

He offered a small smile. "I promise."

Just then, the sound of pounding hooves came from outside. Tauren tugged the thick, black curtains back and peeked through the glass. "Courier Stewart has arrived."

I froze as panic settled in once more. "I'm not ready! And neither are you! You're not even fully dressed. We're going to cause a scandal before we even leave the sector!"

Tauren's chuckle filled the air. "Stewart is discreet. Why do you think I sent for him specifically?" He raised his brows. "Besides, your fellow witches won't bat an eye. They know how we feel about each other. And we *are* hand-fasted. I'm sure they expect much more from us within the next year..."

My cheeks warmed at the thought of being intimate with him.

Or for people across the Kingdom to think, or know, we had been.

Bay once told me that knowing something and seeing it firsthand were very different things.

From downstairs came Mira's voice. "Sable?"

I ran to the bedroom door and slipped into the hallway, closing it behind me. She met me just outside the door. "I have a few things for you," she announced with a beaming smile, holding up a garment concealed by a dark bag. "You should wear this today. The rest, I've given to the Courier."

Mira was a friend I never expected to show up in my life, but one I couldn't imagine living without now. I hugged her tightly around the neck. She squeaked and I eased my grip. "Sorry."

Mira laughed. "I can't wait to see you tonight."

"Tonight? Oh, of course; the coronation will be telecast."

"It certainly will, but we won't be watching from The Gallows. Tauren invited the entire sector to the Coronation Ball."

My mouth gaped at her revelation, and I barely heard the door behind me swing open. I turned around to see Tauren with his arms braced on the door frame. He hadn't bothered to put on a shirt. Mira's jaw unhinged, and I used a finger to gently close her mouth. She immediately forgot I was standing in front of her, too busy ogling my hand-fasted.

A slight swirl of jealousy swept through my veins. My fists tightened, and while I would never hurt her, I couldn't help wanting her eyes off Tauren.

His voice interrupted my inner turmoil. "Will you require a number of carriages, Priestess Mira, or will you all spirit to the Palace?"

"We will appear – in style," she told him. Mira shoved the bagged outfit to me by the hanger and grinned as she strode away. "See you tonight!"

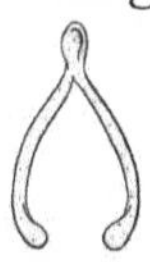

Mira and her magical spiders had crafted a sleek pair of black dress pants. Over it, she'd created a masterpiece of precisely-placed sheer panels and dark, glittering beads.

The tunic was more of a short dress, hugging my curves perfectly. Tauren certainly liked the traveling suit. His eyes swept over me. Often. Bonus: she'd placed my favorite dagger-hiding heels in the bottom of the bag.

The drive to the palace was different. I'd traveled the road before, but never with Tauren beside me to introduce me to every facet of the Kingdom he loved. I was amazed by how much he knew about his people. As the carriage swept through each sector, he taught me.

How the timber mills worked; how strong and brave the men who felled the trees were.

How the factories produced electricity, and how the witches might want to consider adding it in the future.

How his mother had let him pound the head of a hammer into a chisel, which flung small bits of rock into his eyes. He was only five, but he remembered his tears clearing the debris and then taking up the hammer again, undeterred.

He hadn't visited the Children's Ward in Sector Three since his father passed. I promised I would go with him soon, grabbing his hand and making him smile. Of all the powers I'd ever possessed, putting a smile on Tauren's face was by far the greatest.

When we passed through Sector One and Rose's mansion in particular, I tensed. Tauren stared out the window and for a moment, I wondered if he was reconsidering his decision to hand-fast to me. In times of contentment, a year could pass fast, but in times of discontent, it could seem to pass agonizingly slowly.

"I've invited the other invitees, and their families, to attend tonight," he noted, turning to watch my reaction.

"That was kind of you." The words came out snippier than I would've liked, but Rose… well, she could push my buttons like no one else, and I didn't feel like having them pushed.

"You hate Rose almost as much as I do," he laughed.

"You hate her?"

"A match with her would've made sense, given her father's position, but she never would have made me happy."

I wanted to purr when he lifted me onto his lap. I threaded my fingers around the back of his neck, feeling the freshly cut hair at the nape. "Why is that?"

"She's not you. None of them were."

I kissed him, pouring love through my lips instead of through my words. When we pulled away, I finally told him, "She used a love potion on you, you know."

His brows kissed. "Who did? Rose?"

"Yep."

He smirked. "Then she learned a valuable lesson. You, Sable, are more potent than any silly potion." His grip on my waist tightened. He kissed me again and again, and before we knew it, we'd arrived and were stopped in front of the palace.

Courier Stewart cleared his throat from the driver's bench. "Highness, your mother approaches," he warned.

I slid onto the seat like a chastened schoolgirl, pressing my lips together to quench the tingling sensation, all too aware that they were swollen and the skin around them likely red.

Tauren laughed. "You're blushing."

I swatted his arm before he stood and exited the carriage, gallantly proffering his hand. I accepted it

– again – and exited the carriage with careful steps, holding my breath as the Queen descended the stairs.

Annalina hugged her son and then scooped me into her arms. The scent of her lavender perfume clung to her neck and hair. "I'm so happy you accepted. Welcome to our family, Sable."

Tears burned in my eyes, but I held them back.

"Thank you."

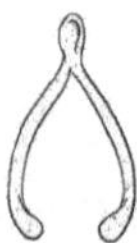

Tauren and I spent the afternoon together. We walked next to the lake, threaded through the woods to the amphitheater, and made our way back to the Night Garden, where we slipped inside the glass walls that were open ever so slightly. The wind was cool, but the sun glorious.

Spending time with him was like a breath of fresh air.

Gone were the moments of uncertainness, the jealousy he and I both experienced. Before, we were consumed by trying to divert the approaching tragedies and the knowledge that both of us were powerless to stop them.

Now, there was only him. Only me. Only calm.

I knew that life never allowed these moments to linger, so we needed to savor them while we had the chance.

The only constant in life was change itself.

When the sun dipped lower and dusky pinks began to streak across the sky, Tauren walked me to my room, the one he'd had designed for me. Courier Stewart had delivered the things Mira insisted I take with me. Given the girth of the dress bag hanging on the rack in the corner, I knew she'd sent a gown worthy of the coronation ball.

I showered and dried my hair, then applied a light dusting of makeup. Once I was satisfied and unable to stand the suspense any longer, I walked across the room to examine the dress.

The zipper purred as it parted, and I pulled the sides open to reveal the gown. The top was strapless, covered completely with tiny, glittering onyx beads. The dress was wider than the bed in this room, comprised of so many airy layers of tulle, I knew it had taken Mira's spiders many hours to weave together. I pulled the dress from the bag and let the layers relax.

In the bag's bottom were heels, encrusted in the same glittering beads as the dress's bodice, and a familiar box. I removed the lid and clasped the necklace Tauren had given me around my neck.

The stones matched our hand-fasting ribbon, one half of which was wound around my wrist. The other half was tied around Tauren's.

I took a deep breath, releasing it slowly. I still couldn't grasp that he came for me, bending his traditions to honor mine.

Never had I felt more at ease about a decision. Accepting Tauren's hand was natural. It felt right. I just hoped the Kingdom's citizens approved of his choice, and of me.

Two knocks came at the door. I knew that knock. I tugged on a robe over my dressing gown and went to answer it.

"Brecan?" I asked, opening the door for him.

"Sorry to interrupt. I know you're getting ready. I just wanted to tell you that I'm happy for you." He gave a small smile, hovering just inside the door frame.

"Truly?" I asked.

He nodded. "If he makes you happy, then I heartily approve."

"He does. Thank you, Brecan." It meant so much that he was okay with the pairing. Brecan – my oldest friend. At times, my only friend. I had been afraid that my choice jeopardized our friendship. "I'm glad you all came to watch and support him in becoming King."

Brecan snorted. "That's not why we're here. I mean, I like the guy and all, but we're here to watch as *you* are crowned, Sable."

My mouth opened slightly. "I don't understand. I think you're mistaken. This is Tauren's coronation, and the ball is to celebrate the new King," I stammered.

"That would be the case had the future King not hand-fasted and pledged himself to you," he replied patiently. "But you're his now, which means you will also be crowned."

My heart began to thunder. "Are you sure?"

He nodded once. "I'm sure."

My mind raced. *Did Tauren tell him that? Why didn't he mention this to me? Does he assume I know?*

Mira appeared behind Brecan and slid into the room. Her eyes widened. "You aren't dressed yet?" she squeaked, taking hold of my hand and dragging me into the wash room. "Wait in the hall, Brecan," she ordered.

Brecan chuckled but obediently left the room, closing the door behind him.

Mira got down to fashionable business and quickly helped me dress. She slid a flat iron down my hair, making it shine and stretch an inch further than it naturally lay, thanks to my unruly waves.

She added a hint of rose color to my cheeks and lips and shadowed my eyes until I looked beautiful, but elegant. Fierce, but merciful.

"Are you ready?" she asked, staring over my shoulder at my reflection. Her hair hung in waves, gently lapping at her shoulders. Her gown looked like the deepest blue of the ocean. It ebbed and flowed in luminescent strands from chest to toe, as if thin streams of foam pushed around its surface.

"You look magnificent, Mira."

She grinned at me through the mirror, her hands tightening on my shoulders. "As do you, my Queen."

twenty-nine

After Mira and Brecan left to guide their Houses into the ballroom, I waited in my room. And by waiting, I mean that I paced until I was sure I might wear a hole through the floor.

Tauren knocked gently and peeked inside. "Are you ready?" he asked, his words fading away as his eyes found me. "My god," he breathed. "You are the most beautiful… I have no words." His mouth hung slightly open. Mine must have matched, because I found I couldn't speak. Dressed in a sleek black tuxedo, complete with a bowtie that matched the glittering bodice of my dress and heels, he extended his hand. "It's time."

"Brecan said that I would be crowned."

"Of course," he answered as if it were the simplest thing in the world.

"What if the people of Nautilus don't approve?"

He shook his head, a smile tugging at his lips. "How could they not?"

My lashes fluttered. I knew he loved me, but wearing a crown beside him would send such a strong message – a message I wasn't sure the citizens were ready to hear. "Tauren –"

He took my hands in his and waited until I looked up at him. "It's just me and you."

But it wasn't. The entire Kingdom was here, along with the highest-ranking military leaders, a smattering of celebrities, and all the other invitees. Not to mention those who weren't present at the palace, but would watch from their homes as the coronation and ball was telecast throughout the Kingdom. The sectors would be filled with parties, public and private, so that people could gather to celebrate the occasion.

"Me and you," I repeated.

"Just focus on me," he assured. "Pretend I'm the only one in the room."

"That won't be difficult," I told him. "When you're near me, you're the only thing I can concentrate on."

Tauren smiled and brought my hand to his lips, placing a kiss on the back of it. Goose bumps spread over my skin as the moths took flight. "The feeling is very much mutual."

Together, we walked to the ballroom where Queen Annalina waited outside. She walked in first and announced us. "I give you my son, Tauren Nathaniel Nautilus, and I give you my new daughter, Sable."

The crowd cheered as two guards swept the double doors open and we entered the room. Tauren and I made our way to the stage, where I could see the colors of the witches blending with the finery of the citizens of the Lower Sectors.

Overhead, the chandeliers dripped light and crystals atop the crowd. The only empty space in the room, the scant trail we'd carved, quickly filled in once we passed by. Tauren squeezed my hand.

The Reverend who had said such kind things at Lucius's funeral joined us. Surprisingly, he blessed the pair of us. I thought he might call our union false or warn us that we should marry in his church instead, but the man was kind, loving, and gracious.

He instructed Tauren on the traits of being a good and moral king, then instructed me on the same traits as they applied to a good and moral queen.

A young girl carried Tauren's crown to the Reverend. He thanked her graciously and she skipped back to her mother with a beaming smile. When the Reverend asked Tauren to kneel, he took a knee.

As he placed the silver crown on Tauren's head, I was mesmerized by its beauty; cut apatite stones and shiny black obsidian stones were inlaid around the metal ring. Tauren smiled up at me, and when the Reverend asked me to kneel beside him, Tauren took hold of my hand.

A matching, more feminine crown that somehow fit perfectly was placed atop my head. Tauren watched attentively, his eyes taking in every movement. When they combed over me, it felt like a caress instead of a perusal.

"You're the most beautiful thing I've ever seen in my life," he whispered. "And I'm the luckiest man in the entire world."

My heart fluttered.

"I love you," I told him.

He smiled. "I love you more."

That night, among my peers and his, Tauren and I danced, toasted, and most of the time, though we were surrounded by an enormous room full of people, it felt like it was just him and me.

One king.

One queen.

One fate.

epilogue

I clutched my stomach, staring into the mirror, mouth agape, listening to the swish-swish sound resonating through my body. Swish-swish-swish-swish. It was strong. I tried to smile, but covered my mouth, unable to believe it.

How will Tauren feel about this?

A baby so soon?

I stared at the new, black ribbon knotted around my wrist. We'd just hand-fasted again, but I had no idea until now that I was carrying his child. I'd gotten queasy a few days ago, but thought maybe the chicken was undercooked or something. I never imagined I was pregnant.

The door to the washroom swung open and Tauren entered. His eyes caught on the hand that rested on my stomach before I could move it away. "Are you sick again?"

"It's nothing." I tried to smile, but I couldn't look at him.

What if he was furious? What if he didn't want children yet? We'd talked about having them, but that was far, far into the future. Not now.

What would happen when the people found out? The purists would be angry. That small, but loud group already hated that a witch sat beside the King. They wanted me out. They would never accept our child.

"Hey," Tauren said gently, tipping my chin up so I would look at him. "What's going on in that beautiful mind of yours?"

I squeezed my eyes shut for a long moment, then took in a deep breath.

"I'm pregnant," I revealed.

We'd made our own vows the night we were hand-fasted. We promised never to lie and never to conceal anything important from one another. It was me and him. Him and me. Against everything else.

His brows rose and then a glorious smile spread over his lips. He tentatively touched my stomach. It wasn't even swollen yet. "Truly?"

I nodded, trying to smile back at him. It wasn't that I was unhappy. It was the other piece of news I dreaded giving him.

"How can you tell?" he asked, wonder lacing his voice. "The sickness?"

I shook my head. "I can hear the beat of his heart."

"His?" he asked, brows raised.

"It's a boy."

"I am so happy, Sable." He hugged me and spun me around, gently setting my feet on the ground. "I'm sorry. Did I hurt you?"

"I'm not a piece of glass, Tauren."

He smiled sheepishly. "Right."

He chatted happily about how we should reveal the news to his mother and Knox and Leah, who would be wed on the first day of spring. Tauren rambled about creating elaborate surprises for them. A cake with blue icing or cyan-colored fireworks. Or both… Or something magical, instead. "Perhaps Brecan and Mira could help with that…" he mused excitedly.

"There's something else," I said hesitantly.

"What is it?" Tauren's brows furrowed with concern. Of all the things I'd said to him since we met, this was by far going to be the hardest. I closed my eyes and gathered every ounce of strength I had.

"I also feel Fate's presence again… in our son."

Tauren sucked in a shocked breath.

acknowledgements

I'm ever thankful to God for his mercy and blessings in my life. I have to thank my family for their constant encouragement, my friends for their support, and fans for loving my characters and stories as much as I do.

A special thanks to Melissa Stevens for designing the perfect book cover, interior, map, tarot card and every other thing related to bringing this book to life visually. And thanks to Stacy Sanford for waving her magic red pen over my manuscript and polishing it beautifully.

Website: www.authorcaseybond.com
Newsletter: http://eepurl.com/gcAu9v
Facebook: www.facebook.com/authorcaseybond
Twitter: www.twitter.com/authorcaseybond
Instagram: www.instagram.com/authorcaseybond
Bookbub Author Profile: https://www.bookbub.com/authors/casey-l-bond

about the author

Casey Bond lives in West Virginia with her husband and their two beautiful daughters. She likes goats and yoga, but hasn't tried goat yoga because the family goat is so big he might break her back. Seriously, he's the size of a pony. Her favorite books are the ones that contain magical worlds and flawed characters she would want to hang out with. Most days of the week, she writes young adult fantasy books, letting her imaginary friends spill onto the blank page.

Casey is the award-winning author of When Wishes Bleed, the Frenzy series, and fairy tale retellings such as Riches to Rags, Savage Beauty, Unlocked and Brutal Curse. Learn more about her work at www.authorcaseybond.com.

Find her online @authorcaseybond.

also by casey l. bond

The Fairy Tales

Riches to Rags
Savage Beauty
Unlocked
Brutal Curse

Glamour of Midnight

The High Stakes Saga

High Stakes
High Seas
High Society
High Noon
High Treason

The Harvest Saga

Reap
Resist
Reclaim

The Keeper of Crows Duology

Keeper of Crows
Keeper of Souls

The Frenzy Series

Frenzy
Frantic
Frequency
Friction
Fraud
Forever Frenzy